Praise for
Catfish Alley

"A tender, wise, unique story of life, love, and Southern women crafted by a skilled writer who understands the struggle to find happiness and the healing power of friendship."

—Lisa Wingate, author of *Beyond Summer* and *Larkspur Cove*

"In the tradition of *The Help,* Lynne Bryant's *Catfish Alley* tackles the racial divide of both 1930s and current-day Mississippi in a page-turning narrative that has, at its heart, the search for personal connections as the path to both survival and understanding."

—Lalita Tademy, author of *Cane River*

"*Catfish Alley* is a bittersweet love song to the union of women and a heartfelt meditation on the old and new wounds of a South that still must tiptoe, still doesn't always know how to move forward, but is determined to try. Lynne Bryant writes honorably and earnestly about women facing each other and themselves."

—Barbara O'Neal, author of *How to Bake a Perfect Life*

Catfish Alley

LYNNE BRYANT

NAL
ACCENT

NAL ACCENT

Published by New American Library, a division of Penguin Group (USA) Inc., 375 Hudson Street, New York, New York 10014, USA • Penguin Group (Canada), 90 Eglinton Avenue East, Suite 700, Toronto, • Ontario M4P 2Y3, Canada (a division of Pearson Penguin Canada Inc.) • Penguin Books Ltd., 80 Strand, London WC2R 0RL, England • Penguin Ireland, 25 St. Stephen's Green, Dublin 2, • Ireland (a division of Penguin Books Ltd.) • Penguin Group (Australia), 250 Camberwell Road, Camberwell, Victoria 3124, Australia (a division of Pearson Australia Group Pty. Ltd.) • Penguin Books India Pvt. Ltd., 11 Community Centre, Panchsheel Park, New Delhi - 110 017, India • Penguin Group (NZ), 67 Apollo Drive, Rosedale, North Shore 0632, New Zealand (a division of Pearson New Zealand Ltd.) • Penguin Books (South Africa) (Pty.) Ltd., 24 Sturdee Avenue, Rosebank, Johannesburg 2196, South Africa

Penguin Books Ltd., Registered Offices:
80 Strand, London WC2R 0RL, England

First published by New American Library,
a division of Penguin Group (USA) Inc.

First Printing, April 2011

3   5   7   9   10   8   6   4   2

 REGISTERED TRADEMARK—MARCA REGISTRADA

LIBRARY OF CONGRESS CATALOGING-IN-PUBLICATION DATA:

Bryant, Lynne, 1959–
Catfish Alley/Lynne Bryant.
p.   cm.
ISBN 978-0-451-23228-1
1. Tour guides (Persons)—Fiction. 2. Historic sites—Mississippi—Fiction. 3. African-Americans—Mississippi—Fiction. 4. Mississippi—Race relations—Fiction. I. Title.
PS3602.R949C37   2011
813'.6—dc22   2010040454

Set in Bembo • Designed by Elke Sigal

Printed in the United States of America

For Annie Lorene Lancaster Bryant

Catfish Alley

Prologue

Thomas "Zero" Clark

It's pitch-black dark. The buzz of crickets and tree frogs is so loud down by the river, I can barely hear myself think. I slip out of my boat and pull it up on the bank, feeling sweat run down my back as I get myself ready for the steep climb. The package is still tucked safe inside my shirt and the laces on my boots are tied tight. These old boots are so full of holes I can feel the black mud of the riverbank oozing in between my toes.

The moon is a fingernail tonight. A snake slithers across my foot and I almost squeal like a girl. The last thing I need is to get bit by a water moccasin. How would I ever explain that to Mama in the morning?

It takes some scrambling, pulling, and fierce scratches from wild blackberry bushes, but I finally make my way to the top of the riverbank. This is the side of the Tombigbee that borders Clarksville. I'm careful to slip behind that wide oak tree on the edge of the property to make sure nobody's outside. Riverview stands there in all her glory, a mansion with fourteen rooms. Even the kitchen out back is bigger than my house and barn put together.

This is where it gets tricky. I'll get paid good money once this package is delivered, or no money, and a lot of rope, if I get caught. Between the climb, the snake, and the cold fear of what Ellen Davenport's daddy or brothers might do if they find a black man under her bedroom window, I'm having a hard time catching my breath.

There's not a light on in any of the windows. Sarah Jane, the maid, told me that John W. and Marie Davenport go to bed early on Saturday evenings because of church on Sunday. Ellen's room is on the second floor at the back of the house with a balcony overlooking the river. The plan is for Ellen to light a candle so I know which window is hers. There's no candle lit. I stand in the tree line at the edge of the wide green yard and wonder if the dogs are locked up for the night. J. W. Davenport has the best coon dogs in the county. The dog pens are farther upriver toward the barn. That's why I put the boat in where I did, to stay away from the pens. If they start barking, this man's goose is good as cooked.

Maybe I'm a little early. The delivery instructions said I'm supposed to get the package to Miss Ellen between midnight and one in the morning. I don't own a watch, but I hear the clock on the First Baptist Church, just three blocks away, strike the half hour. Mosquitoes swarm like black clouds and bite my ankles and bare arms. I don't slap at them for fear of waking the folks at Riverview or those dogs.

There it is! A tiny little flame in a window on the upper east side of the house. As I watch, the balcony door opens about a foot and a woman slips out. She glows like a ghost in that white nightgown. I shiver at the sight of her. Her long black hair hangs down around her shoulders and falls down her back. She holds a candle near her chin and it lights up her face. She's not much of a looker. I surely don't understand what all the fuss is about. But I'm getting paid good money, and Lord knows, I need it.

I study the yard for the hundredth time. I've been over and over my route from the riverbank to the window. Bank to gazebo, around the gazebo to the kitchen, past the kitchen to the rose arbor, around the rose arbor to the chairs, drop down there and crawl over to the house. There's a big set of windows in the sunroom right under her bedroom window. I have to be sure that room is empty, because once I step out, there'll be no hiding.

I take off running, my heart beating in my throat. I crouch behind a big lawn chair to catch my breath—so far, so good. It's so dark she didn't see me cross the yard. That's a good thing. She's still peering out over her candle, studying the night like I'm coming from the trees instead of the ground. I'm fixing to step out into the open when something brushes across my ankles and, again, that little girl scream is in my throat. As it is, I suck in my breath so loud, I see the candle flicker when she turns toward the sound.

A fat calico cat is winding around my leg, rubbing her head on my boot. She starts to meowing and I think that right about now, I could kick that damn cat from here to Christmas, but instead I scratch her behind the ears to get her to shut up her yowling. She starts purring and rolls over on her back so's I can rub her belly. Cat! I didn't count on a cat. I hear a whisper coming from the balcony.

"Who's there? Is that you, Andrew?"

Now what in the world is she doing calling for Andrew Benton? I reckon Andrew didn't tell her he's too much of a chicken shit to deliver this package himself. Next to finding a black man in his yard, finding the likes of Andrew Benton would be the next worst thing for J. W. Davenport. I step out from behind the chair and call to her as quiet as I can.

"Hey, Miss Ellen. It's me, Zero."

From where I stand, I can see the candle flame trembling. The girl is shaking like a leaf. "Zero? What are you doing here? Where's Andrew?"

Good question. Where the hell is Andrew Benton? Not risking his ass in the middle of the night to deliver some mystery package to a white girl. And not just any white girl, but the daughter of the richest man in Clarksville, Mississippi. The money. I got to remember the money. Money means college, and college means a way out. Out of Mississippi, out of working for the white man twelve hours a day. College means a profession, a real profession, like doctoring.

"Andrew asked me to deliver this package to you, Miss Ellen. I've got it here. Now, I'm going to toss it up to you and you make sure you catch it, all right?"

"A package? What kind of package? What did Andrew tell you?"

Sweet Jesus! I don't have time to stand here talking to this white girl *about the woes of her love life with Andrew Benton. I got no interest in their secrets.*

"He didn't tell me nothin', Miss Ellen. He said it was real important that I get this package to you tonight, but he didn't tell me nothin' else. I'm going to toss it up now. You ready?"

"I guess. I still don't understand why Andrew didn't come." She sets the candle down on the floor of the balcony and leans out over the rail, peering into the dark trying to see me. "Is it heavy?"

"No, ma'am, it's not heavy. It 'pears to be just a small box."

"A small box?" She sounds real excited now and holds her hands out. "I'm ready."

I toss the box as gentle as I can toward her hands. She doesn't catch it. The box lands on the ground with a thud. I pick it up and try again. After three tries, she finally catches it. Thank the Lord.

"There now, Miss Ellen. You get back inside. I'll be going."

"Thank you, Zero, good night."

"Yes, ma'am." I nod, then turn and head for the river. I don't know it, but that calico cat has come up behind me again, and when I set my foot down, it lands square on her tail. She hollers like she is dying and I can't help but cuss. "Damn!"

That cat runs off like greased lightning and so do I. As the coon dogs bay at the cat's scream, I run for the riverbank as fast as my old mud-filled boots will carry me.

Chapter 1

Grace

I'm moving slower than usual this morning. My joints ache like they do every year in the fall, but today it's the memories weighing me down, catching around my ankles like tall grass. That Reeves woman calling yesterday has me stirred up.

"Miss Clark," she said, "I'd like to visit with you about your knowledge of African-American history in this area. I was wondering if I could set up a time to drive out to Pecan Cottage and meet with you."

I still don't know what she's talking about. What knowledge? I taught third- and fourth-graders for forty years, but I'm no historian. White folks. Eighty-nine years, you'd think I'd be used to them by now. I said I'd meet with her, but I'd rather be out in the garden. The last of the tomatoes need to be gathered and this old house needs a few repairs before the frost comes.

I prefer for folks to just let me be. A long time ago, I made that promise to keep up Pecan Cottage and I do, with Walter's help, of course. I look out the window to see if he's still out there picking up pecans. Those trees are so old now that they're starting to take more work than he can keep up with. But, Lord have mercy, I'd hate to lose them. They line the whole quarter mile of the driveway, so that coming up on this house is almost a surprise when you pass the last one. It still galls me a little bit not to be able to do all the work myself, even though Walter's been with me a long time. He needed a job and I needed help, but I don't want some white woman poking her nose into my business, asking questions. Just when I think I've made my peace with those old hurts, her calling has got me to thinking about things I haven't thought about in a long time. No use in dwelling on the past.

For most of the years of my life I've focused on my grandma's advice, "Don't let nobody keep you down." I reckon this meeting today is probably what white folks would consider progress. Roxanne Reeves is the director of the Clarksville Pilgrimage Tour of Antebellum Homes. Apparently they now have some sort of new idea for an African-American historical tour and she wants to talk to me about it.

Funny thing is, I've lived in this town all my life, know its people and history better than I know what day of the week it is most days, and I've never toured any of those big old houses. Clarksville was a hospital town during the War Between the States, so most of the houses around here didn't get burned down. Sets my teeth on edge a little bit thinking about the show they put on every year. Those houses are pretty, all right, what with the big white columns and wide porches, big old Boston ferns and wicker furniture out front. I've heard people come from all over the country to see them. They call it a pilgrimage, a journey to a sacred place. Sacred? Can't do much but shake your head at that one.

Come to think of it, I don't know any black folks who are much interested in a tour of houses built before the War. If you're black and you grew up around here, big white houses with names like Shadow Lawn or Riverview or Twelve Gables—which is the one that Reeves woman owns—means someone in your family was probably one of the slaves who helped build it, worked on the property, or did domestic help after Reconstruction.

Now this all-white committee has decided there should be a tour about the black folks. I reckon they are probably trying to do the right thing. How did Mrs. Reeves put it? Oh, yes. They want to "show the contributions of the black members of the community by touring important African-American historical locations."

I can't help but smile while I place coffee cups and cream and sugar on a serving tray. Is surviving a contribution? I wonder. Is doing everything in your power to move yourself and your people forward in spite of white people blocking you at every turn her idea of a contribution? One minute I'm smiling and then that old bitter sadness is pulling down the corners of my mouth and I feel that catch in my throat. Zero tried harder than any of us in those days to make things different, but look what happened.

There are places I can show her all right, although most of them are run-down or gone by now. The problem is that every place I think of has so many stories attached. Will this white woman want to hear those stories? Does she know what she's getting herself into?

Roxanne

This is just so strange. Black people do not live in houses like this. I am sitting on a lovely antique settee in the parlor of Pecan Cottage trying to calm myself down. It's still hot for September, and when I get this nervous I start to perspire. I got distracted by the roses near the front porch steps; my gardening man can never get mine to look that good. And suddenly, that big black man came out of nowhere. There he was, towering over me. It flashed through my mind that I could be attacked and left for dead way out here in the country and no one would ever know. He had a shovel in his hand; he could have buried me, too. Just when I thought I'd better get back in my car quick, the door opened and the old woman stepped out.

"Afternoon," she said. "I see you've met Walter. You must be Mrs. Reeves." He just looked at me then, never said one word, and lumbered off around the house toward the back. Made me shiver. Meanwhile, Miss Clark invited me in. She has very nice manners and she talks almost like a white person, good grammar and all.

I have scrutinized this room carefully. Grace Clark has certainly kept this place up. I can smell reproduction furniture from the porch steps, but this house has the genuine article. I've lost count of the number of pre–Civil War houses I have helped restore in this area and I am certain these furnishings are original to around 1852, when Davis Calhoun built the place.

Of course, I've heard the stories about Grace Clark. But what I don't understand is how an old black woman came to own an entire plantation. She is one of the more educated black people around here, but she's always been private. And since she retired from school teaching, the only time my acquaintances have seen her is when her helper—I guess that must be Walter—drives her into town to go to the grocery store or the bank.

I got here right at two o'clock. I'm never late. Now she's shuffled off somewhere to get coffee. So, here I sit, waiting. I hope she gets back soon; I have at least two other meetings and several errands to run today. Then, I remember: I don't have to rush home to make dinner, because Dudley's gone. When I insisted he move out, I never realized how quiet our big old house would be. Still, I have to keep up appearances. I can't have anyone knowing we're having problems. *Don't think about that now. Focus on this meeting.* I glance at my watch and I get annoyed all over again, thinking about why I'm doing this.

Last Tuesday, we were having a perfectly lovely Pilgrimage Committee meeting when Louisa Humboldt piped up and said, "I have a proposal to make. May I address the committee?"

Thank the Lord, I kept smiling. I can't stand it when people spring topics on me that aren't on my agenda. But she's new to the committee, and frankly, the Humboldts have more money than God, so I felt trapped into letting her talk. Everything was fine until they blew into town from someplace up north—Connecticut, I think. They bought Riverview—I heard they paid cash—which is probably the most beautiful property in Clarksville.

"Of course you can address the committee, Louisa," I said. I tried to sound charming. I've been working on *charming* for years. I think I pulled it off. Besides, if I can get into Louisa Humboldt's good graces, I stand a strong chance of getting the contract to restore Riverview. That would be quite the feather in my cap, not to mention the money.

I remember being in Riverview several years back before the Humboldts bought it—I must have been delivering a food box for the Women's Missionary Union—and I was appalled. Back then that dried-up old spinster Ellen Davenport still lived there. The house looked like something out of *Great Expectations*. Spooky.

"I would like to propose that we create an African-American tour of Clarksville," Louisa said. The whole room got really quiet after that. I looked around, trying to figure out how to respond gracefully. But she didn't stop there.

"I believe that this part of our community is underrepresented in terms of historical accuracy. . . ."

Our community? She's only lived here six months. I've been clawing my way to the positions I have now for twenty years, and in six months she thinks she can waltz in and upset the entire order of things? She's probably one of those people born to money. I still get annoyed with myself for letting her type intimidate me. Will I ever get over feeling like I'm going to be found out? A memory floats by. Something about Louisa Humboldt reminds me of the first summer I helped Mama with her job at the Stanleys' house. I had just carried in a tray of canapés for Mrs. Stanley and her garden club friends. Eight years old, and fascinated by those wealthy women, I remember stopping to listen just outside the parlor door.

"Who was that beautiful little raven-haired girl, Irene?" asked one of the ladies.

"Oh, that's my cook's little girl. She's helping her mama out this summer."

"She's a pretty little thing. A little coonass, I guess."

"Now, Rose, you know I don't like to refer to the Acadians that way."

"Yes, yes, I know. But you don't seem to have the same sensibilities about your colored help, Irene."

"Well, that's different. They're black. This little girl is as white as you and me."

"Yes, but does she speak like you and me? Have you had a conversation with her?"

"Not really. Just a word or two."

"And does she use that thick Cajun dialect like her mama?"

"As a matter of fact, I think she does. You know, I can hardly understand it when they talk. Especially when they're talking to each other."

"See what I mean? They choose to stay backward that way, talking that coonass language that no one can understand."

"Oh, let it go, Rose. She's just a pretty little girl who happened to be born into a poor, backward family."

Just then Mama stuck her head out of the kitchen looking for me. I know my face was red and hot with shame. But when Mama asked me, "What's wrong, Chere?" I couldn't answer. My world had suddenly shifted, and in those short few minutes I realized I had a choice. I was white and I could choose to be like those ladies in that dining room. But I had to learn to speak like they did—and not only that, I had to learn everything I could about how refined white people lived. I vowed to myself then and there that my life would be different. I would not grow up and marry some Cajun boy and live on the bayou cooking gumbo and having babies, like my brothers' wives and my mama.

Louisa Humboldt's daddy was probably paying for her Ivy League education while I was surviving on scholarships at the W. Granted, I married into Dudley's money, but I learned how to act like I wasn't poor. Just thinking again about Louisa and that meeting, I am so irritated I have to get off the settee and move around. I peek around the parlor doorframe to see if Grace Clark is coming. Where did she go?

Louisa Humboldt then proceeded to tell the committee how she thought that someone should research the important African-American historical landmarks in and around Clarksville. And since I'm director of the Pilgrimage Committee, that someone ended up being me. I was so mad I could spit. This was the last thing I needed right now. But I smiled—more charm—and volunteered to interview Grace Clark. I try to remind myself that if I can just get this tour started, the Humboldts will most likely hire me to restore Riverview.

I can feel that nervous twitch starting in my foot. I hope we can get right to the point. I need Grace to be a consultant for this tour, but I just cannot bear her droning on and on about slavery and civil rights and all of that. That's the biggest drawback to planning this African-American tour, all of that unpleasantness. I much prefer to focus on the finer aspects of Southern culture.

What could possibly be interesting about the black community in Clarksville? As far as I can tell, there were no black people with homes or businesses of any distinction. I'm sure Miss Clark will have some ideas. I'm certainly not going to present a proposal to the committee, especially the Humboldts, without something noteworthy to say.

Finally. Here she comes. She's walking slowly and carrying a tray. Are those cookies? There goes my diet. There's nothing worse than a fat woman in a hoopskirt. I've spent years trying to make sure I don't end up looking like Aunt Pittypat.

"Here, Miss Clark, let me help you with that." I move quickly to carry the tray for her.

"Thank you, Mrs. Reeves. I appreciate it. Seems like things are heavier than they used to be."

"Please, call me Roxanne."

"Come on and sit over here, Roxanne. We'll put this on the table and we can sit and visit."

"Yes, ma'am." I place the tray on the table between two wing-back chairs.

"Mrs. Reeves, if this involves putting Pecan Cottage on your house tour, I'm still not interested."

Although I would love for this house to be on the tour, I have sent letters to this woman for at least the last five years and she will not budge. I still don't understand why. It is one of the best-preserved houses in the county. But I have already decided not to push that anymore.

"No, Miss Clark, I'm not here about that. Although I would love to have your house on our tour, I accept your choice not to include it. I'm here for an entirely different reason. It's been suggested that we add an African-American historical tour to the events we host every year. I was thinking that since you've been in this community for so long and, well . . . since you live here at Pecan Cottage, you'd have a lot of knowledge about the history of this area. We thought you might be willing to suggest places we could put on the tour and give us some information about them."

Grace nods at me, then just stares across the room. When I turn to see what she's looking at, she seems to be staring at the portrait of Davis and Marjory Calhoun.

"What kind of history are you interested in?" she asks.

I take a cookie and put it on a napkin in my lap. "I'm not exactly sure. I was hoping you could make some suggestions. My specialty is restoring antebellum homes. I, um . . . I . . ."

"Don't know much about black folk?" she offers.

I just hate being put in this position. How am I supposed to answer this woman gracefully? After all, I don't want to be rude.

"No, not really. Not the local history, anyway. I mean, I know the usual about the slave trade here, and then, after the War, there was Reconstruction and no more slavery. I know that black people had their businesses and churches mostly over near Catfish Alley and that kind of thing. But I don't know about the places that black people . . . um . . . I mean African-Americans would call historical around here."

It feels like this woman is watching me like a chicken hawk. What if I say the wrong thing and offend her? I'm not even sure whether to say "black" or "African-American." They are so particular these days. Sometimes it seems like saying "colored people" like my parents did was easier. My parents may have been poor, but they were careful to teach me never to say "nigger." I'm proud of that. Although people do still use that word around here; even the black people use it. That, I really don't understand.

"It doesn't much matter to me whether you call me black or African-American," Grace says. "I would rather you just call me Grace. And it does sound like you could use some help. Tell me, Mrs. Reeves . . ." She leans forward and looks over her glasses at me. "Why are you doing this? What reason do you have for adding the history of black people to your tour of all those fine old homes?"

I did not expect Grace's question and assumed she would be pleased to have her people represented. Louisa Humboldt should be out here doing this blasted interview!

"Since I'm the director of the tour," I say, "the committee thought I should be the one to talk to you so that when we take the idea to the city planning people for a vote, I am able to answer all of their questions."

"I see. And what do you think about this idea?"

What difference does that make? Here I was thinking I would be the one asking the questions. Just when I was cooling off, I'm starting to perspire again. I hear a big thump outside and wonder if big black Walter comes in the house. I was so sure Grace would be happy to help. I thought maybe she would suggest one of their black churches, or maybe that nice house over on Third Street. I heard it was owned by a black doctor at one point. We could add an extra half hour to the end of the home tour for the handful of people who wanted to see a couple of places that represented black people from the area who made something of themselves. That would make everyone happy. I like that idea. I also like the idea of restoring Riverview.

"I thought this might be a good thing for the community. This way your people won't feel left out." That didn't sound right. Somehow, it seems like everything I say is coming out wrong.

Grace doesn't speak for quite a while. I sip my coffee and eat another cookie—they are so good—and try not to talk. I always talk too much when other people are quiet.

Finally, she says, "I'll help you, but I have a condition or two."

Oh, no! What conditions is this old black woman going to insist upon? What have I gotten myself into?

"What conditions, Miss Clark?"

"I want you to be my driver and my scribe."

"I'm sorry, Miss Clark. I don't understand."

"I want you to drive me around to the places that I think should be on this African-American tour and I want you to write down the stories I tell you."

"Well, I can certainly drive you. I think I have an afternoon free next week." I reach for my planner. Although I don't relish the thought of driving her around, I would rather do that than be trapped in her car with Walter at the wheel. "But I'm no writer. We have a retired English teacher on the committee. Wouldn't it be better if you had her help you with the stories?"

"No. Those are my conditions. You find one morning a week and we'll go out and look at some places. I get around better in the morning before I get too tired, and I'm fond of my afternoon nap these days. Then, during the week, you can write down the stories. You're going to need some stories that people can read so they understand the history, aren't you?"

"Well, yes, that's true . . . but, really, I'm not a writer. . . ."

"That's all right. You'll do just fine."

She has such kind eyes.

I don't see how I could possibly have time for this, with all of my committee meetings and church responsibilities. On the other hand, how hard can it be? A couple of landmark signs and a paragraph or two about the history. Besides, I can get someone to edit it. And if I leave without agreeing to do this, how would that look?

"All right. I can do that. When would you like to get started?"

"How about next Tuesday morning? You can pick me up at nine o'clock. Tuesday would have been Zero's ninety-first birthday."

"Zero? Who's Zero?" I ask.

"My brother."

"I didn't realize you had a brother."

"That's part of the story."

Chapter 2

Roxanne

As promised, I arrive at Grace Clark's house promptly at nine o'clock to cart her around and look at God knows what. This is Ola Mae's day to clean, and I usually like to be there to be sure she does things the way I want, so having to do this today is a little irritating. I know Ola Mae will be able to tell that Dudley's things are missing. I just hope she doesn't talk about it to the other maids. So far, no one knows we're separated. I can barely say that word to myself. How could this have happened? Was it because I gained weight? Got boring? Because I'm over forty?

I think about last night's phone conversation with him and I get that little ache in my chest. He wants to come by for more of his clothes. Funny, the things he says he needs are the clothes he always wears when he wants to make a good impression—that tweed sport coat, his favorite red tie.

"Who are you trying to impress?" I asked him.

"What are you talking about, Roxie? I just need the clothes for work."

"Are you trying to impress your young girlfriend?" I hated myself for asking that. I have been systematically trying to convince myself that what I saw that day last spring couldn't have been what

I thought it was. But when you walk into an off-limits bedroom in your own house during a Pilgrimage Tour, hoping to get a little privacy for a moment, and find your husband with a hoopskirted tour guide pressed against the wall . . . I clinch my teeth together as I remember her pretty face. She's one of his graduate assistants, who oh-so-thoughtfully volunteered for our home tour. She did have the good grace to gasp in horror.

"Oh, Mrs. Reeves," she sputtered. "I'm so sorry . . . uh . . . Dr. Reeves was just helping me get something out of my eye. . . ." She saw pretty quickly I wasn't buying it and rushed out of the room. "I'll just get back to the tour now. . . ."

"I've told you over and over, Roxanne. That was nothing. You've blown it all out of proportion." That's what Dudley said last night. He often says I make too much of things. But then, he's never had to work for anything he has. That easy charm is why I fell in love with him. He just plods along, taking for granted that life will continue to be handed to him. I've always envied his easiness that way. I thought I could ignore their affair, but after four months the tension between us was so thick, he said he couldn't breathe in his own house. He certainly jumped on that faculty apartment the minute it opened up.

When I was young I was so proud of myself for snagging him. I was a graduate student in those days and also struggling to establish myself in the restoration business, desperately wanting to be part of his social class. He was the young, handsome history professor who all the girls swooned over. Why did it have to be a graduate student? Her youth is such a cliché. But then, Dudley never has been very creative. Was I so attracted to him because he never challenged me or my story? He was willing to swallow completely that I was an orphan adopted by the Stanleys, the wealthy couple Mama cooked for. And I was willing to play the role of the perfect faculty wife—the right social circle, the right clothes, the right clubs.

I've begun to wonder lately if all of the effort I've made over the years, not only to get his attention but to keep it, has been worth the cost. I've spent the better part of my adult life working hard to change the way I talk, to get an education, to separate myself from anything related to the bayou, including my brothers. That wasn't difficult after Mama and Daddy died. Monroe and Bill aren't interested in anyone who's not drinking beer and fishing; besides, I'm so much younger than them, I think they actually forget about me. At least that's what I tell myself.

Mama always said, "You was my change-of-life baby, Chere."

Maybe that's why I always felt like an afterthought. As I look up and admire Pecan Cottage, I wonder again how Grace came to be living in a home owned by wealthy whites for generations. I guess we're both usurpers in a way.

I walk around to the back and enter through the screened porch, just as Grace instructed. The smell that meets me takes me back instantly to my mother's kitchen. I stand there for a minute and breathe in the memories along with the scents of coffee, cinnamon, and apples. Then the door to the house opens and Grace appears.

She looks so dignified. Even though she's a small woman, she has a manner about her that makes me think her students sat up and paid attention.

"Good morning, Roxanne. Come on in. I made us some coffee and an apple cake."

I was not expecting to sit down for coffee and can't help wondering if Ola Mae has found all of the instructions I left for her. I'd rather just get started, but how can I hurry along this old woman who has gone to all this trouble?

The kitchen really does remind me of Mama—the good part anyway. After all, it was Mama's cooking that got her the job at the Stanleys' as their cook. If she hadn't gotten that job and started taking me to work with her when I was eight, I never would have had my little epiphany. After that I swore I would never be like her: round and puffy, old and tired at fifty after too many years of cooking for other people. But I do miss her kitchen. I suck in my stomach even as I'm eyeing that apple cake.

"Shall we talk about our plan for today?" Grace asks as she serves me a piece of cake.

"Yes, certainly. Where do we start?"

"We'll start at the first school for black children."

"Where was that?"

"Over on the south side of town, on Ninth Avenue."

I'm trying to place the street. I remember a lumberyard in that area. Delbert Tanner, the owner, sometimes salvages old wood from buildings being torn down around Mississippi. I was there a couple of years ago looking for old beams for Rose Dillard's summer kitchen.

"All I remember on Ninth Avenue South is Tanner's Lumber Yard."

"That's the place. The first school for black children was in what is now a warehouse on the property."

"How do you suppose we're going to tour a place that is a business?"

Grace takes a last sip of coffee, then picks up her purse and starts toward the door. I grab my purse and follow her, moving quickly to keep up. "Miss Clark? Did you hear what I asked?"

Grace stops and turns, pulls a tissue from the sleeve of her sweater, and blots her lipstick. "Yes, I heard. I reckon you will have to sort that out. I'll just show you the places. This is the one we'll start with."

And that's the end of conversation until we're well on the way to Clarksville. Of course, I'm a little uncomfortable with the silence. It just doesn't seem natural. As we drive the country roads back to town I try to make small talk about how bright the sweet gum trees are this year. They really are gorgeous—all reds, golds, and purples. But she doesn't say much, except "mm-hm" or "yes," so I decide to be quiet. Besides, I need to think through how I want to tackle the Humboldts' kitchen. Before she died, that old maid Ellen Davenport actually covered that gorgeous heart pine floor in indoor-outdoor carpet! Scandalous, if you ask me.

I notice when we drive by the Visitors Center at the entrance to town that Louisa Humboldt's car is parked out front. I can't help but wonder what she's doing there. Probably more research. She's convinced that Tennessee Williams was a distant cousin of hers. His daddy was a traveling salesman, so who knows? Maybe he made it as far north as Connecticut. But I doubt it. Last year they moved the house where Tennessee was born to Main Street and made it the Visitors Center. I've tried to tell her there aren't any family records there, but she doesn't listen. I think Louisa is just desperate to have some excuse to call herself a Southerner.

When we reach Tanner's Lumber Yard, I pull in beside a red Ford F350, probably Del Tanner's. The gravel parking lot is full of beat-up trucks. This whole part of town is mostly warehouses and construction supply businesses. I can't imagine children going to school here. Two black men are sitting on the back of a lumber truck just inside the high chain-link fence that circles the yard. They stare at us as we sit in my car looking at the building; I'm feeling strangely self-conscious right now.

I'm not sure how to proceed. I'm fairly sure the particular warehouse where Del keeps the salvaged wood is on the back of the property. It would be quite a distance for Grace to walk. Plus, we would have to go past several large trucks loading lumber. And all of those black men.

"Would you like me to go in and talk to Mr. Tanner about going back to the warehouse? Maybe he'll give us permission to drive back there so you won't have to walk so far."

"I would appreciate that. These old knees are not what they used to be."

As I head toward the office door I smell cigarette smoke, the clean piney scent of newly milled lumber, and the oily smell of old trucks. It's a strange morning for memories. The smells here remind me of Daddy. How he hated working for the oil refinery. Born and raised on the south Louisiana bayou, he would much rather have spent his days in his pirogue fishing and hunting for whatever he could put on the table. My thoughts of him are always bittersweet. His Cajun patois was so thick most people couldn't believe he was speaking English. He smoked like a chimney and drank like a fish, but he was a kind and gentle man. And he loved me fiercely.

Daddy always told me that I needed to grow up and make something of myself, leave the bayou and see what was beyond her waterlogged levees. Mama, on the other hand, said I was too big for my britches, that I thought I was too good for hard work. Thing is, she was probably right. I wanted nothing to do with the life they had. I wanted to get as far away from that swampy, gator-infested place as I could. Daddy's been gone now for more than twenty-five years and I haven't thought about him in a long time. The first time I met Delbert Tanner I wondered what Daddy would have thought of him. More often, these days, I wonder what Daddy would think of me.

Inside the office, a woman sits behind a large metal desk. She looks up as I walk in. She looks so familiar to me; I wrack my brain and finally place her. She was my checker at the Sunflower grocery store just last week. She is probably around my age, mid-forties. Her hair is a strange shade of red, somewhere between legitimate auburn and the color of a pumpkin pie. She is wearing a lavender knit sweater that, I must say, doesn't do much to hide her belly roll and a plaid skirt that looks like something from the sixties. She's friendly, though.

"Good morning, may I help you?"

"Yes. I was hoping to talk to Del. My name is Roxanne Reeves. I did some business with Mr. Tanner back in the spring. He might remember me. Is he in the office today?"

"Yes, ma'am. He is. I'll check with him. Please, have a seat."

While I wait, I wander over to the old black-and-white framed photos on the wall. They show the way the mill and lumberyard looked in the late 1920s. The Davenports still owned the mill then. The secretary tries in vain several times to use the telephone intercom to contact Mr. Tanner. Each time she buzzes through to him, she accidentally disconnects right after he answers. After the fourth try, the office door bursts open and Del Tanner springs into the reception area like a wild cat. He looks older than I remember, his weathered skin almost too tight for his angular frame and his slicked-back hair a yellowish gray.

"Dammit, Ruth! How many times are you going to push that thing? I must've answered you five times!"

"I'm so sorry, Mr. Tanner! I just can't seem to get the hang of it."

"Well, what is it? I've got work to do."

Ruth nods toward me. "This is Mrs. Reeves. She is here to see you."

Tanner looks up in surprise. Apparently, in his tirade, he hadn't noticed me. Now, of course, he is all smiles. He walks over to me with his hand out.

"Hello there, Mrs. Reeves. Good to see you again. Please, come in and tell me how I can help you today."

I follow him into his office and sit in the uncomfortable folding metal chair he offers me. Tanner slides into the chair behind his wide pine desk, leans forward and smiles broadly, showing a gold front tooth. "I remember doing business with you, Mrs. Reeves. You came in about those beams for the Dillard kitchen, didn't you?"

I nod. I bet you remember, I think to myself. That was quite a lucrative transaction for you. Personally, I thought the price was ridiculously high, but Rose Dillard was tenacious. Once she heard that the beams were milled locally in approximately the same year her summer kitchen was built, there was no stopping her. Of course, I'm comfortable negotiating for lumber to remodel a one-hundred-and-fifty-year-old structure, but I'm not sure how I'm going to get that little old black woman waiting for me in the car through the gates of Del Tanner's lumberyard.

"Mr. Tanner . . ."

"Please, call me Del." Another flash of the gold tooth.

"Del . . . You may not know that I am the director of the Clarksville Pilgrimage Tour of Antebellum Homes. We plan the annual spring Pilgrimage Tour, several events related to the history of the area, and the Holiday Home Tour."

"Yes, yes, I know the pilgrimage. Good for business in town, I hear. 'Course those tourists aren't buying lumber"—he laughs at his own humor—"but I support what's good for Clarksville. I didn't know you were the director, though. That must be a big job."

"Yes, it's a pretty big job. . . ."

"Are you needing something for a restoration project? Because I just got in a load of beams from a torn-down house over in Yalobusha County. They'd be perfect for a restoration."

"No, Mr. Tan . . . Del. What I'm interested in is the building you keep that lumber in."

"Come again?"

"It has been proposed to our committee that we include an African-American tour as part of the pilgrimage events."

Tanner rolls his chair back from the desk, crosses his arms, and stretches out his long legs. He looks puzzled. "What's that got to do with me?"

"Are you aware that your warehouse was once a school for black children?"

Tanner laughs and looks at his watch. "No, ma'am, I sure wasn't aware of that. This business has been in my family for more than sixty years and nobody ever said nothing about a school around here. All that building's ever been to me is a storage warehouse for old lumber. Listen, Mrs. Reeves, I hate to hurry you, but I've got a load of pine coming in here in about fifteen minutes . . ."

It starts to dawn on me that this might not work out.

"I won't take much more of your time. What I'd like is for you to let me drive through the gate so that Miss Grace Clark, our consultant for the African-American tour, can show me that building."

"Consultant? You got you some educated nigger from up north to consult? How about you hire me as your consultant? You want to have an African-American tour in Clarksville, Mississippi? I'll tell you where you ought to be touring. Down there at the unemployment office is where you'll find 'em all. I hire them, but I can't keep one on the job. Drink up their paycheck, beat their wives, get thrown in jail, and don't show up on Monday morning."

I wasn't ready for this and I'm not sure how to react. He does have a point about the black people and the unemployment office, but still there are the Humboldts and their insistence on this tour.

"No, we don't have a consultant from the north. Grace Clark was a schoolteacher for many years at the black elementary school and then at Clarksville Elementary after they integrated. She knows a lot about the history of the area."

"Look, Mrs. Reeves, that's all well and good, but I don't have time this morning to escort you and this old black woman around the lumberyard. I'm sorry, but you're going to have to come back another time."

"So you're saying that if we make an appointment, you'll take us through the warehouse?"

"Yes, ma'am. I'll take you through it, or I'll get one of my boys to do it. But I'm going to tell you right now. My lumberyard is not going to be part of some trumped up *African-American* tour." He says *African-American* as if the words are sour in his mouth. "I do that and I'll be out of business in a year." He stands up and opens the door of his office. "Now, if you'll excuse me, Mrs. Reeves."

Grace

When I see the look on Roxanne's face as she comes out the door of the lumber office, I know it didn't go well. Mouth all set in a straight line, forehead all furrowed up. I can't say I'm surprised. I've known the Tanner family since I was a little girl. White folks think the Tanners are upstanding citizens in this community. But white folks are going to think what they want to think. Delbert's daddy, Ray Tanner, has been dead about twenty-five years now, as I recall. His son is just like him, though. Del Tanner might not be a Klansman, but he thinks like one. I wonder for the hundredth time why I'm putting myself through this.

Roxanne opens the car door, throws her purse down on the seat between us, and plops herself down. She grips the steering wheel and looks out through the windshield at that building like she can't figure out what just happened. She turns to me and starts to say something, stops, starts again, and finally just says, "Miss Clark, that didn't go very well."

I figure she might as well get used to it. If this white woman is going to try to head up an African-American tour in the town of Clarksville, she'd better get a little more realistic about what she's dealing with. Poor thing, all caught up in her romantic ideas about Scarlett O'Hara and how people loved their darkies. She's never seen what's right under her nose.

"What happened?" I ask.

"He . . . well, he . . ."

I have a hunch Delbert Tanner probably used some strong words Roxanne is not accustomed to hearing. Her social set prides itself on their enlightened attitude toward black folk. But when it comes right down to it they're just as uncomfortable as Del Tanner's type.

Roxanne is talking now, trying to be tactful. "It sounds like he's very busy today. Something about a load of lumber coming in any minute now. He wants us to schedule an appointment to look at the warehouse . . . Miss Clark, this is just one old building. Aren't there others? I mean, surely there are better-looking places than this?"

Bless her heart. "How about you drive me over to Sanders Café? We'll have a piece of pie and I'll tell you a story about that old warehouse."

Obviously Roxanne Reeves has been taught to respect her elders, even old black women. She doesn't argue.

"All right then, we'll go over to the café, if that's what you want. Did you want to show me anything else today?"

"No. We'll just start here for today."

Sanders Café is one of the few places in Clarksville where you see just about the same number of white folks as black. I figured Mrs. Reeves won't be too nervous about us coming here together. I don't get to town much these days, so I get stopped twice before we're in the door with folks speaking and asking after me. When we walk in, several of the black folk seated around nod and smile. Of course, I've got to chat for a minute with Mary Ellen.

"Hey, Miss Grace! It's so good to see you. What brings you to town today?" Mary Ellen comes around the counter to give me a big hug. She's a sweet girl—I believe she was one of my students sometime in the seventies. Making a good living for herself with this café. She has the place fixed up real nice, even got each room of the old house painted a different color, white curtains in the windows. I like it because it's homey, but mostly because the woman can cook. I've never known a white woman who could cook such good pies.

Mary Ellen glances past me to Mrs. Reeves, but I don't think she realizes we're here together. It occurs to me that I'm too old to be conducting my own little social experiment. But here we are. Roxanne is studying the pies in the case like she's in a museum or something. Probably wondering what I'm going to say.

"Mary Ellen, you know Mrs. Roxanne Reeves, I reckon," I say and look over at the back of her head, where she's still bent toward the pie case. She pops up then and gives Mary Ellen a stiff little smile.

"Hello, Mary Ellen," she says.

"Yes, ma'am, of course," says Mary Ellen, nodding at Roxanne. "How are you today?" Mary Ellen is looking at both of us like we're the strangest pair she's seen in a while.

"Fine, thank you," says Roxanne.

"Roxanne and I are doing some historical work together," I say. "She's looking into the places around here that were important to black folk years ago." Roxanne is looking all fidgety now, picking at something on her sleeve.

"Oh, I see," says Mary Ellen. It's pretty clear to me that she has no idea what I'm talking about, but she's too polite to ask. "Isn't that something?" She seems to not know what else to say, so she moves around behind the counter and adds, "What can I get for y'all today?"

I realize right then that in all my years of coming to the café, I've personally never arrived with a white person to sit down together to eat. They sit at their tables and we sit at ours. Nowadays, you see a mix every now and then, but not much. I wonder about myself. What was I thinking, asking her to bring me here?

We order pieces of Mary Ellen's apple pie and coffee and settle ourselves at a corner table. I think Roxanne is trying to ignore the looks from folks around the room and get this over with.

"So, you were going to tell me about the school," Roxanne says.

"When I was a little girl, my brother, Zero—his given name was Thomas—and I lived with my mother and my grandmother in a small house on the Calhoun plantation. I remember my first day at the Union School. I was so excited. That was also the day my brother got his nickname. . . ."

Roxanne starts to relax around the shoulders a little bit, stops glancing around the room so much. I always could calm the children with my stories. Maybe it will work for her, too.

September 1919

"Grace! Thomas!" Mama hollers. "Y'all get on in here. Breakfast is ready. These biscuits gettin' cold."

I run from the outhouse toward the kitchen, trying to twist one of my braids and pull my new dress into place at the same time. Mama stands in the kitchen doorway and laughs at how excited I am.

"Calm down, girl. You are going to wear yourself out before you even get to school. Go over there to the pump and wash your hands before you come eat. Where's your brother?"

"I don't know, Mama." I push down on the pump handle and shiver as the cold water pours over my hands. I rub on the lye soap, rinse off quick, and stop myself just in time from drying my hands on my clothes. Grandma worked hard on this school dress. I sure don't want to ruin it before I even get to wear it anywhere. Mama waits at the back door and folds me into her skirt for a big hug.

"Maybe Tom went hunting," I say. "Grandma told him she wanted him to get some squirrel for supper."

"*Maybe so. Lord knows I can't keep that boy out of the woods. But he knew this was the first day of school. He better get back here soon, or we'll be having some words.*"

I climb into my chair at our old beat-up kitchen table and tie a dish-cloth under my chin to protect my new dress while Mama fills my plate with biscuits, gravy, and sausage and fixes me a cup of milk coffee. Just as I'm about to eat, Tom comes busting in the back door, out of breath, carrying three squirrels upside down by the tails.

"*Boy, get yourself in here and eat,*" Mama says. "*School starts in an hour and a half and your sister is going with you today. Hang those squirrels up out back. Make sure the dog can't get to them. I'll skin and dress them after breakfast.*"

"*Thanks, Mama.*" Tom slides into his chair and takes the plate she hands him. He looks across the table at me. "*You excited about school, Gracie?*"

My mouth is stuffed full of biscuit, so I nod and smile big. Today is the first day I get to walk through the pine woods and over the creek with Tom. The Union School is the same school where Great-Grandma, Grandma, and Mama went. I even have shoes.

Just as Tom and I are fixing to leave, Mama hands each of us a tin bucket that's got fried apple pies wrapped in wax paper, a piece of the left-over breakfast sausage, and a fat triangle of corn bread. Grandma Clark meets us as we're going out the back door. She's just coming in from picking the last of the tomatoes in the garden. A lot of them are still green, but Grandma'll put them on newspaper in the pantry and they'll get ripe all the way until Thanksgiving. Grandma hands her basket to Mama and then pulls us into her soft bosom.

"*Y'all make me proud now.*"

"*We will, Grandma,*" Tom and I say together.

"*Come on, Grace, let's get going.*" Tom gives me a little push out the door.

I've never been this far from home on foot before. I've only been to town in the wagon twice that I can remember. Tom holds my hand and gives me the older brother speech about how to act at school. The sun is just starting to come up over the cotton fields when we reach the woods. I have to walk careful through the underbrush so that I don't snag my new dress.

It takes us about an hour to get to Clarksville. It's so exciting to see the town coming to life. People are outside on the sidewalks sweeping and wagons are being loaded in front of the feed store. I can even see a big black automobile parked way down the street in front of a tall building. Tom says it's the white folks' bank. We turn, cross the railroad tracks, and head for a long low building with a sign hanging over the wide door.

"There it is, Gracie," Tom says. "You see that sign up there? It says Union School."

Suddenly, all of the excitement I've been feeling all morning turns to lead in my stomach. What if I can't do it? What if I can't learn and I let Mama and Grandma down? Tom must sense how scared I am, because he puts his arm around me and leads me toward the door.

"Come on. It's going to be fine. You're going to love it. Look, here's teacher." Tom points to the tallest colored woman I've ever seen. She looks like an angel. She's wearing a long blue calico dress with little white buttons down the back. I can see them when she turns to say hello to the other students piling into the school. Her dress has a white collar with real lace trim, and at her throat is a round pin with a picture of a face on it. She has smooth, not kinky, hair that is piled up on top of her head. As Tom pulls me close to her, I can smell her. She smells like roses and lemons. She's the most beautiful woman I've ever seen.

Tom plays his part as the man of the family. He pushes me in front of him and grins at the teacher. "Miss Wilson, this is my sister, Grace Clark. She's just starting today."

Miss Bessie Wilson kneels down, takes my hand, and all of my worries slip away. I decide right then and there I will do anything it takes to please this woman.

"Welcome, Grace Clark," Miss Wilson says. Her voice reminds me of the gray doves that coo at twilight. "Are you happy to be going to school with your brother?"

I still can't find my voice, but nod my head real big and follow Tom and the others into the school. I look around, trying to see everything, while Tom takes my dinner bucket and lines it up on the shelf with all the others. The room is wide and bare except for three rows of desks in the middle and a large desk for the teacher at the front.

My grandma has told me our family history with this school so many times, but now it all seems so much more real to me. Grandma came to this school when it was the Freedman's school, the first colored school opened by the Freedman's Bureau after the War. The Calhoun family freed Great-Grandma and Great-Grandpa and they stayed on the Calhoun property to be cotton sharecroppers. Grandma was one of the first children to go to the school in this building. She says it was a hospital for the soldiers during the War.

Grandma always says, "Y'all got to take this opportunity now and make something of yourselves. Can't nobody keep you down if you got an education. Don't you worry about what white people say about you. You just smile and keep on reading. Read every book you can get your hands on."

We don't dare let Grandma down. Mama went to school here, too. She made it through high school before she had Tom. Tom and I want to make it all the way through high school, too.

Tom calls me and motions toward a desk at the front of the room. "You sit here on account of you being a first-grader. I'm a third-grader, so I sit two rows back. You'll be close to teacher, so she can help you a lot."

He makes sure I'm settled into the desk before he hurries back to greet a boy I don't recognize. This boy is dressed in the finest clothes I've ever seen on a colored boy. He and Tom start to whisper and push each other, making eyes at the girls who are huddled in a group in the back of the room, whispering.

I jump when Miss Wilson taps on the desk with her ruler. "Class, come to order now."

Everyone quickly settles down. It gets so quiet I can hear my heart beat.

"We have a new pupil today," teacher says, "Miss Grace Clark. She will be starting first grade. Stand up and say hello, Grace."

This is terrifying. I stand and nod, and stare at everybody's feet. I notice that Tom and I, along with the boy Tom was talking to and one other girl, are the only ones besides teacher who are wearing shoes. I think that I must be pretty lucky to have shoes for school. I'm so distracted by all those dusty feet, I don't hear Miss Wilson tell me to sit down. Miss Wilson nudges my shoulder.

"Grace? You may sit down now."

Everyone laughs and I still can't look up so I plunk myself into my desk, fold my hands, and wait to see what will happen next. It's not what I expect. From the back of the room, there's a loud scream. I turn around just in time to see a big old green bullfrog jump from the desk of one of the prettiest girls in the group I was watching earlier. Tom and his friend have their heads down on their desks turned toward each other, and they're trying to keep from laughing.

"What in the world?" Miss Wilson says. She still hasn't seen the frog. He's sitting on the sill of the only window in the room. He looks like he's saying, "Let me out, please, let me out."

"It was a big old bullfrog in my desk, Miss Wilson. When I opened my desk to get my pencil, it jumped out at me. I'm sorry I screamed." The pretty girl looks worried, like she thinks teacher might blame her for the frog being there.

All of a sudden I remember hearing an odd sound coming from Tom's lunch bucket this morning. And he was carrying it awful careful-like. Maybe he was hunting for more than squirrels this morning. He's sitting up straight now, still smirking around the mouth. No one else moves. From the window, the frog lets out a loud croak. That's when giggles spread across the room. Miss Wilson stops them with one look. She walks real slow back to where Tom is sitting. I don't know how Miss Wilson knows it was Tom, but she does.

"*Thomas Clark, would you accompany me over to the window, please.*"

"*Yes'm.*"

I can tell he's trying to look humble, but he still has that smirk twitching at the corners of his mouth. Tom follows Miss Wilson to the window, and when her back is to him, he turns around, raises his eyebrows, and gives his friend a big grin. At least that other boy has the good sense not to smile back.

Teacher gets to the window where that frog is just sitting there and says, "*Thomas, would you please retrieve the frog and carry him to the front of the room.*"

Tom looks like he's not quite sure what "retrieve" means, but he goes ahead and picks up the frog. It squirms and croaks and tries to wiggle free.

"*You want me to take him outside, teacher?*"

"*Oh, no, Thomas. Since he has decided to visit our classroom today, I want you to make him feel right at home. So you just hold him tight while you write your numbers on the blackboard.*"

Miss Bessie Wilson is a smart teacher. She knows the trouble Tom will get into with Mama when that frog pees on his only school shirt is worse than any punishment she could dole out. Poor Tom stands at the chalkboard, holding that squirming, long-legged, croaking frog under his arm, and writes his numbers. When he gets to fifty, teacher lets him stop. She walks to the left side of the board, where Tom started with number one. I am really proud of myself, because I recognize the first ten of those numbers. Mama's been teaching me at the kitchen table at night.

Miss Wilson points with a long stick to the number one. "*Thomas, what number have you left out that comes before this number?*"

Poor Tom wrestles with the frog, and the class tries to stifle another round of giggles as he looks down at the stream of yellow on his shirt. "*Um, there ain't no . . . I mean there isn't a number before one.*"

"*That is correct, Mr. Clark. And how do we symbolize that amount?*"

More wrestling. Finally, Tom shoves the frog under his arm, and writes a big zero on the board in front of the one. "*It's a zero, Miss Wilson.*"

"That is correct. And do you know what zero means, Mr. Clark?"

"Yes'm, zero means none." Tom looks like he's fixing to cry when that frog adds some brown to the yellow streaks on his shirt. The girls in the back of the room are making disgusted noises. I am mortified. What is he going to tell Mama? How long is teacher going to make him hold that frog?

Miss Wilson gets right up in Tom's face and peers down at him over her glasses. "Please remember this, Thomas Clark. Zero is how much tolerance I have for your antics. Do you understand me?"

"Yes'm."

"And another thing . . ." She pauses and Tom and the frog squirm some more. "Zero is how much progress you will make in your life if you continue to make a joke of this school and everything we have worked to provide for you."

"Yes'm."

"Now, go put that poor creature outside and get back to your desk."

By the time I finish my story about my first day at the Union School, Roxanne has long since finished her pie and coffee. She sits staring at me, seemingly asking for more.

"And after that," I say, as I finish the last bite of my apple pie, "everyone started calling him Zero. Except for Mama and Miss Wilson, of course. It just sort of stuck. And Zero was different after that day. He started talking about making something of himself, getting out of Clarksville, maybe even becoming a lawyer or a doctor."

"And did he?" Roxanne asks.

"Well, now, that's a story for another day." I suddenly realize my old heart can't take any more memories today. "I reckon you'd better get me home. I'll be needing my nap soon."

Roxanne looks a little taken aback, but she gathers her things and looks around the café again while she's helping me up. I'm thinking she's remembered how strange this is, and she's wondering if folks have been watching us. On the way out I stop to speak to another one of my students, who's come in while we were talking, and Roxanne stands patiently behind me waiting. I wonder again how this is going to work out. I can already tell she likes a good story, but how quickly will she tire of mine?

Chapter 3

Roxanne

I turn into the long driveway leading to Pecan Cottage. It is already Tuesday again. The week has flown by. I'm not sure why, but I have felt uneasy all week. Maybe it's because I have so much work to do and here I am, taking another day to meet with Grace Clark. Last week certainly got us nowhere. Del Tanner was just about as rude as a man can be.

Would it have been so difficult for Del to let us take a quick look at his warehouse? You'd think he would be happy to be involved in the pilgrimage. It's not going to hurt him any. All it involves is a historical marker and a few brochures. But he sure doesn't see it that way. He acts like if people know the first black school was on his property, he'll lose business.

I wonder what it must have been like for a six-year-old girl to walk all the way from Pecan Cottage to Clarksville every day. I know she and her brother went through the woods, but I clocked the distance on my odometer from my house in town and it came to a little over six miles. Amazing. A lot of those children had even farther to go, and without shoes. I remember getting on the school bus in the bayou before the sun was up and riding for an hour each way, but at least I didn't have to walk.

Grace has coffee waiting for me again.

"Where are we going today?" I ask.

"I have something special planned for us. We're going to visit my old friend Adelle Jackson. Adelle lives downtown on Fifth Avenue North. Her father was the first black doctor in town, Dr. Albert Jackson."

Good. Now we're getting somewhere. This has got to be better than some warehouse full of lumber. People might actually want to see a house. I try to remember the location. It seems like I dropped Ola Mae off at her cousin's in that area a few times.

"Let's see now . . . Fifth Avenue North . . . I know that street. Isn't there a church on that street, too?"

"Yes, the Missionary Union Baptist Church."

Our drive into Clarksville is quiet, as usual. Grace always seems to be lost in her own thoughts. I wonder if that's the case for most people her age. My mama didn't live much past sixty and I never knew my grandmother, so I don't have much experience with the elderly. Well, except for Mrs. Stanley, but that was so long ago. And then there's delivering the church food boxes. But most of those people are on death's doorstep. Grace Clark's memories always seem as fresh as today's bread. I'm surprised by the number of details she can remember. I decide to break the silence with a question.

"Was this man your doctor when you were a child?"

"You might say that, although I don't remember needing a doctor much as a child. Dr. Jackson and his wife, Anna Lee, lived in the back of his mother's house on Catfish Alley for years. During that time he and one helper built the house you'll see today. Then he opened up his medical practice there." She pauses and stares out the window. "Gracious, the black folks were proud of that man."

Following Grace's directions, I turn on Fifth Avenue North. We drive past an old clapboard church, several nondescript cottages, and finally pull up in front of a redbrick Queen Anne–style house with white gingerbread trim. Wide brick steps lead to a deep front porch that runs the entire width of the house. The porch extends out around a large bay window and three baskets stuffed full of trailing pink petunias hang overhead. The front door is wide and I think it's probably mahogany. It looks hand-hewn.

The house seems a little neglected. The shutters are loose in some places and the paint is chipping. The shrubs are overgrown and the flower beds need weeding. But I am pleased with the potential. With a little care, this place could be beautiful. Funny, in all of my years in Clarksville, I have never noticed this house before.

As I get out of the car, I see two black women and several children watching me from the porch of the house across the street. They are probably curious about why I'm visiting in this part of town. It still feels odd to me to be chauffeuring a black woman around. Whites and blacks don't mix socially in Clarksville. I remember when my school in the bayou was integrated. I was in the sixth grade. Even then, I had goals for myself and I knew better than to mix with blacks. By then I had been going to the Stanleys' during the summers with Mama for a couple of years. Mama would pile us into the old blue truck and we'd rattle down the River Road before sunup when everything was still misted over with fog from the river. We never drove in the main driveway of the plantation. We took the back road and parked behind the barn with the rest of the help.

Everyone except Mama was black. Mama chatted and gossiped with the maid and the gardener like they were old friends. I guess they were, since they'd all been working for the family for years. The black people didn't get to bring their kids, though. I remember one time I asked Mama why. She said the lady of the house was not about to have a bunch of pickaninnies running around the place looking like the Stanleys were still keeping slaves. I was different. I had manners and I needed to learn how to cook.

When I asked Mama why, she was shocked. "Why, because every woman needs to know how to cook, Chere! How a girl gone catch a man if she can't cook?"

But I didn't have much interest in cooking. I was too busy taking in every possible detail I could about how wealthy people lived, ate, moved, and talked. I made it my mission to be as visible as I could to Mrs. Stanley. I wanted her to see that I could be different. Mama let me bring her things like coffee and muffins in the morning. As I got older, Mrs. Stanley started asking me to help her with her correspondence or to bring her things. I copied the way she talked and her manners with other people. She was a lonely person. Her sons had both died in World War II and so she never had any grandchildren. I decided I would become the granddaughter she'd never had.

I refocus my thoughts on the present, go around to help Grace out of the car, and we start up the steps. Before we reach the top, the door opens and a tall black woman, who looks about the same age as Grace, comes out onto the porch. She wipes her hands on her apron as she hurries to meet us. It's surprising how agile she is for her age. When she reaches us she laughs and throws her arms around Grace.

"Gracie! It's so good to see you. This is quite a treat, getting to visit with you twice in one week!"

Grace returns the hug and gives her a big kiss on the cheek. These two old women act like girls with their hugging and chatter.

"Adelle, I would like you to meet my new friend, Roxanne Reeves," Grace says as she gestures toward me. Adelle extends her hand and I shake it. She has a powerful grip for an old lady.

"I'm happy to meet you, Mrs. Reeves," Adelle says. "Y'all come on in the house."

As we follow Adelle, I notice that the wicker furniture on the porch is antique, and in a style popular in the early 1900s. Other than needing some minor recaning, it's in good shape. The windows that I can see as we cross the porch still have their original wavy glass. Good. At least she hasn't replaced them with those ghastly aluminum windows.

The entrance hall is wide with rooms on either side. Adelle brings us into the room off to the left. "We'll sit in here for now and y'all can tell me how I can help you," she says.

We sit at a small oak table laid with china in a pattern I recognize as late-nineteenth-century Appalachian Rose from Tennessee. I can't help but get excited. What other treasures does this woman have in this house? She probably doesn't know what a gold mine of antiques she's sitting on. People might actually want to see this. The room is a little stuffy; those old gold velvet drapes are looking a little threadbare, but they're passable.

"I don't use this room very often anymore, since I don't have many visitors," Adelle says.

"Is this where your father saw patients?" I ask.

"Oh, no. This was where we received guests. Papa saw his patients in the room across the hall. I'll show you when we've finished our coffee. Grace, I have a surprise for you." Adelle removes the cover from a lovely cake plate—probably made in the early 1900s—to reveal a delicious-looking cake.

"Oh, Addie! My favorite." Grace turns to me. "Addie makes the best coconut cake in Mississippi."

"Many more of these Tuesday mornings and I'm going to be as big as the side of a barn!" I say. "I've had more good food since I've been meeting with you than I've had in years."

"Addie's grandmother created this recipe. She worked for Mr. A. W. Spencer over there on College Street. This was his favorite cake."

I put my fork down. "Arvis Spencer, the bank president?"

"No, his daddy, A. W. Spencer the First," Adelle says. "She was his cook and housekeeper."

I feel as though I've stepped back into Mama's world. I never imagined myself having cake and coffee with black service people—or their relatives. Growing up, they were Mama's only friends. I feel a pang of guilt again, remembering her response when I asked her why she was so friendly with blacks.

"You think you better than these people I work with? You think you better than me? You just look out that you don't reach too far, Chere. You might think you can be somebody else, leave behind your family and your roots, but you can't. You as Cajun as your daddy and me and you might as well get proud of it."

But I didn't get proud of it. I did everything in my power to erase it. I kept going to the Stanleys' with Mama all through high school. When I was a junior, we lost Daddy to emphysema. I still remember the rattle of his breathing coming from their tiny bedroom in our house on the bayou. That's the way Mama and I knew he was still alive at the end of the day when we'd come back home. We could hear him waging his battle for oxygen when we walked in the back door.

One day when we returned, the house was quiet. All we could hear was the regular puff of his oxygen tank. We both froze. I followed Mama into the room and we found him sitting there in their bed. He was wearing a cap and a camouflage jacket. His boots were on and still wet. In spite of Mama's insistence that he stay in bed, we knew he had been out on his pirogue for one last ride.

That was the only time I remember Mama not going to work. Daddy died on Wednesday, we buried him on Friday, and Mama was back to work by Saturday morning. And I was there with her. By this point I had gotten close enough to Mrs. Stanley that she had started to let me help her with her restoration projects. She had done everything she could to Oak Grove, and now she and Mr. Stanley had bought a second plantation home, also on the River Road, to restore.

Mrs. Stanley helped me understand that it could undermine a woman's ambition to reveal her poor background. Men could use childhood poverty to show how they had risen out of their humble beginnings and made something of themselves, but "Not so for a woman," said Mrs. Stanley, smoking her long thin cigarette. "A woman can't afford to reveal her flaws. They will always be held against her. She will always be classified as trying to be more than she is. A woman should never expose her soft underbelly."

Mrs. Stanley encouraged me to apply for a history scholarship based on my interest in home restoration. I was shocked when I got a full ride to Mississippi University for Women.

When I left the bayou for Clarksville, to attend the W, I was determined to keep my family background a secret. I kept a cool distance from the other girls and made sure no one ever got to know me very well. I disappeared in the summers to go back home and work as many hours for Mrs. Stanley as I could to save money and help Mama. When Mama died my senior year in college, I went home for her funeral, gave my brothers my key to the house, and turned my back on the bayou for good. I got an apprenticeship with the Clarksville Historical Society working on an antebellum home restoration and a Civil War museum and began to create a history for myself based on Mr. and Mrs. Stanley. Before I realized it, in my mind, they became my parents.

My family tree might be invented, but everyone around here believes it. And I've learned the hard way: Associating with black people, like my mama did, will get you nowhere. I remind myself I've got to stay clear on why I'm here. The people I know in this town think the way I do, so, I wonder: Who will want to take this tour? Will it be black people in the South? Will it be Yankees who come to Mississippi because they think we're backward and don't wear shoes? I'm not sure.

While we're having our cake, Adelle and Grace take turns telling me about the Meharry Medical College, where Albert Jackson took his training. I have to admit it's an interesting story. A white man whose salt wagon gets stuck in the middle of the night in 1876 in the Kentucky hills. A family of freed slaves who take him in and help him.

". . . and then that man, Samuel Meharry, said that someday he would do something to help the black race," Adelle says.

Grace finishes the story. "So, he and his brothers made the donation that started the medical school."

I'm wondering if I could get them to write this stuff down for me—I'll never remember it all—when Adelle gets up, takes Grace's arm, and says, "Gracie, let's show our guest Papa's offices."

I walk behind them through the high-ceilinged hall and Grace and I wait while Adelle fishes in her apron pocket. She pulls out a large brass key and, after a couple of tries and adjustments to her glasses, gets it into the lock on a door I hadn't noticed when we came in. A small brass plate on the door reads *Dr. Albert Jackson*.

"How long did your father practice medicine in Clarksville?" I ask.

"Papa treated patients for fifty-three years," Adelle says proudly as she pushes open the door and stands against it. "Come on in."

I feel myself stepping back in time as I enter the small waiting room furnished with four small wooden chairs. Beyond is an examination room; both rooms are painted a sterile white and I can almost smell antiseptic. Sunlight streams in through the open curtains of the floor-to-ceiling windows and reflects off the glint of steel instruments and glass syringes. Shelves contain neat rows of pill bottles with yellowed peeling labels, and a worn black leather bag sits on top of a small wooden desk in the corner of the room. Adelle has kept her father's office as if he might walk in the door any minute and say, "Bring in the next patient."

"When Papa was not much more than a boy, he apprenticed

with an old white doctor over on College Street who helped him learn how to mix medicines and treat wounds and such," Adelle says. "White people didn't like seeing coloreds around the doctor's office, so he had my papa treat them out behind his house. Papa saved every dime he could to go to medical school. On the day Papa was headed for the train station to leave for Nashville, Dr. Smith handed him an envelope with two hundred dollars in it. Every time Papa told that story he said it was the most money he had ever seen in one place at one time before or since!"

As Adelle and Grace stand in the middle of the room, they suddenly become quiet. Grace walks over and picks up a tattered book with a frayed leather binding. "Addie, do you remember the time Junior and Clarence Jones brought Zero to see your daddy? We must have been about eight years old."

Adelle smiles. "Of course I remember. I always thought of that as the day you and I became the best of friends." Adelle turns to me and says, "Mama and Papa had just started letting me go to the Union School that year. Grace and I were both in second grade. My brother, Junior, and Grace's brother, Zero, were in fourth grade."

"Zero was ten years old," Grace adds. "I remember now because it was his birthday. Grandma baked him a chocolate cake and his birthday present was a whole nickel. He was so proud of that nickel. As we were walking to school that day he was telling me what he planned to do with that money."

September 1921

Zero and I walk down the dusty road toward Clarksville. The sun is just coming up. As we turn to take the path through the woods, Zero stops to check his pocket once again.

"Come on, Zero. We're going to be late for school. You better not let

Mama know you brought that money with you to school. If she finds out, she's going to tan your hide. What if you lose it?"

"I ain't going to lose it."

"Don't say 'ain't.' Grandma says it makes coloreds look ignorant."

"Then I know a lot of ignorant white folks, too."

"Grandma says that doesn't matter. What matters is that we take pride in ourselves."

Zero sighs. "I've got big plans for this money."

"What are you going to do with it?"

"I'm going to start a savings account."

"A savings account? What's that?" I switch my dinner bucket to the other arm and pull my sweater closer around me. The air has a little nip of fall in it.

"Over at the Penny Savings Bank, you can open up an account in your own name and put money in it. And when you keep it there for a long time, they start paying you for it. Teacher said it's called interest."

"What are you going to do with all of that money?"

"I'm going to college. I turned ten years old today. I figure it's time I started thinking about my future. I'm going to be a doctor, like Dr. Jackson."

"Adelle's daddy?"

"Yep. Look what a nice house and nice things they have. Adelle always wears shoes. She even had a new winter coat last year. I want to have a house of my own someday. And I want to be a professional man, with an education."

"How come you picked doctoring? You can't even stand to skin squirrels. Mama always does it for you."

"That's different. Besides, I'll get used to it when I leave and go take my training."

I don't like the thought of Zero going away. I can't imagine life without my brother.

"Are you going to come back to Clarksville and do your doctoring?"

"I don't know. Sometimes I think I'll leave town. Maybe go someplace where people treat coloreds better. I've heard of such places. They're mostly

up north. Teacher even told me of a place where whites and coloreds go to the same school."

"I don't believe you. You're just making that up."

"No, I'm not. That's what teacher said."

Miss Bessie Wilson is never wrong.

"I'm going to be a teacher when I grow up." I try to sound as sure of myself as Zero.

"Teaching is a fine job for a girl. At least until you get married."

"What makes you think I'm going to get married?"

"I don't know. I just thought you probably would. Most girls want to."

"Miss Wilson's not married."

"Yeah, that's true. Wonder why she never got married. She's pretty enough."

I ponder this as we walk the last mile through the woods and work our way across the tracks and down the street to the school. We can see from a block away that everyone is gathered outside. As we get closer, we smell burned wood. All the schoolkids are gathered in small clumps, whispering and talking quietly. Miss Wilson is speaking to a short round white man with a big gold star on the coat of his crumpled black suit. I've never seen him before, but I think he's the sheriff. You don't see whites around this area of town much, not even the sheriff.

I scoot in beside a group of girls my age and find Adelle Jackson. Adelle and I are getting to be friends since Adelle started coming to the Union School this year. We both love to read, and Adelle even offered to share some of her books with me. I've never known anyone who actually owned books before.

"What happened?" I whisper.

"Somebody tried to burn down the school last night. We got that rainstorm and I guess it must have put out the fire before it could burn the whole school. When Miss Wilson saw what happened, she sent Elroy Davis over to get the sheriff. He's been here talking to her for about twenty *minutes. He and that other man have been walking around and around the school like they are looking for something."*

The other man is near where the fire started to burn around the front door. The sheriff watches him while he takes his handkerchief out of his pocket and wipes his face. It's cool today, but the sheriff looks agitated and hot. The man near the door of the schoolhouse walks over to where Miss Wilson and the sheriff are standing. He's holding something small wrapped in a handkerchief, but I can't see what it is. The sheriff and the other man and Miss Wilson talk for a few more minutes; then the men get in a big black car and leave.

Miss Wilson turns toward us. Her face is pale and ashy-looking and she has a black smudge down the front of her dress. One small strand of hair has come loose from her bun and she reaches back to tuck it in. I realize this is the only time I've ever seen her look afraid. She takes a deep breath and looks down at the ground like she is gathering herself; then she calls to us to come inside. School is in session.

What a strange day it is, with the smell of burned wood and the breeze blowing in from the open door. Even though it's scary to think someone tried to burn down the school, I can't help but be excited for the end of the school day. Mama has given me permission to visit Adelle at her house over on Fifth Avenue. Adelle is going to loan me a book by Mr. Charles Dickens called Great Expectations. Miss Wilson says I will love it. Zero and I agree that while he goes to the bank to talk to Mr. Morris about a savings account, I will go over to Adelle's house. Zero promises he'll be by in an hour to pick me up for our walk home.

The Jacksons' house is so beautiful I have to be careful not to walk around with my mouth open. I didn't know coloreds could live in a house like this. It's made of brick, has a staircase and big windows, and a real library. Adelle takes me into a room where one whole wall is filled with books. Adelle says her daddy is especially fond of books. He's been collecting them for more than thirty years. Adelle's mama brings us tea cakes and milk, and I decide I could just stay here forever. I get so caught up in the house, and the cookies, and the books that I don't realize how late it's gotten until Adelle's mama comes back to ask if I'll be staying for supper.

"Oh, no, ma'am," I say. "My brother is going to be back here to get me by four o'clock."

"Honey, it's already five fifteen. Do you think he meant five o'clock?" Mrs. Jackson sounds worried.

I am shocked. First of all, because all that time slipped away without me noticing, and second, because Zero is never late. He prides himself on being on time. Plus, he knows Mama will be madder than a wet hen if we're late. As it stands, we won't be home in time for him to milk the cow before supper.

"Grace, where did your brother go this afternoon?" Mrs. Jackson asks me.

"He said he was going over to the Penny Savings Bank. He was going to see Mr. Morris about opening a savings account. He got a whole nickel for his birthday. I don't know why he's not here yet." I twist a braid in the back of my hair, trying to think what I should do.

"Mrs. Jackson, can you tell me the way to the Penny Savings Bank? I'd better go check on my brother."

I try my hardest to sound brave, even though the thought of walking the streets of Clarksville alone to look for Zero scares me to death. Mama told me to never go out on the streets by myself. Just last week, a colored girl from down by the river cut through the yard of the white Baptist church on Main Street on her way to work at the Riverview House. A white woman saw her and told her boss lady. That colored girl almost lost her job.

Mrs. Jackson gets a stern look on her face. "Adelle, go knock on your father's office door. Tell him that I need to see him. Tell him it's urgent."

Something in her voice frightens me even more. I hope I haven't gotten Zero in trouble. What if these nice people go look for him and he's goofing off somewhere, maybe meeting his friend for a Coca-Cola over at Mr. Green's store? What if I'm not allowed to see Adelle anymore?

A large handsome colored man comes into the room behind Adelle. He's wearing a white coat over his white shirt, with a tie and suit pants.

His shoes are black and polished shiny. I've never seen a man with shiny shoes on before. He kneels down beside me and looks at me over the top of his spectacles. His voice is gentle.

"Grace, we haven't met. I am Dr. Albert Jackson," he says; then he gives me his big hand to shake. I take his hand and try to fight the tears I feel starting to form under my eyelids. "Grace," he says, "do you think your brother might have forgotten the time, maybe gone over to Green's for a soda pop or a piece of candy? Adelle tells me he got a nickel for his birthday today."

I'm so overwhelmed I start to blubber and stutter. "I don't know, sir. He's usually on time. He knows Mama will be upset with us if we're late. She's cooking his favorite supper tonight and Grandma made him a cake, and we have to milk . . ." I finally burst into tears and Dr. Jackson puts his arm around my shoulders. Mrs. Jackson and Adelle are patting me, too.

"Don't worry, Gracie," Adelle says. "I'm sure he'll be here soon."

Just then there's a loud banging on the front door. Before Dr. Jackson can reach the door, it bursts open. I hear loud voices coming from the hall, and Adelle and I rush to see what's going on. I get to the hall first and I take in a big gasp. Two boys, one of them Adelle's brother and the other someone I don't know, are lunging into the doorway with Zero barely held up between them. Bright red blood drips from a long gash across Zero's cheek. His nose looks crooked and blood oozes from his nostrils. One of his eyes is swollen shut and his clothes are dirty and torn.

"Zero!" I holler, and run to his side, trying to help the boys hold him up. "Zero, what happened?" He looks like he's trying to say something to me, but I can't understand him. Dr. Jackson steps in.

"In here, boys. Get him up on the table." Dr. Jackson looks calm and in control. I try to follow him into the room but he stops me. "Now, Miss Grace, you just go with Adelle and let me take care of your brother. He's going to be fine. You just go on with Mrs. Jackson and Adelle." He eases me toward the door. The last thing I see as Dr. Jackson closes the door is a tear running down Zero's face from his good eye.

Things happen in a blur after that. I sit with Adelle in her bedroom upstairs, while Mrs. Jackson sends Junior out to our house in their wagon to fetch Mama. I worry that Mama will be terrified and I keep getting up and going to the window to watch for her. Mrs. Jackson brings us some supper on a pretty tray with flowers on it. There are dishes with flowers on them, too, and cold milk in crystal glasses. If I wasn't so worried about Zero, I might feel like I was at a party. Adelle tries to help by reading to me from Mr. Dickens, but I can't concentrate. Every sound out on the street makes me jump.

Finally, after what seems like hours, there's a soft knock on the door and Dr. Jackson comes in and sits down next to me on Adelle's bed.

"Grace, your brother is going to be fine. He took quite a beating today, but I've gotten him stitched up and I gave him some medicine for the pain. He's asking for you. I think you better come and see him before he goes off to sleep again."

I follow Dr. Jackson down the stairs and he takes me into a big white room, where Zero is lying on a narrow bed, covered with a quilt. Dr. Jackson guides me close to the table and reaches out to gently touch Zero's shoulder. "Zero, here's Grace."

Zero opens that one unswollen eye and gives me a weak smile. "Hey, Gracie," he whispers. I notice his words are all slurry. "Don't get Mama all worried now, you hear?"

I don't know whether I'm crying because I'm mad at him or worried about him, but I nod my head and stand there not knowing what to do. He reaches out from under the quilt to take my hand. "I'll be all right, Gracie," he says. "Don't you worry . . . ," and he drops my hand as he dozes off.

We hear a horse's steps and the crunch of gravel outside and Dr. Jackson walks over to the window and peers between the curtains. "Your mama is here. How about we go out on the front porch to meet her?" he says. When Dr. Jackson opens the door for us to leave Zero's room, Adelle is standing right outside waiting for me. She puts her arm around me and gives me a quick squeeze. Right then I think how lucky I am to have a friend like Adelle. She steps back beside Mrs. Jackson as I run out on the front porch to meet my mama.

Roxanne

I feel the bond between Grace Clark and Adelle Jackson. I wonder what it would be like to have a friend like that, someone you've known practically your whole life. It occurs to me that no one knows me that well. Of course, I've made sure not to get too close to anyone; otherwise people might find out about my background. But it would be nice to have a friend to confide in; maybe someone who could tell me what I ought to do about Dudley.

But then, as far as I can tell, neither one of these women ever had a husband and child to complicate their lives. I look at them and I can't imagine that either of them would ever fall head over heels for the wrong man. Was Dudley the wrong man? He seemed to fit everything I needed perfectly at the time. Was I so ambitious that he simply served as a vehicle for me to complete the story I made up about myself?

Having children was certainly a part of my story that didn't work out according to plan. I always thought that Dudley and I would have our first child about a year after marriage and then maybe one or two more, two or three years apart. Everything seemed to be moving right along according to schedule. I got pregnant right away and Dudley was delighted. Milly came along in February and it was wonderful. I loved being a mother, knowing that things would be so different for my little girl. She would have genuine social status. I poured myself into mothering her. I even began to wonder how I would be able to love the next child as much as I loved Milly.

But there never was a next child. The same cancer that killed Mama because she ignored it for thirty years started early in me.

My dreams of surrounding myself with beautiful children disappeared along with my uterus and ovaries. No son for Dudley. No more daughters for me.

I never confided my sense of loss to anyone. Instead, any conversation with women in the community could so easily be turned to the subject of Dudley, or a home I was restoring, or my daughter, Milly. Deflecting attention from myself had become a habit very early in my life and I never broke it. Dudley's parents were so indulgent, of him and of Milly, that it was easy even with my own child to gloss over my particular past. Milly has always been a happy, contented person. She must have gotten that from her father. She doesn't seem compelled to ask questions. She takes her secure place in the world for granted. All through school as she was growing up, I focused her attention on Dudley's family. It was fairly easy to just say that my Louisiana parents died young and I was taken in by the Stanleys.

I see a lot of myself in Milly. She's very interested in appearance, but she doesn't have to work as hard at it as I did. She really does have wealthy grandparents. She really was a debutante and a sorority member at Ole Miss. It's all part of her reality, not a fairy tale. Milly has no problem allowing me to indulge her; having everyone's attention is her birthright. It's probably my fault that the child has been on the fast track since conception. She was even born two weeks early. She whizzed through high school, finished college in three years, married her prelaw boyfriend this past summer, and is now complaining about being bored and trying to decide between opening a boutique and going to graduate school. I always dreamed that we might go into business together. After last night's phone call, I have serious doubts about that.

"Hey, Mama," she said in her distracted tone. I can always tell when she's doing something else during our phone calls. I could even hear magazine pages turning. We chatted randomly about nothing—mostly clothes, home decor. I haven't told her anything, of course, about the problems between her father and me. She did ask what I'm working on now. I told her about the tour.

"An African-American tour? You're kidding, right?" she said.

"No, I'm really not kidding. The committee wants to launch it next spring."

"Ew. Sounds depressing. What is there to tour?"

"So far, not much. A couple of interesting houses, maybe," I equivocate, surprised at myself for feeling a little defensive. I might not like it, but this tour is part of my work.

"But you don't really know any black people . . . well, except maybe Ola Mae. How are you getting your information?"

"From a woman named Grace Clark, who taught school here forever. She's retired now, but she's helping me out." Of course Milly doesn't know her, because Milly has been in all-white private schools her entire life—until Ole Miss, that is. She seemed to seamlessly mesh herself into an integrated environment in college. Although she never brought home black friends, there were two black girls in her sorority.

"So, how does that work, exactly?" Milly asked. "Does she just sit and tell you about these places? Or, I mean, like, do you have to actually go see them?"

I took a deep breath, already imagining her response to my answer. "Miss Clark has insisted that I drive her to the places and that I write down the stories that she tells me."

"Wow! So let me get this straight. You actually go to the black parts of town and visit these places with this old black lady. Are you, like, the only white person there?"

"Well, I've only been to a couple, but yes, pretty much. . . ." I think about telling her about my experience with Del Tanner, but decide not to.

She's laughing now. She's so smug in what she thinks is her enlightened racial attitude.

"Oh, Mama. I would love to be a fly on the wall when you are touring around with an old black woman. That would be a sight to see."

I manage to change the subject and get off the phone, feeling even more frustrated and confused. Am I angry because I'm having to do this or am I angry at Milly for thinking I can't?

Adelle puts her arm around Grace's shorter bony frame and gives her a comforting squeeze. It's obvious that standing here in Dr. Jackson's exam room eighty-one years later still brings back some painful memories for Grace.

Grace looks up from the exam table and shakes herself slightly, as if trying to wake up. "I guess you'll be wanting to see the rest of Dr. Jackson's office and the house now. Adelle, be sure and take her in there and show her the library," she says, walking out of the office, talking over her shoulder.

"Just a minute," I say, following her. I can't seem to help myself. "You stopped in the middle of the story. What happened to Zero? Who was his fight with?"

She pauses, but she doesn't look at me. "I'll finish the story, but first I've got to sit down. Y'all complete your tour while I rest in the parlor. When you're done, come meet me."

Adelle shows me through the rest of the Jackson home. It's not an antebellum, but it's an attractive Victorian. I wonder how both these women ended up as old maids, but I decide not to ask right now. My list of questions about these women just keeps growing— and their history is not even part of this tour.

"Miss Jackson, how do you feel about your family's home being part of an African-American tour of Clarksville?" I ask, after we finish the tour and head back to the parlor.

"If you can put together something like that in Clarksville, Mississippi, I would be happy to have y'all tour this old house. There are a lot of memories here for me, some good, some bad.

Since I walk around with a couple of ghosts all the time, it might be nice to share them with someone else for a change."

This makes the hairs on the back of my neck stand up. She sounds so matter-of-fact. "Ghosts? You're not serious, are you?"

She doesn't answer me. She just chuckles low under her breath. *Maybe Zero died that day, right there in that exam room.* We get back to the parlor, where Grace dozes in a chair by the window. She wakes up when we come into the room.

"How did you like the rest of the house?" she asks.

"It will be a good house for the tour," I say. "Authentic antiques, interesting history. Now, Miss Jackson, about those ghosts."

Adelle and Grace look at each other and smile, but I can't read them. They seem to share a secret.

"You wanted to hear what happened to Zero, remember?" Adelle says.

These women are maddening! They leave stories unfinished. They make me wait until the next visit, as if I have endless time for this. Who would have thought I could ever get so roped into the stories of old black women?

We settle into chairs in the sunny parlor.

"Do you remember how I told you that Zero got a nickel for his birthday?" Grace asks.

"Yes, ma'am, I remember. And he was going to start a savings account at the Penny Savings Bank." I wonder if that bank is still around. That might be a good place to put on the tour.

"That's right. Well, he was on his way to the bank that day, with that shiny new nickel in his pocket, when he was stopped by two white boys. We found out later it was Ray Tanner and one of his buddies."

"Tanner? The same Tanners that run the lumberyard?"

"Yes, Ray Tanner was Delbert Tanner's daddy."

"And he beat up your brother? Why?"

Grace shakes her head and sighs. "Zero was admiring that shiny new nickel and not paying attention to where he was going. He looked up and those two white boys were standing in front of him blocking his way. Later that day, when he was able to talk, he told me that Ray Tanner said, 'What you doing, nigger? Where'd you get that money?' Zero said he was a little scared, but he thought they would just go on about their business. He also told me later that he probably could have made it easier on himself if he had just given them the money without a fight."

"Given them the money?" I'm appalled.

"They said to him, 'Don't no nigger need money. You probably stole it, anyhow. You give that money back so's we can find who it belongs to.'"

"That's horrible! You mean they beat him up and they took his money? All for a nickel?"

"Well, I reckon mostly they beat him up because . . ." Grace pauses and smiles. "He told them that he was saving to be a doctor and to get out of town so he wouldn't have to deal with . . . excuse my language . . . redneck assholes like them."

Grace and Adelle both laugh. The pride they share for Zero Clark is obvious.

Grace continues. "My brother never was very good at keeping his mouth shut or his head down."

"Did someone do something? Did you go to the police?" I ask. They only laugh harder. "Why is that funny?"

Adelle replies first. "Mrs. Reeves, you'll have to forgive two old women. Sometimes you learn to laugh or you'll be crying all the time. There was no point in calling the sheriff. This was a white boy that beat up a black boy. They wouldn't have done anything. Zero didn't want to call attention to himself. My papa tried to get him to at least tell the sheriff, but Zero said he just wanted to forget it."

"My brother never even told our mama what happened," Grace adds. "He told her that he got into a fight with some boys at school and lost the nickel from his pocket. Oh, Lord, she was angry. She didn't whip him because he was already so beaten up. But she did make him do extra chores for a month. And she didn't let either one of us go to school for a week."

"So she never knew that Zero was innocent?" I ask.

"No. I believe Grandma knew, though. She always knew those kinds of things without us telling her. She had a way about her. Don't you know she had Zero load her into the wagon and she went to town with him herself? Told Mama she had business to attend to. She and Zero went to the Penny Savings Bank and opened that savings account after all. It was a proud day for my grandma and for Zero."

I sit in silence with the two old women. They are remembering Zero. I'm turning it all over in my mind. Del Tanner must have come by his mean-spiritedness honestly. His daddy sounds every bit as prejudiced, if not more. How could he take a nickel, just one small nickel, from a boy who had so little? All of it is about what black people deserved and didn't deserve. I'm not sure I can hear many more of these stories. Milly's right. They are so depressing.

Chapter 4

Roxanne

As I set out to pick up Grace this morning it's raining—pouring rain, actually. I pull on my raincoat and make sure to grab a couple of umbrellas. Of course, she hasn't told me where we're going today, so I'm trying to be prepared for anything. I called her earlier to see if she wanted to cancel and wait until next week. I can't believe I was actually a little disappointed thinking we might not have our Tuesday morning together.

"Cancel?" she said. "Why would we want to do that? I'm not sweet enough to melt and a little water never hurt anybody."

So, here I go, in a steady downpour, dodging the deep holes in the gravel drive, squinting to see through the fog that has settled in over everything.

When I arrive I rush from the car to Grace's back porch door, hurrying to put my umbrella down before I get drenched trying to get in the door. Grace is waiting for me, as usual, with hot coffee and delightful smells of something baking in her kitchen. Today's treat is something Grace calls cathead biscuits.

"Why are they called cathead biscuits?" I ask, trying to fluff some of the water out of my hair.

"I'm not sure. That's what my grandma called them. I think it's because they are as big as a cat's head. Here's the butter, and I've put out some of my muscadine jelly from last year. We had the best muscadines I've seen in a long time."

"I wish I knew how to make jelly," I say as I slather the biscuit with a generous helping. "It's such a pretty color." I take a bite and the jelly tastes even better than it looks, tangy and sweet all at once. "These are the best biscuits I've ever had."

Maybe even better than Mama's, I think. My mind wanders to Ponchatoula strawberries . . . Mama and an old black woman in the Stanleys' gleaming kitchen, stirring up batches and batches of bright red jam. It was a Saturday in May and I was thirteen years old, doing everything I could to steer clear of the sweltering hot kitchen. Mama and her friend, Miss Ethel, were telling stories about their husbands while they worked. The kitchen was filled with the sound of their laughter and the overpoweringly sweet scent of strawberries. I volunteered to come with Mama that day, but I had no interest in jam-making, like Mama thought.

Mrs. Stanley was hosting a bridal shower for the granddaughter of one of her friends and I was dying to see what a rich girl's bridal shower was like. Although Mama and Miss Ethel were complaining about Mrs. Stanley deciding to have a party on jam-making day, I was thrilled. Mainly because I got to help set up the trays of finger foods that would be spread across the dining room sideboard. Each time I carried in a tray, I peeked into the parlor and listened to the polite "oohs" and "aahs" coming from the room full of women. I was so impressed with how sophisticated it all was and I couldn't help but notice the difference between my own mother's raucous laughter and storytelling and the sedate interaction of the ladies during the bridal shower. I was especially fascinated with the bride and her friends. They whispered and giggled over each new crystal goblet or serving piece. I managed to avoid learning anything about jam-making that day. And here I am now, regretting that, too.

"You all right?" Grace asks.

"Oh, yes, I'm fine," I say, almost wishing I could tell her about Mama and Ponchatoula strawberries.

"I tell you what." She refills her coffee cup and pulls a chair up to the kitchen table. "After we get done with all of this running around Clarksville, digging up bones, you and I will have a lesson. I'll teach you how to make jelly and cathead biscuits. I may even share my recipes with you."

"I would like that." I'm surprised by this realization. "So, where are we going today?"

Grace stirs sugar into her coffee and gazes out the wide window of the kitchen eating area at the rain. "We are going to a very special place today. The Queen City Hotel."

"Where is that?" I have been in Clarksville for more than two decades and it still amazes me, the places I've never heard of. But then, why would I? I don't talk to black people except to give them instructions on the services I need. Ola Mae has been working for me about fifteen years now, and I really don't know anything about her or her family. Today, for some reason, that strikes me as sad. What kinds of stories could Ola Mae tell?

"The Queen City Hotel building is on the corner of Fifteenth Street and Seventh Avenue," Grace says. "Robert Webster built it in 1909, four years before I was born. Robert belonged to the Webster family. After the Civil War, he got himself a job working at the white hotel as a waiter. He scrimped and saved for thirty years to build that place."

"What do you mean when you say he 'belonged' to the Webster family?" I ask, deciding to take one more biscuit. I'll have to get on the treadmill again this afternoon.

"He was a slave. Born into slavery and freed by the Webster family after the War. He was thirteen years old when the War ended. That's when he went to work for the Gilmores, the white folks who owned the hotel downtown for white people. He saw what it was like for coloreds to never have a place to stay. They couldn't stay at the white hotel, you know."

"Yes, of course." I guess that just fell out of my mouth, because I can tell right away it was the wrong thing to say.

Grace looks at me with raised eyebrows, as if she's thinking I agree with segregation. She continues, shaking her head. "White folks did not want to mix with colored people anywhere. Not the hotels, not the restaurants, not the stores. If colored people hadn't built these places I'm showing you, they might as well have stayed in the field and picked cotton the rest of their lives."

Once again, I am at a loss for words. Suddenly, I feel guilty for being white. And what am I supposed to do with that feeling? The War is over and the blacks got their rights, so why do we have to dwell on the past? Of course I know about slavery and segregation. I just choose not to dwell on them. I prefer to appreciate the beautiful aspects of the Old South, like the gracious lifestyle, the lovely columned homes, the wide-skirted dresses with corsets and crinolines, rococo furniture. Capturing and restoring the beauty of the Southern plantation lifestyle is my specialty. And I've worked damn hard to get where I am. People flock from all over the country to see that lifestyle re-created once a year at the annual Clarksville Pilgrimage Tour of Homes.

This African-American project is tainting all of that for me and I resent it. Why did I ever let Louisa Humboldt convince me to do this? I don't need the Riverview restoration job that badly. How will I ever reconcile the two tours? People leave the Pilgrimage Tour laughing and smiling and talking in bad Southern accents. How will people leave this tour? Depressed and feeling guilty, probably. Maybe this whole tour should have been left to black people to figure out.

I can feel Grace watching me with those calm dark eyes of hers, as if she knows what I'm thinking. Suddenly, I don't have much of an appetite and I put down my biscuit. Better to press on, get busy. That always works.

"Shall we get going? I can't eat another bite." I rise and clear the dishes. "How about if I wash these up real quick before we go?"

Grace doesn't stop me. She just smiles and pats my shoulder. "Thank you," she says. "I'll go powder my nose and get my purse." She takes a step, then stops. "Oh, and we'll pick up Adelle on the way. Then after we see the Queen City, we'll go over and see Mattie Webster."

Before I have a chance to ask who Mattie Webster is, Grace walks slowly out of the kitchen and leaves me there with the dishes and my thoughts.

On the drive to the Queen City Hotel I'm lost in the rhythmic drumming of the rain on the roof of the car and the voices of Grace and Adelle trading stories about their brothers, Zero Clark and Junior Jackson, in the spring of 1924.

"Yes, both of those boys turned thirteen that year and they were both itching to get out of Clarksville as soon as they could," says Grace.

"And you had gotten all moony-eyed over Junior already," teases Adelle.

I glance over at Grace, who's nodding her head. She sighs.

"It's true. I had the biggest crush on Junior that an eleven-year-old girl could have. Adelle, do you remember that day Mama let me go to town to pick up something for her at Green's store? I think it must have been sugar. I reckon she needed it right then, because Zero was working for Green and he could have just brought it home. But she sent me."

"Oh, I remember," says Adelle. "I was down on Catfish Alley with my mama that day. We were buying catfish for supper. You came bursting out of Green's store all puffed up and about to cry because those boys were ignoring you, telling you to scram and get home." Both women laugh, and then Grace tells her story.

March 1924

Junior, Zero, and I are sitting on the curb, drinking a root beer out back of Green's store on Catfish Alley. It's Saturday afternoon in the springtime. The sun is warm on my face and I can smell Miss Mabel's catfish from Jones's Café across the street. Mama sent me to town for sugar. She's got to have it for a cake she's making tonight. Fine with me, because I get to see Junior. Junior and Zero will both turn thirteen years old this year and they're itching to be somewhere bigger than Clarksville. Why do boys always want to be somewhere besides where they are?

Zero stocks groceries and sweeps the sidewalks for old Mr. Green and Junior has a job over at the Queen City Hotel. Junior's papa always planned on him following in his footsteps and becoming a doctor. But he doesn't want anything to do with doctoring; crazy thing is, it's Zero who wants to be a doctor. Every chance he gets, he's running errands for Dr. Jackson, or offering to clean his clinic.

Junior eats, sleeps, and breathes music. Ever since the day Louis Armstrong first came to the Queen City Hotel last summer, and played to a Saturday night crowd of every colored person within forty miles, Junior has been saying that playing music is what he's got to do.

Mrs. Anna Lee Jackson, Junior and Adelle's mama, is a musical person, so I reckon Junior came by it honest. They even have a piano in the front room of their house. They're lucky. Their mama taught them both to play the piano when they were little. Adelle plays for the Missionary Union Baptist Church on Sundays. But Junior . . . Junior plays jazz piano. He's talking about Louis Armstrong again.

"I'm telling you, Zero, you've got to come hear Louis Armstrong next time he comes to town. He's got this big smile and he dresses really nice,

like a white man. And what he can do with that trumpet. He had people dancing and singing. It was something to see. I want to do that, Zero! I want to play jazz piano for a band! I'm going to get out of this town and travel with a band like Mr. Armstrong's."

"Why you always talking about leaving, Junior? What's wrong with Clarksville? I think it's nice here," I say.

"Be quiet, Gracie," Zero says. "You don't know what you're talking about."

Zero's always trying to look big when he's around Junior. I get real quiet and sulk.

"That sounds great, Junior, but I got a plan in mind myself," says Zero. "I'm going to medical school. I want to be like your daddy. Except, I'm going to leave Clarksville, too. I'm going to a place where a colored man doesn't always have to go in the back door, or wait behind the white people to get served."

"And where is that?"

"I'm not sure. Someplace up north. Or maybe out west. Maybe I'll move to California and be a doctor there."

"California? You can't go all the way to California!"

"Why not?"

I look over at Junior. I don't think he knows why not. He's quiet for a minute. I don't think he knows where California is.

"Your grandma ain't ever going to let you go that far away from home."

"That's right, Zero," I say stubbornly. "Grandma wouldn't stand for that."

Zero frowns at me. "Don't you have to get home, Grace? Get that sugar for Mama?" Zero takes the last swig of his root beer. "Anyhow, Grandma's not going to be around forever, you know. Besides, I still got to finish high school and college and go to medical school." He turns back to Junior, trying to ignore me. "Your daddy told me maybe I could go to the same medical school where he went in Nashville, Tennessee."

"I tell you what, Zero. You be a famous colored doctor and I'll be a famous jazz musician and we'll meet back up in Clarksville when we're old and tell stories."

"That sounds good to me," Zero says and leans back on his elbows, smiling like he's thinking about being famous.

"You know the last time Louis Armstrong and his band were here, there was a big fight out in the alley behind the hotel," Junior says.

Zero looks at me and motions for me to leave. "I'm not ready to go yet, Zero, and you can't make me," I say. "'Sides, I want to hear what happened at the Queen City."

"She ain't hurting nothing, Zero," says Junior. "Let her stay."

Right about then I want to kiss Junior Jackson, but that would ruin everything. He only thinks of me as Zero's little sister.

"Okay, okay. So what happened?" Zero asks.

"A Tanner is what happened."

"Ray Tanner got in a fight at the Queen City Hotel? I didn't think he'd be caught dead at a colored hotel."

"Not Ray. It was his daddy, Rufus. Rufus has got him a new girlfriend since Ray's mama passed two years ago, and she talked him into bringing her to the show. Says she loves jazz and she doesn't care what color the musician is—she just wants to hear the music."

"How do you know all of this stuff, Junior?"

I can tell that Junior gets a kick out of showing off all the good gossip he knows from working at the Queen City. He's looking real smug right now.

"I just keep my eyes and my ears open. You'd be amazed at what white people say. They don't really see us, you know. So they don't think we hear all of their gossip and such. So anyhow, here comes Rufus Tanner waltzing in the front door of the Queen City Hotel, looking around like he owns the place. I just happen to be passing through the lobby when he comes in with his new girlfriend. She looks to be about twenty years younger than him, got on a short dress, her hair all cut off. She's a pretty woman, smiled real big when she saw me. I didn't look at her, though. I know those Tanners and I don't want to get my ass whooped."

"So let me get this straight. Rufus Tanner shows up at the Queen with his girlfriend to see Louis Armstrong? Did he talk to you?"

"Oh, yeah, he stopped me right there in the lobby, even though I was trying to lay low and stay out of his way. He says, 'Hey, boy! Where's that there nigger band you got playing tonight? My woman here's wanting to hear them.' So I point to the bar at the back of the hotel and tell him that the show is starting back there in about half an hour."

"What happened then?"

"Then he and that woman go back to the bar. I keep working because I've got a lot to do to help the band get ready for the show. I'm helping unload the instruments out of the car, so I'm in and out of the back door from the alley. I'll tell you something, though. Things changed when Rufus Tanner walked in with that woman on his arm. At first, everybody got real quiet and sort of moved out of the way to let them pass. Then that woman flashed this big smile and said, 'Evening, y'all. Please don't anybody get up. We're here to enjoy the show, just like you.' Rufus didn't say nothing. He just followed her like some big old bloodhound. Some folks relaxed after that, but not the ones that know the Tanners very well."

By this time, we've been sitting back here for a while. Zero turns to see if Mr. Green is looking out the back door of the store. "Hurry up and finish the story, Junior," Zero pleads. "I got to get back to work before old Green comes out here and sees me. What happened to start a fight?"

"So the show started and, brother, what a show it was. The horns, the piano. I'm telling you, it was so good that folks was dancing and twitching. That white woman was shaking her skinny little ass right in front of all of those colored men and Rufus was standing there with steam coming out his ears."

My eyes must be big as saucers right now, but I keep quiet because I don't want the boys to remember I'm here.

"He didn't stop her?"

"Last I saw, he tried. But he had a flask in his pocket and all evening he'd been drinking that home brew he makes, so he was too drunk to even get hold of her."

"She didn't dance with a colored man, did she?"

"Naw, she didn't go that far, but she got right up by the stage, you know. So's the musicians could see her real good, and that's when it happened."

"What?"

Just then Mr. Green pokes his head out the back door of the store. "Zero Clark," Green says in his big gruff voice.

"Yessir," Zero answers.

"Get your black ass back in here and get to work. I'm not paying you to sit on the curb all day drinking my soda pop and talking to Junior Jackson."

Zero gets up quick and grabs the broom. "Yessir," he hollers. "I was just taking a quick break. I'm going to sweep out the storeroom right now." Zero motions for Junior to follow him, and I tag along as we go out to the storeroom in back.

"Quick, finish telling me what happened," Zero whispers.

While Zero makes a big show of sweeping near the door, Junior and I pin ourselves up against the wall just inside out of sight. I'm so close to Junior right now my heart is about to beat out of my chest. But it's like he doesn't even know I'm there.

"She got right up near the stage, you know?"

"Yeah, yeah, I got that."

"And she kept making eyes at this bass player. Finally, he looked up at her and gave her a big smile."

"What's wrong with that? She smiled at him first, didn't she?"

"Zero, you dumb ass! This is Rufus Tanner's girlfriend."

I can't believe how hardheaded my brother is, even after getting beat up by Ray Tanner just three years ago and coming close no telling how many times since.

"Nothing happened until after the show," Junior continues. "I saw Rufus stumble out to his car with that woman. He put her in the car and told her to get on home. Told her he would be home later; he was going to meet up with the boys and have a drink. Well, I'm telling you, that's when I started getting a bad feeling."

Zero stops sweeping. "What? Why'd you get a bad feeling?" We all peek out the storeroom and see Green walk out the back door of the store and throw a box on the garbage pile. Zero sweeps like the devil.

"Something about the look in his eye. Plus, he didn't head over to J.T.'s, where he usually meets up with his buddies. He headed around to the back of the hotel instead."

"Uh-oh," Zero says.

I can tell from Junior's tone that something bad is fixing to happen. Zero stops sweeping and stands there, leaning on the broom.

"What happened then?"

"When I saw him heading to the back, I knew there was going to be trouble. So I scooted out through the bar and grabbed John Luke. You know him; Mr. Webster hired him to make sure things don't get out of hand when folks start drinking too much." Zero nods. "I told John Luke it looked like there might be a fight out in the alley. I figured if anybody could take care of old Rufus Tanner, it would be John Luke.

"So the bass player, he's out there in the alley with some of the other musicians smoking cigarettes and winding down. That's what they do after a show. They get real excited playing that music and they have to wind down." Junior is acting all smart again. He's proud of knowing these things about the musicians because he watches them so close.

Zero's getting impatient. "Look, Junior, just get to the point. What happened?"

"Old Rufus came into the alley, drunk as a skunk. He started staggering toward that group of musicians, hollering, 'I'll teach you not to look at my woman like that, nigger! Who you think you are, looking at a white woman that way?' Those boys just got kind of quiet-like. They didn't run and they didn't try to fight him. I think they probably been through this before."

"What about that bass player?"

"That's the problem. He got up in Rufus's face and said, 'Maybe you better keep your woman at home then. 'Cause she the one looking at me!'

*Rufus really got mad then. His face turned red like he was about to ex-
plode. Just as he was about to fight that bass player, John Luke stepped out
into the alley and got between them."*

*"What'd you do?" By now, Zero's forgot about looking like he's work-
ing.*

*"I just stood there and watched, like everybody else. Rufus stood about
even with John Luke's chest. You know John Luke is big as a tree. John
Luke said, 'Now, Mr. Tanner, we don't want no trouble here.' He's talking
real quiet like to Rufus. Then that crazy colored man tried to get in Rufus's
face again.*

*"You should have seen the look that John Luke turned around and
gave him. Anyway, John Luke told Rufus he better go home and sleep it off,
ain't no colored man would ever think of going after his woman. Rufus, he
backed off then, but he was muttering to himself all the way back down the
alley. I followed behind him, keeping way back just to see where he was going. He headed over to J. T.'s then. And do you know that crazy bass player
tried to follow him? Them other boys had to hold him back."*

*"Don't he know he's in Mississippi?" Zero asks. "He'll be hanging
from a tree instead of playing that bass."*

*I shudder when I hear this. I've heard stories about the lynchings,
Mama and Grandma whispering when they think I'm not listening.*

*"Yeah, I figure he's pretty lucky nothing happened," Junior says. "And
I heard them boys say he'd better be glad Mr. Armstrong didn't know
nothing about all that. He probably would've fired him. He can't afford no
trouble like that on the road."*

*Just then the back door of the store slams and old Green yells, "Zero,
what the hell are you doing out there, plucking chickens? Get your ass in
here. We got customers and I need some help!"*

*"Yessir, Mr. Green. I'm coming." Zero looks at me suddenly like he's
forgotten I'm there. "Gracie, you get on home now, and don't you tell
Mama and Grandma what you heard us talking about or I'll . . . I'll . . .
anyhow, just get on home."*

After Mr. Green and Zero get inside the store, Junior and I sneak out of the storeroom. I feel so grown-up sneaking around with him. That is, until his parting statement.

"I've got to get to my job at the Queen City Hotel. It's Saturday night and there'll be music for sure."

I'm so thrilled that he's actually talking to me. "It sounds so exciting, Junior. I would love to hear Louis Armstrong play!"

Junior gets that little-boy excitement on his face, but then he seems to remember who he's talking to and puffs up his chest. "Not a place for little girls, Gracie. You'd better get home now, like Zero said. Your mama'll be wondering where you are."

Grace

The rain has let up a little bit as we sit in Roxanne's fancy big car in front of the Queen City Hotel. The black folks sitting on the porch swing next door crane their necks, trying to figure out what a white woman is doing in this neighborhood.

I realize just how sad the Queen City looks. The roof has obvious holes where huge oak limbs broke through during past storms. Several of the windows in the upper two stories are broken out and the ones on either side of the wide double doors are boarded up. It looks like the last paint color was some ugly shade of green, and it's obvious from the peeling that even that paint is at least twenty years old. The wide brick steps are crumbling in places, and what's left of the azaleas and roses are overgrown and spindly.

I break the silence. "When I was a girl, this was a fine hotel. People all over the county were so proud of this place. There weren't many hotels for black people in those days, you know."

"I guess I never really thought about it before," Roxanne says. I shake my head before I can stop myself. She probably helped get the white hotel, the Gilmore Inn, on the national register of historic places. She knows a different history, and sometimes I wonder if she'd rather stay ignorant.

She got herself into this; she'll hear a lot more before it's over. "They had signs posted on the front of the Gilmore Inn that said *No Colored.* That's why Robert Webster built the Queen City. Before the handful of black hotels in Mississippi were built, those musicians I was telling you about slept in their cars, or in people's barns. It was rare for them to actually get to sleep in a bed."

"What happened to this place? Why has it been allowed to get so run-down?"

"Oh, it's one of those family stories. Robert Webster, Sr., died in . . . let's see . . . seems like it was in the early fifties. His son, Robert, Jr., operated the hotel for about eighteen years. Then, in the late sixties, after the Civil Rights Act was passed, and things opened up just a little bit, black people started being able to stay at the hotels and motels that had previously been just for white folks. It still wasn't easy, mind you. They still got turned away in some places. But there was a different attitude then.

"Black folks stopped coming to the Queen City and it ran on hard times. It's been a boardinghouse off and on over the years. When Robert, Jr., passed, he left the hotel to his wife, my good friend Matilda Webster. She's over in the Pineview Nursing Home now, so she can't keep it up. Her oldest son and his wife died in a terrible car accident when their daughter, Billy, was in high school. Billy lived with Mattie until she went off to college. The hotel will go to Billy in the will, but she doesn't care anything about the place or its history. So . . . here it sits."

"Do you think Matilda Webster will want to talk to us about this property?" Roxanne asks.

"I don't know. Mattie's not much on history, either."

"Stay here," Roxanne says as she throws open the car door and pops up that big umbrella of hers. She climbs out of the car and runs across the muddy grass to the hotel's porch. She sets her umbrella down and cups her hands around her eyes to peer in the window near the door. She even picks her way around the side and struggles through those scraggly old azaleas in the rain to stand on her tiptoes and look in the side window that's not boarded up.

"Would you look at that?" says Adelle. "She's acting right interested in this old place."

"We'll see," I say. I'm still not sure about this woman.

She disappears around the back for several minutes and then comes hurrying back to the car. Gets in all out of breath.

"This place has incredible potential," she says, all excited. "I don't know a whole lot about the buildings in this particular era, but I can tell from some of the woodwork and finishes that it could be really beautiful. When do you think we can go inside?"

I have to admit, I'm a little surprised by her enthusiasm. I look over at Adelle and she smiles like she's saying, *I told you so.*

"We'll need to get the key from Mattie," I say. Truth be told, I'm not sure this woman is ready for Mattie Webster. But I keep this to myself. Come to think of it, might be interesting to see Roxanne Reeves and Mattie Webster in the same room. "I tell you what," I say as I make the decision, "let's head over to Pineview and see if we can get Mattie interested."

"I don't believe I've visited this particular nursing home before," Roxanne says as we approach Pineview.

"No, I reckon not," I say.

Not many white people come to this side of town. I imagine all those old people she knows from the Junior League and the Garden Club live in those nice senior citizen centers with manicured lawns and flower gardens with rocking chairs on the porch.

There's nothing manicured about Pineview. It's a simple one-story brick building with four wings jutting out from a central nursing station. As Roxanne and Adelle and I walk through the sliding glass doors into the sterile-looking lobby, I can see Roxanne trying not to crinkle up her little nose as the smell of age hits her head-on. I don't know why Mattie Webster insists on staying in this run-down place, either, but she's stubborn and there's been no changing her mind.

It's as if Adelle is reading my thoughts. "I don't know why Mattie thinks she has to stay here," she complains. "With all her money, she could be in one of those nice places over on the other side of town."

"Now, Adelle, you know Mattie likes it here," I say. "She doesn't give a hoot about those fancy homes. You and I better count our blessings. If we have to go into a home, this will probably be all we can afford!" I think then about Pecan Cottage and how I probably should count my lucky stars that I can live in a big old house like that. I just hope I keep my faculties about me. If I have my way about it, they'll take me out of there in a pine box.

As we stop to hug and love on our old friends and neighbors parked in their wheelchairs along the long corridor, Roxanne trails behind us, looking uncomfortable.

Pineview is a right gloomy place, but I swear all of that gloom disappears when we walk into the room labeled *Matilda Webster*. Mattie's got the walls painted a warm yellow the color of butter. She's hung some flowered curtains at the window and she has them open to let in the late-morning sunshine that has temporarily broken through the clouds. Through the window, I can see that bright red bird feeder Billy gave her for Christmas. Birds are all over that thing, pushing at each other to get to the food.

Mattie insisted on bringing her own furniture from the hotel; I believe it's called Art Deco style. I remember Roxanne mentioning some kind of word like that when she got back in the car after looking in the windows at the Queen City. I'm certainly no expert at decorating style. Roxanne stops and bends down to look at the table by the door. And, of course, she stops to study the pictures. Mattie's got pictures of herself and Robert, Jr., with all the great musicians who came to the hotel back in the day: Mr. Louis Armstrong, Pearl Bailey, James Brown, B. B. King, Duke Ellington. Oh, those were the glory days of the Queen City Hotel. You can tell from the pictures how beautiful it was then.

As usual, Mattie is dozing in her big old wing chair in the corner. She's got her record player going, and Billie Holiday's voice fills the room. Mattie's wearing her red pantsuit and her hair is combed into tight curls that frame her face. Mattie Webster always was a beauty. We used to say she looked like Lena Horne with those high cheekbones and light skin.

Adelle and I tiptoe over and pat Mattie on the arm.

"Mattie, dear, wake up. It's Grace and Adelle come to visit," I say softly into her ear. Her eyes open and she looks confused at first; then she recognizes us and smiles with that mouthful of white teeth of hers.

"My girls!" she says in her deep voice. "How y'all been?"

Mattie reaches up and puts an arm around each of us as we stoop to kiss her cheeks. She sees Roxanne standing there, just inside the door, pulls Adelle down to her and asks in a loud whisper, "Who's that white woman?"

I walk over and take Roxanne's arm and guide her closer to Mattie. "Mattie, this is Mrs. Roxanne Reeves. She is the director of the Pilgrimage Tour here in Clarksville. She wanted to meet you."

Roxanne smiles politely.

Mattie scowls. "Home tour? Why does she want to meet me? Ain't nobody in my family ever worn no hoopskirt! Why you bringing some white woman running a show about big houses with slaves running around waiting on white people hand and foot to see me?"

Adelle always gets nervous when Mattie starts acting like this.

"Now, Mattie," she says. "Be nice. Mrs. Reeves here wants to talk to you about the Queen City Hotel."

"The Queen City? Since when do they want a black hotel on the home tour? Ain't that the wrong side of town for all those Yankees from up North? They might get the wrong impression about how black folks live if you take them over to my side of town, you know. Ain't that right, Grace?"

I smile. Mattie always did have a wicked sense of humor. Adelle is still patting Mattie's arm and looking horrified. Roxanne stands there with her mouth open, trying to figure out what to say. I think I might enjoy this.

"Roxanne here is trying to start an African-American tour, Mattie. Let people see some of the historical places of black folks in this area. We thought the Queen City Hotel should be part of that tour. We thought we might get the key from you so's Roxanne can look inside the place."

Mattie is still scowling. She reaches into a crocheted bag hanging over the arm of her chair and pulls out her Jim Beam. Roxanne's eyebrows shoot up as Mattie picks up a coffee cup on the table beside her chair. She hands the cup to Adelle.

"Pour that out for me, will you, Adelle?"

Adelle obediently carries the cup over to the sink and rinses it out. She gives the cup back to Mattie, who proceeds to pour herself a drink. A look of sadness suddenly comes over Mattie's face.

"I'm afraid the Queen City Hotel is not in any shape for tourists. Most places around here where black folks did business back in our day are either all shut up or have been torn down. Why would anybody want to tour that?" Mattie looks directly at Roxanne for the first time, her black eyes challenging, her mouth set in a defiant line.

Poor Roxanne! She looks like she's about to cry. Here she is trying to do the right thing by the black folks and we are just not cooperating. I almost feel sorry for her. I reckon right now she wishes she was at home worrying over what kind of lace to sew on the next dress she's having made for some little white girl working in the tour. But Mattie's not done with her yet.

"Mrs. Reeves, come over here and sit down."

She points with her gnarled old fingers to the bed beside her chair. Roxanne obeys, just like Adelle did. That's what people do when Mattie Webster speaks. Adelle and I pull some chairs from over by the sink closer to Mattie. This should be good.

Mattie studies Roxanne for what seems like forever before she finally asks, "Just what kind of information are you planning to give to the people who take this tour?"

Roxanne looks at us as if we'll answer, but we are as curious as Mattie is to hear her answer.

"Well, um . . . I'm not sure yet, Mrs. Webster. I'm just trying to learn about places around here myself." Roxanne fidgets and clears her throat. "I'm planning to have the traditional historical markers that list the year the structure was built and a short amount of information about it. Those would be placed near the street where people could see them from a car. . . ."

Mattie interrupts. "So this is going to be a driving tour. People just get in their cars and drive around on their own?"

"No, ma'am, not exclusively. I was thinking we would do a guided tour. Have someone with a good knowledge of the area conduct the tours and explain about the locations. Um . . . maybe the Queen City could be a bed-and-breakfast . . . or some kind of place for meetings."

I decide to chime in. "Adelle has agreed to let her house be on the tour. They'll be talking about Dr. Jackson."

Mattie looks from Adelle to me and back.

"Y'all are like sisters to me. We've been through more together in the years we've known each other than I ever thought a human being could bear. How can you want to have people tour all of those places where all of our memories are? How can you stand to have them talking about how wonderful everything was when we know the truth?" There is a hard edge to Mattie's voice. "Especially you, Adelle, after what happened to you. And, Grace, what about what happened to Zero?"

Adelle looks down at her hands and doesn't say a word. I stand up and go over to the window to study the birds. I don't know what to say. Mattie's right. Every place I take Roxanne Reeves has some memory of my own or my people. They aren't all bad. It's just that, with memory, I can't have one kind without the other. They all come to me together these days. This woman is just doing her job. She doesn't have any idea what she's opened up. Oh, Lord, she's talking again.

"Ladies, we don't want to deliberately dredge up any painful memories for people. We want to showcase the successes of the black, um, African-American people in this community. I guess we thought it would help y'all feel more included, um . . . not ignored."

Mattie snorts. "Mrs. Reeves, it don't work that way. You might be able to dress your little white girls up in pretty hoopskirts and have them sashay around the big house telling people about the fancy furniture and the big parties and the barbecues on the lawn. But you can't tell the history of the black people of this community and leave out the pain. They are one and the same." Mattie's getting her dander up. She pours another finger of Jim Beam.

I can tell Roxanne doesn't know what to say, so I decide to try again. I'm still not sure why I'm doing this.

"Mattie, you're right: A lot of things have happened over the years, good and bad. But can't we—"

"People need to know, Grace. People need to understand. Is this tour going to help people understand, or is it just another gimmick white people have come up with to make it sound like things have always been fine down here? Make it sound like we're just complaining all the time and not willing to work hard?"

After a moment I reply, "I don't have the answer to that yet, Mattie. Adelle and I just brought Roxanne here so that you could tell your part of the story. And we thought this tour might help your Billy get interested in Clarksville again. Maybe inspire her to figure out something to do with the old place. Roxanne told me there's money available to fix up places like the Queen and other historic places that have gotten run-down."

"Billy's not going to come down here and fix up the Queen. She's got no interest in that old place. She's hardly got the time to come see her grandmother. It's different where she lives up in Chicago. She gets some respect up there now. It's not like here."

Adelle, who has been sitting there listening quietly, speaks up. "We can't live our lives hating, Mattie. It just doesn't do any good. You remember what my papa always said?"

"Yes, I know, I know. 'Keep moving forward.' But your daddy was an educated black man. He was a doctor. He didn't have the same problems as the poor working black folks around here."

"Now you just hold on a minute, Mattie Webster!" Adelle snaps. It makes everybody jump. "It wasn't always easy for my papa—"

"Sisters, sisters!" I say, interrupting Adelle. "Let's not argue among ourselves. Let's remember the good times. Let's tell Roxanne about the night Louis Armstrong played at the Queen City."

Adelle and Mattie both nod. I always could distract them.

"What happened?" asks Roxanne.

"Grace, you tell it," says Adelle. "You're the best storyteller."

"All right then," I say. "It was so exciting! Mr. Louis Armstrong was booked for the Clarksville Auditorium, but Robert Webster talked him into doing a late-night show just for the black folks. We couldn't go to the show at the auditorium, you know."

"What do you mean you couldn't go to the show at the Clarksville Auditorium?" Roxanne asks.

I'm beginning to think this woman is a little thick in the head. When is she going to understand? "They didn't allow colored people to go there."

"Not even to hear a black musician?"

"No, we weren't allowed in. But it didn't matter that night because we were going to have our own show! And the best part was that Mr. Louis Armstrong himself asked Junior to play that night. Adelle and I had just graduated high school and Zero was working to save money for Alcorn State—"

Adelle interrupts me. "I was just beside myself because Zero wasn't there to take me to that show."

I think of Zero's beautiful, smiling face, looking at me across Grandma's kitchen table that afternoon. I was irritated with him because he was going to be late, if he made it to the show at all. He kept saying he had business to attend to. "Don't you fret, Grace," he said. "I'll try to get there, but this is something I need to do." Everything changed after that night. But Roxanne doesn't need to hear that part of the story.

Chapter 5

Grace

Adelle and I are upstairs in her bedroom primping. Adelle's taking longer to get ready than me, even though Zero's not here to take her to the show.

"Ain't you girls ready yet?" Junior calls up the staircase. I step down to the landing and peer over the rail so I can see him in the foyer, pacing back and forth.

"You just hold your horses, Junior. We'll be down in a minute," I call down to him. I can see him looking in the mirror, fixing his tie. Mrs. Jackson walks through on her way to the kitchen.

"Don't you let me hear you say 'ain't' again," she scolds, and then smiles up at him. She brushes a piece of lint from his jacket. I can see from the landing that she's got tears in her eyes.

"You look so much like your father," she says as she stands on her tiptoes to kiss his cheek.

"Are you sure you and Papa can't come tonight, Mama? This is my big chance to break in. Just think, Mama, Louis Armstrong! I'm going to play piano with Louis Armstrong. Do you have any idea how famous he is?" Junior is lit up like a Christmas tree with excitement.

"Now, Junior, you know your papa has patients he has to visit. But we'll be thinking about you. I know you're going to make us proud. Besides, you know this kind of music isn't exactly what your papa likes."

"I know, Mama, but if he would just come hear it one time. It gets in your blood, you know." Junior starts tapping his foot, then moves his shoulders to a rhythm in his head. "And then before you know it, you just got to move!" He grabs his mama and swings her around the foyer, scat singing the rhythm of the music.

Mrs. Jackson laughs and throws her head back. I stand at the stair rail watching the two of them. Lord have mercy, I love to see Junior Jackson move! He will never be as serious as his daddy. I think his mama secretly loves that Junior wants to play jazz music for a living. Now that Zero's talking seriously about college, maybe Junior's daddy will ease up on him just a little bit. After all, Zero's like another son to Dr. Jackson. Zero has worshipped Dr. Jackson since the day Junior and the boys brought him here after he took that beating from Ray Tanner and his gang.

Finally Adelle is ready and we walk slowly down the stairs to show off our finery. Mrs. Jackson and Junior look up to watch us, and we giggle as Junior lets out a low whistle.

"Whew, Lordy, don't y'all look fine!" I can't help but notice Junior never takes his eyes off me. I get that same little quiver inside that I always do when I'm around him.

My new dress is white with a blue ribbon around the waist and I've got my hair done up in that new curled style. I'm even wearing lipstick, which is rare. I hope it'll make Junior want to kiss me.

"Oh, Mama," Adelle whines, "I feel like such a third wheel. I hardly get to see Zero anymore and he's never here for the important things."

Mrs. Jackson puts her arm around Adelle. "Now, sugar, you know Thomas is working as hard as he can to save money for college. He'd be here if he could; you know that."

"I know, I know," Adelle says. "I just miss him, that's all. There won't be anyone there for me to dance with tonight."

"I'll dance with you, sis," Junior offers. "That is"—he puts his arm around me—"if my beautiful date doesn't mind."

I smile and push him away. "Don't be silly, Junior Jackson. Of course

I don't mind. Besides, once you get up on that stage, you're probably not going to even know Adelle and I are there for the rest of the evening. We'll be lucky to get a ride home, won't we, Adelle?"

We laugh and make our way out to the porch. As we're getting into Junior's old Model T, Dr. Jackson drives up. He waves at us, and Junior calls from the car window, "Sure wish you would come to the show, Papa. It's going to be great."

Dr. Jackson smiles stiffly and nods his head, as if he can't quite hear what Junior is saying.

"Let's go, Junior," Adelle says. "I don't want to be late!"

The Queen City Hotel is already crowded when we arrive. Colored people from all over Mississippi, Louisiana, and Alabama have driven in to see the show. There are old cars, new cars, trucks, wagons, and even a few mules tied in the shade of the big magnolia trees out back. Robert Webster himself is standing out on the front porch of the hotel, wearing a fine suit and shaking hands with everyone coming in.

Adelle and I look around for our friend Mattie Johnson. Mattie will be dateless tonight, too, since her beau, Robert Webster, Jr., will be helping his daddy keep everything running.

Adelle spots her first. "There she is, over there by the door. Oh, my, look at her dress!"

Mattie Johnson is wearing a red, close-fitting dress that flares out at the bottom and a matching cloche hat. She outshines us, as usual, with those perfectly placed curls and stylish clothes.

"Isn't it exciting?" Mattie asks as we rush over to greet her. "It's like Mr. Webster threw a graduation party just for us before we all split up."

"Let's not talk about anybody leaving tonight," I say. "Let's just have fun."

In a few days I'll start a job at the garment plant to save money for Tougaloo College. I'm still determined to be a college-educated teacher. I'm scared, excited, and worried all at the same time. I'm not worried about Mattie, though—she'll be fine. She and Robert, Jr., are already talking *about getting married. The worry part is mostly about Adelle and Junior. Adelle is going away to Tuskegee, Alabama, for nursing school. I'm going to miss her so bad, I can't stand to think about it.*

And then there's Junior. I'm so fiercely in love with Junior Jackson I can't see straight, and he doesn't even know it. I know I should give him up and find a man who's planning to settle down and stay in Clarksville, but I can't make myself do it. I've breathed the same air as Junior for so long, listened to his music and his dreams for so many hours, not loving him would be like forgetting to get up in the morning.

"Tonight is Junior's big night," Mattie says.

"That's right," I answer. "And nobody deserves to shine more than him."

Junior has worked for Mr. Webster at the Queen City Hotel since he was thirteen years old, on top of practicing with every two-bit band that blows through Clarksville, just to get the experience. And this is his big chance. I remind myself not to say anything that might make him nervous.

"Here comes Mr. Sunshine now," Adelle says of her brother as he returns from parking the car. Junior is so handsome tonight with his smooth new suit, white shirt, and red tie. If only Zero could be here to see him.

We crowd into the dance hall and find the seats Junior marked for us last night. The table is right in front of the stage, seats usually reserved for the white people who sometimes decide to come to the show. We aren't sure how Junior managed to get us this table, but we're not complaining. He pulls out chairs for us.

"Ladies," he says in his most suave voice, "may I get you some refreshment from the bar?"

We order root beers and look around at the crowd while Junior heads to the back. We wave and hug and laugh with our friends. It's not often, other than at church, that we see this many colored folks gathered together, familiar faces and strangers alike. Even though it's crowded, hot, and noisy, we are so excited we can't sit still. Before Junior gets back to the table, the band members start to come in and warm up their instruments, and a hush falls over the crowd as the trumpets squawk and the clarinets squeak. It doesn't last long when people realize it's not Mr. Armstrong yet.

Junior comes back, grinning and holding two icy root beers. He sneaks a bottle of beer out of his pocket, turns the chair around, and sits facing the back of it. He's already starting to sweat. I can see the beads forming along his lip and on his forehead.

"Are you nervous?" I ask. I'm thinking conversation will calm him down.

"Nah," he says, but I don't believe him. "It's just hot in here with all these folks pressing in. I'm hoping they'll open the doors when they get started, let a little air in here."

Just then the band strikes up a fast-paced melody and the crowd settles into their seats, swaying and tapping their feet to the music. After the first number, Robert Webster walks to the microphone.

"Ladies and gentlemen, put your hands together for none other than Satchmo himself, Mr. Louis Armstrong!"

We are on our feet, hollering and clapping and whistling. Junior is snapping his fingers and grinning, and I think how I've never seen him look so handsome, or so happy. Mr. Armstrong starts with "When the Saints Go Marching In" and we stand through the whole song. Before long, couples start breaking off out of the crowd and filling the small dance floor at the back of the hall, or dancing in the aisles between the lined-up chairs.

It's such a joyous feeling to be here with the man I adore and my very best friends. I think I might burst with happiness. Tonight, I believe anything is possible. Zero will become a doctor and Adelle will finish nursing school. They'll get married and have lots of babies. Maybe Junior will even decide to stay in Clarksville and play right here at the Queen City. And then, maybe Junior and I . . . I stop myself. I can't get my hopes up that much.

The first set ends and Mr. Armstrong takes a break. Junior excuses himself and we see him talking with Mr. Webster back by the bar. When he returns, he's glowing.

"Mr. Armstrong has asked me to sit in on the next set!"

We all jump up and hug him at the same time. "We're so proud of you," Adelle says.

"I knew he'd ask you to play for him," I say. I try to catch my tears before he sees them as I reach up to kiss his cheek. Junior gives me a look like he never has before. It feels like my heart is going to stop. It seems as if he wants to say something, but just then a member of the band steps up and grabs his arm to tell him it's time to go.

Junior disappears and we settle back into our chairs to wait. From where we sit we can see the musicians returning one by one to the stage in the dim light. The piano is on the far right of the stage, and Junior comes in and takes the bench, lightly fingering the keys of the instrument he has played for so many years. My eyes are so glued to the stage that I gasp and turn when I feel someone touch my arm.

There before us are Dr. and Mrs. Jackson, looking elegant and poised, and maybe a little uncomfortable. We squeal with delight to see them. They part slightly and Zero steps in between them, his eyes fixed on Adelle. The love between them is clearer than ever as he takes her in his arms and kisses her.

Our greetings are short because just then the lights come up and Mr. Armstrong steps out onto the stage.

"Ladies and gentlemen," he says in his raspy voice to the hushed audience, "tonight, appearing for the first time onstage with my band, we are honored to have on the keyboard your own Mr. Albert Jackson, Jr." Mr. Armstrong turns and points at Junior, who stands up from the piano bench and bows. Everyone screams, but one voice is heard above everyone else's.

"Tear it up, brother!" yells Zero.

Junior turns toward the table and sees not only his best friend but also his parents sitting in the glow of the low stage lights. He smiles so wide, I think his face will crack, and he sits down and rips out a series of chords that fires up the band and gets Mr. Armstrong tapping to the beat. Before we know it, the band is in full swing and the whole place is pulsing with the rhythms of Louis Armstrong's jazz.

. . .

I have to shake myself and recollect I'm in Mattie's room at the nursing home, I'm so lost in my memories. That August night in 1931 was so full of promise. I can still feel the way my skin tingled when Junior sat down at that piano. I remember how the black folks were so proud of Junior. We were all so young and full of dreams. We refused to believe that life could turn on a white man's whim. I look over at Adelle and Mattie and they're also gone in memory. Roxanne looks at me, waiting for me to finish the story.

"Junior had never been better. He played his heart out that night. I was so proud of him," I say. "That's also the night I knew I'd lost him for good." Mattie and Adelle nod. I see their sadness for me.

"What do you mean?" Roxanne asks.

"There was no keeping him in Clarksville after that. Within a month he hit the road with Louis Armstrong and his band. I didn't see him again for three months."

Mattie agreed to let us borrow a key to the Queen City Hotel, so on the way back to Adelle's house we stop by again so Roxanne can go inside and look around. Adelle and I decide to get out and go in with her this time. She looks very serious and her forehead is all furrowed up as she walks carefully around the old lobby. She opens doors and examines the floor and the walls like she's a fire inspector. We decide not to go upstairs, since we're not sure that old staircase will hold us.

Adelle and I wait and watch while she does her examination. I think Adelle is as lost in thoughts about what this place meant to us as girls as I am. I remember the late 1920s, when we were falling in love with each other's brothers. Me with Junior—especially when he finally started to notice that I was not just Zero's annoying little sister anymore. It was mostly Sunday afternoons when I was able to spend time with him. He would come out to our house and pick me up in his daddy's car and drive us into town. We always came to the Queen City Hotel on those afternoons. Mr. Webster allowed us to sit out on the lawn under that big old magnolia tree and court.

"Addie, do you remember how old Mr. Webster would sit and watch us from the back porch?" I ask.

Adelle chuckles. "I sure do. I think he must have had some kind of arrangement with my mama and your grandma to make sure we behaved ourselves."

Roxanne wanders back over to where we're standing. She has pulled a notepad out and is writing something in it.

"What year did you say this hotel was built?" she asks.

"I believe it was 1909," I answer.

"Mm-hm," she says, still looking around. "You know . . . I just wonder . . ." She almost seems to forget we're standing here waiting on her. Then she looks back at us and says, "You know, it's a shame to let this beautiful old building sit here falling apart. Is there anything that it could be used for in the community? A bed-and-breakfast maybe? Or a country inn?"

"I don't rightly know," I answer, and Adelle just shakes her head.

"There's not much call for a bed-and-breakfast in this part of town, Mrs. Reeves," says Adelle.

Roxanne has a little set to her jaw, like she's just made up her mind about something. "In order to get money for restoration, there will need to be documentation of how this property will be used for the community's benefit." She looks at Adelle and me like we're supposed to have an answer.

"I don't really know how you go about that," says Adelle, and I shake my head in agreement with her. "But you're right. It would be a shame to let this old place go." Adelle walks slowly over to the big double doors that open onto the back porch. She stares out the doors for a long time, while Mrs. Reeves brings me over and points out some of the details of the staircase railing that are apparently historically significant. I watch Adelle out of the corner of my eye, wondering what she's thinking.

I walk over to her and put my arm around her waist. "What you thinking about, Addie?" I ask, as Roxanne finally stops poking around and comes to stand beside us. We're all watching the rain drip off the eaves of the porch. It's so quiet in here all you can hear is the steady drip of the leaks in the roof into the buckets Billy has taken the time to set around the lobby.

"I was thinking about that Sunday afternoon when Zero asked me to marry him," she says.

August 1931

Adelle

This year everything has started to feel different. Used to be, the minute church service let out, the boys were off, running around, playing ball or racing to the creek to catch tadpoles. Grace and I always help the older women get the food laid out, wishing we could be tearing around and being silly like the boys. But today, both Zero and Junior are helping set the tables up and hanging around after the preacher says the blessing.

The four of us have been coming with our families to these all-day singings with dinner-on-the-ground our whole lives. Grace and I are especially excited today because we're having the singing in two different places, since we've got so many people. The older folks will be over at the church, but Mr. Webster agreed to let us young folks use the Queen City for our singing. Right now, everybody's here under the trees down by the river for dinner. There's so much food spread on those wooden planks and sawhorses, they look like they might break in two.

I look up from unwrapping a chocolate cake and Zero is standing in front of me acting all shy, which is not like him. "Would you like to sit together for dinner?" he asks, looking at his feet for some reason.

At first, I don't quite know what to say. I'm thinking, of course I want to sit together. Isn't that what we always do—our family, Grace, Zero, and their grandmother? But then I realize he means just us, separate from my mama and papa. I look at Grace and she sort of shrugs her shoulders like she's not sure why he's asking, either.

He must think I'm hesitant, because he says, "Gracie and Junior, too . . . they could sit with us, I mean."

Junior nods, looking over my shoulder eyeing the food, distracted as usual. Grace just looks at him and waits. She adjusts her collar and smooths the front of her dress. She's so patient with Junior. Any of the boys around here would love to be eating dinner with her, but she has her heart set on my crazy brother. The only things Junior seems to have a heart for are music and food. He seems to suddenly realize that we're all staring at him.

"Oh, yeah . . . Gracie," he says, charming her with his smile, "how 'bout it?" Zero rolls his eyes in exasperation. This is obviously not how he planned this, but Grace, as usual, puts everyone at ease.

"Yes, I'd love that," she says, placing her arm through Junior's. "Let's eat."

Zero offers his arm to me and we walk over to get in line behind the old folks and our parents. I glance over at my mama and realize she's watching me. Grace and I are eighteen years old now, and the boys are twenty. Both her grandma and my mama keep telling us that we need to act like young ladies around these boys. They don't want folks talking.

We fill our plates and find a spot under a gnarly old oak tree that's particularly shady. We're mostly quiet for a while except for making small talk about how good everything is. The boys lay into their plates of food like they haven't eaten in a week. Gradually we begin to talk about last night's show and how great it was for Junior to play with Mr. Armstrong. I'm feeling so grown-up today, sitting here with our beaus under this big old spreading oak tree. And Zero even offers to bring us more food. I decide that's definitely courting behavior. Of course, Junior, my stupid brother, is starting to fall asleep. Poor Gracie! I don't know why she puts up with him. But it does give us a chance to talk while Zero's gone.

Grace and I are giggling over how much chicken and dumplings Junior has consumed already. He's leaning against the trunk of the oak tree we're all sitting under, rubbing his belly and groaning. Zero is headed back over to the long tables spread with food. "Oh, and Zero . . . get me some more of your grandma's fried chicken, please," I say. I bat my eyes at him and give him my prettiest smile. Zero is looking particularly handsome today in his white Sunday shirt and gray serge pants. He takes such particulars with his clothes, you would never know it's the only good set he has. The only other clothes he owns are work overalls.

"And I need one of Miss Mamie's fried apple pies," Grace calls before Zero takes two steps away. He shakes his head and grins, working his way through the groups of folks scattered around the grassy riverbank on blankets and under trees.

"Lordy, how do you girls eat so much?" Junior asks. "I ain't going to be able to do any singing this afternoon. I got to have me a nap." He slouches down and puts his hat over his face.

"You always say that," says Grace, leaning over to knock his hat off. "And then you end up singing louder and longer than anyone else."

"He does," I say and laugh. "And he also reads music better than any of the rest of us."

Junior picks up his hat and puts it over his face again. "Y'all wake me up when it's time to sing."

"Zero's not talking so much about going to California these days," I say to Grace as we watch him stop to help one of the elderly ladies out of her chair.

"I know." She nods. "And I think the whole reason he's changed his mind is you."

I blush then, feeling a little quiver of excitement. "Do you think so?"

"I do. I think he's smitten with you. And he knows you don't want to leave your mama and daddy."

"You're right. I don't." I squeeze Grace's arm as I say, "Oh, Gracie, I hope it's true. You know Mama married Papa when she was eighteen."

Grace frowns and pulls away. "But what about nursing school? What *about how we said we were going to be different from these other girls around here?" Junior snorts and turns his head in his sleep. Grace is temporarily distracted from fussing at me. She bats away a fly that's buzzing around Junior's face. "He wouldn't be so tired if he hadn't stayed up all night talking with those musicians," she says.*

"Of course I'm going to nursing school," I say. "But, to tell you the truth . . ." I lower my voice to a whisper. "I would marry Zero today if I could . . . so I wouldn't have to worry about being such a good girl anymore . . . if you know what I mean."

Grace's eyes get big and she looks at me like she's shocked. "Why, Adelle Lee Jackson, you little hussy!"

"Shh, now," I say, grinning at her. "Here comes Zero."

We sit up and act all innocent as Zero passes around the food he's brought back. We munch contentedly, watching the people milling about laughing and talking. When we've finished eating, Zero stands up, stretches, and looks down at me.

"Um . . . Grace, if you'll excuse us . . . Adelle, I was wondering if you'd like to take a walk down by the river before the singing starts?"

I'm startled by this, since Zero knows how strict Mama is about me being alone with a boy, even him, now. As I'm figuring out how to answer, he says, "I did ask your daddy's permission. He and your mama said it was fine, as long as we stay in sight."

Grace turns to me and grins, giving me a little wink. "You go ahead, Addie. I'll stay here with Mr. Sleepyhead."

Zero and I walk along the bank of the river, mostly in silence. I'm still a little off balance by how different things feel between us today. What happened? I find myself more conscious of his shirtsleeve against my arm and his hand against my back when he says, "Let's stop here for a minute."

We look out across the Tombigbee River, at the calm brown water, and I imagine us coming here with our children someday, letting them play in the mud on the riverbank. Zero stoops down and picks up several rocks and begins skipping them across the water. I watch and think how graceful he is.

"You know that I'm saving money to go to college as soon as I can?" he asks, not looking up.

"Yes, I know," I say, feeling my heart start to beat faster, wondering where he's going with this.

He squats again for another rock and pauses there, staring at the river. "And then I'm going to medical school."

"Yes."

"I can't let anything stop me. And, well . . ." He seems a little flustered, but I let him sort it out. He stands and turns to me. "It's just that I have to do this, Adelle. I want to be able to support my family. I want my kids to have a house like your daddy provided. . . ."

"I understand," I say. Why does he look so worried? I've never doubted for one minute that he'll do everything he's planned.

"What's wrong, Zero?"

He stands and glances back toward the church folks. I look, too, and I can see his grandma deep in conversation with my mama. Mama lifts her hand and motions for us to come back. I ignore her.

His words come out all in a rush as he stands up and comes over to me. "It's just that I'd like us to have an understanding. . . ."

My heart is in my throat now as he takes my hands and turns so that his back is to our people, shielding me from their view. "I was hoping that when I'm done, and when I'm ready to provide for us, that you and me could . . . get married." He pushes the last words out as if he's been holding his breath.

I don't know whether to laugh or cry. It seems like such an impossibly long time. College, then medical school. I'll be so old by then. He must see the confusion on my face. He drops my hands and thrusts his hands into his pockets.

"Will you at least think about it?"

I realize then that he thinks I'm hesitant. I laugh at the thought that he can't see I'm crazy for him. He starts to turn away.

"No, wait." I reach for his arm. "Yes, Zero. That's what I want, too . . . to marry you." I take a deep breath. "I'll wait as long as you need me to."

Mama's calling my name now. Zero and I both turn and shout, "Coming!" at the same time. When we see our folks start to pack up the dinner, Zero grabs my hand and pulls me behind a huge tree near the riverbank. He gently places his hands on either side of my waist and leans down for a kiss. It's a sweet kiss, full of promise.

"I love you, Addie Jackson," he says.

"I love you, too, Zero," I say, throwing my arms around his neck.

As we start back to join our families to prepare for the afternoon filled with singing, my heart is about to burst with joy. I feel like it will be obvious to everyone that Zero and I are truly a couple now. I'm so preoccupied with my own thoughts that I don't notice anything strange until Zero suddenly stops.

"I'll see you at the singing," he says, and he's gone, walking toward a group of men I now notice are standing apart from the women, who are busily packing boxes and baskets with leftover food. All the contentment I was feeling is instantly replaced with a sharp sting of fear. My papa and Mr. Morris are talking to two white men. In the distance I can see a truck parked on the road. Two white boys are sitting in the back of the truck. I find Mama wrapping leftover corn bread in wax paper.

"Mama, what's going on?"

She looks up at me, then glances in the direction of where Papa stands quietly listening as the white man shakes his finger near Papa's face. The look on her face matches the feeling I have in my stomach.

"That's John Davenport from the mill, and A. W. Spencer from the bank. They're having a word with your papa," she says, as if this is an everyday occurrence. But I can tell from the way her hands are shaking that she's not as calm as she's trying to look.

"A word about what?"

"I don't know, child," she says sharply. "Here, help me pack this food." She hands me a cake to wrap and I take it, still watching the men. Zero has joined the group now and, as I watch, he walks over near my papa, looking defiantly at the white men. Papa never takes his eyes off John Davenport as his arm comes out and gently pushes Zero back.

"Where's Junior?" I ask, thinking that he should be there with Papa, standing up, like Zero, to these white men.

"He and Grace left already to help get the hymnbooks ready over at the church."

I finish wrapping the cake and help Mama carry the boxes to our car. The truck with the white boys in the back is parked nearby, and as Mama and I approach, the boys whistle and make rude comments.

I start to say something and Mama stops me. "Just ignore them," she says.

"But, Mama, they shouldn't be talking to us that way."

"I know it, child. But sometimes it's better to keep your head down and your mouth shut."

Everything inside me rebels at this statement, but I trust my mama. So I stay quiet and feel all of my earlier happiness and excitement draining out of me through the big hole that's opened up in my perfect day.

Grace

"So what were those men talking to your father about?" asks Roxanne.

"I overheard Mama and Papa later that evening when we got home," Adelle replies. "Papa said that John Davenport had somehow gotten wind of Papa and some of the other colored businessmen trying to get more colored folks to vote. He told Mr. Spencer and they decided to come by and have a talk with Papa."

"About what?" Roxanne asks. She hasn't caught the irony in Adelle's voice.

I decide to jump in. "You see, Roxanne, those white men didn't want the colored folks to start voting, acting like we had rights."

"But they couldn't stop you. What did they say?"

Adelle answers with a sigh. "It was just another of those thinly veiled threats. I remember that night how Papa almost spat out the words when he told Mama what they'd said. 'We wouldn't want trouble stirred up in our little community, now, would we, Dr. Jackson?' I was afraid for Papa after that."

I nod in agreement and Roxanne doesn't say a word. I don't think she knows what to say. As we're driving home, I can tell she wants to ask more questions about Zero. But I just can't bring myself to talk about Zero more than a little bit at a time. I want her to know how special he was. I want her to see him through my eyes, not white folks' eyes.

We get back to my house after seeing Mattie and Adelle home, and Roxanne walks me to the back door with that big old umbrella of hers, and then she plops herself down in the rocking chair on my screened porch.

"I think I'll wait on the rain to let up a little bit before I head back," she says.

I think she just doesn't want to go home. I don't know much of her story because we've been so focused on mine, and I'm not sure I want to know. Probably none of my business anyway. But she sure seems lonesome.

I go over and sit beside her in the other rocker. "Are you married, Roxanne?" I ask. I figure this is a safe enough question. She wears a wedding ring and a big old diamond on her left hand.

She sighs and says, "For now, I am. My husband and I are . . . separated." She seems to have a hard time getting this out, but then she rushes to say real quick, "But no one knows . . . in the community, that is . . . and, well, I haven't exactly told my daughter yet, either."

"So you have a daughter, do you?" I ask.

This makes her smile. "Yes, her name is Milly—Millicent, actually. She married last summer. A really sweet boy from Natchez. They met at Ole Miss. He's going to be a lawyer." The way she says this, I can tell she's real proud.

"I see, and what's your daughter going to do?"

"Oh, I don't think she knows what she wants. She's not as driven as I've always been."

I look over at her and realize that she's got tears starting down her cheeks. She's trying to wipe them off her face without me noticing. Probably embarrassed to be crying in front of an old woman like me. I reach in my pocket and pull out a clean handkerchief and hand it to her. I'm a little surprised when she takes it. She dabs at her eyes and glances at me.

"Thank you," she says. "I'm not sure what's wrong with me today. I don't usually talk about such personal things."

"I can understand that," I say. I'm thinking to myself that Lord knows I don't want to tell any more of my stories today. I decide to see if maybe she just needs a little prompting. It's clear to me that she could use a talk. I'm trying to sort out what question to ask. "Is your daughter close to her daddy?"

"Oh, yes, very close. She thinks he hung the moon. That's why I haven't said anything. I just hate to disappoint her that way."

"That sounds like a big old burden to be carrying by yourself," I say.

"What do you mean?" she asks.

"Your daughter's a grown-up married woman now. Surely she knows that things happen between men and women sometimes. Misunderstandings and the like."

"Maybe. I guess I've always protected her from anything unpleasant."

"You got some of your lady friends you can talk to about things with your husband?" I ask. Surely she's not going to talk to me. She hardly knows me.

She thinks about this for a while, and I notice she dabs at her eyes some more. Then she takes a deep breath and her voice is a little stronger. "I don't really have friends that I talk to about . . . you know . . . me. To tell you the truth, Grace, seeing you and Adelle and Mattie makes me realize I've never had a friend like that."

I nod and rock, thinking how I don't know what I'd have done without those two. "That's a shame," I say. I'm not sure how to respond, but I'm curious. "How come you never made good friends? You move around a lot growing up?"

"No. We didn't move around. As a matter of fact, my parents were born and died in the same town."

"Was that here in Mississippi?"

"Um . . . no . . . it was Louisiana."

For some reason she seems hesitant. I sit waiting. Don't want to push her. I can almost feel her wheels turning. What could be so hard to talk about? Suddenly, she completely changes the subject back to Zero. Here we go again. "So, it sounds like your brother, Zero, was able to go off to college. That must have been quite a feat, especially during the Depression," she says, raising her eyebrows, trying to get me to talk some more.

Somewhere along the way, I guess I've given her the impression that Zero changed his mind and left Clarksville after all and lived out his days somewhere else, happy being a doctor. What if he had never gone to Ellen Davenport's house that night? Things might have turned out differently. He labored at that sawmill all those long months, saving every penny, even though Ray Tanner treated him worse than the dogs hanging around there begging for scraps from the dinner buckets. But Zero kept saying he was so close. And that night, he said how that was forty dollars closer to him making tuition, all two hundred dollars, for a whole year.

I guess I'll never know what really happened. It seems I should be resigned to that by now. So many things changed for me during those years when I left Clarksville. Tougaloo College was my salvation. Zero believed Alcorn State would be his.

"So where did you say Zero went to college?" Roxanne asks.

"Alcorn State College in Itta Bena," I say. Just then Walter knocks on the screen door, wanting to ask me something about the yard, and Roxanne jumps like the boogeyman got her. Walter wouldn't hurt a fly, but she'll never know that long as she keeps running off every time she sees him.

"I'd better get on home so you can have your nap," she says, and scoots past Walter real quick, grabs that umbrella, and heads for her car.

Chapter 6

Roxanne

I'm sipping on an RC and trying to piece together what I have so far for this African-American tour. Not much. A schoolhouse-turned-lumber-warehouse, a doctor's house, and a dilapidated hotel. Great. I feel the knot in my stomach growing. I have to report to the committee tomorrow and this is pathetic. I try to scribble some notes about Dr. Albert Jackson. What was the name of that black medical school he went to?

My house is too big and too quiet—that's the problem. Sitting here in the kitchen I remember what it was like before Milly married and left last summer. There was a constant flurry of activity—wedding preparations, dress fittings, flower selections. I loved that time with her. I finally got to experience all of the parts of a wedding that I never had since Dudley and I eloped, much to his mother's chagrin. Penelope Reeves was apoplectic when he brought me home to meet her. She disguised it well, being the genteel type, but I was, of course, terrified. What could I do to prove myself worthy of the Reeves name? Having Milly helped. She wasn't tainted by an uncertain past. It always bothered Dudley's mother that she couldn't pin down my ancestry. Thankfully, she threw all of her energy into Milly and I dodged her social bullet. And, in the meantime, I built a social circle for myself that even she couldn't question.

Now, not only is Milly gone, but Dudley is, too. How naïve I was to believe he'd never cheat on me! But then, he's always had everything he wanted—money, education, even this house he inherited from his family. None of it means as much to him as it always has to me. *What should I do? Should I take him back?* I can't fathom why that young woman would put up with him and his tiresome obsession with Civil War history. The knot in my stomach tightens more. I wonder if he loves her. Was all that business about being tired of waiting on me to forgive him just an excuse? *Stop it,* I tell myself. *You've got work to do.*

Thankfully, the phone ringing interrupts my downward spiral about Dudley. It's Louisa Humboldt. She barely lets me say hello before she launches in.

"You all are just not going to believe this!" she says in that stupid attempt at a Southern accent. "I think Riverview has a ghost! Won't that be special when we get on the Pilgrimage Tour?"

"How about that? Really?" I'm trying to act interested since my bid for her restoration project went in last week. Everybody and his brother around here has a ghost. One more is not going to increase the tour attendance. But I let her rattle on.

"Do you remember the old woman who died here? What was her name?"

"Davenport. Ellen Davenport." I picture fat old Ellen Davenport. She practically ate herself to death, I've heard. I can't imagine her flitting around anywhere, unless ghosts can roll. The story I heard was something about her pining away for years for a boy who married someone else. I seem to be surrounded right now with women, alive or dead, who spent most of their lives alone. Is this some kind of sign? Is this what's going to happen to me?

"Well, I kept hearing something last night up in the attic."

"You know, Louisa, you probably have bats," I say. I don't want her to get her hopes up.

"No, I'm sure it wasn't a bat. Because, listen to this. Today, I was poking around the attic. There's a ton of old stuff up there. And I found a trunk full of letters and a diary."

I'm thinking Ellen Davenport probably kept a diary of everything she ate for sixty years. "Uh-huh," I say, reaching for my RC.

"It's Ellen Davenport's diary and it starts in 1926. I think she must have been about sixteen years old." Louisa is so excited she's forgetting to try to sound Southern.

"Mm-hm," I say, stifling a yawn. I think I'll take a nap. It's still raining and I don't feel like writing today.

"Well, anyway, I want you to look at it when you come here for the committee meeting tomorrow. You might recognize some of the names. There's only one, so far, that looks familiar to me."

"Oh, really," I say. "And who is that?"

"Um . . . let me see . . ." I hear shuffling in the background.

"Tanner . . . Ray Tanner? Isn't that the name of that lumber business over on the south side?"

That makes sense. The Davenport family was in the timber business for years. They probably worked with the Tanners. I think again of Del Tanner's refusal to let us look at his warehouse and grit my teeth. Louisa is still yammering on.

"And let's see, there's an Andy Benton—apparently, she was in love with him. And there's a funny name . . . someone named Zero?"

I almost drop the phone. "Zero Clark?" I ask.

"I don't see any last name. She's just writing something about Zero delivering a package . . . Her writing is really difficult to make out."

I promise Louisa I will look at the diary first thing tomorrow after our meeting and hang up. I stop myself before dialing Grace Clark's number. She seems so mysterious about her brother. Maybe there are things in that diary she doesn't want known. I'll just see what it says and then decide whether or not to talk to her about it next Tuesday.

Chapter 7

Del Tanner

As I sit on a barstool at Dewey's sipping a cold Bud, I try to figure out how the hell I got myself into the mess I'm in. We Tanners been running the lumberyard since Daddy took it over in 1941, the year before I was born. Lumber's always been plentiful and profitable. But I've never been able to make the business work as well as my daddy. Folks around here always talk about him. "That Ray Tanner," they say, "he had such a good head for business." I'd like to tell them, Daddy didn't have to deal with all these worthless niggers. Back in Daddy's day, black men wanted to work and you could get a good day's labor out of them.

What I can't sort out is how I'm supposed to pay the damn health insurance or workman's comp on a bunch of employees who would just as soon spit on me as work. It used to be, the boys were loyal. They were willing to work for what the Tanners could pay. Glad to have a job. Now, I can barely keep anybody for six months before they up and quit.

If that ain't enough, Alice is on a tear about building a new house. She keeps complaining that we need to live in a better neighborhood. The last thing I want to do is move. When Daddy built the Tanner house, it was in a prime part of town, near all of the right people and all of the right places. Then those developers started building up subdivisions on the south side of town. Good for business, but all the white people started moving out there. I can't abide the thought of selling my daddy's house to some nigger. It just ain't right. But if I don't, I'm going to end up in the middle of an all-black neighborhood.

And if that ain't enough, that Reeves woman shows up the other day with that old woman waiting outside in her car. Asking about my warehouse and some damn school. That's the last thing I want to hear about. I'll burn that warehouse down before I turn it into some tourist attraction for a bunch of Yankees. Let'm all burn in hell.

Dewey walks in from the kitchen behind the bar, drying a glass. I order another Bud and study my options. I could sell everything and move, get out of the lumber business completely. Alice's brother up in Memphis told me if I ever needed a job, I could work for him, but I don't know nothing about farm equipment. Or, I could sell the house and use the money to support the lumberyard for a couple more years until things turn around. Me and Alice could move in with her mother for a while, maybe build a new house in one of those subdivisions when I get a little ahead.

The thought of living with Alice's mother is just about more than I can stand. That woman is the orneriest old bitch I ever met. I've spent the better part of the past forty years of my married life staying out of that woman's way.

Nope, neither one of those ideas is even tolerable. I'm going to have to get a loan. I'm just going to have to go down there to the First National Bank of Clarksville and meet with a loan officer. Hopefully, it'll be one of the boys I know from high school. One of them will probably do me a favor. My credit's been mostly good until the last couple years. And I've never asked for much before.

Yep, that's what I need to do. I finish off my second Bud. It's all going to work out. Alice will see. And maybe I'll look into selling the old place. Things are bound to be looking up soon. I've lived in this town my whole life and I provide a good service for people. Alice teaches Sunday school at the First Baptist. I even show up there myself on Easter and for the Christmas program. Yessir, how can a banker—who's probably one of the boys I grew up with—refuse me? I feel so much better, I tell Dewey to bring me another Bud.

After a shower and shave, I put on a clean shirt and think about a tie, but decide I don't need that. Those boys up at the First National Bank of Clarksville know me. A. W. Spencer and now Arvis Spencer, the president of the bank, have been working with us Tanners for as long as I can remember. When I was a boy, I'd go to the bank with Daddy, and sit in a big soft chair while he met with A.W. Of course, Daddy was growing the business enough to pay back the advances the bank made him ahead of time. And he ran the lumberyard before all of the rules about how much you have to pay: health insurance, workman's compensation, and all of that malarkey. It's enough to drive a man out of business these days.

Construction should pick up after the first of the year. I heard rumors that a new contractor's coming to town looking to build a couple subdivisions with one hundred to one hundred and fifty houses each. This could be a great boon to Tanner Lumber if I can get that contract. I just need a small loan to tide me over until then.

I walk up to the front counter and a young girl wearing a suit greets me real polite-like. When I ask to see Arvis, she smiles in a snooty businesslike way and asks me if I have an appointment. I am not expecting to need an appointment to talk to old Arvis, so I tell her no. I tell her that I just stopped by to chat with him. She smiles again. This girl sure does smile a lot. She tells me to have a seat. I go over to one of the chairs in the big wide lobby and I look around to see if there's anybody there I know. Thankfully, since it's early, there are only a couple other people, who I don't know, in the lobby. The girl from the front counter talks on the telephone for a few minutes and then she comes over to tell me that Mr. Spencer will be right down. He's upstairs in a meeting.

That's more like it. He knows my family. Of course he's going to want to talk with me. I wait patiently, my cap in my hand. Finally, I hear the ring of the elevator bell and low voices of men having a business conversation. I see Arvis Spencer in his expensive suit in the middle of a group of men that are all dressed like him. One of them, to my surprise, is black. Now this is strange. Since when did old Arvis Spencer start hiring blacks at the Clarksville Bank? I'm going to have to have a conversation with him about that.

Arvis looks up and sees me, so he breaks free from the group and comes over to shake my hand.

"Good to see you, Delbert. It's been a long time." Arvis's voice is one of those deep, booming ones.

"Yessir, it has. I haven't had much call to visit the bank."

"What can I do for you, Del? I've got just a few minutes before I have to be in a meeting over at City Hall." Arvis looks over my shoulder at the group of men waiting for him.

"Oh, well, I won't keep you long. I just needed to talk to you about a small loan for my business. . . ."

"Not a problem, my man," Arvis says, clapping me on the shoulder. "I've got a fine loan officer here who will sit down with you and help you out." Arvis turns and hollers to a man from the group who got off the elevator. "Jack, come over here and meet Del Tanner."

The black man leaves the group and heads over toward us. What? He has to be kidding! He is going to leave me in the hands of some nigger for the most important business decision of my life? I don't know what to say. What is Clarksville coming to? I nod and shake his hand. Arvis says his name is Jack Baldwin. Then I nod again as Jack says I should meet him in his office over on the east side of the lobby.

"Arvis," I say quietly, as Jack walks away, "I don't believe I want to do my business with a stranger. Haven't you got somebody else who can help me? You yourself used to work with my daddy."

I don't think Arvis realizes how serious I am. He laughs. "Del, Jack Baldwin is a very good loan officer. He's one of the best I have. I stole him from a bank in Tupelo, as a matter of fact. He'll take good care of you—don't you worry."

And without another word, Arvis claps me on the back again, goes to join the group of men waiting for him, and they're out the door.

What else can I do? I sure as hell can't go to another bank. Granddaddy and Daddy both dealt with First National their whole lives. I walk over to the office that Jack Baldwin had motioned toward. I look in and he's sitting behind a huge desk. I just hope he ain't one of those arrogant ones that think they're hot shit because they got themselves a big job where they could tell white people what to do. Why, this man even has one of those young white girls bringing him stuff. Bet he likes that all right.

Jack Baldwin gets up out of his chair. "Come in, Mr. Tanner. Please, have a seat. Can we get you anything? Cup of coffee?"

I shake my head and ease myself into the chair across the desk from Baldwin. I notice he's got a picture on the desk of a good-looking black woman and two kids. There's a bunch of framed important-looking papers on the walls. Near as I can tell, this man has won a lot of awards for his work. But I still don't trust him.

Baldwin asks me what he can do for me, so I explain my situation as best as I can without letting him know how bad it really is. It wouldn't do for him to start spreading around town to other blacks that Tanner Lumber is having problems. They might start taking advantage of me even more. They always do. Apparently, I don't give him enough information, though, because he keeps asking the same questions over and over. Finally, I get tired of the whole damn thing.

"Can you help me, or not?" I ask.

"Mr. Tanner," Baldwin says, real calm-like, "I'm pretty sure that we can, but I'm going to need more documentation from you. It's just part of the process. Your business value has to be appraised by a professional business appraiser before I can loan money on it. It's just part of the regulations we're required to follow." Baldwin hands me a piece of paper with a list on it. "If you'll get these documents in order for us and get them back to me within the week, I'll get that appraisal scheduled for you."

I take the list and get the hell out of there. Damn! Back in Daddy's day you didn't have to go through all of this bullshit just to get a simple loan. Besides, I'm good for it. Why can't it be like it used to be when two men, two white men, agreed and shook hands? Now that banking is integrated like everything else, it's just too damn complicated. And to top it all off, I don't know where half of the shit on this list is. I'll have to go home and get Alice to help me look for it. I hope to God she has a better idea where Daddy kept all the old records than I do.

Chapter 8

Roxanne

At least the front façade of Riverview hasn't been tampered with, I'm thinking as I walk up the steps to the marble-floored portico. The massive white columns are still in good shape and the original ironwork from 1850 is intact. That's a start. The front door is standing open behind the screen door, letting in the warm October sunshine, and Louisa has placed some gorgeous gold and deep purple chrysanthemums in pots on either side of the door.

It's so irritating to be nervous about this meeting. I've been a member of the Pilgrimage Committee for at least fifteen years, and director for two. Yet this African-American tour has got me so ruffled up, my palms are sweating. There's not one woman on this committee who knows any more about the history of black people than I do. So what am I worried about? It occurred to me last night when I was tossing and turning again that Louisa is just trying to get the black vote for her husband. I've heard rumors that he'll probably run for mayor next year. Wouldn't she just love that? *Ellery Humboldt, Candidate for Mayor, Establishes First African-American Tour.*

I'm surprised, but it matters to me that I get this right. It was so much easier when it was just one more item on my list of have-todos, but since I've gotten to know Grace and her friends a little better, it does matter. I find that very annoying. I'm still trying to get my head back into my role as pilgrimage director when a young black man in a white butler's jacket answers the doorbell. Louisa and Ellery Humboldt have enough money to employ plenty of people at any function they have. I happen to know for a fact that the caterer she uses is Bayou Belle's. The young man who answers the door is tall and handsome with a brilliant smile and a Creole-accented voice as smooth as butter—probably one of Belle's sons.

Belle Robicheaux moved up here from New Orleans in the fifties and has built a small empire catering functions like this one. And for an extra fee—which I could personally never afford—she'll send some of her children to serve and answer the door. *At least she's making good money from wealthy white people who want to put on airs.* Now, why did I think of that? That's never occurred to me before. Usually I'm trying to figure out how I can afford to have servers at one of my parties. Of course, I'm the one who gave Belle's name to Louisa.

As I step inside and look around, I have to admit, Louisa has exquisite antiques. Her collection, along with what was left in the house after Ellen Davenport died, is impressive. It's been just six months since she and Ellery purchased the house at auction from the Davenport estate. I know they have plans to put it on the tour in the spring, but I'm not sure the restoration can be done by then.

The problem is that the Davenports did some expensive, but terribly inappropriate, remodeling to the old home. Ellen had Berber carpet laid in the bedroom she used downstairs and had a bathroom installed that looks like something out of a catalog for assistive devices. Of course, there's what she did to the old summer kitchen to accommodate her live-in sitter, and then there's the new kitchen her parents tacked on to the back of the house around 1940 that's just ghastly.

Riverview is one of the older homes in this area, with a wide, sloping back lawn that looks out over the Tombigbee River. People will be interested to hear how it was situated here because the river was the main thoroughfare to transport cotton during the days before the Civil War. Riverview is also another one of the homes that wasn't damaged by the Union soldiers because it served as a hospital during the War. After being neglected all those years by the Davenport family, it's looking a little shabby. I notice that the walls and woodwork need some refurbishing.

I'm hoping Ellery Humboldt, Louisa's husband, won't be here today. He tends to be underfoot a lot, since he's much older than she is and retired from a lucrative law practice in Connecticut. They've already hosted at least two parties since they moved to town, and I find him obnoxious. Too bad Dudley's gone, or I could get him involved in one of those long, drawn-out conversations with Ellery about his collection of Civil War memorabilia. Ellery especially likes to wear his vintage Rebel uniform, which fits him to a tee since he's such a small man. He actually wore it for their Christmas party, and Louisa was in hoopskirts.

They both like to think of themselves as benevolent plantation owners. It always feels to me like they're trying to play parts out of *Gone With the Wind*. I feel that old green-tinged twinge of jealousy when I think of Louisa Humboldt's parties, which, I have to admit, are some of the best I've seen during my years in Clarksville. She even had the dress she wore at Christmas made from actual bolts of green satin she found in Charleston. The fabric was stored in locked trunks that had gotten lost in a warehouse on the docks.

On the night of the party, women were surrounding Louisa like flies on sugar. "Yes, isn't it amazing?" she said. "These bolts of fabric were going to be smuggled across the blockade so that the Southern ladies could still have nice dresses, but the ship never made it out of Charleston. My antiques broker heard about the trunks and called me. I bought them sight unseen. People always say that I have the best luck when it comes to an antique find!"

Louisa and Ellery have enough money to employ a large staff of service people, and I've noticed that they tend to drop the Southern drawl when giving directions to them. Given my work lately with Grace Clark, I'm experiencing a surreal sense of time as I stand in the entrance hall. I wonder how many slaves the original family at Riverview owned, and then I fast-forward to the early twentieth century—Grace's day. *Who were the hired help that worked here then? Did Grace and her family know any of them?*

I shake myself slightly. I have to get a grip! I'm about to be in the middle of a very serious conversation about the style of dresses that the young girls who will be guiding tours for Riverview will be wearing. I can't afford to risk my position of authority by getting sidetracked wondering how long it took a slave woman to iron that same dress with a heavy iron heated in a fire in a one-hundred-plus-degree summer kitchen!

But I do wonder. And I wonder where that woman slept and how many children she had and how many of those children were the progeny of the master. I wonder if there are any half-white ancestors of Riverview slaves still living in Clarksville. I search my memory about the family that originally built Riverview. I can't think of them right now, probably because my mind is just too crowded with all of this other stuff.

I peek into the parlor, where soft music is playing and six women twitter like colorful birds as they stand around the exquisite mahogany and satin furniture. Louisa spies me and smiles. She's still a good inch shorter than I am, even in those three-inch heels, not to mention the height of her swept-up bleached blond hair. She detaches herself from the rest of the group and approaches me in a cloud of L'Air du Temps and bourbon. She isn't a pretty woman, but she's wealthy, so everything about her is designed to give the illusion of beauty. I wish I could pull that off. She takes my hand and presses it between hers.

"Roxanne Reeves, we're so glad you're here," she gushes. "Johnny"—she waves to the young man who answered the door— "take Mrs. Reeves's things." It occurs to me that this same young man might have been the butler for the last party of hers that I attended. I didn't even notice him then, but now I find myself wondering what he thinks of all of these over-accessorized white women trying to hold on to our little eddies in the small pond of Clarksville. Are we as invisible to him as he is to us? Johnny obediently takes my sweater and purse with a courteous nod, and Louisa ushers me into the room as if I'm royalty. "Ladies, look who's here! It's our very own pilgrimage director."

I smile as everyone stops talking and looks up. This is awkward. I've been in meetings of various sorts with these women for years. It's embarrassing to be treated like some sort of special guest. They all know as well as I do that Louisa Humboldt is just trying to get her house into the spring tour. Making me even more uncomfortable than the introduction is knowing that all of these women are just waiting like hopeful buzzards to see what my decision will be.

Everyone on the committee knows that I'm a stickler for authenticity. I carefully review each and every home on the tour to be sure that the owners can explain any modern changes and that, as much as possible, details from the antebellum period are preserved. I can see from looking around this room that the Humboldts are well on their way to furnishing this house with period-appropriate furniture. Ellen Davenport's cheap reproduction pieces that still lingered in December have been removed and replaced. From the fainting sofa in the corner to the harpsichord under the window, the antique furniture is dead-on. But then, Louisa is quite the collector. Between the discomfort of being on display and the fear that Louisa might be a threat to my job, I'm breaking into a cold sweat.

I decline the milk punch that yet another young black person, a girl this time, offers and ask for coffee instead. Milk punch is deadly for me this time of day. It's a delicious concoction made from Maker's Mark, sugar syrup, vanilla, and heavy cream. The whole mixture is frozen overnight and then thawed just enough for pouring. I know if I have milk punch my judgment will be clouded, and I need to stay clear.

I'm anxious to get my hands on that diary Louisa found, but I'll have to wait until she and I are alone. Hopefully, she hasn't broadcast it to the whole group. As I maneuver into the room I overhear a group of ladies in a heated discussion. The woman currently holding forth is Elsie Spencer, my longtime nemesis and the wife of Arvis Spencer, the president of the First National Bank of Clarksville. Elsie has made an art form out of snobbery. I find myself simultaneously drawn to her like a beetle to a bug light and yet repulsed by the swift, bloodless executions I have seen her perform on her unknowing victims' social lives. For years, I've spent tremendous amounts of energy being sure that I stay under her murderous radar.

Elsie fancies herself quite the genealogist. If she ever finds out that my only claim to class or money is my husband's—possibly soon to be ex-husband's—family, not my own, I might as well move to Biloxi and go to work in a casino. Somehow I've always managed to skirt the question of Who are your people? by giving her vague responses that are really more about the Stanleys than my own parents. And they *are* both dead. That much is true. It's just that Mama died of cancer gone untreated for years and Daddy smoked and drank himself to death. They're both buried in a small Catholic cemetery in the bayou. Daddy is not tucked neatly under a white headstone in a particularly beautiful corner of Arlington Cemetery, like I *might* have implied.

"So, it's not enough that her husband has gotten a high-profile position at the bank, but now she wants to volunteer to help with the Pilgrimage Tour," Elsie is saying to Dottie Lollar, one of the two women listening to her in rapt attention.

"A black woman in the Pilgrimage Tour?" asks Dottie. "How can that be? What would she wear?" Dottie nibbles nervously on a cheese straw, looking like an anorexic squirrel.

Elsie nods. "That's what I thought. Now, I'm not prejudiced, but how can a black woman wear a Southern day dress with hoop-skirts? That just wouldn't look right. And we can't very well ask her to wear what slave women would have worn." Elsie shakes her head and sips her punch. "I tell you, it's a dilemma." She looks up, sees me, and moves toward me. The other women tag along. *Oh, Lord! I don't want to be in this conversation!*

"Here's our director now. I'm sure she will have a solution for this problem."

I try to look interested as Elsie describes the bank function she was attending. "Rita Baldwin is the wife of that black man, Jack Baldwin, who Arvis swears is going to make him a heap of money. Apparently he was a widower and Rita is his second wife. I think he met her in Atlanta. She was in some community service job—I forget what. Anyway, so Rita approached me and asked if she could help with the spring tour, maybe even be a guide." The other women are looking distracted since they've already heard this story at least twice. "Well, I made up something about an application process and being on a waiting list, but I'm telling you, Roxanne, I just didn't know what to say! We've never had this happen before." Elsie shakes her perfectly coiffed head and pats the corners of her mouth with her cocktail napkin. "So I told her she should contact you about how to proceed."

Of course, this is typical. Take the credit if it's something positive, and pass the problem on to me if it's not. I'm already in a difficult situation with this African-American tour. Elsie is a powerful woman in this community, and if I can't keep her support, then I might not get reelected for this position next year. Elsie was also one of the three people on the committee who voted against the African-American tour. I'm remembering what she said in that meeting: "It is not necessary to have an African-American tour. It will introduce the wrong element to Clarksville. It just doesn't fit."

By the wrong element she meant more black people. I can see her obvious glee in putting yet another such situation in my hands. Elsie's plotting my demise. It's as clear as the crystal cup she's sipping her milk punch from.

I make up some inane comment to put Elsie off as—*thank the Lord*—the butler announces that lunch is served. Everyone moves across the hall into the dining room. I notice that the original patterned carpet is still in here, and the huge gilt rococo mirror that I've admired over the years still hangs over the fireplace. We all find our place cards and take seats around the perfectly laid-out mahogany dining table.

"I've seated you next to me so that I can bend your ear about that diary," Louisa whispers as I sit to her left and she waits for the butler to pull out her chair at the head of the table.

"Good, I can't wait to hear about it," I say, thinking that's truthfully the most interesting thing I'll hear today.

The lunch is excellent as usual. I stuff myself on Belle's crawfish étouffée and am eyeing the bread pudding on the sideboard when Louisa clinks on her glass.

"Ladies, we should come to order now. Our director is ready to start the meeting."

I take one last longing look at the bread pudding being served to the others and pull the agenda from under my plate. I take a deep breath, mostly because I'm nervous today, which I'm usually not, and also because I ate too much. I launch into today's topics.

"The attire for the Holiday Tour, the treasurer's report on the ticket prices for spring, and finally . . ." I look down, adjust my glasses, and clear my throat. "My report on the African-American tour." I hear a short rumbling of hushed conversation after this last item and decide to push on.

"Dottie, we'll start with your report on the Holiday Tour," I announce.

Dottie Lollar pulls her reading glasses and a small notepad from the expensive designer bag hanging on the back of her chair and sets the glasses on her minuscule turned-up nose. She tucks a strand of hair behind her ear and launches into her usual perky soliloquy on the local home owners who have volunteered their homes for the annual Christmas tour. I remind myself to think "Holiday Tour." Two years ago we had a Jewish family buy one of the homes traditionally on the tour and we had to start calling it a Holiday Tour, but none of us have gotten used to that yet. I find my mind wandering as Dottie goes on.

"So I've looked into caterers for the cookies. There's the black woman over on Martin Luther King Drive that makes the best date nut balls I've ever put in my mouth. But then there's also Sanders Café, where we've gone for the past five years. Anyway, the decision was so hard that our little subcommittee decided to hold a contest in October to choose the best cookie. Won't that be fun? I'm just so excited about it. . . ."

The meeting rambles on at its usual sluggish pace. Each woman reporting seems to feel compelled to include some story about the difficulty she's having with a dressmaker, or a caterer, or a cleaning service. I find my mind wandering to what Grace would think of this meeting if she were here. Would she be impressed with how detail-oriented we are and how high our standards are? Or, rather, would she shake her head at our sense of entitlement?

Finally, we get to my report on the African-American tour. Louisa's looking at me expectantly and I can't help but notice that

Elsie Spencer is talking behind her hand to her minion, Dottie Lollar. I make my voice sound matter-of-fact and, I hope, positive.

"So far, we have three very interesting historical sites for our African-American tour." The ladies stop talking among themselves and look at me as if they're surprised.

"We have the first African-American school. . . ." Granted, that's a little bit of a lie, but I'm still convinced I can work around Del Tanner somehow. "The home of the first black doctor in Clarksville, Dr. Albert Jackson. And a very important African-American hotel called the Queen City Hotel." I end my report by telling them that I will follow up next month with a more extensive list and finalized plans. I'm now holding my breath, hoping no one asks questions. Louisa is nodding, looking impressed. Of course, Elsie is staring at me with those beady green eyes.

"Roxanne, darling," she says, "is the Queen City that run-down old building over on Fifteenth?"

I'm squirming now. "Yes, it is a little run-down, but there's a plan in the African-American community to do some restoration." Another lie. *God is going to strike me down with lightning.* "I thought I might approach this Rita Baldwin you mentioned earlier." I'm proud of myself for having this brainstorm. "Maybe she can convince her husband to get behind this project."

"Oh," Elsie says. "Well, I hope so, because my maid says she won't even drive through that area, it's gotten so bad with gangs and all, and she's black, of course." Elsie immediately starts talking in whispers with the women seated next to her.

I decide not to respond to this last comment, and since no one has any other items for discussion, the meeting draws mercifully to a close. As the ladies drift toward the door I stay at the table and press Louisa's arm.

"Have you got that diary for me?" I ask.

"Yes," she says. "It's in here." She gets up and walks over to the sideboard and opens a drawer. "Maybe you can read it better than I can, you being a Southerner." I'm wondering what that has to do with reading handwriting. "I can't make head or tail of it. I was hoping it might have some information about the house . . . you know, for the restoration and all."

I feel a tremor of hope now. Maybe she's trying to tell me I'm going to get the job. I notice that Elsie is staring our way, probably wanting to stick her nose in what we're doing.

I quickly tuck the diary into my purse. "I'll read it over and be in touch," I say, turning my back toward Elsie. I say my good-byes and make my way toward the door. Little does Louisa Humboldt know that I'm not nearly as interested in the details of the River-view mansion as I am in the black man called Zero.

I can hardly hold my eyes open, but I am determined to read at least a little bit of Ellen Davenport's diary tonight, so I take the worn leather-bound book and crawl into bed with it. I'm still exhausted from that meeting today, and I realize that I'm looking forward to my next get-together with Grace Clark more than anything I have to do related to the pilgrimage or the committee people. What a strange turn of events this has been.

I snuggle into my pillows, taking the ones from Dudley's side of the bed, too. After all, he's not here to use them. For a moment I'm sad not to have his long, lanky frame sprawled out beside me. If nothing else, his presence always gave me a sense of security. I try to push the thoughts away and pick up the diary. I feel something tonight that I haven't felt before, and I can't identify it. I sit here, the diary open on my lap, my sleepiness fading into wakeful-ness. Longing, that's what it is. I'm longing for something . . . or someone? I examine the possibilities and realize it's not Dudley. I think about sex with him. That was fine until I found out about the graduate student; then I lost all my confidence. No, it's not sexual . . . It's more about having a relationship with another person who really knows me, not for the role I fulfill—like wife, or mother, or chairperson. Once again, I push the nagging thoughts away. I need to try and decipher a little of this diary before I sleep.

The pages are yellowed and swollen as if it was dropped in water at some point. The handwriting is loopy and girlish. I try to imagine Ellen Davenport as a young girl. The older Ellen Davenport, whom I visited years ago, was a lonely old spinster who was eating herself into oblivion. *Dear God, please don't let me turn out like that!* Maybe I should call Dudley. *Stop that!* I turn to the first page. . . .

Ellen Elizabeth Davenport

Clarksville, Mississippi
1931

AUGUST 7, 9 P.M.

Mama gave me this journal for my sixteenth birthday. She said I should use it for writing poetry, but I've had it for two years now and never written one word of poetry, so I decided to write about what's happening to me right here, right now, in Clarksville, Mississippi. I can't tell anybody my secret and I feel like I'll explode if I don't write it down.

Andy Benton wants to marry me! We met yesterday, like we do every week, at the sawmill. Until I started secretly meeting Andy, it was always so boring to have to go down there each Thursday and bring Daddy lunch. He could care less about seeing us, but Mama insists. She says she wants Daddy to feel supported. Sounds like hooey to me. I think she just wants to check up on him.

Anyway, if I hadn't gone down there with Mama, I

never would have met Andy in the first place. I noticed him because that awful Ray Tanner was yelling at him about something. I had stepped out onto the porch of the office to get some air and Ray didn't see me. Andy looked at me over Ray's shoulder and smiled. Then Ray just yelled at him more for smiling.

So every week, while Mama and Daddy are talking after lunch, I say I want to get some air, and I go out on the shaded side of the porch. Then Andy comes up next to the building real close, so no one can see him, and talks to me for a few minutes.

And now, after meeting for only a few weeks, Andy has practically begged me to marry him! I can't believe it! He's just so adorable with his freckles and blond hair. I think we'll make beautiful babies together. Maybe I'll let our children read this so that they'll know how exciting it was when their daddy and I ran away together. Andy says he only works at the mill because there's no other place to find work now. Still, I know Daddy would never approve of me marrying him. He and Mama have this idea that I will marry some distant cousin on my mother's side. They think I'm not pretty enough or smart enough to catch a boy on my own, but I'll show them.

I have to be careful now. Andy is my secret and I don't want anyone to take him away from me! Andy thinks I'm pretty. He even said so. We're going to run away and get married and he'll find work down in New Orleans. He'll make lots of money and someday we'll come back and Papa will see that he should have been nicer to Andy.

As much as I love Andy, I don't want to be stupid. I told him I have to see a ring first to be sure he's serious. If he can come up with the money to buy me a ring, then I'll know he really wants to marry me. So, I'm waiting, waiting, waiting.

August 13, 8 p.m.

Still no ring yet. Today at the sawmill he said he's working on it. He tried again to get me to run away with him without an engagement ring, but I said no. I wish I could tell Mama how I'm holding out for this. She would be proud of me. I think Sarah Jane knows something is different. She's been watching me real close. I never could keep secrets from her very well. She's been with our family so long she's practically like a sister to me. But if I tell her, what if she tells Mama? I might just have to take that risk, because I might need her help. I just don't know what to do!

August 14, 8:30 p.m.

I told Sarah Jane today! I think she was happy for me just a little bit, I could tell. But she told me I'd better be careful. She's worried about me, but I told her I'll be just fine. I'm completely in love with Andy and we're going to be so happy together. She says I don't know what I'm getting into, that I'm used to having nice things and plenty to eat. But I told her that I'm stronger than she thinks. I am a little worried about cooking, though. Sometimes I hang around the kitchen and watch Josephine cooking our meals, but I've never really done it myself. It doesn't look too hard. It's just so hot in there, I'm not sure I could stand the heat. Maybe Andy and I could afford to hire just one person. Maybe Sarah Jane would leave and come work for us! I'll ask her about it tomorrow!

August 20, 9:30 p.m.

It's really going to happen! Andy told me today that he's saved enough money to buy the ring and pay the justice of the peace. I told Sarah Jane, but she didn't look happy for me at all today. As a matter of fact, she's been downright sullen lately.

She doesn't talk much and goes off by herself whenever she's not cleaning or serving at the table. I don't understand it. I know she works for us, but I thought we were friends, too. She won't talk to me about whatever's wrong. But I can't let her stand in the way of my happiness. Andy says he'll bring the ring Saturday night between midnight and one in the morning. That means I'll just have to stay awake, because if I fall asleep I might miss him! And then, our plan is to meet early Monday morning behind the feed store. He's going to borrow his brother's car. We'll drive over to Yalobusha County to Itta Bena and get married and then we'll board the bus headed for Louisiana and our new life together! I better stop writing and get packed.

AUGUST 23, 1:30 A.M.

The strangest thing happened tonight. Andy didn't deliver the ring himself and I still don't know why. He had Zero Clark deliver it. Of course, I've known Zero since I was a little girl. He's friends with Sarah Jane. She makes eyes at him every time he makes vegetable deliveries to Josephine from the Calhoun farm. And until Daddy bought a car, he always took care of our horses when we visited the Calhouns. But I sure didn't expect to see Zero under my balcony at half past midnight! It liked to scared me to death!

The ring is pretty enough. It's a very small silver band, but it's a start. At least I know Andy's serious now. The note inside the box only says, "I'll explain later. Meet me behind the feed store at five o'clock Monday morning." I only have to get through the rest of today and then I'll be with Andy forever!

Chapter 9

❧

Roxanne

Rita Baldwin and I just ordered our food and I can't help but notice how Mary Ellen Sanders keeps glancing in our direction from behind the counter. I find myself remembering those Sunday nights as a little girl when Daddy let me stay up late and watch *Candid Camera* with him. He loved the absurdity of it all—seeing people make fools of themselves. Even then, I cringed at the horror of being caught on camera looking so foolish. Today, trying not to stare at Rita Baldwin's impeccable skin and nails or the suit she's wearing that fits her full body so well, I feel like at any moment a cameraman will step up and say, "Roxanne Reeves, smile! You're on *Candid Camera*!" Then Allen Funt will step out and explain how they wanted to capture the awkwardness of a white woman like me having lunch with a black woman.

How would we look? Like two businesswomen having a working lunch? Like friends? Probably not, since I'm not sure what that looks like. I'm asking myself for the hundredth time why I invited Rita to lunch. Is this my little vendetta against Elsie Spencer? Am I just asking to *not* be reelected as pilgrimage director next year? Maybe, in the end, what it boils down to is curiosity. Rita is about my age, well-dressed, articulate. I wonder if she can tell that I'm sizing her up. As we return our menus to the waitress, I'm about to take control of the conversation in my usual manner when Rita beats me to it.

"I'm glad we got a chance to have lunch. The reason I wanted to talk to you personally is to get your sense of what it will be like for a black woman to participate in the Pilgrimage Tour in Clarksville. So far, I'm not sensing a lot of openness about the idea from the women I've met."

I'm so caught off guard by her directness that I'm pretty sure my mouth stays open for several seconds before anything comes out. This was not at all what I expected. Who is this woman? How do I answer her, knowing that I'm supposed to be discouraging her, even making up some reason to keep her out of the pilgrimage? All because it might be awkward for Elsie Spencer or Dottie Lollar? I stumble for words. "I . . . well . . . I'm sure it would be fine . . . well, maybe not fine, but . . . um . . . challenging . . . different. . . ." I'm so mad at myself right now. I'm coming off as incompetent and addled. Why didn't I figure out what to say ahead of time?

"Challenging because?" she asks, dumping artificial sweetener in her tea and stirring. She's not going to let me off the hook easily.

Okay, I tell myself. Settle down. Don't be so frazzled. It feels like this woman can see right through me. I take a deep breath and make myself stop fiddling with my napkin. After all, I initiated this lunch. I've come this far. Why not try honesty for a change? Dammit, just the bald-faced truth.

"Here's the thing, Rita," I say, taking a sip of my own tea and looking her in the eye. "There are no African-American owners of antebellum homes in Clarksville—except for Grace Clark, that is. And I'm still not sure about her story. You would be the first to actually purchase one." She nods. "And the women who are on the committee . . . well, let me just say that they are less than enthusiastic about your becoming a member."

"And you?"

She just doesn't let up! How do I feel? I'm staring at her, knowing she's waiting for an answer, and I realize that I honestly don't have one. A few weeks ago this conversation would not have even taken place. Instead, I'd have done everything in my power to avoid Rita Baldwin until she gave up. I decide to try my strategy of keeping the conversation off of me.

"I guess what I don't understand is why. Why would you want to own a home that was built by slaves? Believe me, I love the whole antebellum era. I've spent years learning how to restore these places to their former grandeur. Plus, I know everything from how many petticoats they wore under those hoopskirts to what type of food they served at parties. People around here pride themselves on being able to tell stories of their great-great-grandfathers and the battles they fought during the Civil War. They talk about how these houses have been in their families for generations. Or, as in the case of people like the Humboldts, who moved here from Connecticut, they have an intense fascination with the Civil War and they're just thrilled to be part of the whole thing. But why would you—"

She interrupts. "Why would a black woman want to be part of all of that?"

"Exactly. Especially when it's all so connected with slavery. The black women I've met through working on this African-American tour don't have anything good to say about the pilgrimage. They seem to think it paints this overly romantic picture of the Old South."

"I agree."

"Then why do you want to be a part of it?"

"The same reason you're putting together this African-American tour. There's another history here. One that's untold."

With a twinge of guilt it occurs to me that she must think this whole African-American tour was my idea, instead of something I'm doing to get a lucrative restoration contract. It's also beginning to dawn on me what she's trying to do. In my naïveté, I thought she simply wanted to be like us. . . . Like them? I'm so confused. Did I think she wanted to be like white people? Is she not like white people now? She must see my confusion as I ask, "Rita, what is it that you do? For a living, I mean? Elsie Spencer mentioned that you did something with community service?"

Rita's smile is polite but there's an edge to her voice. "Ah, yes, Elsie Spencer. I met her at a bank employee barbecue a couple of weeks ago. She couldn't extricate herself from me fast enough after I mentioned the pilgrimage. I got the impression the only black women she's ever had conversation with were holding a dust rag at the time."

I find myself feeling a little defensive. Of Elsie Spencer? Am I crazy? "Well, I don't know about that—"

"Come on, Roxanne," she interrupts. "Are you going to tell me that this little town's social register looks any different from any other small town in the South?"

I'm at a loss here. She's right. The pilgrimage is mainly about social status—white social status. She's still talking, and I have to admit, I'm drawn to her confidence.

"When I met Jack I was running a nonprofit center for kids in Atlanta. I loved it, but I fell into it accidentally. After Owen, my first husband, died, I needed to do something with my time. Our girls were in college, so they didn't need me. Owen was a pediatrician, so I knew a lot of people in organizations that worked with kids. It was easy to get involved. But I was a history major in college and what I've always wanted to do is start a museum. . . ."

At first I feel a twinge of excitement to finally meet another woman with a similar educational background. However, that's immediately followed by fear. She's black, after all, and that changes everything. Doesn't it?

"My great-great-grandmother was a slave," Rita continues. "I grew up in a poor family on the black side of the tracks in Macon, Georgia. I got to college on a United Negro College Fund scholarship, and my mama couldn't have been more proud. This isn't about me trying to be like white folks. Jack and I are in a financial position to buy this kind of house and maybe, just maybe, by doing that, we can tell the other side of the story."

"What does Jack think about all of this?" I ask.

"I'm Jack's second wife, you know. We had both lost our spouses when we met. His first wife died three years ago. She was born and raised here and, although she was lovely and smart, she stayed within the expectations of this community. So, Jack thinks I'm a little crazy, but he loves me enough to let me try it. I know I'll get flak from blacks. Half of them will say I'm selling out to the white man and the other half will be proud of Jack and me for what we're trying to do. In the end, we have to do this the way that's right for us."

I shake my head. I'm impressed with her passion and it's obvious she's prepared herself for this decision. It's just that she's talking about shaking up everything. Here I am caught between a white woman from Connecticut who wants us to tell the history of the black community and a black woman from Atlanta who wants to be part of what has been an all-white event for sixty years. I'm not so sure I'm ready for this. Isn't this new tour enough? Where will it end?

"You know, people around here don't usually talk this openly about . . . race," I say carefully. "I'm just not sure how it will be received. Not that it matters, of course." I hurry to say this last part. For some reason I like that she believes I'm more open than most people in town.

Rita nods and leans forward. "I know it's complicated. But if we spend our lives staying within the limits of the black community—

limits, I might add, that are made by white people—how is it any different from before desegregation?" She's very matter-of-fact about this. I'm not sensing anger from her. No . . . it's pride, actually . . . and determination.

"I'm no political activist, but I do want young people, like my new stepchildren and my own daughters, to see me mix with whites. Not because I'm trying to 'act white,' but because I can do anything I want to do."

I have to ask the question. It seems shallow, but I have to know. "Do you plan to wear a costume and give tours of the home you buy?"

"You mean, how the hell are you going to pull off having a black woman in a hoopskirt?"

"Well . . . yes," I answer, grateful for the interruption of the waitress to fill our tea glasses. When I look up at Rita again, I find that she's laughing so hard her shoulders are shaking. It's contagious and I find myself laughing, too, not sure whether to be relieved or more confused. Is she laughing at me?

She catches her breath and dabs at her eyes with her napkin. "If I put on a hoopskirt and stays, my grandmother would roll over in her grave. Not to mention, can you see this figure in one of those getups?" She motions toward her full curves. "To tell you the truth, Roxanne, I haven't figured out that part yet. Do I recruit young black girls to dress as slaves, while the young white girls are out front on the lawn being belles and waving their fans? I don't know how to present what it really was like and deal with this race issue, but I'm damn sure going to try to figure it out."

I find myself suddenly seeing the Pilgrimage Tour from a different perspective. One I've never considered before. Maybe instead of an elite social status event it could truly be about history—all of the history. Maybe Rita and I can figure this out together. Maybe it's time for something new in Clarksville. Most of all, maybe it's time for something new for me. I feel more hopeful than I have in a long time. Rita grew up poor and she just admitted that to me as if she wasn't ashamed of it. Where did I go wrong? Why have I thought it necessary all of these years to hide my background? Mrs. Stanley's words echo through my mind again . . . "A woman can't afford to reveal her flaws . . . They will be held against her." Maybe Mrs. Stanley was mistaken.

"I want to help you," I say, realizing that my hands are shaking. "I do know of a property that will probably come on the market next spring. And I think it might be perfect for what you have in mind. It's one of the few properties around here that's kept some of the slave quarters intact."

"Good," she says, smiling at me. "I would appreciate that." She looks down at her plate, then back up at me. I'm uncomfortable with the silence; something is hanging unsaid between us. She's the first to break it.

"I want you to know that I realize this . . . relationship with me probably puts you in a difficult position . . . with your friends, that is."

Right now, I am so tempted to blurt out, *What friends?* I've spent the past twenty years focused on building an image, not relationships. But I'm not sure I can trust this woman. What if she laughs at me? I feel a strong pull to share my story with her, to finally tell someone who might actually understand. But what if she doesn't? What if, instead, she's repulsed by my lies, by my total focus on appearing to be from a pedigreed Southern family? No, I decide the risk is too great. I actually think I might want this woman to be my friend. How can I ever unravel this web of lies I've made without unraveling my whole life? But then, isn't it unraveling already?

"Oh, don't worry about that," I reply, trying to appear nonchalant as I change the subject to my own agenda. "Since we're talking about history, have you heard of the Queen City Hotel?"

· · ·

Today Grace and I are going down to Catfish Alley to the site of the Penny Savings Bank, where young Zero was headed that day with his nickel when he got waylaid by Ray Tanner and his gang. I fell asleep last night reading Ellen Davenport's diary and picturing Zero Clark standing out under the balcony at Riverview in the middle of the night. Zero must have been around twenty years old then. Funny, I'm beginning to feel more familiar with these people than with my own family. As a matter of fact, I don't know this much about my own parents' histories.

I've decided not to mention the diary to Grace yet. For some reason, she seems very private about her brother. When I arrive at Pecan Cottage, she is ready and waiting for me at the door.

"Hello, Grace. No coffee today?"

"We'll have coffee," she says as she walks toward my car. "Just not here."

It turns out she's made arrangements for us to meet the man who owns the buildings that were once home to several African-American businesses on Catfish Alley. This includes Jones's Café, where, according to Grace, the catfish was fried that gave the street its name.

As we turn onto Fourth Street South, Grace points to a row of brick buildings on the right that don't appear to be in use now. The windows in two of them are boarded up and there's some kind of gang graffiti on one of the walls. Another building still shows what's left of an old 1940s advertisement for RC Cola. I remember noticing the sign before, because RC is my favorite, but I never really paid attention to this part of town. This street, or alley as it used to be called, is usually only a thoroughfare for me to get to other parts of town.

We stop in front of a small barbershop that appears to be still open for business. A red candy-striped barber pole stands outside and the sign in the window says *Jones Barbershop—Haircuts $5.00.*

Through the wide plate-glass window, I see three chairs, two of which are occupied by black men. Once again, I'm feeling very uncomfortable. I'm not accustomed to being around black men, except when they're doing lawn maintenance or service work of some kind for me. There is a black man who bags my groceries at the Piggly Wiggly, but I don't really talk to any of those people.

Grace, of course, is serene, as usual. I take a deep breath. If an eighty-nine-year-old woman is not nervous, why should I be? But then, these are *her* people, not mine.

When we open the barbershop door, a cowbell clanks over our heads, announcing our arrival. The shop is small, but very clean. It smells of shaving soap and Old Spice cologne. I recognize the smell from Daddy's shaving mug that always sat on the bathroom shelf. A baseball game plays on a small TV that is mounted on the wall in the corner of the shop. The volume is up so loud it's a wonder anybody hears us walk in.

There is one middle-aged, very clean-cut-looking man in the back barber chair, draped with a white cape. Behind him stands a tall lean man with graying hair and mustache, a pair of scissors poised over the head of his customer, while he looks intently at the small television screen. The third man, younger and dressed in baggy shorts and a T-shirt, sits on an old sofa nearby.

As the wooden door slams shut behind us, the barber looks up and smiles.

"Well, look who's here!" He excuses himself from the other two men, who both stand up and nod politely in our direction. I am impressed with their courtesy and I begin to relax a little. The barber comes over and warmly shakes Grace's hand.

"Gracie, it's so good to see you again." He turns to the other two and says, "Fellas, y'all remember Miss Grace Clark, the best teacher the Clarksville Union School ever had. Miss Clark, this here is Jack Baldwin."

The older man who was getting the haircut nods politely and says, "Union School, fourth and fifth grades."

"Yes, I remember you," Grace says. "Jackie Baldwin. You were quite a cutup in school. I was always proud to see you do so well. And I heard at church last Sunday that you had moved back from Tupelo." Grace turns to the younger man. "And you must be Jack, Jr. I remember you from Clarksville Elementary, too."

"Yes, ma'am," he says.

I stand behind Grace, trying to be unobtrusive. I'm wondering if I should mention to Jack Baldwin that I had lunch with his wife. Would she have told him? Grace moves to stand beside me.

"Gentlemen, I would like to introduce Mrs. Roxanne Reeves. She is putting together an African-American historical tour for Clarksville. Roxanne, this is Mr. Clarence Jones. He owns this barbershop and most of this block of buildings," she says. She motions proudly to Mr. Baldwin. "Jack Baldwin here has recently been appointed as a loan officer at the First National Bank of Clarksville. He was one of my last students at Union before we integrated with Clarksville Schools in 1971. And this is his son, Jack, Jr."

Jack and Jack, Jr., both shake my hand, and the older Jack says, "Rita told me about meeting with you the other day, Mrs. Reeves. She said y'all had a mighty fine conversation."

"Yes, it was good to visit with her," I say, wondering what he thinks a "mighty fine" conversation entails.

Jack turns to Grace. "My new wife has got her heart set on us buying one of those old houses—the ones like yours, built back before the Civil War. She's got it in her head that she wants to do some history thing." He shakes his head. "I surely don't understand it."

"Well, how about that!" says Grace. "She'll fit right in with what Roxanne here is trying to do."

"Yes, ma'am," Jack answers, and there's an awkward silence as we all try to figure out what to say next.

Grace pats the younger man on the shoulder and asks, "What are you doing these days, Jack, Jr.?"

"I'm going to Mississippi State, Miss Clark. I'm a senior there, studying business."

The older Mr. Baldwin glows with pride as his son speaks. "He's going to come work with me at the bank when he finishes school. Keep it in the family, you know?"

"That's just wonderful," Grace replies.

Grace spends a few more minutes chatting with the men about common acquaintances, while Mr. Jones finishes Jack Baldwin's haircut. When he's finished, Mr. Jones escorts us back to the kitchen of his home, which adjoins the back of the barbershop. The other men open up Cokes and keep right on watching the ball game, as if they were home in their own family rooms.

We sit down at an antique red Formica table in Mr. Jones's spotless kitchen. I can't help but admire the vintage 1940s fixtures. There are cookies in a jar on the table and coffee cups are set out for us on the counter near the coffeepot. A set of double windows looks out over the alley, and I can see a small vegetable garden in the back. This little apartment has such a homey feel. It's all so cozy and comforting that I find myself starting to relax.

"What a lovely place," I say. Frankly, I'm surprised at how well kept it is. "Mr. Jones, are you married?" I'm thinking that there has to be a woman to keep a place as neat as this.

"I'm a widower, ma'am. My Ernestine died about ten years ago." He has a look of deep sadness in his eyes. He must have loved her very much. Grace reaches up and pats his arm.

"We all miss Ernestine," she says, turning to me. "I went to the Union School with her. And Clarence was a good friend of my brother Zero's back in our young days. He grew up on a cotton farm just outside of town. He started cutting hair when he was a teenager and opened this shop when he was in his twenties. He's been cutting hair here for more than sixty years."

"So y'all are about the same age?" I am still incredulous at how long-lived these people are. I can never tell their ages by looking at them.

"That's right. Clarence will be ninety next year, if I'm not mistaken." She looks to Clarence for affirmation and he nods.

"Yes, ma'am," answers Clarence. He walks slowly to the counter and pours coffee. He moves well for his age. He lowers himself into a kitchen chair, looks directly at me, and smiles. I get a sense of quiet confidence from this man. He seems completely at ease with himself, a quality I always envy.

"So how can I help you ladies?"

"I was hoping you could tell Mrs. Reeves here about some of the businesses black folks had down here on Catfish Alley over the years. I know most of them are closed now, but since you own a lot of this block, I figure you know the history best," Grace says.

"Well, let me see now," Mr. Jones says, scratching his chin thoughtfully. "Right here next to the barbershop, there used to be a café. It was called Jones's Café. Miss Mabel fried the best catfish and hush puppies in town. You could smell it all the way over to Main Street. Even white folks come over here to get Miss Mabel's catfish." He laughs. "They come in the front door, too. Not like we had to do if we went to some white restaurant." At this last statement, Clarence reaches over and nudges Grace gently, and she shakes her head, laughing softly. He pauses to sip his coffee, frowns, and reaches for the sugar bowl in the middle of the table. "I got the sugar diabetes, you know. Ernestine never would let me put sugar in my coffee, but I'm telling y'all, I do love me some sweet coffee.

"Now, 'cross the street here was the Penny Savings Bank, and then there was the lodge for the Knights of Pythias upstairs over the bank." He pauses. "Oh, and Green's Grocery was on the other side of Jones's," he says, looking at me and motioning right and left.

"The Knights of Pythias?" I have no idea what that is.

Grace pitches in. "In the twenties, black businessmen and clergy established several secret societies. They were similar to some of the white organizations, but since black people couldn't join the white societies, they formed their own. Adelle's daddy, Dr. Jackson, set up the Knights of Pythias."

"What kinds of things did they do?" I ask, thinking this might be a good way to highlight the philanthropy of early-twentieth-century African-Americans.

Grace and Clarence give each other an odd look. It's as if they aren't sure how to answer me. I get the impression that they're trying to decide if they should make up something or tell me the truth.

"I reckon Gracie better tell you about the lodge, Mrs. Reeves," says Clarence. "I never did have much patience for trying to work on things peaceably like Dr. Jackson did. Especially after what happened."

I look at Grace. Her mouth has tightened into a thin line as she shakes her head. She looks down at her coffee cup. "This is not one of the good stories, Roxanne," she says. "Zero was bound and determined to get to Alcorn State College one way or another. He took a job at the sawmill that summer—"

"Were y'all still living out on the Calhoun property?" I interrupt. I'm still curious about how she came to own Pecan Cottage, but I don't have the nerve to ask that yet.

"Oh, yes. The Calhouns deeded our little house on the back of the property over to Grandma when she and Mama were still working for the family. Said they wanted Grandma to feel secure that she had a place to live in her old age. Grandma was the Calhouns' cook and Mama was a housemaid and helped take care of the Calhouns' twin daughters. My mama loved those little girls like she did Zero and me. She used to love to dress them up in those beautiful little dresses Mr. Calhoun ordered all the way from New York. We were all sad when we lost those little girls to polio. They were only three years old. That near about broke Mrs. Calhoun's heart. Grandma said she was never the same after that. She never had any other children.

"Our mama died when we were young. I was only twelve and Zero was fourteen. My grandma raised us after that."

I think of my own mama then, ignoring symptoms I can't even imagine for all those years. I make a mental note to talk to Grace more about our mamas—when we're alone. "What about your father?" I ask this tentatively, not knowing, for some reason, if this is too personal.

"Sugar," she says, looking at me over her glasses, "that's another story for another day."

I know Grace well enough by now to know when to stop asking questions. This is one of those times. However, she has just made me more curious than ever. Anyway, we've gotten off subject. "So you were telling about Zero and the sawmill?" *Is this the same sawmill mentioned in Ellen Davenport's diary?*

"Oh, yes, I knew I got off track somewhere. So Zero goes to work at that sawmill because he says the money's good and it's only for one summer. I told him then that he shouldn't get mixed up with any place where Ray Tanner was, but he wouldn't listen. Always was hardheaded about Ray Tanner. Said he was all talk.

"That was August 1931. I remember it like it was yesterday. Everything started to change after that summer. Zero was working two jobs—Green's store and hauling lumber for Davenport Timber. Those Davenports were the richest folks in town, and rumor was, Ray Tanner was trying his best to work his way up in that company. Ray's daddy, Rufus Tanner, had worked there since he was a boy, but he didn't make much of himself. He drank up his whole paycheck. Junior and Zero used to tell us stories about old Rufus Tanner and his brawling. But Ray was different. Had a mean streak and he didn't care what it took to get what he wanted. He'd already made it to supervisor by the time Davenport hired Zero.

"Do you remember me telling you about the Louis Armstrong show over at the Queen City?" Grace asks me. I nod, waiting for her to go on.

"That night after we got home I tried to sleep, but I was still too wound up. So, I was in the kitchen getting some cold butter-milk out of the icebox when Zero came tiptoeing in through the back door. I was surprised because I thought he had gone to bed the same time I did. We had church the next morning. I remember looking at the clock on the kitchen wall, and it said two o'clock in the morning. I knew he wouldn't be seeing Adelle that late at night. He was trying to be real quiet, took his shoes off at the door. . . ." Grace pauses and chuckles to herself. "I liked to scared him to death when I said, 'What do you think you're doing?' I thought he would jump out of his skin, he was so twitchy and nervous."

"What was he so jumpy about?" I ask.

Grace shakes her head and exchanges glances with Clarence. "He was still a ball of nerves from what he'd just done. When he told me, I thought right then about waking up Grandma and telling her the whole story. Because if she'd ever known that Zero was up in the middle of the night delivering packages for a white boy to his rich sweetheart, she would have tanned his hide right then and there, even if he was almost twenty years old!"

"Package?" I ask, thinking to myself that it is true. It *was* Zero who delivered the ring to Ellen Davenport that night.

"Yes, he was close to saving the money he needed for that first year of college, and Andy Benton offered him forty dollars to de-liver a package to Ellen Davenport." Grace frowns and sighs. "Zero never should have gotten himself mixed up in that mess."

Clarence and Grace are both silent. I sense there's much more to this story than they're telling. Clarence reaches over and squeezes Grace's hand. She sits up straighter and says, "Clarence, we should tell Roxanne how Zero ended up at Alcorn State."

"That's right, Gracie," he says, and turns to me. "I was right here on Catfish Alley the night Zero came looking for Dr. Jackson. I'd finished up my work and stopped into Jones's for some supper. That's when I saw Zero starting up the stairs to the rooms over the bank. He told me the whole story. . . ."

August 1931

Zero

Sweet Jesus, I got trouble now. After I was feeling so good, too. Met up with Andy Benton yesterday morning. Told him I made his delivery, how Miss Ellen acted all innocent like she didn't know what was in that box. We laughed about that one. He paid me the other twenty dollars and I was thinking that was a pretty easy way to make some money after all. When lo and behold today if I don't meet up on the road with Ray Tanner driving the Davenports' big old car and Miss Ellen sitting up in the backseat, bawling her eyes out. I have to stop the mule, I'm so surprised. She and Andy was supposed to be in Yalobusha County today getting hitched.

As soon as I can get that pile of lumber unloaded I hightail it back to Clarksville, get the mule pastured and the wagon put up, and then I head back to Riverview and sneak into the summer kitchen to find Sarah Jane. It's hot as hell in there and Josephine is cooking greens, standing over a big iron pot, stirring, the sweat dripping off her face salting them more than the fatback. She says she can't be worrying about Sarah Jane. Says that girl's been moping around looking like she swallowed something rotten. Says she's not worth a damn and don't want to work. Josephine gives me a glass of sweet tea and shoos me out of the kitchen.

Just as I'm heading for the river, I see Sarah Jane coming round the back of the kitchen. I call to her real quiet and she comes over behind that big old live oak. She must be feeling sassy today 'cause she says, "You better not let your little bitch Adelle see you talking to me, boy. She'll be jealous, might turn her little nose up at you." Sarah Jane's been sweet on me for a long time, but she knows Adelle's the only girl for me.

"Oh, come on now, Sarah Jane," I say. "I just need to ask you a question."

"What you want?"

"Why is Miss Ellen bawling today in the car? I met up with Tanner today on the road and she's in the backseat crying like she's dying or something."

"Why you care what's wrong with Miss Ellen?"

"No reason. I'm just curious."

"Curious, my ass," she says to me. "You done got yourself mixed up in that business between her and Andy Benton, ain't you?"

"You don't know anything," I say, but she knows I'm lying.

"I hate Andy Benton. I hate Ray Tanner. I hate all them white mens," she says, and she starts crying then, tears rolling down her face making trails in her sweat. I feel bad then, like I done something to hurt her, when all I want to know is what happened.

"Did something happen to you, Sarah Jane? Did somebody do something to you?"

I reckon she softens up to me a little bit then, 'cause she starts telling me how Mrs. Davenport came dragging Ellen by her arm into her room, while Sarah Jane was in there cleaning. Ellen was dragging a suitcase behind her screaming how her mama done ruined her life, how she loved Andy Benton and how she was going to marry him no matter what they did. And then later on, Sarah Jane tells me, she overheard Mr. and Mrs. Davenport talking.

"He said to her, 'You know, I really appreciate Ray Tanner looking out for our Ellen,' and she said to him, 'Yes, I hate to think what could have

happened if Ray hadn't stopped them.' And then they talked about how bad for the family and the business it would be if Ellen married that low-class Andrew Benton."

"They didn't say anything about me, did they?" I ask.

Sarah Jane looks down at the ground, starts running her bare toes over one of the roots of the tree. I grab her by the arms then and have to stop myself from shaking her. "What did they say, Sarah Jane?"

"Zero, you got to get out of here!" she says, looking real scared now.

"Why? What did he say?"

"He said Ray Tanner says you was mixed up in this somehow and Mr. Davenport thought he was probably going to let you go."

I breathe a little easier. I can find another job. But when I look at Sarah Jane, I know she's not finished yet.

"That ain't all, Zero. Then he says Ray Tanner says let him take care of you." Sarah Jane's voice has gotten all high and squeaky, and she's breathing real fast. "Zero, Ray'll kill you if he has half a reason. He want Miss Ellen for hisself. Thinks marrying her'll get him Mr. Davenport's business someday."

"What did Mr. Davenport say?"

"He said that's fine with him. He told Ray he don't want to hear no more about it. Just do what he need to do."

I wait 'til it gets dark and I head over to Catfish Alley. Tonight's the meeting and I know Dr. Jackson will be there. I'm hoping he'll help me figure out what to do. I know he's not going to be happy with me. He doesn't like it when I get mixed up in white folks' business. He's always saying how we've got to make ourselves separate, make our own way. Doesn't he know that's what I'm trying to do? Only this time it's backfired on me. And I'm starting to believe Ray Tanner's just a mean enough son-of-a-bitch, if he thinks I might get in his way at the sawmill, no telling what he'll do.

I come from the alley, and just as I'm starting up the stairs to their meeting room, Clarence hollers from across the street. He's coming out of the café and he cuts across the street.

"Hey, Zero. What you up to tonight, sneaking around like you hiding from somebody?"

I stop and tell Clarence what's happened and how I've got to see Dr. Jackson. Clarence says he'll wait for me.

"But how're you going to get in there?" he asks.

I tell him I hid under these stairs as a kid and watched the members go in here so often I got their secret knock memorized. I take a big deep breath and knock, two times real quick and two times slow. The door opens sudden and old man Green is standing staring me dead in the eye.

"What you want, boy? What you mean coming up in here interrupting our meeting? Get on outta here." He looks over my shoulder like he's afraid somebody's going to see him.

"I promise, Mr. Green, nobody saw me come up here. I've got to talk to Dr. Jackson. It's urgent. Can you please let me come in?"

"You just stand right there, boy, and I'll have him come out here and talk to you."

"Please, Mr. Green," I say. "It's real important nobody see me." He must have seen how scared I was, because he let me come just inside the door and wait.

From where I stand, I can see into a big room with ten or twelve colored men sitting around a big table, most of them smoking and talking real serious. They don't have any liquor, so this is not a drinking club. I can't figure out what they do in here. Green goes over and whispers in Dr. Jackson's ear. He jerks his head up toward the door and, directly, Dr. Jackson comes out and shuts the door behind him. He grabs my shoulders and looks down at me over his glasses.

"Zero Clark, what are you doing here?"

I try real hard not to sound like I'm as scared as I am. All of a sudden, my mouth goes as dry as cotton and I can't think what to say. I just stand there looking at him, trying to find some words.

He gives me a little shake. "What's happened, son? Is somebody chasing you? You look like you've seen a ghost."

I finally find my voice. "Dr. Jackson, I did something that wasn't real smart and now I think I might be in trouble. . . ."

Roxanne

"Dr. Jackson knew the dean at Alcorn State," Grace says, picking up the story.

"They were both secret members of the N double A C P," Clarence adds.

"I don't understand. Why would they be secret members?" I ask. All this secrecy and hiding are so strange to me. It seems to me that these men were probably being overdramatic.

"Wasn't safe for a colored man to openly join an organization like that if he lived in Mississippi," Clarence replies. "Quickest way to get your house or business burned down by the Klan."

"The Klan?" I ask. Now this is a different story. I know a little bit about the Klan and none of it's pleasant. My mama used to tell me tales that made my toes curl. But Daddy always said she was exaggerating.

"Yes, ma'am, the Ku Klux Klan," Clarence says, looking over at Grace. "They was real active around here in the twenties and thirties. Those white men were joining up like folks getting saved at a tent revival. They wanted to be sure colored men didn't get to vote or have property rights, legal rights, such as that."

Grace nods and continues. I notice how sad her eyes look. "Dr. Jackson was always trying to work for change and he insisted on doing it peacefully, but he had to be careful. And when Zero told him what he'd done, Dr. Jackson knew that it wouldn't be long before Ray Tanner would be coming after Zero. It wasn't clear how Ray would get him, but it was mighty clear that he would.

"Dr. Jackson made special arrangements to get Zero admitted to Alcorn State right away. When he brought Zero out to the house that night to pack, Grandma made coffee and we all sat at the kitchen table and Zero told her the whole story. He was so ashamed, mostly because he had to get Dr. Jackson involved. He was so determined to make it on his own. But this time he'd gone too far."

Grace sighs deeply. "Grandma just sat listening. I could tell she was struggling, but she stayed calm. I know that my grandma loved me, but Zero had a hold on her heart like no one else. When Zero finished and Dr. Jackson told her the plan, Grandma nodded and sipped her coffee for a few minutes. Then she got up and left the kitchen. None of us knew where she'd gone or if she was coming back. Zero and Dr. Jackson and I sat there and looked at each other, not knowing what to do next.

"Directly, she came back into the kitchen carrying an old cigar box with a rubber band around it. She sat down and pushed it across the table toward Zero. 'I reckon you'll be needing this now,' she said. Zero looked at her and then at us. 'Go on, open it,' she said. So he took off the rubber band and opened it up and there must have been a hundred dollar bills stuffed into that box.

"I'll never forget it. She looked at Zero, who was sitting there with his mouth open, and said, 'Zero, when you were ten years old and we took the wagon down to the Penny Savings Bank so you could open a savings account, you told me you was going to make something of yourself, maybe even be a doctor like Dr. Jackson here. That day, I decided I would start a little savings myself and I told the good Lord if he would let me live to see you go to college, I would help you. So I been saving a dollar a month, sometimes two if the Calhouns gave me a Christmas bonus, since you was ten years old.' By now, we were all crying, even Dr. Jackson. Zero got up and hugged Grandma real tight, kept thanking her over and over, saying he was sorry he had to leave like this.

"And that's how he got to Alcorn State that fall," Grace says, getting up and taking her coffee cup to the sink. "Clarence, I surely do thank you for giving us coffee and showing us around," she says. "Roxanne just might be able to add Catfish Alley to this tour she's making. Isn't that right, Roxanne?"

I take this as my cue that we're done here. As usual, I feel the disappointment of the window to Grace's past slamming shut on any further questions. This story has taken hold of me and I want to know so much more about Zero, but I say, "Yes, ma'am, I think this area would be a nice addition to the tour." I shake Mr. Jones's hand, thank him for his hospitality, and dutifully follow Grace to the car.

When I get back home, I pull the diary back out to see if there's more to the story than Grace has told me. For some reason, I always feel like she's leaving something out. Is she afraid to tell me? Once again, it takes me what feels like hours to make out what Ellen Davenport wrote. What a sad story! All these years I never realized she was heartbroken.

AUGUST 24, 2 P.M.

My life is over. Daddy found us out. And it's all because of that horrible Ray Tanner. Right in the middle of our ceremony with the justice of the peace, he walks in and insists that Daddy would never approve of our marriage. He actually threatened that justice of the peace and Andy, too. He had both of them so scared that my wedding got stopped right then and there. I've never been so humiliated in all my life! And the hardest thing was that Andy didn't even protect me. He let Ray Tanner put me in the back of his car and drive me all the way back home. It was horrible. I don't even know where Andy went! Mama and Daddy were furious, especially Daddy. Mama just dragged

*me up to my room and told me to stay here. Sarah Jane brought
me some supper a little while ago, but I can't eat. What will I
do now? The man I love has been taken away from me and I'm
destitute. I can't even write anymore.*

SEPTEMBER 30, 8 P.M.

*It's been a long time since I wrote anything in this journal.
My life is nothing but a series of long dull days. I've had no
letters from Andy. Nothing. He might as well have never lived.
Sarah Jane is no help, either. She heard that he might have
gone to New Orleans. Our New Orleans! I'm trapped. I don't
have any money of my own and Mama and Daddy watch me
all the time like I'm some criminal escaped from Parchman
Penitentiary. I guess I'll just live here and be an old maid. I
don't want anyone else. Ray Tanner tries real hard to be nice to
me, but he makes me sick. I just want to spit in his face. Mama
says I have to be polite, that he was just trying to do what's best
for me. She says they all are but they don't know what's best for
me! They don't!*

Chapter 10

Del Tanner

Alice and I are poking around in this damn old dusty attic, trying to find those documents that banker Jack Baldwin said I have to have. We been up here looking for two hours and ain't found shit. Still chaps my ass to think I got to come up with the original deed to the lumberyard. What if there ain't one? Then what'll happen?

"I'm going downstairs to fix some supper," Alice says. "I got to get out of this dust for a while. You come on down in a little bit, you hear me?"

I grunt a reply as I sort through some old lumber brochures in a cardboard box. Nothing here. I'm in the last corner of the attic. We've been through everything and I'm trying to think where else I could look. But we put everything of Daddy's up here after he died. Didn't want to deal with it, had a business to run. Mean old bastard. Never would give me all the information I needed. He's probably laughing from his grave at me now.

I'm fixing to give up and go downstairs to eat when I spot that old shoe trunk. I'm sixty years old, but seeing the trunk still gives me a start. That trunk used to sit in Daddy's room. It was always locked and I was always curious about it. I used to think Daddy probably hid his whiskey in there. I remember being around ten years old, sneaking into Daddy's room and trying to open it. Daddy caught me and pulled off his belt and beat me with the buckle. Said he'd teach me not to mess with things that didn't belong to me. Even now, I find myself looking around before I reach for the trunk.

It's about two feet by three feet and about a foot deep. Daddy probably got the trunk from Granddaddy Rufus. That's how long I can remember it being around. Things weren't much better between me and Daddy when he died than they'd been all my life, so of course he never mentioned this trunk or wanting me to have it. *Well, Daddy, as usual, you wouldn't want to do nothing to help old Del out, would you?*

I pull the trunk out from under the pile of old quilts and study the lock. It would be fairly easy to break, provided I can't find a key. I suddenly remember the handful of keys that black nurse at the hospital handed to me the night Daddy passed away.

"He never let these out of his sight," she said.

I'm trying to picture what I done with those keys. Damn if I can remember. I pick up the trunk—must not be much in it; it's not very heavy—and make my way down the attic stairs.

"Alice, do you remember that set of Daddy's keys that the nurse gave me after he died?" I holler.

"Yes, the ones she said he never let out of his sight?" she answers from the kitchen.

"Yeah, what did we do with those?" I come into the kitchen, carrying the trunk.

"I think you put them in your desk somewhere. God knows, you've got so much junk in there. Come on and eat." She's carrying a plate of corn bread to the table and stops. "What in the world is that?" she asks, pointing to the trunk.

"I found this under some old quilts up there. It used to be Granddaddy's and then it was Daddy's. He always kept it locked.

I'm thinking that maybe the key is with those we got after he died."

I go into the little room where I keep my desk and business papers and set the trunk down. Alice is still hollering for me to come eat before the bread gets cold, so I decide to look for the keys after supper. Just as I'm finishing up, I get a call from one of my suppliers and I forget all about that trunk.

Chapter 11

Roxanne

Grace and I are standing in the vestibule of the Missionary Union Baptist Church. The church is constructed of wood in a simple style. Three steps lead up to a narrow porch with a wider overhang over the front door. Just inside the door is a vestibule area that houses a row of coat hooks, an umbrella stand, and one of those boards with rows to slide in numbers that report last Sunday's attendance and the amount of the offering collected. I remember the thrill I got as a little girl when I was allowed to do that job in our church in the bayou.

I can't help but notice the heart pine floors. They glow like Tupelo honey from years of foot traffic. I know what some people would give to have floors like this in their homes. Through the vestibule door is a small sanctuary with two sections of wooden pews worn to a satin patina from years of holding backsides clothed in Sunday best. The pews are stocked with hymnals, offering envelopes, and fans advertising the local black funeral home. I have attended the Clarksville First Baptist Church for decades, but I've never set foot in a black church in Clarksville before.

I find myself beset with a memory of being about six years old and Mama taking me with her to visit the Baptist church of one of her black friends from the Stanley plantation. Details flood through my mind as I stand beside Grace in this little church. The same style pews, but filled with color—hats, dresses, men in suits in Easter egg hues. And the sounds! The organ and the deep, rich voices that seemed to soar to the ceilings and fill the whole building with melody. It was glorious and terrifying all at the same time. I remember the little black children wanted to touch my hair, and I wanted terribly to touch theirs, too, to feel that springy texture between my fingers, but instead we just stood and stared at each other from behind our mothers' skirts.

This church has a similar small choir loft with a baptistery, a piano, an old organ, and the pulpit. We are approaching the pulpit area when a black man crawls out from behind the first choir seat. I jump and let out a little squeal before I can control myself. I wasn't expecting to see anyone in the church on a Tuesday morning.

Grace smiles calmly, in her usual way. The man is obviously just as surprised to see visitors, but his smile is wide and welcoming, and, I can't help but notice, very attractive. His skin is very dark and smooth and he is wearing a baseball cap, which he instantly pulls off. He looks young. I assume he's probably the church janitor. He approaches us and takes Grace's hand.

"Miss Grace, how good to see you this morning! I'm sorry I didn't hear y'all come in. I was down there behind the choir seats looking for Eva Randall's earring. She called me this morning in a dither. Her deceased husband, Earl, gave her those pearl clip-ons for their fiftieth wedding anniversary, and she is just in a state about losing one. Even said she might have to stop singing in the choir!"

I'm still wondering who this handsome young man is. Maybe he's not the janitor; maybe he's a young deacon. Grace chuckles softly as he describes Eva's plight.

"Eva gets herself stirred up, all right, Brother Daniel. I hope you find that earring. It would be a shame to lose that wonderful alto voice of hers from the choir." Grace turns to me and draws the man near her. "Reverend Daniel Mason, I would like for you to meet a friend of mine, Mrs. Roxanne Reeves."

So this is the minister? I'm surprised. I thought he would be Grace and Adelle's age. I shake his outstretched hand, and I can't help but notice those gorgeous deep brown eyes and the way his forearm ripples with muscle.

"I'm pleased to meet you, Mrs. Reeves. How do you come to know our most important church member?"

Grace squeezes Reverend Mason's arm and laughs. She is as excited as a schoolgirl around this man.

"Oh, now, stop that. I'm one of the oldest, but certainly not the most important."

I am impressed with their easy comfort with each other. I'm sure this minister has no problems winning the support of the ladies of the church. As my mama would have said, he is a sight for sore eyes, for a black man, that is.

"Miss Clark is showing me around some of the African-American historical places in the community," I answer.

He nods. "And, of course, she brought you here. This church has been around for a long time, Mrs. Reeves." He motions to the front pew. "Please, won't you have a seat?"

Grace and I settle ourselves on the front pew and Reverend Mason pulls up the piano bench and sits facing us. I can't help but notice those muscular thighs and the supple ease of his movements. I have to shake myself. *We're in church, for mercy's sake!* The reverend is saying something.

"Miss Grace knows the history of our church much better than I do, Mrs. Reeves. I'm afraid I'm still learning."

Grace nods and rests her arms on her handbag in her lap. "Reverend Mason has only recently come to us from up in Chicago. This is his first time to pastor a Southern Baptist church."

"Oh, really," I say. "I'm Southern Baptist, too. I am a member of the Clarksville First Baptist Church."

"Yes, I know of it. I believe I met your minister at one of the interfaith meetings last month," he says.

"What I meant to say," Grace says, "is that this is Reverend Mason's first time to pastor a church in the South. We're actually Missionary Baptist."

"Yes, Miss Grace has been trying to help me with the ins and outs of the Southern black community," Reverend Mason says. "Unfortunately, I've trodden on several toes already." Reverend Mason and Grace share conspiratorial smiles.

They spend the next half hour telling me the history of the Missionary Union Baptist Church. It's the oldest church in Mississippi, established as a meeting place during the days of slavery. Back then, they tell me, there was no church building. The church consisted of a collection of branches and underbrush gathered into an arbor-like semicircle. The slaves stood within the brush arbor to worship. Years later, after the War ended and during Reconstruction, this wooden structure was built. The church has survived since 1871 and there are many stories about obstacles the members have overcome.

I listen to how the black people worked and scraped and volunteered in order to have a building for worship. Now, I'm an expert on the history of the local white churches and their white benefactors: the Catholic church on Fourth Street was built by a wealthy steamboat magnate because his only daughter decided to become a nun; the impressive First Methodist Church was built with slave labor by a famous white planter who moved his family here from New Orleans; and my own church, First Baptist, was built in 1853 by the ancestors of the current president of the Bank of Clarksville. But none of those stories match the endurance and spirit of the people who built this little church.

I realize I've grown so accustomed to the grandeur and amenities of my church that I can't imagine sitting through Sunday service in one of these hard wooden pews with no padding or listening to the organ without an echoing sound system. Yet this church has the kind of warmth and peacefulness about it that makes me want to sit down and stay. I feel a lump in my throat remembering again that day so long ago with Mama. I've never had that kind of emotional experience in my own church. I tell myself, even before seeing any more, that this church has to be on the tour.

Grace decides to remain in the pew and "have some quiet time with the Lord" while Reverend Mason takes me on a tour. There isn't much to see. Two or three small rooms behind the sanctuary were the original Sunday school rooms. Behind the sanctuary, a new fellowship hall was constructed in the 1950s. Reverend Mason says it's used for everything from choir practice to Sunday night socials. He points next door to a small bungalow-type cottage.

"That's the parsonage over there. It was built in 1910 by the same man who helped Dr. Albert Jackson build his house."

"Does your wife like Clarksville?" I ask, finding myself surprisingly curious about this man.

Reverend Mason grins and shakes his head. "Oh, I'm not married. My house companions are a fourteen-year-old beagle named Ruby and an equally old cat named Harriet. Believe me, though," he says, laughing, "if the ladies in my church have anything to do with it, I'll be married off before I'm here much longer. They just can't believe that I don't have a woman to take care of me."

I find myself liking this young man from Chicago who doesn't have one trace of a Southern accent, but the best manners and the friendliest, not to mention most handsome, smile I have seen in a while.

"I recently met another of Grace's friends," I say. "Matilda Webster. She has a granddaughter living in Chicago. According to the ladies, she's in some powerful city position up there. Maybe you know her. I think Grace said her name was Billy . . . Billy Webster?"

He laughs softly. "I never met Billy Webster while I was living in Chicago, but I definitely know Mrs. Matilda Webster. She's an interesting woman. I visit her in the nursing home every week, and she is always talking about Billy."

"I'm hoping to get to meet Billy myself," I say. "Are you familiar with the old Queen City Hotel?"

"No . . . ," he says, looking puzzled. "Should I be?"

"No, no," I answer. "I was just curious." I decide I'll keep my ideas to myself for now. Another thought occurs to me. "Does a man named Jack Baldwin attend your church?"

"Yes, I do know Mr. Baldwin, and his wife, Rita. Real nice folks. He's a banker, I believe. Why do you ask?"

My plan just might work, but I need to arrange a few more details first. "Oh, just wondering. I had lunch with Rita a couple of weeks ago and then I met Mr. Baldwin last week when Grace and I went down to visit Clarence Jones on Catfish Alley." I sound so casual talking about being social with blacks, I don't even recognize myself.

Reverend Mason smiles. "Yes, I know Clarence—wonderful barber, but not much of a churchgoer."

We end our tour and return to the sanctuary, where we find Grace dozing in the sunlight slanting through the stained glass window over the choir loft. I gently touch her arm and she wakes instantly.

"Gracious, I must have dozed off. I was praying, and before you know it, I fell asleep."

"We're done with our tour now," I say, feeling a little sad to be leaving this peaceful place.

"Brother Daniel, thank you for showing Roxanne our little church," Grace says.

I walk along behind them as we leave the church, noticing how attentive he is to her and how much she seems to enjoy it. Why did Grace never marry? Were there not other men after Junior? Did she wait all her life for him?

I shake hands with Reverend Mason after he helps Miss Grace into the car. Closing the car door, he peers into the window and looks across at me.

"Let me know if there's anything I can do to help with the tour, Mrs. Reeves. I'm just new enough in this community that I can get by with asking for things that some folks won't." He grins. "At least once anyway."

I look in my rearview mirror and see him waving as we drive away. It hits me that my whole perspective on black men is changing. How strange.

Billy Webster

I love Chicago. I've got a great job and great friends. No man yet, but I'm still hopeful. Today is one of those beautiful, crisp fall days—at least it's not the dead of winter. I've never gotten accustomed to the cold, windy winter weather here. On those days just walking from the taxicab to the airport doors is enough to chill you to the bone. Even now, I'd rather be home in my cozy downtown apartment, sipping hot chocolate in front of a fire. Instead, I'm boarding a plane and headed to Mississippi to see Gran.

It's the right thing to do, I tell myself for the thousandth time. It's just so depressing to go home. Gran sits in the Pineview Nursing Home day after day. Just sits there. Granted, she has her room fixed up nice and it's her choice to stay there. I've tried for years to convince her to come and live with me in Chicago, but Mrs. Matilda Webster wants nothing to do with it. So, every three or four months here I am on a plane to Mississippi.

Yesterday, on the phone, Gran mentioned the old hotel again. This is the other bone of contention between us. I want to sell it and at least get the money for the land it's on, but Gran refuses. She says all of her memories are there and, as long as she's living, she will not sell it. Now Gran's talking about a tour. Says some white woman from Clarksville is organizing an African-American tour and wants the Queen City Hotel to be part of it. I snort at the thought of that, and the woman sitting next to me in the airport waiting area looks at me curiously.

That place is so run-down it looks more like some of the projects on Chicago's South Side than a hotel. Daddy always said the Queen City was fine by comparison to where blacks usually had to stay back in those days. Of course I've heard all of the family stories about the heyday of the Queen City Hotel. It's all interesting and nice, but I don't have much interest in history. Why anybody would want to tour an old hotel that represented segregation at its worst is beyond me.

The nasally voice announces our flight and I board the plane with the other faithful folk returning to the South. I find my seat and sleep until the pilot announces our arrival in Jackson, Mississippi. My best friend, Travis Sprague, and I were out far too late and drank far too much last night. But the jazz was hot and Travis was buying, so I couldn't refuse. In Jackson, I rent a car, as usual, and drive down to Clarksville. I take my usual route down the Natchez Trace, admiring the fall color with the car's air conditioner on full blast, since it must still be ninety degrees down here.

When I walk into Gran's room at Pineview, I'm surprised to see a tall black man facing her chair and holding her hand. She's looking up at him like he's good enough to eat, and I have to agree from what I can see from behind. That is one fine-looking man. Gran looks past him, sees me, and squeals in delight. He straightens quickly and turns. It's been a long time since I've seen a man who made me catch my breath. Most of the guys I've met so far in Chicago are players, not really serious. I've gone out with a few white men, but I quickly realized that I'm just not attracted to white men. But this man. Oh, my!

Ease up there, sister, I tell myself. I settle down and focus on my grandmother. "Hey, Gran," I say as I move past the stranger to kiss Gran's cheek.

"Hey there, baby girl," she says. Her obvious pleasure in seeing me always makes the trip worth every cent. "I want you to meet my new pastor, Reverend Daniel Mason. Brother Daniel, this is my granddaughter, Belinda Webster."

I have to stifle my disappointment. *A preacher? This must be God's idea of a joke.* How could he put this gorgeous man right in front of me, close enough right now to notice how good he smells, and make him a preacher? I wonder what I did to make God angry. Probably not visiting my grandmother enough. I smile and take his hand. *Those eyes!* Even behind the glasses, they're warm and sexy.

"Good to meet you, Belinda. Your grandmother has told me a lot about you. She's very proud of you, you know."

"Please, call me Billy," I say. "Gran, I hope you haven't been telling this minister any of those made-up stories you like to tell."

Gran laughs. "No, baby girl. Everything I've said about you and your high-powered job is true. I've just been telling the reverend about the Queen City and how I want him to help me talk you into taking a look at it again. Reverend Daniel says he'd love to see it."

I haven't seen my grandmother this animated in years. What is that twinkle in her eye? Is it just from being around a handsome man or is it something else? And here we go with this discussion of the Queen City again. I think I might as well nip it in the bud, right now.

"Gran, we've been over this before," I say, pulling up a chair beside her and plopping my bag down on the bed. I turn to the preacher. "Please, Reverend Mason, sit down, won't you?"

"I can only stay a minute. I have other folks to see. Please, call me Daniel." He moves a chair near the two of us and I can't help but watch as he bends that tall muscular frame into the small chair. I look up and realize Gran is watching me. She actually winks!

Oh, Lord. "Rev . . . Daniel, what my grandmother doesn't realize is what poor condition the Queen City Hotel is in. You see, it's in an area of town that's not too great and it's been vandalized. The roof leaks. . . . Anyway, it's just not something you would want people touring—"

Gran interrupts me. "There was a white woman over here the other day talking about putting the Queen City on a tour. An African-American tour. She just might have some ideas about what we could do with it. I was telling Brother Daniel about the days when your grandfather ran the hotel and all of the famous black musicians and athletes and such who stayed there. He still wants to see it for himself," Gran insists.

"I believe I met her," Daniel says. "Roxanne Reeves?"

Gran nods. "That's the one. Little bit uppity. Don't think she's very comfortable around black folks, but she's trying. I let her borrow a key to take a look at the place. Grace Clark tells me she's quite taken with it."

Daniel nods in agreement. "Yes, ma'am, I agree. I got that impression from her, too." Daniel Mason looks at me with an expression as eager as a little boy's. I wonder what it would be like for him to act that interested in me. "I really would love to see the place, if you have the time," he says.

There are those eyes again! I look from Gran to Daniel. It seems as if they are conspiring against me. And I'm so confused.

Who is Roxanne Reeves and what African-American tour? Gran loaned out a key to the place? Gran reaches out and takes my hand.

"Brother Daniel's father was a jazz musician and he plays, too."

"Really?" I ask. "What instrument?"

Daniel looks embarrassed. "Oh, I just play a little on the horn, nothing much. I grew up with jazz, and when I came in here and saw all of these pictures"—he motions toward the pictures Gran has hanging on just about every inch of her walls—"I was amazed at all of the jazz greats who came down here."

"I gather you're not from Mississippi," I say.

"No, no. I'm from Chicago."

Now this is just too strange. Another cosmic joke. A good-looking intelligent man who plays jazz and is good to old people, and he leaves Chicago, where I live, and moves to Mississippi, where I wouldn't be caught dead living, *and* he's a minister? It's enough to make a grown woman cry. But Gran is looking at me with that pleading look in her eyes, and this man is so handsome, how can I refuse? I can at least show him the place; nothing has to come of it. But I'll do it on my terms.

"All right, Daniel. How about I come by and get you and we'll go over to the Queen City? When do you get off work, uh . . . I mean, when are you available?" It occurs to me that preachers might not keep office hours like regular people.

He smiles, and, of course, Gran looks extremely pleased with herself. "Would this evening work for you? I have a church meeting at five, but I'll be done around six."

We settle on six thirty for me to pick him up at the parsonage. I assure him that I know where it is. It's been a long time since I was in church, but not long enough to forget its location. He kisses Gran on the cheek and says he will see her in a few days, politely shakes my hand, and makes his exit.

I turn from walking the preacher to the door and Gran is

watching me with a wicked gleam in her eye. "Enough to make you want to move back to Mississippi, isn't he?" she says.

I act nonchalant, waving my hand. "Oh, Gran."

"You have to admit, baby girl, that is one good-looking preacher."

Some things, as hard as I try, I cannot hide from Gran. Interest in a man is one of them. I don't know what I'm worried about anyway. It's not like Gran is going to have a chance to interfere much in my life. I'll be gone in a couple of days and I probably won't see the preacher again for a year.

It's starting to drizzle when I ring the doorbell at the parsonage behind the Missionary Union Baptist Church. Standing on the porch looking over at the old church, I remember all of the Sundays and Wednesday nights I spent there as a child. There was always some activity—Sunday school, choir practice, dinner-on-the-ground, singings. It was such a big part of my life growing up. Next to the hotel, it was the place where I spent most of my time. But then, everything changed. When I was a senior in high school I lost both my parents in a car crash. I think I walked around in a fog for that entire year. It was Gran who saved my life, helped me decide on a college, was my rock when I started working in the Clarksville City Council office, and finally encouraged me to take the job I was offered in Chicago.

College changed my view of the world, opened me up to new possibilities. Moving to Chicago was the best decision of my life. I'm not hampered there by being the same small-town girl, the granddaughter of Robert Webster, the girl who grew up at the Queen City Hotel. I'm just Billy Webster, an intelligent, well-educated administrator for the city of Chicago. It suits me. But every now and then I get a longing. I just can't quite put my finger on what it is.

When Daniel Mason opens the door, I decide I have that long-ing figured out. It's sex. He stands there in a pair of faded jeans that fit just right, a soft corduroy shirt, and a smile that does that thing with my breath again. *Dammit!* I find my voice to respond vaguely to his invitation to come in. I stand in the doorway watching as he gently herds an ancient-looking dog away from the door. Now I have to add "loves animals" to the growing list of reasons why I like this man. *Will it ever end?*

"You'll have to excuse Ruby," he says. "She's half blind and so she tends to want to stand and sniff everyone who comes to the door."

"No problem," I say with a laugh. "I love dogs. I would have one if I could, but I'm never home."

He smiles as he nudges Ruby toward a well-worn dog bed in the corner. "I can't imagine life without Ruby. She and I have been together fourteen years now."

"No wife?" I ask, then immediately wish I hadn't. Of course, I want to know, but, as usual, I probably could have found a more tactful way to ask.

"Almost," he replies, not seeming to mind the question. "I came close back in Chicago, but it didn't work out. You? A husband, I mean." I feel my knees go a little weak when he looks at me.

"No, too busy, I guess. My hours are long and . . ." I realize I don't have much of an answer. "Well, anyway . . . are you ready?"

We chat about Chicago as we drive the short distance to the Queen City Hotel. I ask Daniel how he ended up in Mississippi after living in Chicago all his life.

"My father is the reason I'm here," he says with a smile. "He was the minister of a small church in our neighborhood, so I grew up playing with my Matchbox cars under the church pews and helping him and my mother every Sunday get the church ready for service."

I smile at the thought of Daniel as a small boy on his belly on the cold floor of some Chicago church, pushing toy cars through a city made of the underside of wooden benches. I turn up the windshield wipers to deal with the heavier rain.

". . . so I guess I came naturally to the ministry. But the reason I'm so drawn to the South is Saturday nights in our basement. That's when my father became a different man. Daddy and his cronies were all transplants from Mississippi or Louisiana, and they put together a small jazz band. As far back as I can remember, I would sit on the basement steps and listen to them play records of the jazz greats like Louis Armstrong or Miles Davis on this ancient turntable and then try to copy them. Daddy played the trumpet, and he had friends on the sax, the trombone, and the piano." He laughs. I think I could listen to the sound of his laugh every day and never get tired of it.

"During college, after my father died, I made a road trip through the Mississippi Delta with some friends. We saw the towns and places where the blues were born and we visited the small churches along the way. . . ." He drifts off, caught up in his memories. "Anyway, I knew then that I would pastor a church in Mississippi someday. And when this opportunity came up, I had no ties to keep me in Chicago. It seemed like the right time."

I shake my head. *How can an intelligent, well-educated—not to mention single—black man want to move from Chicago to Mississippi?* "What about the racism, and the poverty, and just the general backwardness of things down here?" I ask, realizing my incredulity at his decision is probably showing.

"Billy, I know about all of that." I'm thinking how I love the sound of my name when he says it. "But you and I both know there's racism everywhere. And being poor sure doesn't keep folks from coming to church around here. I've met several church members who are really proud of this community."

"That I know," I say, sounding more sarcastic than I intend to.

He leans forward to look as we turn on to Seventh Avenue. "Take this tour, for example. If this hotel was on the African-American tour, just think how exciting that would be for folks around here." His enthusiasm is almost contagious, but not quite. He hasn't seen the hotel yet. But I'm pleased to find him open and surprisingly normal. I realize I'm talking to him like a real person, not like a minister at all.

When we arrive at the hotel, the drizzle has turned to steady rain. We sit in the car looking at the old dilapidated building. The wide front porch is sagging, as are the steps leading up to it. The boarded-up windows look bleak. I realize the rain is probably pouring in through leaks in the roof in several places.

I reach over into the backseat and pull out an umbrella. "I'll come around to your side of the car and get you."

"No, no, that's okay," he says, studying the hotel. "I'll just run for it."

I find myself disappointed. I had been entertaining a brief fantasy about being under the umbrella with him. "All right, but be careful—those steps are caving in."

I climb the treacherous porch steps just behind Daniel and dig in my bag for the keys to the hotel. I unlock the door and we step inside, shivering from the chill that's settled in. The dim light of the rainy afternoon casts long shadows across the wide lobby. I notice immediately that there is a new leak near the counter. I retrieve one of the buckets that I keep in the closet by the front door and place it strategically under the drip.

"Looks like you've done that before," Daniel observes.

"Yes, I don't know why we keep trying to hold this old place together. Gran won't let me sell it. Even though I want to get rid of it, I just can't stand to see these old wood floors get destroyed. Every time I come home, I come over here and empty the buckets and set out new ones."

"Sounds like you've got some attachment to the place?" Daniel asks.

"Well, I do have some good memories here of my father and my grandfather. But my life isn't here anymore. It's in Chicago."

Daniel nods as if he understands. "Will you show me around?"

We go through the first floor, starting with the lobby and ending with the kitchen and the bar with the small stage. He stands for several minutes on the stage, looking around, completely engrossed in some picture that seems to be playing in his mind. I wander around the room I have seen so many times before. Occasionally I steal glances at Daniel. He seems to be completely at ease, no pretense, no attempt to impress me. This both disappoints and pleases me. He's probably just imagining the famous jazz and blues musicians who once graced this stage.

"Let's do this, Billy," he says suddenly.

This man has no idea where my thoughts went just then! Quickly I realize he's referring to something about the hotel.

"What do you mean? Do what?"

"Let's turn this place into a community center. It could be great," he says as he starts pacing around the old lobby, pointing. "We could put meeting rooms over here, maybe a little coffee shop . . . I'm sure we could find some funding. And I'll work in my spare time. Maybe I'll get some of the teenage boys in the community to help me. It will be good for them. We could get this place back in shape, fix the roof, replace those doors. . . ." He seems lost again in his thoughts and his excitement about the possibilities for the old hotel.

I can't find any words. I never in my wildest dreams expected the preacher to offer to fix up my old hotel. This is crazy.

"Oh, I don't know, Daniel. I couldn't let you do that. There's so much work to be done, and then who's going to take care of the place? I'm in Chicago and Gran's at Pineview. . . ."

He steps close to me and interrupts me by taking my hand. Suddenly, I can't breathe. "Don't worry, Billy—it will be great. Don't you see? We could get the community involved and we could save this place. It would be great to have it on a tour. Just think what kind of boost that could be for the black community." He's even more handsome when he's excited. *What is happening to me?* I have to get out more often.

"Okay, okay," I say, pulling my hand away. "We'll talk about it. I still don't see how you're going to salvage this place, but we can talk."

"I tell you what," he says. "Let me buy you dinner over at the catfish place, and we'll talk about it some more before we approach your grandmother."

I agree. I have to eat, right? After a quick tour of the upstairs rooms, we're on our way to the Catfish Cabin. What am I getting myself into?

Grace

We finally have ourselves one of those cool fall days. I think how nice that is because Halloween is usually so hot around here. I'm having my second cup of coffee on the front porch so I can look at the pecan trees that line the road up to my house. Those old trees are glowing gold today and the ground is just covered up with pecans. I'm going to have to get Brother Daniel to make an announcement down at the church for folks to come out here and pick them up. It would be a shame for them to go to waste, but Walter can't keep up with all of them.

The pecan pie for the cake walk at the church Harvest Festival this afternoon is in the oven, and I've sent Walter out to cut some flowers. I didn't really get to enjoy my first cup of coffee this morning like usual because Mattie Webster was calling me on the telephone before the sun was even up good, all excited about her granddaughter Billy and Brother Daniel.

"Gracie, you ain't going to believe what happened yesterday," she said.

"What's that?" I said, a little irritated because I usually don't like to talk that early in the morning.

"Brother Daniel was here visiting me when Billy got in from Chicago, and you should have seen the eyes she was making at that man! And him studying her, too, like she was the finest thing he'd seen in a very long time."

"Now, Mattie, that's the preacher you're talking about."

"Well, he's a man, ain't he? And you know how good-looking my Billy is. Anyway, Brother Daniel and I talked her into showing him the Queen City Hotel."

This surprised me. "I thought you didn't want the Queen City on the tour."

Mattie snorted. "To tell you the truth, I don't give a plug nickel whether the hotel is on that so-called African-American tour or not. What I care about is Billy, and as far as I can tell, she couldn't find a better man than Brother Daniel. If I was a little bit younger, I'd have a crack at him myself. Why, he's so fine, he reminds me of the time . . ."

Mattie had me laughing like she always does and I told her to be sure and let me know how it goes with Billy and Brother Daniel. I can't see Billy leaving Chicago to move back to Mississippi for a man. And it would be a sad day if we lost Brother Daniel. But these things tend to work themselves out. The Lord moves in mysterious ways.

I think over the places I've shown Roxanne Reeves: the old Union School, Dr. Jackson's house, the Queen City Hotel, Catfish Alley, the church. Kind of a pitiful collection of places, I guess. But I can't imagine my life without any of them. And it's been interesting to watch Roxanne over these last few weeks. At first, she was so jumpy and nervous all the time, I thought I'd have to tell her to find somebody else to help her. But the more we spend time together, the more relaxed she gets. I think she's right comfortable with me now. And I could tell she was especially struck with Clarence Jones and Brother Daniel. White women sometimes get ideas in their heads about all black men being dangerous. If she had only known all the good men I've known in my life.

It would make a big difference if Brother Daniel could talk Billy into putting the Queen City on the tour, but there's so much work to be done there. And there's not much chance of getting the Union School—not with Del Tanner owning the property.

I'm not sure that my old heart could stand any more dealings with Del Tanner anyway. I've spent the better part of my life trying to stay away from that family. I push myself out of the chair to go in and check on the pie. No matter how old I get, I remember Zero every time I make a pecan pie. It's Grandma's recipe, and whenever she'd make it Zero would hang around the kitchen begging for the first piece. She'd fuss at him about cutting it too soon, before it was set up good.

Lord knows, I wish Zero had stayed away from those Tanners. No one could ever prove anything, not in Mississippi. But I've always known in my heart that Ray Tanner had something to do with what happened to Zero. I take the pie out of the oven and set it on the table to cool. Maybe I'll get Walter to take me by to see Adelle today. We could go to the Harvest Festival together. I always find it soothing to be with Adelle. She loved Zero as much as I did. I know she wouldn't want me to have anything to do with Del Tanner. She had to nurse his daddy, Ray, when he was dying with emphysema. That was enough. I still don't know how she did it. She was even there when he died, and he was a mean old cuss every second until he took his last breath.

I come back out on the porch, and Walter is headed for the house holding a basket full of mums. He's been in an ornery mood today. Doesn't like Halloween much.

"You got my mums there for me?" I ask, taking a look in the basket he hands me.

"Yes'm," he says, as he starts to walk away.

"Why, Walter, these are all cut so short. I can't put these in a vase." Walter just hangs his big old head and looks at the ground. He knows better. How many times have I had him cut flowers for me for church?

"Now, you just get back out there and cut some more. And leave the stems long enough for that tall green vase of mine." He takes the basket and turns. "And this time go out there behind the barn and cut some of those nice sunflowers back there to go with them."

"Yes'm," he says without looking at me.

I try to be understanding because I know Walter hates this season. I've told him at least three or four times that this Harvest Festival is nothing like the Halloweens he remembers, but he won't hear it.

Children can be pretty hard on other children like Walter. He's always been what folks called different. As I watch him working on a second bunch of mums, I remember him as a third-grader, all full of smiles and just as helpful as a boy could be. But that's about as far as Walter was able to get in school. He kept going until the tenth grade and the teachers kept passing him on through. There wasn't anything called special education in those days. He tried so hard to fit in and make friends with the other boys, but they treated him badly, and I think Halloween must have been the worst. Those boys were always playing mean tricks on him.

After the Calhouns died, back in the seventies, I finally moved up here to this big old house to rattle around in it all by myself.

Thankfully, they left an account open at the bank for me to pay the taxes. I hired Walter full-time and let him live in the little house where I grew up. His mama and daddy passed away not long after the Calhouns, so it all worked out just fine. Walter's been a big help to me. He doesn't have much book smarts, but he can do anything with his hands. I've been able to keep this place running, and with the Lord blessing me with such good health, I don't need any hired help besides Walter just yet. I feel a stab of worry thinking about what's going to happen to Walter after I'm gone and remind myself that I need to look into some arrangements for him.

I finish my coffee and take my cup inside. Time to get ready for the Harvest Festival. I wonder if Brother Daniel invited Billy. I chuckle to myself. That would just tickle Mattie Webster pink!

Chapter 12

Del Tanner

I am bone tired. But I've got to sort out that damn trunk and see if I can find any of those legal papers. I'm still pissed off at having to go through all of this rigmarole. That banker, Jack Baldwin, is just trying to make my life miserable because he can. Daddy wouldn't have had to go through all of this. His word was all he needed.

I dig in the deep drawer on the side of my desk and finally find the ring of keys I threw in there after Daddy's funeral. I find the heavy silver skeleton key that I think belongs to the trunk. I try it, and sure enough, the lock gives way easily. Finally, something goes right.

Opening the trunk, I feel like Daddy is in the room with me. I'm breaking a sweat and my hands are shaking. Memories of being a boy are grabbing hold of me and I have to stop for a minute.

I remember Daddy standing over me, tall as a tree, the sun behind him so I couldn't clearly see his face. I was just coming up from the riverbank near the sawmill. I must have been about eight years old. That would have made Daddy about thirty-nine years old. I had started helping out at the sawmill, picking up scrap lumber and doing odd jobs. But that day I sneaked off early to go fishing with a new friend I made. His name was Joe and he was the son of one of the mill workers. The problem was Joe was colored.

Daddy spied me and Joe coming back from the river, holding a stringer of crappie between us. We were planning to split the catch and surprise both of our mamas with supper.

"What the hell do you think you're doing?" Daddy boomed.

I remember getting this sick feeling of dread in my stomach. I looked at Joe and he looked at me and he quick dropped his side of the stringer and ran off. I can still see those fish, lying there in the sawdust, their dead eyes staring up at me from the ground.

"We was just fishing, Daddy. We got done with our chores, so we went down to the river for a little while. Caught some good crappie. Look." I pointed to the fish on the ground, hoping to distract him from whatever reason he was so angry. When Daddy got mad, I was never sure what set him off.

He grabbed my arm and shook me so hard I dropped my fishing pole. "Boy, what do you mean going off and fishing with niggers? Ain't you got no pride? Don't you ever let me see you messing around with them again, you hear me?"

"Yessir," I said, bracing myself for him to hit me. It didn't come yet. He wasn't finished yelling.

"You see that boy there? Look at him."

Daddy shoved my shoulder and I turned around to look at Joe, who'd done run over to stand by his own daddy. Joe looked scared, too. Only his daddy stood with his arm around him. I remember thinking he looked like he was protecting him. I nodded my head to let Daddy know I was listening.

"If you start making friends with niggers, pretty soon they're going to think they're as good as you. And then the next thing you know, they're going to take your job, and then they'll take over the whole town." Daddy jerked me around again to face him. "So you keep with your own kind, you hear me?"

"Yessir," I said, real quiet, and I was wondering what job I was going to have that a nigger couldn't do.

After that, I didn't have no more colored friends. I made sure to find the boys whose fathers thought like mine did. It was easier that way. Together, we reminded each other that we were better than blacks—smarter, richer—and that it was our God-given responsibility to be in control. That made our daddies proud. That's just the way things are around here. And ever since I took over Tanner Lumber, that's how I've run my business. I make sure the blacks stay in their places. And now I'm having to follow instructions from one just because I need money.

I take off the lock, open the trunk, and start going through the top tray. There's stacks of old receipts, bills, lumber brochures, and almanacs. Daddy always was a stickler for reading the almanac. I find a brown envelope marked *Tanner Lumber*. Good! Maybe these are the papers I need for the loan. Then I notice another envelope, thick and yellowed, stuck in the fabric lining on the side of the tray. I might not have seen it, but the fabric has started to disintegrate with age.

I decide to start with this one and I notice it's addressed to Mr. Ray Tanner and has the address of the lumberyard on it. The postmark is 1932. There's no return address.

I open the envelope and pull out what looks to be a postcard. The back of the card is faceup when I slide it out of the envelope. The writing scrawled across the yellowed message area is hard to read, but I can make out the date, December 1931. I can read the first word of the message. It's Daddy's first name, Ray. The rest of the writing is smeared and blurry.

I turn the postcard over and find myself looking at a photograph of a young black man strung up from a huge tree. His body is suspended in the air from a tree limb that reaches out over the water of a river below. That tree looks like the old live oak behind that big house downtown that overlooks the Tombigbee. River-view, I think. I always pass that tree when I'm fishing down there. Underneath the tree, with big grins on their faces, is a group of five men, hands on their hips or in their pockets, looking at the camera with pride, like a man looks when he poses with the first deer he's ever shot.

The man in the front of the group, the one who looks to be the leader and is actually holding the black man's feet to keep him still for the camera, is smiling the broadest. I pull the postcard closer and adjust my glasses. I recognize the face and my stomach turns in on itself. Smiling at me from a photograph of a lynching in 1931 is my own father, Ray Tanner.

I can't get that picture postcard out of my mind. In every black man I look at—at work or around town—I see that boy's face, all puffed up and hanging from that tree, nose bloody, eyes swollen shut. It turns my stomach. I can't concentrate on nothing. I don't even associate myself much with blacks, except for hiring them for the lumberyard. I make it a point not to. Daddy raised me to be suspicious of them and make sure they always stayed in their places. Daddy was a son-of-a-bitch, but I never thought of him as a mur-derer. Until now.

I've always been comfortable with what Daddy taught me. He always said we didn't have to go around talking about it, but that it's clear in the Bible that God created colored folks as a lesser race. They're meant for service. That's just how God made things. They just ain't as smart as white people. Daddy always said, "Just be-cause slavery ain't legal no more don't mean niggers are equal." All through the years, even through all that business about civil rights in the sixties, I never questioned Daddy's word.

I think about that loan officer, Jack Baldwin, who's still waiting on me to produce a deed for the property. He seems smart enough.

I find myself wondering if anybody ever threatened his life. I have to stop this! This is craziness. This is just the way it is and who knows? Maybe that hanging all those years ago was justified. It probably was, I tell myself. Daddy wouldn't string up some black man for no reason.

This last thought makes me feel a little better and I decide to stop in to the café downtown for lunch. I have my usual fried chicken, butterbeans, and corn bread, followed by a big piece of apple pie. I'm just coming out of the café, finishing a conversation with two of my buddies from the county extension office, when a sign catches my eye. I realize I ain't really noticed it before. I say my good-byes to the two men and stand there looking at this sign that hangs over the door to an upstairs office. The office is one of those small places on the second floor. There's a hardware store on the first floor and you get to this office by one of them narrow staircases from the street.

The sign says *Purvis Photography*. I know I've seen that before somewhere, but I can't place it. Then I remember. *Purvis Photography* was on that postcard of Daddy's I found. But there's something familiar about this place, too. Could this be the same place I went to get that high school senior picture Mama insisted on? I walk closer to the door and read the sign painted on the upper glass window of the door. *Purvis Photography Serving Clarksville Since 1922*. I'm pretty sure this is the same place I came to get my picture taken. I try the door, but it's locked.

Then I notice the sign says *For Sale by Owner, Tours by Appointment Only*. I pull a small pad of paper out of my shirt pocket and write down the phone number. I'm not sure why I'm doing this. I ain't going to call these people. Hell, they ain't going to remember a postcard from 1931. But then, they might keep records. I shake off that sick feeling again. I got work to do.

I'm late for supper again this evening. Alice ain't happy. When I open the back door into the kitchen, she's standing at the sink washing dishes. She don't even look up. I try coming up behind her and kissing the back of her neck. She likes that. But she pushes me away with her elbow.

"Where have you been?" she asks, never taking her eyes off the casserole dish she's washing.

"Last minute, some of the boys making a delivery today from over in Alabama wanted to go over to J.T.'s for a beer. We got to talking and one thing led to another, and . . . well . . . the time got away from me," I say. What I don't say is that I was trying to get that picture postcard out of my mind. It's like some ghost keeps creeping up behind me. I needed a few beers just to stop my hands from shaking. This whole thing has me all out of sorts.

"Supper's in the oven if you want it. Just be sure you don't leave dishes for me to wash. I'm going to bed." And with that Alice walks out of the kitchen, leaving me standing by the sink.

I pull the plate of food out of the oven, pour myself a glass of tea, and take both back to my office. I have got to make myself look for that deed. I sit down at the small desk and stare at Daddy's trunk sitting across the room from me. I left the postcard in there, and I didn't look at anything else the other night because I just had to stop. That postcard was enough for one night. I try to eat, but I just can't seem to bring the fork to my mouth. I push the plate away and dig in my pocket for the key to the trunk.

This time when I open the trunk, I set that envelope with the postcard in it aside real quick and keep on looking through the rest of the papers in the tray. I breathe a sigh of relief when I find the old file folder labeled *Tanner Lumber*. The file contains the documents I've been searching for. I turn back to my cold supper and take a couple bites of corn and meat loaf. At least Daddy kept something useful. I'm still wondering what else is in that trunk. I smile to myself, thinking he's dead now and he can't do a damn thing about me looking through the whole thing.

I pull out the shallow tray to see what's underneath in the larger hollow of the interior. I set the tray on the floor next to the trunk and look inside. What appears like a set of sheets or maybe a table-cloth is folded up real neat on top. I reach in and touch the fabric and it feels like rough cotton. I take a side of it and pick it up. As it falls open, I notice that it has two openings cut in the front for eyes and it's sewn like a hat with a sharp point. I look in the trunk again and pull out a long white robe. The robe has a big red cross on the front of it. All of a sudden I realize that what I'm holding in my hands is a Ku Klux Klan hood and the robe that goes with it.

I can't move. I just sit there staring at the robe. I know about the Klan. A man can't grow up in Mississippi without knowing about the Ku Klux Klan. But I've always steered clear of anything to do with them. I figure I got enough to worry about without trying to terrorize a bunch of niggers or Jews. As long as my boys do what they're told and turn out a good day's work, I'm fine with that.

So my daddy was a member of the Klan. That explains that postcard. Only he wasn't wearing this getup in that picture. I wonder what else he might have done. I'm getting that sick feeling again and I have to drink some tea. I think about Daddy lying in that hospital bed, still smoking like a chimney through that tube in his throat, cussing any black nurse who came in his room.

Them nurses was real patient with him, too. I remember one in particular. She was black as night and tall and skinny, but she was a kind woman. She just ignored the old bastard when he cussed her and called her nigger to her face. It was her who washed Daddy's body and got him ready for the funeral home. I remember how her being so calm helped me when Daddy's hatefulness made me want to get the hell out of that room and never come back.

Why had he hated them so much? What happened that night when the black man in the postcard was lynched? I put my hands on my head and squeeze. I've got to get these questions out of my mind. Without thinking any more, I pull the notepad out of my shirt pocket and pick up the phone. I dial the number I wrote down earlier for Purvis Photography. The phone rings several times, and I'm fixing to hang up when a man's quavery voice answers.

"J. R. Purvis. May I help you?"

I ain't prepared with what to say. "Uh, yessir . . . I'm calling about an old photograph I found . . . It was, uh . . . a postcard of my father's . . ."

"The photography business closed more than forty years ago, sir," the old voice answers.

"I was, um, well . . . I was wondering if you keep records . . . if I could talk to somebody . . ."

I hear the person on the other end of the line clear his throat. Then in a much stronger voice, he asks, "What's your name?"

"Delbert . . . Delbert Tanner."

It's quiet for a few seconds and then he says, "Tanner . . . hm . . . my father knew some Tanners. Are you related to Ray Tanner?"

"Yessir. He was my father."

"And he's dead now?"

"Yessir, he is. About those records . . . ," I start to say.

"What few records my father kept are stored at the old studio on Main Street. I will see what I can find. Come by tomorrow afternoon at one o'clock sharp. I'll be waiting for you."

I'm fixing to tell him I can't come tomorrow because I've got work, but he's already hung up.

I decide to park down the street at the old feed store. Folks around here know my Ford, and this way I have less chance of someone seeing it parked right in front of Purvis's place. I ain't ever felt no reason to care about who sees my comings and goings, but today I find myself looking around to make sure I ain't going to meet somebody I know. I just want to get in and out of Purvis's studio as quick as I can. Daddy died more than twenty years ago, but he was only in his sixties when he passed. There are still people alive in this town who knew him, who probably even knew about the things he did. But I sure as hell don't want to talk to anybody about this.

It all seems so shameful now. I ain't no nigger lover, but I sure don't want it known around town that my own daddy lynched one. That's why I got to get my hands on the negative of that photograph and make sure it gets burned.

When I'm sure there ain't nobody watching me, I go in the glass street door and climb the skinny stairs that lead up to the studio. At the top there's a small landing and a wooden door with faded lettering that says *Purvis Photography, J. R. Purvis, Photography for All Seasons* painted on the door. I have this crazy thought in my head to wonder what the lynching season was.

I open the door and come into a barely lit reception area with a small wood desk that's bare except for an old black rotary dial phone and a black hat, the kind the old men around here wear. A waiting area has a sagging floral settee and two old worn-out wingback chairs. There's a little table under the wide window that overlooks the street. It's got a vase of them artificial flowers on it that are coated with so much dust you can hardly tell what color they are. This place looks exactly the same as it did when I came here for my high school portrait. I'm looking out to see the view to the street, when I hear footsteps coming from the back and someone clearing his throat.

The man who comes in is tall, about my height, and a big man. He fills out his black suit coat like one of them blown-up balloons you see on TV at Thanksgiving. He's got a thick shock of wavy white hair, and when he gets near me, I realize he's pretty old—at least eighty, I'd say. That must be his hat on the desk.

His voice is deep and he acts real stiff. "Mr. Tanner?" he asks. I nod and he holds out his right hand. "I am J. R. Purvis, Jr.," he says, giving me a quick handshake. I notice his hands are dead cold and soft like a woman's. "I'm sorry, but I don't think I'm going to be able to help you. My father was an atrocious record keeper." He don't smile. He just stands there with both his hands folded in front of him and waiting for me to answer. He screws up his face into a frown and looks up at my cap.

I reach up and quick pull off my John Deere cap. "Yessir," I say. I shuffle my feet, feeling nervous.

"Have a seat, Mr. Tanner."

I sit down in one of the old chairs, trying to place this man. I know I've seen him somewhere before. Purvis don't sit down, and now I'm feeling like a schoolboy with the teacher standing over me. He still ain't said nothing. Not much for shooting the shit, I reckon, so I figure I might as well get this over with. I'm starting to wish I never came here.

"Mr. Purvis, I was sure hoping you'd have some records or negatives of pictures your daddy took back in the early thirties."

Purvis responds real fast, like he had his answer all planned out before this meeting. "My father was not a very efficient record keeper, Mr. Tanner. We have a few files on the marriage, graduation, and baby photographs, but that is the extent of it. I'm afraid that if you want reproductions, you'll need to see a professional photography restoration specialist. What type of family photograph were you interested in investigating?"

All of a sudden, I realize why he looks familiar. I've seen his picture in the *Clarksville Dispatch*. This man is that big-ass lawyer in town who tried that murder case up in Tupelo with all the hype back in the seventies. No wonder he acts like he's got a rod up his ass. I'm trying to remember the details of the case. Something about a black man killing an old white woman. He was the lawyer for the black man. Then I realize Purvis has just asked me a question.

I look down at my green and yellow cap, twisting it in my hands. "This ain't exactly a family photograph, Mr. Purvis . . . I mean . . . my daddy was in it, but . . ." I'm not sure where to go from here. Has this guy looked at old J. R. Purvis's photographs? Does he know that his daddy photographed lynchings along with all them weddings and high school graduations and baby pictures? I reach in my shirt pocket and pull out the postcard. "This is the picture I'm interested in."

Purvis barely glances at the postcard I'm holding out for him to see. He clears his throat again and says, "I'm sorry, Mr. Tanner. There seems to have been a mistake. My father did not take that photograph, nor do we have any records of any such photographs." He turns around, walks to the desk, picks up that black hat and sticks it on his head. Before I can say hello or kiss my ass, he's opening the door, saying, "Now if you'll excuse me, I have clients to see."

I realize I've been dismissed. I start to tell him that J. R. Purvis's name is on the postcard and so is the date, but this son-of-a-bitch is so cocksure, I don't have the balls to argue with him. I walk out of the studio and head down the stairs. I stop for a second, listening to Purvis pull the door closed behind him and turn a key. I look up and see him start down the stairs, laboring over each step. "Good-bye, Mr. Tanner," he says.

"Um, yessir. Good-bye," I say, feeling again like a schoolkid, slapped on the hand by the teacher. As I'm walking back to my truck I'm wondering what exactly just happened and why the conversation with Purvis seems so strange. It's like he's hiding something, but why? I walk a block, then turn to look back at the studio. A big old Mercedes pulls up. The driver hops out and takes Purvis's hat while he gets in the backseat. The driver closes Purvis's door and drives off.

Three hours later, I'm back at my office trying to get some work done, but I'm still stewing over my meeting with Purvis. Why was he so short with me and why was he so stubborn about that post-card not being done by his daddy? Maybe Purvis really didn't take the picture. But why would his name be on it then? I don't under-stand why you'd make a postcard of something like that anyway. Looks to me like you'd be setting yourself up to get caught. But then, maybe those boys weren't worried about getting caught back then. I think again about the way my daddy talked about being a young man in Mississippi. My whole life Daddy complained about every step that blacks took toward being more equal with us.

I remember when he was in the last months of his life, living with us, before he went into the hospital. He'd sit on the porch in a rocking chair, playing checkers and yakking with his old buddies when they came by to visit. I was trying to keep the business going and I couldn't stand being around the old man for very long at a time. Alice was a saint to take care of Daddy those last few months. I wonder what all Alice heard Daddy talk about. The old man got plumb out of his head toward the end. Seemed like he talked more about his younger days than anything else.

Maybe it's time I talked to Alice. Lord knows, I don't need to be worrying about this now. My business is on the line, I'm trying to get the bank to give me a loan, and all I can think about is who the boy was that Daddy strung up from a tree more than seventy years ago. Disgusted with myself, I lock up the office and head home.

Chapter 13

Roxanne

"Grace, I've been wanting to ask you something for a long time," I say. We're sitting on the screened-in porch of Pecan Cottage, enjoying the late-afternoon breeze as we go over the details of the tour. I've drafted a preliminary program and brought it by for her to look at.

"What's that, sugar?" Grace asks, continuing to study the program through her thick glasses.

"How is it you came to own Pecan Cottage? I mean, I know you'll understand when I say that I don't know of any black women in this area who own antebellum homes . . . well, not like this one . . . or not because they inherited them from family, um . . . white family . . . I mean . . ." I am just not sure how to ask this and I'm getting frustrated. Fortunately, Grace interrupts.

"You want to know how an old black schoolteacher comes to own a house that was in a white family for six generations?" Grace asks.

"Yes, I do."

Grace sits back in her rocking chair and lies down on her lap the program she's been studying. She takes off her glasses and absently begins to clean the lenses with the bottom edge of her sweater. "Do you remember me telling you that I grew up in a little house down on the back of this property?"

"Yes, ma'am. You said your mama worked for the Calhouns."

"Yes, she did. And my grandma before her. My great-grandma was a slave of the Calhouns and she and her husband stayed on after the War and started sharecropping. Her daughter, my grandma, worked for the Calhouns as a cook. My mama grew up here, too. Grandma insisted that Mama finish high school—she was always fierce about education, even though there wasn't much available to a black woman in those days. You could graduate when you were sixteen if you went straight through. Mama did what Grandma wanted and finished high school, but then she ran off with her sweetheart, Monroe Clark, came back here a married woman.

"Mama had my brother, Zero. Then two years later she had me. Then, as I told you before, Mama died when I was twelve. All my life I thought Zero and I had the same daddy."

"You mean you didn't?" I'm surprised by this. "But you didn't mention your mother getting a divorce. . . ." I stop myself, realizing I've made another assumption.

"They didn't divorce. The man I always thought was my daddy died when I was just a baby. But Mama and Grandma had always told me stories about him. So Zero and I grew up out here living near the Calhoun house, helping out at parties, playing in the woods near this house. I helped Mama clean and Grandma cook. Zero helped out around the yard and the barn. He took care of the horses and parked the cars later on when people started driving cars."

I can hear the sadness in Grace's voice. "Miss Grace, I'm so sorry. If this is too painful to talk about . . ."

Grace shakes her head. "No, no. It's all right. I'm old and only the good Lord knows how much longer I'll be around to tell these stories. It's a good thing for me to tell them now. But before I do," she says, getting slowly up out of her chair, "I need to get something that I want to show you." Grace leaves the porch and goes into the house. She's gone for several minutes.

I'm beginning to wonder if I should follow her in and offer to help, when she reappears holding what looks like a yellowed envelope and sits down again in her chair. She continues without missing a beat.

"So my grandma raised us after Mama died, you see. I came home every day after school to help out around the house and to help her with her work. The Calhouns paid me two dollars a week. I was so proud when my savings started to mount up. Zero started working as soon as he could pick up a broom, for old Mr. Green down at Green's Grocery on Catfish Alley. He wouldn't get home until after dark most nights. We kept his supper on the stove. But he was just as determined as I was to save for college. Grandma had always told us how important education was, so she couldn't complain a whole lot about him not being at home much.

"You remember how I told you about Dr. Jackson helping to get Zero out of town after that business with Andy Benton?"

I nod. "Yes, ma'am."

Grace's voice cracks a little then and she takes a deep breath. "We rushed around that night and got Zero ready to leave for Alcorn State, and I think that's when Grandma started getting pains in her chest. I remember noticing her holding her hand over her heart, but she never complained. We didn't have the modern medical treatment and the medicines then that we have now, you know. Plus, Grandma kept ignoring it, saying she had just eaten too many bitter greens or too much onion.

"I found her one morning, just two days after Zero left, slumped over the table in the Calhouns' kitchen. I had come into the house to ask her a question and noticed the smell of burning biscuits. She had put a batch of biscuits in the oven for the Calhouns' breakfast and sat down at the kitchen table to drink a cup of coffee. The doctor said he didn't think she suffered much. The Lord took her mercifully fast. Within a week, Zero had left for college and I had to bury our grandmother. I tell you what, Roxanne, I had never been so lonely in my life! Everybody I loved was leaving me—Zero was off to college, Grandma died, Junior had already gone on the road to play his music, and Adelle was going to Tuskegee for nursing school."

I feel the old familiar pain in my own chest. My mother died when I was just a young woman. There have been so many times when I miss her. Wished I could talk to her, ask her advice, or cry on her shoulder.

"What did you do then?" I ask.

"After Grandma died, Zero tried to convince me that he should stay and not go back to college, but I told him absolutely not! He had worked too long and too hard to quit now before he even got started good. I had a little money that Grandma left to me in her will and I offered to take over Grandma's job for the Calhouns until I could save enough money for school. I had my heart set on going to Tougaloo College, you see, and becoming a teacher.

"Then one afternoon in late September, about a month after Zero left and Grandma died, Mr. Calhoun knocked on the door of my little house. He had what looked like an old letter in his hand and he said, 'Grace, I wonder if you would come up to the house. Mrs. Calhoun and I need to talk to you about something real important.' Well, I'm here to tell you that just about scared the living daylights out of me! I thought for sure they were going to tell me I had to get off the property."

"I thought you told me that your mother got the deed to that house in old Mr. Calhoun's will?" I ask.

"She did. And it passed on to me. But you have to remember, I was a young girl then, only eighteen years old. And it was 1931. I didn't know but what he could make me move off of his property, him being the landowner and all."

"Yes, you're right. I can see how you'd be scared."

"I came up here to the big house. As a matter of fact, we sat right where you and I are sitting today. I remember because there was a cool breeze that evening. Very unusual for September. We talked about how it smelled like rain and we laughed about how Grandma could always tell when it was going to rain by the way her knees ached.

"I was a might shaky when I sat down, but Mr. and Mrs. Calhoun were smiling and friendly, so they put me at ease a little. And then Mr. Calhoun pulled out that letter he had in his hand earlier and started to tell me about it."

September 1931

"Grace, Ruth and I have some news for you," Mr. Calhoun says, and he looks at me over his small round spectacles. He's holding a yellowed-looking piece of paper in one hand and an old envelope in the other. From where I sit, I can't make out any of the writing, but the stamp on the envelope must be foreign. It isn't like any postage stamp I've ever seen around here. I cross my ankles and try to keep my hands still. What could this be about? Are they unhappy having a colored woman living alone on their property? Are they thinking about hiring someone else? Are they unhappy with my work? I try to keep the panic down.

All the way up here when I was walking from the little house, I've been thinking of other jobs I could do and who might be hiring in town. There's always the garment plant. That's what I'd planned in the first place. Maybe I could take the little bit of money that Grandma left me and go to nursing school with Adelle. The problem with that is I don't want to be a nurse. I don't have the stomach for it. I want to be a teacher. I've always wanted to be a teacher.

Mr. Calhoun looks at Ruth, who smiles at me reassuringly, and then back at me. "As you know, your grandmother kept her will in my father's safe."

"Yessir, I did know that. She always said it would take a lot longer for Pecan Cottage to burn up than it would our house."

"That's right. I remember her saying that. Anyway, after Daddy died and my older brother died and I realized that I was going to inherit the place, I spoke to your grandmother about her will and she said that she would like to just keep it right where it was. So we left it there for safe-keeping."

"So is this something about her will?" I ask. "I mean, I thought all of that was settled?"

"No, no," he says. "Everything is fine with the will. But when we were looking in the safe for your grandmother's will, we found a letter tucked inside your grandmother's document. I had never seen the letter before and it has to do with you and your family."

I'm racking my brain for what might be contained in this mysterious letter. I sit silently waiting for Mr. Calhoun to continue.

"As you probably know, I had an older brother, Gerald, who was a pilot for the French air force during the Great War."

I nod. "Yessir, I remember seeing the photograph of him in his uniform, standing in front of an airplane. I always liked it when I got to dust the parlor because I could look at all of the photographs. . . ." I stop talking, realizing I'm bordering on nervous chatter.

"That's right. And we lost Gerry when he was shot down over France. But apparently before he died, he dictated a letter to a French nurse. That letter is what I found folded into your grandmother's will. My father must have known about it, but neither Ruth nor I had ever seen it before. It is a little difficult to read, but I've read it over several times and I would like to read it to you now, if that's all right."

I nod, still wondering what this could possibly have to do with me.

Late-afternoon rain clouds have rolled in and occasional streaks of lightning spark the sky, followed by a distant rumble of thunder. Mr. Calhoun switches on the lamp beside the wicker chair he's sitting in and begins to read. . . .

August 11, 1918

Dear Mother and Father,

I fear that I might not see your faces again in dear old Mississippi and I have persuaded a nice nurse who has been taking care of me to write a letter for me. Don't worry, they are able to keep the pain under control with morphine, although I must admit, it makes me a little foggy at times, so please forgive me if this letter seems disorganized.

I have on my conscience a terrible thing that I did before I left to join the French air force and I must tell you. I've heard so many of these Catholic boys around me calling for priests to confess their sins before they die. I know that we Baptists don't believe that we need priests and such, but I cannot die knowing that the truth has not been told about what happened five years ago between myself and Monroe Clark.

The truth is I slept with Monroe's wife. Mama, I'm ashamed to have to admit this to you. I know that you raised me to be a good Christian, but I confess I was tempted and gave in to temptation. The bigger shame is that she was not willing. I came on her alone one day up at the big house doing some of her chores and I forced her into one of the upstairs bedrooms and took her. I didn't hurt her, I swear. Nevertheless, I know what I did was wrong and I have asked God to forgive me for it. I'm sorry to say that I will never have the opportunity to ask Mary herself for forgiveness.

I didn't realize that Mary was pregnant because by then I had left for North Carolina to learn to fly airplanes. I came home for a short time later that year, and when I saw Mary with her big belly, I made myself believe the baby was Monroe's. And Mary, of course, would have nothing to do with me.

Monroe, as you know, always hunted with us boys to help carry the guns and manage the dogs. One night, while I was home visiting, we were getting ready to go coon hunting and I noticed Monroe hadn't shown up yet. One of the boys said his wife was having her baby. After the hunt I had started back out of the woods, and just when I got to the road, Monroe drove up in the wagon. He was carrying a gun and he pointed it straight at me. He said his wife just had a healthy eight-pound baby girl. When I tried to congratulate him, he said that the midwife told him that there wasn't any way a baby could come out looking that white and be his child. I reckon Mary finally told him what happened between her and me.

I tried to talk him down, honest I did. I told him it was all going to be all right, that I would help them out best I could. He said he didn't want to look at his daughter every day and think about a white man raping his wife. He just kept pointing that gun and coming closer and I got scared and shot. He fell down and didn't move. I just stood there scared to death. I've killed a lot of men in this war, but it never felt like it did that night when I shot Monroe Clark.

The boys heard the shot and came out of the woods behind me. I was still shaking when they knelt down beside him and felt his pulse and told me he was dead. I made up a story about him being mad at me about a hunting dog and pulling a gun on me. What was crazy is that they believed me. Not one of them questioned me a bit. We loaded Monroe in his wagon and took him to the colored hospital and told the doctor it was a hunting accident.

I'm telling you all of this now because I don't think I'll survive this injury, and I left Mississippi right after all of this happened, so I never got a chance to make any arrangements for that little girl. I don't even know what her name is. But I can't go to my grave knowing that I have a child in this world and not let

*you know. She's probably about five years old now and I want to
be sure that you take care of her. I realize that what I've done has
caused shame for our family, but please don't make the wrong I've
done even worse by refusing to acknowledge my daughter.*

I'm forever in your debt. I beg your forgiveness as I do God's.

Your loving son,

Gerald

Roxanne

"Lord have mercy, Grace! What did you do? How did you feel?" I'd
been listening with rapt attention as she read the letter.

"Looking back on that day after all of these years, I think what
I felt was shame. I didn't know it then. Right then, at that moment,
all I could feel was anger. I sat there just stunned, and Mr. Calhoun
put that letter down and said, 'Grace, we think my father was embarrassed by all of this business and hid this letter. We never knew
it existed until now.' I just looked at him. I didn't know what to say.
After all, these were the bosses. These were the people my family
had been working for more than eighty years. We were friendly,
but we weren't in the habit of revealing our personal feelings to
them.

"Mrs. Calhoun chimed in then. She started to tell me how they
had talked and that they wanted to make it right somehow. At that
point, I couldn't listen anymore. My head was spinning. The man I
thought was my daddy wasn't. My mother had this happen to her
and I never knew. And worst of all, I was now just another illegiti-
mate colored girl with a white daddy who wouldn't claim her. I'm
telling you, Roxanne, all I could think to do was run. I ran out of
that house and back to my grandmother's little house and just sat
there all night crying my eyes out and trying to make sense of it all.

"By the time the sun started to come up the next morning, I

had made a plan. I packed what few clothes I had in my grandmother's old suitcase and I walked to the bus station in Clarksville. I bought a ticket to Jackson."

"Why Jackson?" I ask.

"Because Tougaloo College is only ten miles north of Jackson. I had decided, by hook or by crook, I was going to get out of Clarksville and, even if I had to beg them to take me, I was going to go to Tougaloo and become a teacher."

"Did you know anyone there?"

"No, and I had never been that far away from home in my life, either. It was quite an adventure for a young girl."

Grace stops telling her story and sits rocking quietly. It's so quiet out here all I can hear is the rustle of the wind through the red and gold leaves of the sweet gum trees outside the porch and the occasional soft thud of pecans hitting the ground near the driveway. I look at Grace, trying to determine if she's dozed off, but her eyes are open and she starts to fold the letter she has just finished telling me about and put it carefully back in its yellowed envelope. I'm holding my breath, hoping she's not finished. There's so much more I want to know.

It's shocking to me to find out she's half white. She doesn't look it. As far as I can tell her features are like most black people I've seen. Her skin is certainly not any lighter. I study her features surreptitiously. I've never really noticed, but maybe she has some resemblance to the Calhouns I've seen in the photographs. I remind myself to examine that family photo more closely next time I'm in the parlor. I remember that day I first met Grace, several weeks ago now. I was studying the family pictures that day. Who could believe then that I would end up feeling so close to this small, fragile woman who's taught me so much?

Grace looks up as I gently pose another question. "What was it like?"

She raises her eyebrows. "What's that?"

"What was Tougaloo College like?"

She sits up straighter in her chair and her eyes sparkle. "It was the best and the worst time of my life," she says.

September 1931

Grace

It's so hot and dry today, the wagon wheels leave a cloud of dust behind as the kind colored farmer who gave me a ride from the Jackson bus station drives his mules on down the winding dirt road. I set Grandma's old suitcase down and brush the dust off my dress, wishing I'd just stayed on the back of that wagon. Maybe I could go home with that farmer, find a new family and new life. I'm a hard worker. I could pick cotton. No one would know me. No one would know this terrible secret I carry about myself.

As the dust clears, I can see a brick arch and the words "Tougaloo College" displayed in the curve of the arch. Once again, I wonder how I'm going to make this work. I don't have much money and I haven't even applied for the fall semester. All I could think about when I got on that bus this morning was getting away from the Calhouns and Clarksville. I still can't take in the idea that my father was Gerald Calhoun. I've never known a father, colored or white, but Mama and Grandma always told me my daddy died when I was a baby. They always said it was a hunting accident.

Now I find out the man who fathered me died in a hospital somewhere in France. A white man. And not only that, I find out that I looked so white the day I was born that Monroe Clark lost his life over it.

I look down at my arms and hands as I stand there on that dirt road in the hot Mississippi sun. My skin is as black as Mama's was, as black as Zero's or Grandma's. There's never been any reason for me to suspect I might have any white blood. Then it strikes me. It's my nose. Grandma and

Mama always said I had such a pretty nose. But they never said why my nose is long and sharp and not wide and flat like theirs. I always thought it was just a twist of nature, a fluke. I reach up to touch my nose and run my fingers along the bridge of it. I silently curse my nose and Gerald Calhoun for forcing himself on my mama the way he did.

Mama and Monroe Clark probably had big dreams for our little family. But Gerald Calhoun took that away from them. I spit in the dust, feeling contempt for the man who ruined my mother's life, and right then I decide I will not let him ruin mine. If only I could talk to Junior. I miss him every day and he knows nothing about all of this. But I don't even know where he is right now. I feel hot tears stinging my cheeks.

But I've felt sorry for myself long enough. So I wipe my face with the handkerchief from my pocket, pick up my little suitcase, square my shoulders, and strike out down the long driveway and through the arch to Tougaloo College. I stop to look overhead as I pass through the arch. A mockingbird flies over my head and lands on top of the arch, looking down at me with quizzical eyes. I stare at the bird and think of Mama, rocking me to sleep at night when I was a little bitty girl, singing, "Hush, little baby, don't say a word. Mama's gonna buy you a mockingbird . . ." I'm flooded with the memory of my mother, her smell, her kind eyes, and I feel those tears coming again.

I remember asking her, "When are you gonna buy me a mockingbird, Mama?"

"Hush, child," Mama would say. "It's just a song." And she would keep singing, "If that mockingbird won't sing, Mama's gonna buy you a diamond ring. If that diamond ring turns to brass, Mama's gonna buy you a looking glass . . ."

Once again I brush away those tears with the back of my hand. I don't have time for sadness now. I came here to get an education. I can't let Mama and Grandma down. In the distance I see a large white house with columns and a generous front porch. This must be the Tougaloo mansion I read about in the pamphlet my teacher in Clarksville, Miss Wilson, showed me. As I get closer to the building, I can see that the entire second floor of the mansion has a series of multipaned windows across the front. I think how beautiful it is.

A quiver of excitement runs through my body and I smile with pride to think that this is a college, a real college, just for colored people. The mansion reminds me of the white people's homes I've seen in Clarksville. As a matter of fact, a white cotton planter built this mansion back before the War. The closest I've come to seeing the inside of any of the Clarksville houses, other than Pecan Cottage, was to go in their back doors for some errand I might be running for the Calhouns. I realize then that I've worked for the Calhouns all my life and I've never been in the front door of Pecan Cottage.

I resist the instinct now to go around to the back door of this grand old house. I set my jaw and march up the wide front steps. I'm busy admiring the arched window over the door when the door opens and I find myself face-to-face with a colored woman different from anyone I've ever seen before. She's dressed in a dark well-fitted suit. I know that her shoes and clothes are the latest fashion because Adelle and I have seen clothes like this in the Good Housekeeping *magazines that Mrs. Calhoun lets us have when she's finished. Her shoes are good leather, polished and shining, with pointed toes and a smart little heel. Her hair is combed in a straight bob with short bangs and she's wearing red lipstick. I notice that her skin is lighter than mine and very smooth. Her smile is immediate. She looks so young that I assume she's one of the students.*

"Why, hello there," she says. "May I help you?"

I'm suddenly very self-conscious of my dusty, old-fashioned dress and worn shoes. I decide that I'd better make up for what I lack in appearance by showing some spunk. I set my suitcase down and extend my hand.

"Hello," I say in my bravest voice. "I'm Grace Clark. I would like to be a student here."

The beautiful woman smiles again and a slight look of surprise crosses her face. She motions toward two wicker chairs on the shady porch. "You look hot and tired, Miss Clark. Please, have a seat. It's cooler out here on the porch right now than it is inside." She calls back over her shoulder through the still open door, *"Marjory, could you please bring my guest a glass of iced tea?"*

I move to the chair and stand in front of it, waiting for the woman to join me. I marvel at a colored woman asking someone to bring something to her. Other than my experience fetching and carrying for Mama or Grandma, I've never seen a colored woman have someone wait on her. The woman joins me and sits down.

"Please, sit down, dear. You look exhausted. Forgive me, I didn't introduce myself. I am Dr. Inez Prosser. I am a member of the faculty, in charge of teacher education."

I'm so overwhelmed I can't speak. This young woman is the very person I need to see and I've had the good fortune to meet her even before I got through the doors of the college! I feel Mama and Grandma watching over me like angels. I do think it's strange that Tougaloo College would put a doctor in charge of teachers. I didn't even know women could be doctors. This is all so exciting and very confusing.

"Now, Miss Clark," Dr. Prosser is asking in a businesslike tone, *"have you applied to the college and been accepted?"*

While I'm searching for a way to answer this question that will not make me look completely incompetent, Marjory appears with a tall glass of iced tea. I thank her as I take the tea and feel the cool sweat from the glass on my hands. In my excitement I forgot how hot and thirsty I was after the long bus ride here, not to mention the ride on the back of the farmer's wagon the ten miles from Jackson. I try not to gulp all of the tea down at once. Dr. Prosser is waiting patiently for me to answer. I take a deep breath, sit up straight, and hold my shoulders back. Grandma always said, *"Start out like you can hold out."* I figure I'd better start out honest with this impressive doctor woman because I just don't have the energy or the inclination to live a lie.

· · ·

Roxanne

"So right then and there I poured out my whole story to Dr. Inez Prosser," Grace says. "You probably didn't know this, but Inez Prosser was one of the first black women in this country to earn a doctoral degree."

"No, I didn't know that," I answer. Of course this is just one of the many things that I don't know about black history. I've never had any reason to care about black education or anything related to it. Funny that it's now interesting to me. Because of my friendship with Grace Clark, I have a sense of what Inez Prosser must have gone through to get as far as she did academically.

Grace continues. "She was such a kind woman. Of course, I had shown up without papers or an application. I was so distraught, I told her that I would do whatever it took just to stay there—mop floors, wash dishes, anything. Right then and there she called for Marjory and sent her to the college cafeteria to get Miss Crump."

"Who was Miss Crump?" I ask.

"She was just about the meanest, orneriest woman I ever met." Grace laughs. "But she saved my life. She gave me a job that very day in the kitchen. She saved my pride and gave me a chance to earn my keep."

"And did you get admitted?"

"Yes, I did. Dr. Prosser was so gracious. She took me under her wing and helped me with everything. She talked me through the admission process step by step. She made sure I got registered for classes." Grace pauses and leans forward in her chair. "I would have done anything to make her proud of me." I can feel the intensity of her gratitude to Dr. Prosser.

Grace leans back and sighs. "Then one day she called me into her office. I was terrified. I just knew that I had done something wrong or someone had come to take me back to Clarksville."

"Why would anyone do that?"

"Oh, it was just a young girl's foolishness to think that. I was always looking back over my shoulder, thinking someone would find me out. Someone would tell the world I was just a poor colored girl from Clarksville and I didn't deserve to get an education. But that's not what she wanted, of course. She wanted to tell me that she had received a letter from the Calhouns. They had set up a fund for me."

"A fund?"

"Yes, Dr. Prosser sat there quietly that day, waiting for understanding to dawn on me, I reckon. I must have seemed thickheaded, because I remember she said to me, 'Grace, do you know what this means?' and I said, 'No, ma'am, not really.' 'Your entire education is paid for,' she said. I'm here to tell you, Roxanne, I could hardly take that in. And then, I got angry."

"Angry?" I can't imagine why Grace would be angry when a college education had just been handed to her.

"Yes, you have to remember how young and stubborn I was. I stormed around Dr. Prosser's office, talking about how this was guilt money and how I wasn't going to take it and how they couldn't buy my silence."

"What did Dr. Prosser do?"

"She just sat there, real patient, and let me do my ranting. Then, when I paused to take a breath—by now I was crying—she said very quietly, 'Are you done?' I told her I was, and I plopped down in the chair in front of her desk and buried my head in my hands and just bawled my eyes out. I missed my mama and my grandma so much. And I missed Zero, and Junior, and Adelle, too. Even though Dr. Prosser was so kind, I felt so alone."

Grace shakes her head at the memory. "Dr. Prosser let me cry for a little bit. Then she told me something I've never forgotten."

"What was that?" I ask.

"She said, 'Grace, every now and then life brings us a gift. We don't earn it. We don't work for it. It's just part of the mystery. Why, that gift is the very origin of your name . . . Grace! Take this gift and use it. Don't let your anger or the mistakes of other people stand in the way of your dreams!"

My heart fills up and I feel a tightness in my throat, thinking of the Grace Clark I've grown so fond of as a young woman struggling with her pride and anger. And, I realize, I'm confused. She finds out she's half white, yet feels that's the very thing about her that somehow betrays her people. Given that I'm constantly looking over my shoulder, wondering who will find me out, I'm at a loss to understand this. I promise myself that, soon, I'm going to talk to Grace about my background. Just not today. "Did you take the money?"

"I did. I was able to earn my bachelor's degree at Tougaloo College with the fund the Calhouns set up for me."

"I guess you quit your job in the kitchen?"

"Oh, no." Grace frowns. "I told you, Gladys Crump saved my life. I worked for her in that kitchen until the day I graduated."

Chapter 14

Billy Webster

As I push through the glass doors of the Pineview Nursing Home, I realize I still have that stupid grin on my face. I need to get myself together before I see Gran. She will start firing questions from the minute I step into the room. I don't know why I'm worried. Yes, I've enjoyed getting to know Daniel Mason. Yes, it was fun having dinner with him and then seeing him in his element at the Harvest Festival. That was a trip! I haven't been to a small-town church social event in decades. Yes, he's intelligent, witty, good-looking—sexy. But! He's a preacher and he lives in Mississippi, and I don't. I won't . . . can't?

Gran is in her chair, all dressed up, looking like a spider waiting for a fly. I can tell she's ready to spin her web around me and pull me in. Suddenly feeling trapped, I rush over to the window.

"Good morning, Gran. It's a little stuffy in here, don't you think?" I ask, opening the window with a view of the bird feeder outside. "Look at all those birds. You must enjoy watching them at the feeder—"

Gran interrupts my nervous chatter. "Belinda Louise Webster," she says, "get over here and give your old grandmother a kiss."

I walk obediently over to her and bend to kiss her cheek. As

I'm pulling away, she grasps my hand. "Tell me how things went at the Queen City with Brother Daniel," she says.

Of course I'm not surprised she would ask this. I've prepared my answers carefully. I don't want to get her hopes up and then see her disappointed.

"Okay, okay! Just let me sit down first," I say, breaking her grip on my hand so that I can pull up a chair near her. I drop my purse on the floor and slouch into the chair, stretching my legs out in front of me. "Doesn't that breeze coming in the window feel nice?" I close my eyes, remembering why the fall is my favorite time of year down South.

Gran will have none of it. "Girl, I'm old as Methuselah and I don't have time to wait around for you to talk about the weather! Now, get on with it! What happened with you and the preacher?"

I sit up, having been put on notice. "Well, Gran, I think it went all right . . . He was very interested in the place . . . has some ideas. . . ." Gran can tell I'm hedging.

"What kind of ideas?"

I sigh. This is the part I feel so uncertain about. Might as well get it over with. "He wants to get the bank involved, get some estimates . . . on the work it would take to . . . you know . . . restore the hotel. He thinks it would make a great community center." I watch carefully for her response.

Gran nods and doesn't look surprised. "And what did you say to that?"

"I told him that I supposed getting a couple of estimates wouldn't hurt. He says there's a contractor who's a member of the congregation who might do an estimate, and then he wants to involve some of the teenagers at the church to help do the work. There's also Jack Baldwin, who works at the bank."

Gran chuckles. "I reckon he got real excited over that old hotel, didn't he?"

For a moment, I forget to hide my feelings from Gran. "He did, Gran. You should have seen him. He was like a little boy with a new model car. He had all of these ideas and he talked about them all through dinner. . . ." I'm remembering how animated Daniel was as we talked over catfish and hush puppies.

"So you had dinner with him, did you? What happened after that?" She has a wicked look in her eye as she winks at me.

"Gran!" I say, with my best attempt at sounding dignified. "Don't be ridiculous! We just had dinner and talked about the hotel and . . . well . . . maybe a few other things, but anyway . . . that's it. I told him that we would allow him to look into what the repairs would involve. You do agree with that, right?" I'm trying to steer the conversation back to the hotel.

Gran nods her head. "I reckon it won't hurt, but it sounds like a big job to me. Does he really think it could be ready by next spring?"

"Well, maybe not completed, but at least well under way. He told me yesterday that he'd already made arrangements with the contractor to take a look at it."

Gran doesn't miss a beat. "Hold on a minute. You talked to him yesterday?"

"Well, yes. I dropped by the Harvest Festival for a little while and—"

Gran interrupts me. "You? You, Miss Big City Girl, went to the Harvest Festival down at the church?" Gran's laugh is infectious. "Baby girl, you must be in love!"

I feel the blush climbing my throat and I'm laughing along with her in spite of myself. "That's silly," I say, strangely exhilarated. "Of course I'm not in love after one dinner at the Catfish Cabin and one Harvest Festival . . . but, okay, I admit it, I haven't met a man as appealing and as handsome as Daniel Mason in a long time." I sigh and get up to search in Gran's tiny refrigerator for one of the diet sodas she always keeps there for me.

I look at Gran as I wander back to my chair; her expression is serious. "You know what they say, darlin', about a good man being hard to find."

"You're telling me! But why here?" I realize I probably sound like a whiney little girl. "My life is in Chicago. I love you, Gran, and please don't take this wrong, but I could never see myself living in Mississippi again."

Just as Gran is about to respond, there's a knock on the door and Gran's two best friends, Miss Adelle and Miss Grace, arrive in a commotion of hugs and old-lady kisses. These two women have always been like two doting great-aunts to me. For a moment I find myself wondering if I'll end up an old maid like them. Maybe that wouldn't be so bad. They're happy, right?

I suddenly have an image of myself as an old woman sitting around a card table with a bunch of other black women the same day every week to play the same card game at the same time of day, just as these three are about to do. I want to run screaming from the room and jump on the first plane back to Chicago and marry the first man I see when I get off the plane!

Miss Adelle and Miss Grace are accompanied by a well-dressed middle-aged white woman. She and the ladies are all smiles with each other, like she's one of their old friends. Even Gran shakes her hand and nods a welcoming response to her greeting. This strikes me as odd. I've never known these ladies, especially Gran, to associate with Junior League types. Miss Grace introduces her as Mrs. Roxanne Reeves, the woman who is responsible for the development of the African-American tour. So, this is the person stirring up Gran with ideas about the Queen City. I step over to shake her hand when Miss Grace introduces me.

"Roxanne is going to join us for cards today," says Miss Grace. Roxanne doesn't look too certain about that, if you ask me. She's shaking her head.

"I really don't know about that. Maybe I'll just watch for a while," she says, pulling some papers out of her bag. "I've written up some information on the Queen City Hotel I was hoping to go over with you, Mrs. Webster—and maybe with you, too, Billy?" She looks hopefully at Gran and me. I can tell she's the kind of woman who doesn't spend much time sitting around playing cards. I wonder if she ever takes off those panty hose.

"Billy," Gran says, ignoring Roxanne's request, "pull that card table out of the closet and set it up here in front of my chair." I follow Gran's instructions, even though she really didn't have to tell me. Anytime I've been here to visit on what happened to include a Saturday afternoon, I've gotten roped into playing bid whist with these ladies. They've been meeting every Saturday afternoon for as long as I can remember. When I was a little girl, they took turns going to each other's houses. Some of my best memories are the days they would come to Gran's house across the street from the Queen City. She let me sit under the card table with my dolls, listening to their chatter overhead. Since Gran moved into the nursing home, they've made Pineview their regular meeting place.

I'm relieved to be out from under Gran's interrogation about Daniel Mason, for now anyway. As I slide the old table out of the closet, I'm feeling more relaxed. Miss Adelle is over by the sink starting a pot of coffee and Miss Grace has Roxanne moving chairs. Miss Grace is taking the top off of what I'm hoping is one of her buttermilk pound cakes and searching in Gran's cabinet for paper plates.

I realize how much I'm enjoying myself. I have women friends in Chicago—I've even tried to teach a couple of them to play bid whist—but it's not the same as being surrounded by these nurturing old women. I love listening to the stories they tell and the way they laugh and joke the whole time they're playing. But today I'm wondering what they plan to do with this Reeves woman. She's perched on one of the chairs, watching everyone, still holding those papers in her hands. She looks more like the bridge type to me.

Roxanne turns to Gran. "So y'all play cards every Saturday?" she asks, trying to make conversation.

"Yes, ma'am," Gran answers.

"Do you always play the same game?"

"Oh, yes," Gran says, and winks at Adelle, who's come to sit near her. "Same game for almost sixty years now, and Addie and Gracie are still trying to beat me."

"Now, don't you listen to her," says Grace from where she stands cutting cake. "Mattie Webster just forgets how many times she loses."

"My daddy taught me when I was just a girl," Gran says. "Daddy was a Pullman porter and he learned it on the train. Then I taught Addie—"

Miss Grace jumps in. "Then Addie taught me. But I really perfected my skills"—Gran lets out a snort at this—"when I was at Tougaloo College. We would play for hours—"

Miss Adelle interrupts. "And I perfected mine when I was at Tuskegee in nursing school."

Gran laughs. "You educated girls ain't got nothing on me. I can still whip both of you."

I sit back in my chair, watching and listening, smelling the coffee brewing, my mouth watering at the thought of Miss Grace's cake, feeling contented just to be here with them. I wonder if Daniel Mason drinks coffee. . . .

Grace

We've settled into our card game and I'm enjoying myself. Mattie is in an unusually good mood, and I'm guessing it has to do with her granddaughter, Billy, spending time with Brother Daniel.

Whenever he's brought up, I get a kick out of watching Billy try to hide her feelings about him. I think she's sweet on him.

Roxanne doesn't want to play bid whist with us. Right now, she seems content to watch us and ask questions every now and then. We're between hands and decide to take a break and have some cake and coffee. Roxanne reads the information she's written up about the Queen City to Mattie, and Billy is telling us about Brother Daniel's plans.

"...so he's planning to get the contractor out there to see it on Monday," she says.

"Junior would be so proud to hear that the Queen City will be on this tour," says Adelle.

I nod my head. "Yes, that's where he got his start," I say, remembering what wonderful times we had there.

"Whatever happened to Junior?" Roxanne asks carefully, as if she's afraid of what the answer will be.

Adelle and Mattie both look at me. Billy, who probably hasn't heard this story, echoes the question. "Yes, Miss Grace, where did Junior go when he left Clarksville?"

It occurs to me that before it's over with, everything about those months in 1931 is going to come out. I probably should have known this would happen when I started dragging up old stories, talking so personal to Roxanne Reeves. Somehow I fooled myself into thinking we could just stick to the pleasant stories related to the places I suggested for the tour, but I reckon I was wrong. My thoughts turn again to that time in my life. Lord, that was a hard year! I don't want to think about it on a nice day like this, when we're having so much fun. But Roxanne and Billy are looking at me, waiting for an answer.

"The last time I saw Junior, it was about this time of year. . . ."

· · ·

November 1931

Grace

I finished the last of my chores and Miss Crump doesn't have anything critical to say about my work today, which is a miracle, so I leave the dining hall and run down the path through the cedar trees and scoot in the back door of my dormitory. I need to check my mailbox before I go back to my room to study.

Right after I arrived at Tougaloo, I wrote to Zero at Alcorn State and Adelle at Tuskegee to tell them everything that had happened. I've been exchanging letters with both of them every few weeks. Zero is working hard at Alcorn and won't be leaving the campus to visit Clarksville until things have had time to quiet down after all of that business with Ray Tanner and Andy Benton. Adelle and I are planning to see each other back in Clarksville during the holidays. I'm hoping for a letter from her today saying that I can stay with her family over Christmas. I can't bear the thought of going back to my little house behind Pecan Cottage yet. None of us has heard anything from Junior.

I round the corner to the hallway where our mail slots are, pulling off my kitchen hairnet, holding my bobby pins tightly between my lips, and I stop dead in my tracks. My mouth falls open and all of the hair pins hit the wood floor, sounding like rain falling around me. Junior Jackson is standing by the mailboxes, leaning against the wall with his hat in his hand. He's got on the same suit he was wearing the last time I saw him, but as he turns toward me, I notice he's grown a mustache and he looks a little tired around the eyes. For just a second we stand there frozen. He's looking at me like he's not sure what to do and I'm still not believing it's him I'm seeing.

"Hey there, Gracie," he says in that sweet low voice of his, and before I can think about it I'm throwing myself into his arms, and he drops his hat as he picks me up and twirls me around, holding me so tight I can't breathe. I'm already crying and he's got his face buried in my neck. I can feel that scratchy little mustache against my skin and I can smell the mixture of his cologne and cigarettes.

I'm suddenly aware of my surroundings, although the hallway is still deserted. "Put me down, Junior," I whisper.

He sets me down slowly and looks like he's about to kiss me, but I turn my head and look around to see if someone's coming. "What are you doing here?"

"You are one hard-to-find woman, you know that?" he says.

His voice echoes through the hallway and I put my finger to his lips to quiet him. "They don't let men in our dormitory. How did you get past the front desk?" I happen to know that Vidalia Swenson is on door duty tonight, and she gets an evil pleasure from the authority that gives her. If one of us girls signs in even thirty seconds past curfew, she runs the risk of being written up if Vidalia is in charge.

Junior grins in the devilish way he always does and I feel my heart speed up. "I convinced that nice girl named Vidalia Swenson to let me wait here for you."

My suspicion is that this is just another testament to Junior's charm. "How'd you get her to do that?" I ask.

Junior smiles and looks a little sheepish. "I sort of let her believe that I'm your long-lost brother from Alcorn State."

I shake my head, laughing. "Junior Jackson, you always could get anything you wanted."

He reaches around my waist and pulls me close. "I've missed you so much, Gracie. Let's go someplace where we can talk." He lets me go and bends to pick up his hat.

I scoop up my bobby pins from the floor and tuck my hairnet in my pocket, wishing I could look in a mirror and check my hair, even put on a little lipstick, but there's no time for that now. I slip my arm around Junior's as we walk circumspectly past Vidalia toward the front doors of the dormitory.

"Why, Grace Clark," she says in her syrupy Atlanta accent. "You didn't tell me you had such a handsome big brother." She bats her eyes at Junior with a come-hither look. I'm surprised at how territorial I instantly feel. I have to stop myself from telling her to back off.

"Yes, isn't this a wonderful surprise for me?" I say as I give Junior's arm a tug. I somehow think he's enjoying this. "We're just going out on the grounds to take a walk and catch up."

"You be sure and be in by curfew, now." Vidalia calls to our backs as we step outside.

"Oh, don't you worry, Miss Vidalia. I'll be sure to have her back on time. I can't have my sister falling down on her school work," Junior says.

We both burst into laughter as the door closes behind us. It's a cool fall evening and I let Junior pull me close, feeling his warmth and aching for him to hold me and kiss me. I'm intensely aware of how limited my time with him is. I glance down at my watch. It's already six thirty and the freshman evening curfew is at eight o'clock on weekdays. The sun is almost gone and the clouds are making the late-evening light cast a luminous glow from the burnt orange leaves of the big oaks we're walking under. I decide to take Junior to my favorite thinking spot. It's a little place I've discovered under the pine trees down by the pond on the back of the campus.

As we walk, we take turns telling each other what's happened since August. Junior is full of stories about his experiences with Mr. Armstrong's band, and I tell Junior about what happened with Zero and how I came to be at Tougaloo so much sooner than I thought I would be. We sit down side by side on a bed of pine needles near the pond as Junior tells me about the places he's already seen while traveling with Mr. Armstrong. The reason he's here tonight is because the band made a stop in Jackson, and when he called home to talk to his parents, they told him he could find me here. I feel a pang of sadness, realizing he's completely satisfied with his new life.

"I still can't believe my good luck," he says, taking my hand and kissing the palm. "But I miss you every day, Gracie." He pauses. "I . . . I want us to be together. I know it might be too much to ask, but I want you to come with me. I want us to get married and go on the road together." His voice trembles with excitement. "Just think about the fun we could have! And I'm making enough money now to support us. Mr. Armstrong even talks about doing shows overseas! Imagine us, Gracie—going to Europe!"

I turn to look at him. I've forgotten to breathe and my body is aching with love and desire for him. These are exactly the words I've always wanted to hear from Junior Jackson. Somewhere in the back of my mind, pushed into a corner, are the words I should say to him about the other things I want, about my college education, about my obligations to Dr. Prosser and the Calhouns. But he kisses me softly and gently cradles my head as he lays me back on the ground. Right then I forget about Dr. Prosser and the Calhouns, about my studies, or becoming a teacher. I even forget about Vidalia Swenson and curfew.

For once, my mind goes quiet, and the loneliness and fear I've been feeling for months is replaced with the welcome weight of Junior's long lean body on mine, his kisses covering my face and breasts, and our lovemaking on a pine-scented carpet of needles near the pond behind Tougaloo College.

Roxanne

Of course, the first question I want to ask is what happened next. But I'm always the one with the questions. Right now it seems obvious—Grace never married, so she must have refused to go with him. As I listen to this petite, wise woman talk about Junior Jackson and watch her expressions, I can see glimpses of the young girl who made love with him on a bed of pine needles so long ago. My heart aches to think she wasn't ever able to throw caution to the wind, to run away with her lover and find a new life.

Billy Webster asks the question I don't. Billy is an interesting woman—tall, beautiful, confident. She must be in her mid- to late thirties, a Chicago career woman from what Mattie tells me. I envy her easy closeness with these women, the way they dote on her. I want to be part of their closeness, but I find myself keeping a little distance, still uncertain, torn between wondering if I fit in and wondering if I want to.

"Miss Grace, that's so romantic!" Billy says. "What happened?

Did you run away with him?" Billy takes our plates and brings the coffeepot over to pour warm-ups. Adelle and Mattie are watching Grace. It's obvious that they know the answer, but this time they're letting her tell the story.

"Oh, no, child," Grace answers. "But, oh, how I wanted to." Grace looks at Adelle and Mattie for affirmation and they nod. "I didn't want to lose him, but I didn't want to throw away my own dreams, either, and I couldn't let Dr. Prosser down, not after all she'd done for me. So I put him off, asked him to come back at Christmastime and visit me. I told him that we could talk about it again then. We were all planning to meet at Christmas, and I was hoping to convince him to stay."

I'm accustomed by now to Adelle's long silences, so when she looks up from shuffling cards and speaks, I think we're all surprised.

"And then everything fell apart because of what happened to me," she says.

"Now, Addie," Grace says. "We don't have to talk about that. You know that was not your fault." Grace reaches over and takes Adelle's hand and gives it a squeeze.

Mattie abruptly leans forward in her chair. "Help me up, Billy. I got to use the ladies' room." Billy moves quickly to help her grandmother out of her chair. Mattie refuses Billy's assistance with walking to the restroom. "I got it from here. You see if anyone wants some more cake."

I look back at Grace, and she's shaking her head at Adelle, as if to silence her again. Suddenly, the atmosphere in the room feels uncomfortable. It's as if whatever Adelle is not saying is floating there among us like a dark cloud in an otherwise pristine day.

We all make small talk while Mattie is gone, and we refuse Billy's offers of more cake. Mattie returns and settles into her chair and instructs Adelle to deal the hand. I glance at my watch. I know it's getting late, but I'm hesitant to leave.

Adelle starts to deal and stops. She studies the cards as if she's trying to remember what to do with them.

"Addie?" Grace asks.

"That Christmas changed everything, didn't it, Gracie?" Adelle says.

"Things were already changing before that, Addie."

Mattie looks from Grace to Adelle and coughs. "Girls, I think we need to get on with our card game," she says. "How about I deal?" She takes the cards from Adelle, and Grace continues to watch her. Billy and I are both silent. I'm trying to figure out what's going on. What's so hard to talk about?

"Grace," Adelle says, taking a deep breath, "I think we should talk about what happened."

"Oh, Lord," Mattie says, setting the cards down. "Billy, look in that little refrigerator over there and bring me a Coke." Mattie brings out the same bottle of whiskey she was working on the day I met her. Billy looks over her shoulder at Adelle as she rummages in the refrigerator for soda. None of us can take our eyes off of her. Billy brings Mattie the Coke and a small glass of ice.

"Sweetie, if you want to talk about it, we'll talk about it," Grace says gently.

Mattie shakes her head and mixes whiskey and Coke. Billy hands her a spoon, which she pushes away. I tear my eyes from Adelle long enough to see Mattie stick her long, black, gnarly finger in the drink and give it a stir. I can feel the tension among the three women, but I don't understand it. We're all watching Adelle now, waiting.

She looks up at Grace, who nods, as if giving her permission to go on. Adelle begins, "We were all so excited to get home that year. . . ."

Chapter 15

Adelle

As the bus travels through the western Alabama countryside, I stare out the window thinking of home. I can see my house, my warm bed, and the faces of Mama and Papa greeting me at the door. It's not usually this cold, even in December. The seats for coloreds in the back of the bus don't get much of the heat from up there at the front.

My whole body aches from lifting patients and cleaning floors, so even this lumpy old bus seat feels good, but I'm so excited to get home I can't sleep. Nurse's training at Tuskegee is the hardest thing I've ever done. The hours are endless, and on top of the hours in the hospital for training, they hire us out at least three weekends a month to nurse sick folk out in the country. It's hard to believe that four months have gone by since I started nursing school and I haven't been home once, until now.

I know it will be a wonderful Christmas. I feel all warm inside as I think back to Mama's letter saying how she's decorating the house and how Papa cut the largest cedar tree he could find in the woods near Clarksville. Even better, Gracie's coming home. Mama said in her letter that Junior probably won't make it. He's still on the road with Mr. Armstrong's band and Christmas is his busiest time of year. But Gracie and I know better! I'm thinking maybe, after what happened last month when he visited her at Tougaloo, she's convinced him to come home.

Most of all, I can't wait to see Zero. I've gotten only two letters from him in the whole time I've been away. Papa and Mama say I shouldn't worry, that he's just busy. But there are those moments when I can't help wondering if he's met some other girl and forgotten all about me. I know it's silly but I can't help it. I miss him so much.

It's funny with Zero. He doesn't think about wedding plans like I do. It's as if he's just always known we would be together for the rest of our lives. He says he's going to come back and take over Papa's medical practice, and I'll be his nurse until we have babies. We even talked about building a house and where our children might go to college. Our dreams are big. Sometimes I worry they're too big. I also feel guilty because I have the man I want, if he hasn't forgotten me, that is. But Grace is still waiting, hoping Junior will come back to Mississippi.

I shift my weight and try to get more comfortable. They added three rows to the white section of the bus because of the Christmas crowd of travelers, so I'm crammed into one seat with three other women. I'm still wearing my nursing uniform because I left in such a hurry to catch the bus. I just yanked off my cap, threw my two outfits and my books into the suitcase and ran for the bus station. Mama and Papa aren't expecting me until tomorrow afternoon, but I got an unexpected extra leave day, so I flew to the station to catch the earliest bus I could. I smile as I think about my plan to walk the few blocks home from the bus station and surprise them.

I must have finally drifted off to sleep, with my head resting against the window, because I wake with a start to the sound of the bus driver's voice announcing, "Clarksville." Still yawning and shaking myself awake, I go around the side of the bus to get my suitcase. I shiver with the cold and pull my nursing cape closer around me. My watch says eight o'clock. Mama and Papa are probably just now settling into their chairs by the fire to read. If I walk fast, I can be home before they start nodding off.

It's so good to be on the familiar streets of Clarksville again. As I take the same route from the bus station to our house on Fifth Avenue North that I've taken all my life, it seems like nothing has changed. The lights are out at Jones's Café, since it closes earlier in the winter. All I can think of is surprising Mama and Papa and finding out whether or not Zero is coming home. I barely notice the two men leaning against the building in the alley across from the barbershop.

My suitcase is too heavy. I probably shouldn't have brought all my books home, but I need to study. I pause and transfer the suitcase to my other hand. That's when I notice the footsteps behind me. I turn, thinking it's probably just people leaving the pool hall, but it's not. Cold fear grips my belly when I see two white men step out of the shadows of the alley. I step up my pace, trying not to look as scared as I feel. It's nothing, I tell myself. Just keep going. My heart is pounding out of my chest and my suitcase suddenly feels like it's made of lead. For a second I think I should just drop it and run, but then I decide I'm being silly.

Suddenly, they're right beside me, one on either side. They press their shoulders so close to me I can smell the cigarette smoke and the sour scent of moonshine. It's so dark on this part of the street that I can barely see their faces. But as soon as the one on the left opens his mouth, I know. Ray Tanner.

"Hey there, little nigger nurse," Ray says to me. He looks across me at the other man and says, "Pete, this here's the one I told you about. This is the one Zero Clark is sweet on." The other man nods and grunts. Ray slurs on, "He'll come running like a pig to slop for this one."

I try to ignore them, and walk faster to get to the next corner. Only three blocks until home, I tell myself. Just stay calm. But now, Ray and the other man move in front of me and block my way. Ray Tanner's ugly pitted face leers down at me, and the other man grabs my suitcase when I try to go around them.

"Hold on there, little nigger nurse," Ray says, his breath reeking of whiskey. "I need me a nurse. I'm hurting. I got me a hard-on that just won't go away." He tries to grab my breast as the other man, a man I recognize but can't place, laughs and throws my suitcase to the side. They force me into the alley.

I push Ray's hand away from my breast and start to run, but he catches me and pushes me against the wall of the building, clamping his filthy hand over my mouth.

"Pete, show our little nurse here what we're going to do if she makes any noise."

My scream stops when I see Pete flash his hunting knife. Ray presses himself into me until I can feel his erection through my clothes. He rips my uniform open and sticks his hand down between my breasts. I struggle to break free of his grip and try to get my knee in a position to hit him in the balls, but he's too quick. He gets his leg in between mine and pushes me down in the dirt of the alley.

"Hold her, Pete," Ray says. "We'll show Zero Clark what happens when he messes in white folks' business."

Pete comes around behind me, jerks my arms above my head, and holds his knife to my throat. The last thing I remember hearing is Pete laughing while Ray Tanner unbuttons his pants and pulls up my dress.

When I come to, what I notice first is the stink of catfish guts. I realize I'm lying beside a trash can in the alley near Jones's Café, and everything that happened comes to me in a rush. I still smell Ray Tanner's rancid sweat on my body, but worse, I feel the shame of what he's done to me between my legs. I raise myself up to look around, and the pain that shoots through my head almost makes me faint again. I reach up to touch my forehead and I know, even in the dark, that what I feel is blood. I have to get myself home.

I rise slowly to test my legs. Dragging my suitcase, I start down the alley, forcing myself to focus on Mama and Papa. They're sitting by the fire right now. Mama is exhausted from decorating and cooking all day, making the house perfect for me, preparing my favorite foods. I reach the end of the alley and furtively cross the street. No one can see me like this. It's too shameful.

Think about Mama and Papa, I say to myself again. Papa will say they're working me too hard at Tuskegee. Mama will look at my calloused hands and kiss them. She'll rub them with Vaseline and make me wear cotton gloves to bed. I stop and duck behind a big hydrangea bush, the rattle of *its dried blossoms sounding loud in the winter stillness. Is someone coming? Was that footsteps? The blood from the cut is running into my eyes, so I reach up with the end of my cape to wipe it away. Two more alleys and I'll almost be home.*

My legs are refusing to move and my suitcase feels like it's full of bricks. A dog barks from the yard across the street. I have to move before anyone wakes up. Zero . . . I'll think about Zero . . . My legs move slowly, my feet dragging in the dirt of the alley.

Zero, who's followed in Papa's footsteps ever since the day Clarence Jones and Junior brought him to the house all bloodied up . . . it was Ray Tanner who beat him up. This thought stops me dead in my tracks. Zero can never know about this . . . I have to keep it a secret . . . have to come up with a story . . . I feel the despair and the dirtiness closing in on me again and I push myself forward. Think about Zero—he'll make a wonderful doctor and we'll come back here and get married. Mama and Papa will dote on our children. I'm almost there. I can see our front door, but I need to go around to the back . . . I'm too dirty for the front door. Mama will have cleaned the rugs. . . .

I drag myself up the back steps. Home . . . the blood is in my eyes again. I drop the suitcase and crawl toward the door. I don't have the strength to stand anymore. I can only bring my hand up to scratch at the door. Before things go black again I notice that I've left blood on the white door.

Mama is screaming. I hear her calling for Papa. I tell myself, Quiet, just stay quiet. Don't tell them anything. The shame would kill them.

"It's all right now, baby, Mama's got you, Mama's got you," Mama is saying. She pulls my head into her lap. I feel the tears running into my ears as Papa bursts out of the back door. I'll be safe now. Papa will protect me.

"Anna Lee," he says to Mama in the low, calm voice he gets in an emergency, "go to my exam room and get the table ready."

Papa scoops me up like a hurt puppy and Mama rushes off to follow his instructions. "Hang on, sweet girl, hang on," he says in my ear.

Quiet, I remind myself. Stay quiet.

The exam table is ice cold. I have no control over the shaking of my body and my teeth are rattling together so hard, the pain in my head is almost unbearable. Mama covers me with a blanket and tries to warm me with her body, but Papa sends her to the anteroom for supplies to stitch up my forehead. Stitches? I wonder how deep the cut is. Papa is pressing his hands into my legs and arms. I know he's checking for broken bones, but his touch makes me shake harder, and I want to scream. But I'm locked into my mind and my body, and words won't come. I won't let them. Not yet.

"Can you tell me what happened, Adelle? Who did this to you?" Papa is asking.

I flinch when Papa wipes the blood from the cut across my forehead. For a second the crazy thought occurs to me that I'll have to style my hair differently to hide the scar. Will Zero like it that way? Will he still want me?

"This is a clean cut," Papa says. I close my eyes again. "This was done with a sharp knife."

Mama is at my side, and I grip her hand tight as Papa finishes cleaning and stitching the wound and covers it with clean white gauze. I can tell how helpless she feels as she says over and over, "My baby, my sweet baby." I open my eyes to look at her and she is studying me, even as she tries to soothe me. Her eyes are roving over my dirty uniform. Somehow she knows. I feel it. How can she tell? Is it Ray Tanner's stink? Do I look different?

When Papa finishes with the dressing, Mama looks at him, as they stand opposite each other over my body. "Albert," she says, her voice stern. "I want you to bring Adelle upstairs to her room. I'll help her out of these muddy clothes." She smiles at me, but I can see her fear. She lets go of my hand and blots the tears out of my eyes with her handkerchief. "I'll get you cleaned up, baby. Don't you worry." She must know.

"But I need to do a more thorough examination," Papa insists. Worry creases his face into deep lines. But Mama won't have it.

"Albert, I need for you to bring Adelle upstairs," she repeats. "She needs me to take care of her right now."

I pray Papa will give in. I can't stand the thought of being touched any more. *Every part of my body feels like it's bruised. I just want to be in my bed and pull the covers over my head. Papa doesn't argue. He lifts me into his arms again and follows Mama upstairs to my room. He lays me gently on the same bed I've slept in all my life. But everything's different now and I feel like a stranger in my own room.*

"Now, Albert, you go and get Adelle some medicine that will help her sleep. I'm going to wash her off and get her into a nightgown," Mama says, taking charge. "Oh, and light that heater. It's cold in this room."

I close my eyes and feel myself moving far away, moving to a place deep inside myself where no one can touch me.

Roxanne

The warm feeling of companionship I was experiencing before Adelle told her story is gone. All I can feel now is cold, sick anger. I want to hit something, or someone. Del Tanner's face comes to mind as I remember his gold-toothed snarl and the words he said that day Grace and I visited him a month ago. *"My lumberyard is not going to be part of some trumped-up African-American tour."* I wonder if Del Tanner knows that his father raped Adelle. Do men like that talk about such things to their sons? Brag about them?

I wonder if this hatred and violence toward black people is something inherited. Would Del Tanner be the same way today if there was no possibility of being prosecuted? I had been thinking that I'd approach him again about his warehouse being on the tour, since it did once house the original Union School for black children. I was hoping maybe he'd soften, reconsider letting us include it. But I can't imagine having anything more to do with him now. How could I stand to be in the same room with him, knowing what his father did? Knowing Del himself probably would have condoned it.

Everyone in the room has gone silent. Adelle's face is expressionless. It's as if she's frozen. Grace is holding her hand and they're staring off in the same direction. It's like they're looking into the same pool of memories. Mattie takes a long sip of her drink and shakes her head. Billy is blotting tears with a tissue. She's the first to speak.

"I hope somebody nailed that asshole's dick to a tree," she says. Startled by her outburst, we all turn to look at her. Personally, I agree with her. She's just expressed what I would say if I used that kind of language. I don't understand the expressions on Grace's and Adelle's faces, though. Adelle clears her throat.

"I'm so sorry for ruining this fine afternoon with that terrible story. I never should have dragged all that up," Adelle says.

"No, no," Billy says. "Please, don't apologize, Miss Addie. . . ."

"I don't like to hear them, but I reckon those stories have to be told," says Mattie, setting her glass down with a thump. "We have to remember."

I'm wondering why you would need to remember something as horrible as that. What good could that possibly do?

"It's true," says Grace. "You can't let that stay inside you and fester."

"I suppose you're going to tell me that he was never prosecuted, that there was never anything done," says Billy, a bitter edge to her voice.

Grace and Adelle look at each other. Adelle looks down at her hands. Mattie looks up at me. Why is she looking at me that way? Suddenly, I'm very conscious of being white. I feel like I represent the enemy, and I want to crawl under my chair. Why am I feeling this way? I'm just as angry at Ray Tanner as they are!

"Baby girl," Mattie says, turning toward Billy, "you know things were different back then."

Billy sighs and reaches up to rub her eyes. "I know, I know you always say that. . . ."

"It was my fault," says Adelle.

"What the hell are you talking about?" Mattie asks. "That white man raped you, Addie! Have you lost your mind?"

"What I mean is . . . I refused to say who did it."

"You're kidding," I say. This falls out of my mouth before I can stop it. And I had been doing so well at staying quiet until now.

"She had her reasons," says Grace.

"I don't remember much about those days right after it happened," Adelle says.

"I'll never forget them," Grace responds.

December 1931

Grace

From the minute I got the message from Mrs. Jackson yesterday, I've been in a panic to get to Adelle. Miss Crump released me from work early and Dr. Prosser herself helped me pack and drove me to the bus station. I got off the bus in Clarksville today and came straight to the Jacksons' house. Dr. Jackson answers the door looking exhausted and worried.

"She won't speak to us, Gracie," he says as he hugs me close. I can hear the anguish in his voice.

I look up as Mrs. Jackson rushes down the stairs to embrace me. "I'm so glad you've come, Grace," she says. I notice she looks tired, too, and older somehow.

"How is she?" I ask, taking off my coat and hat and hanging them on the hall tree.

"She won't eat anything. I've tried to coax her with all of her favorite foods, but she just sips a little tea or water and pushes the food away," Mrs. Jackson says as she takes me by the arm and we mount the stairs. "Every time I touch her, she trembles all over. . . ."

"Anna Lee," Dr. Jackson calls, "I'm going out to check on Maylou Johnson. Her rheumatism is acting up again, but I'll be right back."

"All right, Albert," she calls over her shoulder.

"And I might check in town again to see if anybody's heard anything," he says, just before closing the door behind him.

"He's been beside himself since we found her on the back doorstep," Mrs. Jackson whispers. "He'll only leave for a little while at a time, and then he's right back here, pacing outside her door. She won't even let him come in the room. He just so desperately wants to do something, to find out who did this to her, but she won't talk to us. I'm hoping she'll talk to you."

Mrs. Jackson and I enter Addie's room quietly. The curtains are drawn and the room is dim in the late-afternoon winter light. I can see the glow of the gas heater and smell Addie's favorite tomato soup from the tray near the bed. Addie is lying on her side with her knees drawn up toward her chest, facing away from the door. I walk around the bed and pull up a chair beside her. Mrs. Jackson hovers behind me. In the shadowy light I can see the bandage across Addie's forehead and a dark bruise on her cheek.

"Addie," I say softly, clasping my hands together in my lap and leaning forward. Even though she's taller than me, she looks so thin and fragile right now. I want to wrap her up in my arms and hold her tight, but after what Mrs. Jackson said, I'm careful not to touch her.

Adelle opens her beautiful eyes. They're her best feature. Zero always says she has the eyes of a young doe. Today her eyes are glazed and dull. When she recognizes me, a depth of sadness crosses her face that breaks my heart. I instinctively reach for her and have to stop myself. Slowly she pulls her hand out from under the quilts and extends it toward me. I drop to my knees beside her bed and take her hand with its long graceful fingers, calloused from the hard work of nursing school, in both of mine and press it to my cheek. We're both crying now.

After a few minutes, Adelle tries to sit up.

"Let me help you," I say, carefully supporting her shoulders as I test her response to the physical contact. Adelle allows me to help her sit up, and she pats the bed beside her.

"Sit beside me, Gracie . . . please," she says in a small, scratchy voice.

"Thanks be to Jesus!" Mrs. Jackson whispers. "She's talking to us, Grace! Baby girl, is there anything we can get for you? Are you hurting anywhere? Are you hungry?"

I sit quietly beside Addie, trying to keep myself calm, even though seeing her in pain makes me so angry at whoever hurt her, I want to scream. I'm hoping Mrs. Jackson will calm down, too. I think she's making Addie more anxious. I'm surprised when Addie's voice comes out stronger.

"Mama, I'm not hungry, and the medicine you gave me earlier is still helping. But I need for you to leave Grace and me alone for a little while." Mrs. Jackson looks crestfallen, but turns toward the door.

"And, Mama," Addie says softly as Mrs. Jackson looks back at her. "Thank you."

After the door closes behind her mother, Adelle takes a deep breath and sits up straighter. Although I'm full of questions, I'm silent, fearful of saying something that might cause her to go mute again. I can hear the low hiss of the heater and the pinpoint tapping of the rain turning to sleet on the roof outside. Finally, Adelle speaks.

"I'm going to tell you what happened and then I don't want to talk about it anymore . . . ever again."

"But, Addie . . ."

"No, I mean it, Gracie. . . ."

"All right," I say, thinking she doesn't really mean it. She just feels that way right now.

I listen as Adelle recounts her trip from the bus station, how she planned to surprise her parents. The walk from the station was just a few blocks. Her voice drops to a whisper and I have to strain to hear her as she tells how Ray Tanner and Pete Hatfield came out of nowhere and dragged her into the alley. She hangs her head in shame as she describes how she tried to scream for help and how Pete held her at knifepoint. Her voice turns bitter and cold as she recalls what Ray Tanner said to her before he raped her.

"I thought they were going to kill me, Gracie. I remember thinking I'd never see any of you again." Adelle starts to weep quietly and can't talk. I hold her close, both of us crying. After a few minutes, she stiffens and pulls away from me.

"You don't have to talk anymore," I say to her.

"Yes, I do. I have to tell you this." I nod as she continues. "I tried to kick Ray Tanner in the groin, and that's when Pete cut me. After that, all of the fight went out of me. When it was over, they ran off, and all I could think about was getting home without anyone seeing me. So I kept to the alleys and stayed behind bushes the last few blocks. When I got to our back door, I think I must have fainted."

"Yes," I say. "Your mama told me you were facedown on the porch when she found you."

"I didn't even go to my own front door, Gracie," Adelle whispers. "I was too ashamed to go to the front door of my own house."

I can feel her shame as she looks down at her hands. My own anger seethes inside my belly like boiling water. I want to run screaming from this room and tell the whole town what Ray Tanner did. I want to see him tied up and dragged to the courthouse. I imagine Junior holding him while Zero punches him in the face and stomach. I never knew I was capable of such violent thoughts. It occurs to me that if I feel this way, how will Zero feel?

"Addie," I say. "Zero knows about the attack. When I found out, I called Alcorn State and got word to him. He'll be here today on the six o'clock bus."

Adelle's body begins to tremble and she turns and grasps both of my arms. I'm surprised at how strong her grip is. "He can't know what happened, Grace. We can't tell him about the . . ." Adelle can't bring herself to say it.

"But we have to tell him! He loves you. He'll want to know the truth," I say.

"Don't you see, Grace? If he knows, he's going to feel like he has to do something. And there's nothing anyone can do. You and I both know that Ray Tanner will deny all of it. No one saw what happened. It would be my word against his, and who's going to listen to a colored girl?"

I don't want to believe this. I try to argue. "But . . ."

"But nothing, Grace." Adelle is insistent, and I turn away from her fierce eyes. "Look at me!" she insists. "If Zero knows what happened, he'll go after Ray Tanner. And you know how long Ray Tanner has had it in for Zero. That's just what Ray wants him to do."

I nod and then try again. "Yes, you're right, but . . ."

This time Adelle shakes me. "I'm afraid, Gracie. I'm afraid if Zero finds out what really happened, he'll get himself killed!"

"What did you do?" Roxanne asks.

I look at Adelle. "I went to the bus station that night and picked up my brother and I told him the story that Addie made me promise to tell."

"What was that?" Billy asks, looking back and forth between Adelle and me.

Adelle raises her chin and tightens her mouth in a stubborn line, but doesn't respond. I answer, watching Adelle. "She made me promise to tell Zero and her parents that she was robbed. She made up this story that she had thirty dollars in her suitcase that she'd earned from doing independent nursing jobs on her days off from Tuskegee. She had me say the men who hurt her were colored men after her money. They pushed her down and she hit her head on a pipe and was knocked out. While she was out, they ransacked her suitcase and stole her money. She even said she didn't recognize them, that they weren't from around here."

"You made her say all of that?" Roxanne asks Adelle. She sounds shocked.

"I sure did," Adelle replies. "I knew what would happen if Zero knew the truth."

Chapter 16

Billy Webster

Monday morning and I'm back in Chicago, but my mind is still in Mississippi. I'm staring out of my tenth-floor office window in the City Planning Department. A light snow has begun to fall, driven sideways by gusts of wind off the lake. I just hung up the phone with Daniel Mason. He called to say that the contractor and a local black architect are going to draw up some plans to take to the bank. Jack Baldwin has agreed to take the idea forward to Mr. Spencer. Daniel's also started to generate some interest among the young men from the community to help with the work. I still feel the warmth in his voice when he talked about the boys.

"Some of them have actually heard of Louis Armstrong. I told them a little about the early days of jazz and the black men who were the first musicians to play the music that people all over the country eventually became crazy about. You know, Billy, at first they acted all tough and like they didn't care, but then they started to ask a few questions, and now I think they might actually be starting to get interested—realizing they have a heritage they can be proud of."

I'm impressed, once again, with Daniel Mason. He has a way with people. And although I'm the first to be skeptical of anyone's intentions, he seems to care about those kids and the black history of Clarksville. I still can't understand why he would leave a high-energy city like Chicago for a small town. I would absolutely dry up there. For one thing, there's nothing to do in Clarksville—no theater, no jazz clubs, no nice restaurants to speak of, unless you count the Catfish Cabin. But then, every Southerner can fry catfish.

I remember the fire in Daniel's eyes when he talked me into restoring the Queen City the night we had dinner together. I could use a little more of that fire. I certainly haven't met a man who sparks my interest the way Daniel Mason has. I shake myself and get up to pour a cup of coffee. *What the hell am I thinking?* When I left yesterday I told myself that I was leaving thoughts of Daniel Mason in Mississippi. Nothing can ever come of that, anyway. I need to get my mind off of him and back on my work.

I flip through the files on my desk. Permit requests, new trash route proposals, traffic light replacements, all the usual stuff. None of it seems very interesting today. Maybe I'll try to focus on one of the requests and get at least something done before the staff meeting at nine. The top file is a permit request for a new jazz club opening on the South Side. Once again, I find my thoughts drifting to my conversation with Daniel about the beginnings of jazz and how so many musicians from Mississippi and Louisiana migrated to the South Side of Chicago.

I also think about the conversation with Gran and her friends during Saturday's card game. They talked about how proud Junior Jackson would be of the Queen City Hotel. But they didn't finish telling me what happened to him. We got sidetracked into what happened to Miss Adelle. I shudder at how horrible that must have been for her, hiding what happened and living in the same town all of her life with the man who raped her.

We all got so sad and quiet after that conversation. I really had been enjoying myself playing cards with the ladies. I had even been getting a kick out of watching Roxanne Reeves hanging out with

Gran and her friends. But the fun went out of the day after they told those stories. When Miss Grace finished, I decided that I needed to get out of there for a while, and I think Roxanne was just waiting for a cue. She left to bring Grace and Adelle home. So we never got back to the story of Junior Jackson. Did he tour Chicago? Is he still alive? He'd have to be almost ninety by now, so probably not. As I gather up my papers for the meeting, I have an inspired thought.

My best friend, Travis Sprague, is a huge fan of jazz. He owns tons of old records and spends just about all of his spare time searching for classic jazz to add to his collection. He might know of a Chicago musician named Junior Jackson. I pick up the phone to call him. I can be a little late to the meeting.

Travis and I agreed to have a drink after work. Now we've drifted over to Andy's, our favorite jazz bar on Wilson Street, to catch the eight o'clock show.

"It's been too long since we caught a show, Billy," Travis says in his raspy voice as he lights a cigarette.

"Yeah, I know. I work too much sometimes," I reply, swirling the olive in my martini.

"What you been doing with yourself? You been on vacation?"

"I've been down in Mississippi visiting Gran. I had to stay a little longer this time. Had to do some business with that old hotel that Grandpa used to run."

"Did you finally talk her into selling it?" Travis asks, a note of disappointment in his voice. I told him about the Queen City Hotel several years ago when we first met. He's nagged me ever since not to sell it or let it be torn down. For years, he's been trying to convince me of its historical significance, but I just haven't been able to get interested.

"You'll be happy to know that I've been talked into restoring it. We may turn it into a community center," I reply with a sly smile. "Maybe even have a jazz program for kids."

"Well, how about that!" Travis grins. "How did that happen?"

I stir my martini and take a sip. "There's this white woman down there trying to start up an African-American tour of Clarksville—"

Travis interrupts, almost choking on his beer. "Hold on a minute! You mean to tell me that a white woman talked you into restoring the Queen City?"

"Not so fast, Travis. I'm not done yet. One of Gran's old friends brought this woman over to the nursing home to meet Gran and they talked Gran into considering it. I wasn't there at the time, but when I got there to visit last week, it was all she could talk about. Plus, there was the preacher."

Travis sets his cigarette down on the ashtray and laughs. "This is getting good. The next to the last person I would think of who could talk you into anything would be a preacher."

I pull the olive out of my drink and pop it into my mouth. I grin at Travis. "This is not just any preacher."

Travis knows me well enough to catch the look and nods. "I see. So what's so special about Mr. Preacher Man that he could make you change your mind so quickly?"

I sigh. "Crazy, isn't it? I mean, really. Here I am in Chicago, doing just fine. I have a great life, a great job. . . ." I motion with my glass toward Travis. "Great friends. And I go and find myself attracted to some backwoods preacher in Clarksville, Mississippi. I must be losing my mind!"

"Hold on now, Billy. I know you. You've turned down more men in the ten years we've been friends than most women ever get an opportunity to meet. So there must be something special about this guy. Tell me about him." Travis stubs out his cigarette and motions for the waitress. "But first, let's get another drink."

Over more drinks, with a great jazz ensemble playing in the background, I tell Travis about meeting Daniel Mason, about his interest in jazz, and the way his passion for his work shows through.

I tell him about the irony of Daniel being from Chicago and moving to Mississippi. Then I remember what I was going to ask Travis about.

"By the way, Gran and her friends mentioned a piano player from Mississippi who traveled with Louis Armstrong and possibly ended up in Chicago back in the thirties. He would be ancient now, maybe ninety, if he's still alive. His name is Albert Jackson, Jr.; they call him Junior. Ever heard of him?"

Travis looks thoughtful, turning the name over in his mind. "Jackson," he murmurs. "I know of a Slider Jackson." He brightens. "I bet it's the same guy. He's a legend. One of the best slide piano players I've ever heard. I got to hear him about ten years ago. He agreed to do a show for a fund-raiser I went to. I don't think he plays anymore. Retired. Even then he had some pretty wicked arthritis in his hands. Maybe he's your guy."

"Maybe so. Wouldn't that be crazy? Junior Jackson grew up in Clarksville and is the brother of one of Gran's best friends. Do you think we could find him? I'd like to talk to him. Maybe see if he would consider coming to the Queen City for some kind of start-of-the-renovation ribbon cutting or something."

"Wow, you really are getting into this, aren't you?"

"You know me. If I do something, I don't do it halfway."

Travis grins. "Let me see what I can do. I'll talk to some friends of mine and see if I can find out any more about our friend Slider Jackson."

"That would be great. Gran would be so excited." What I'm really thinking is how pleased Daniel would be. The whole time the second set of music is playing, I'm imagining his excitement when I tell him that I've found Junior Jackson. He'll wrap his arms around me and pull me close. Between the music and another martini, I forget for a little while how far I am from Clarksville, Mississippi.

Chapter 17

Roxanne

Ola Mae and I are getting the house ready for the Junior League meeting later today. She usually comes on Tuesdays to clean, but the extra money it will cost for her to help me today is so worth it. I've got ten leaguers coming over to make magnolia Christmas wreaths for the Holiday Tour and I'm not near ready. Plus, I decided at the last minute to invite Rita Baldwin. I've got a knot in my stomach over that spontaneous decision. Spontaneity is certainly not my strong suit, and today I'm remembering why. I'm mad at myself for not being better prepared since I've known for months that this was my year to host the wreath-making party— but with everything else going on, I'm not my usual organized self.

I feel really good about this project, though, since the money goes to buy Christmas presents for the kids at Children's Hospital in Jackson. And everyone relaxes and has a good time. *Usually* they do anyway. Even though Rita is a member of the Junior League in Atlanta and it's perfectly acceptable for me to invite her as a guest, I know there will be plenty of raised eyebrows. Of course, that's how Louisa Humboldt got in with the group. Elsie brought her as a guest. But she's white. Why do I keep running headlong into these black-white issues? I can't ruminate on all of this right now.

I remember that I need to check the liquor cabinet to make sure I have enough Grand Marnier for the cranberry punch recipe I'm trying this year.

As I walk into the dining room and open the liquor cabinet, I hear the kitchen door open and close and the sound of keys being tossed on the table. It must be Milly. Oh, my word! I really don't have time for this today.

"Hello! Where is everybody? Mama?"

"I'm in the dining room," I call. "Come on in."

"Oh, hey, Ola Mae," I hear her say. "What are you doing here today?"

"Wreath-making party," Ola Mae answers, probably knowing that's all she needs to say and Milly will understand.

"Is it time for that already? My goodness, this year has gone by so fast! I can't believe I've been married five months already."

"No, ma'am," Ola Mae answers. My guess is Ola Mae's not up for much chatting, either. But then, with her usual easy grace, Milly asks, "How's that grandbaby of yours?"

I can practically hear the glow in Ola Mae's voice as I listen to bits and pieces of their conversation. Milly has never known a time without Ola Mae, and, unlike me, Milly keeps up with Ola Mae's family and when her kids are having babies and whatnot. I realize how comfortable my daughter is with the order of things between herself and a black housekeeper, something I've never quite grasped. It occurs to me that I've spent many years trying to create a barrier, make myself somehow above Ola Mae. Milly hasn't had to do that. She just takes her social status for granted.

"Hey, Mama," Milly says, strolling into the dining room, eating a cheese straw and bending to kiss my cheek. "I see you're getting ready for a party." She plops down at the table and watches as I pull out bottles of liquor, searching for the right one. "I guess you had to run Daddy off for the evening."

I almost drop the bottle of Grand Marnier. Does she know? Did Ola Mae whisper something I couldn't hear? "Yes, sometimes these parties do run late." I'm hoping I don't sound as nervous as I feel. "What are you up to today?" I ask as I put the bottle of liquor down on the sideboard and start digging for napkins in the drawer.

"Just a little shopping downtown. I have to go to some stupid law school fund-raiser with Bobby and I don't have a dress that fits." She reaches down and pinches what is probably a quarter inch of skin at her waist. "I think I'm getting fat since I got married. Bobby and I must be eating out too much."

It occurs to me that, like me, she's never really learned to cook, but fat? "Milly, you are not fat. If you were any thinner, I'd be worried about you."

"Mama, you always say that," she says, finishing the cheese straw and brushing the crumbs from her fingers onto her jeans. "What's Daddy going to do tonight? I was hoping to catch both of you at home. Doesn't he usually come home early on Mondays?"

Is now the time to tell her? Why does everything always happen at once? My heart is racing and I'm already nervous about this party and inviting Rita Baldwin, and now this. "Would you look at the time!" I say. "I'm sorry I can't chat today, darling. I'm so far behind on getting ready."

"Okay, okay," she says, following me into the front parlor. Ola Mae comes in to light the bayberry-scented candles I like so much. "Do you think Daddy's at the university?" Milly asks.

I suddenly get a vivid picture of Dudley in his office sitting in that big leather chair with a blond graduate student, probably only about two years older than my own daughter, straddled across his lap. A wave of nausea and anger hits my stomach like a fist, and I stop in the middle of the room, not remembering why I came in here. When I turn I find Milly and Ola Mae both watching me.

Ola Mae turns away and starts fiddling with a lamp, but Milly continues to look at me expectantly.

"Mama, are you okay? You look really pale. Ola Mae, don't you think she looks pale?"

Ola Mae looks up from the lamp. "You might be a little peaked, Miz Reeves. You want me to get you an RC?"

"No, no, Ola Mae. Thank you, but I'm fine."

"All right, then. I'm going back out to the kitchen to check them pecans I got in the oven."

I take a deep breath and sit down in the nearest chair, trying to keep my voice even. "Things are a little different with your daddy and me these days, darling. He's . . . um . . . not living here right now."

"What? Not living here? You mean he's moved out? What happened? Why? Did you ask him to leave?" I imagine I hear an accusing tone in her voice, whether it's really there or not.

"Milly, I really can't get into it all right now. I have so much to do and . . . well . . . your daddy and I . . . we just needed some time apart. That happens sometimes, you know." I realize that my words probably sound like lame excuses to her. I stand up and square my shoulders, remembering to stay in mother mode. "I really don't want to talk about it right now," I say, going over to Milly and putting my arm around her shoulders, nudging her gently toward the kitchen. "I'm sure everything is going to be fine. Just give your daddy a call. He'll be thrilled to hear from you." As we walk into the kitchen, Ola Mae glances up from the oven, where she's pulling out toasted pecans, and frowns at me. I ignore her stare, picking up Milly's keys and handing them to her. "Let's have lunch one day next week and we'll talk."

"But, Mama. . . ."

I can't believe I'm practically shoving my daughter out the door, but if I have to talk about this anymore I'll burst into tears. She must see the determination in my face, because she stops arguing.

"All right." She sighs, picking up her purse. "I don't get it, but I guess it's none of my business, since I'm just your only daughter and all. . . ."

I bite my lip, hard, and decide not to respond to her barb. She turns the doorknob and looks back over her shoulder. I'm frozen in my spot and I can see Ola Mae out of the corner of my eye standing there holding the pan of pecans. We're both watching Milly.

"I'm grown-up now, Mama. I can handle it . . . whatever's going on. You just need to talk to me."

I nod, unable to say anything as my daughter yanks open the door in frustration and leaves, slamming the door behind her. I can't stop the tears now, even though I'm embarrassed to be crying in front of Ola Mae. I sit down at the kitchen table, unable to set aside the flood of mixed emotions whirling inside me. As I sit there with my head in my hands, watching tears drip onto the tablecloth, I hear Ola Mae set the pan on the cooling rack. The refrigerator door opens, and I look up between my fingers to see her work-roughened hand set an RC in front of me and pop the top. "I'll be in the butler's pantry if you need me," she says as she leaves the kitchen.

I look up, grateful for her kindness, wanting desperately to talk to her, but immediately realizing that I can't do that. Has it come to this? I've got all of these things going on and the only person I can talk to is my maid?

I struggle to get everything into perspective. I'm going to be entertaining in a few hours. At least I won't have to give a report today on the African-American tour, although I'm sure Louisa Humboldt will ask me about it. On top of what's just happened with Milly, and not knowing what to do about Dudley, I've just been so sad all weekend thinking about Adelle Jackson being raped. Saturday afternoon, after we dropped off Adelle, I asked Grace how in the world Adelle was able to live and work in the same town as Ray Tanner all those years. I knew things hadn't worked out for her and Zero, since he apparently left Clarksville, but why in the world would she stay here?

"That's just the sort of person Adelle Jackson is," Grace said. "She finished her nurse's training at Tuskegee, came back home, and worked in the colored hospital until they closed it in 1969. Then she transferred to the Clarksville Hospital. Worked there until she retired in 1978."

"Didn't she ever run into him? You know, see him on the street?"

"White folks didn't mix much with colored then, and Adelle didn't go to the places where they did mix—like the speakeasies or the dance halls." Grace was quiet for a while, then spoke again. "Funny thing was, she nursed him when he was dying from emphysema."

I can't believe this! "That can't be! Couldn't they get someone else? Couldn't she refuse to take care of him?"

"Roxanne, there wasn't anybody else to do it. Adelle said they were lucky to have one nurse to twenty patients on the night shift in those days. And she always worked the night shift. What's more, if she'd refused, she'd have lost her job."

I get mad all over again, remembering that conversation. The injustice makes me sick inside. I'm having a hard time with everything I've learned about the lives of the black women I've met. I don't know what to do with the feelings—guilt, anger, sadness, and even some envy of their closeness and the way they look out for each other. I try to put it out of my mind and focus on this party. I realize it's cold in the house and I'll need to build a fire in the dining room fireplace. Dudley usually did that. Damn him again for what he did! I wonder if Ola Mae knows how to lay a fire. I blow my nose and go looking for her.

Ola Mae is up on a stool in the butler's pantry searching for the punch bowl and cups, and I start digging around in a drawer trying to find the silver ladle. I start to talk ninety miles an hour about everything we need to get done, like I always do when I get nervous. I've never really noticed before, but it hits me today that Ola Mae never has anything to say. She just says "uh-huh," or "yes'm," or "no'm," but she never participates in the conversation. I'm realizing that the reason she doesn't is probably because I've never really wanted to hear anything she has to say.

As I'm rummaging through the drawer, I glance over at her knobby old brown knees with her rolled-down stockings just below and say to them, "Ola Mae, do you go to church?"

I see her knees relax from the strain to reach the top cabinet. "Ma'am?"

"I said, do you go to church?" I repeat louder. I think she's getting hard of hearing.

"Why, yes'm, I go to the Missionary Union Baptist," she says. I can feel her looking down at me, but I keep focused on the silver drawer.

"Then you know Reverend Daniel Mason?"

"Yes, ma'am." I can tell she's not going to offer anything without me asking, but then what should I expect? We've never had a conversation before, other than what needs to be done around the house. She pulls out the punch bowl and backs down the steps of the stool with the bowl balanced in one hand. She's watching me now, probably suspicious as to why I'm asking her questions.

"I was just curious," I say. "I've been working with Grace Clark, you know, on an African-American tour, and she introduced me to the reverend. He seems real nice." I finally find the ladle and turn to find her staring at me, the punch bowl still in her hands, her mouth open slightly.

"What?" I ask.

She looks away. "I'm going to put this bowl in the kitchen, and I'll come back for the cups." I see her shaking her head as she walks toward the kitchen. I decide to follow her.

"I suppose you know Grace Clark, and maybe Adelle Jackson?"

She sets the bowl down carefully beside the sink and looks at me. "Yes, ma'am. I've known those ladies all my life. They're fine women, both of them."

I pick up the freshly pressed tablecloth draped across the kitchen chairs. "Help me with this, will you?" Ola Mae and I spread the green linen cloth over the dining room table, and I smile to myself, thinking about the wreath-making process. At least that will go as planned. Each of the ladies will bring different items to add to the wreaths. Our magnolia wreaths have become famous around here. Every year we sell out, long before Thanksgiving. This year we'll be doubling our production, so we have two sessions planned.

"Your church will probably be on the tour, you know," I say as we smooth out the cloth. I rattle on about what I learned about the history of the church and how nice I think Reverend Mason is.

"Uh-huh," she says.

I'm getting frustrated, realizing she's not willing to have a conversation with me. I try to put her more at ease. "I'm interested in your perspective on this. . . . What do you think about the Pilgrimage Committee planning an African-American tour?" I'm still busy pulling napkin rings out of a drawer in the sideboard, and when she doesn't answer, I assume she's still thinking, so I keep talking. "I mean . . . is that something you think you . . . or your friends might be interested in?" When she still doesn't answer, I look up. She's turned, facing away from me, and her shoulders are shaking. I realize she's laughing. I'm confused.

"What's so funny?"

"I'm sorry, Miz Reeves," she says. "But you and I ain't had two words of conversation other than about what you need me to do around here in the last fifteen years I been working for you, and now you want to chat me up like I's one of them Junior League ladies. And then you want to know what I think about the African-American tour. . . . It just struck me as right comical, that's all."

"I fail to see why this is so funny, Ola Mae," I say, feeling defensive. "After all, I'm trying to help the black community. . . ."

She's laughing harder now—the kind of laughing you do when you're in church and you know you shouldn't, but you can't stop yourself. She doesn't make any noise when she laughs, but her eyes are tearing up and her whole body is shaking. I find myself smiling, even though I'm still upset with her.

"Would you please stop laughing at me and tell me why this is so funny?"

She puts her hand over her mouth and pulls her lips down, trying to stop her laughter, and takes a deep breath. "I just got to picturing all those white ladies sitting around one of these fine mahogany dining room tables talking about whether folks should tour our little church before that big old Catholic cathedral, or maybe after, and I just got tickled. Then I thought about the way they do up the young white girls in those hoopskirt dresses for the pilgrimage, and I got to thinking about them asking some of the young black girls I know to dress up like black folk did back in the day, and I got tickled by the thought of that, too."

I plop down into a dining room chair, exasperated. "I know . . . I know . . . you're right. This is exactly what Rita Baldwin said. By the way, do you know Rita, too? I've invited her today."

I stop counting out napkin rings and look up at Ola Mae. She's shaking her head. "Okay, what is it now? You can't believe I invited a black woman to the Junior League meeting, right?"

Ola Mae nods. "Things are sure getting more and more peculiar around here, Miz Reeves."

"It's all so complicated. I'm trying to do this right, and every time I turn around, I feel like I'm stepping on someone's toes. Louisa Humboldt is all fired up about this tour, but she's from Connecticut and has no clue what the other women on the committee, like Elsie Spencer and Dottie Lollar, are saying. And then there's the black women, who seem to think I'm just doing this out of some self-serving need to get another star in my crown or something. . . ."

Ola Mae just stands there. I can feel her uncertainty about how to handle me. "Miz Reeves, what you expect? You doing something that's gonna upset the way things been around here. People don't take to that too easy. Black folks don't want to be no charity cases, and white folks don't want to face the fact that black folks' history ain't pleasant to look at. So you done got yourself caught up in the middle."

"So what do you think I should do, call the whole thing off?"

Ola Mae doesn't respond as she heads back to the butler's pantry. I follow like a dog on her heels. She remains silent for a while as she pulls punch cups off the shelf and hands them to me. Finally she stops, climbs down off her stool, and looks me dead in the eye. "No'm, I don't think you should call it off. If Grace Clark and Adelle Jackson is behind this thing, then that's enough for me. I don't know Mrs. Baldwin very well, but she seems like a real nice lady. I got to admit, she's different from most of the black women around here. I don't think she's going to put up with much from your white ladies' club." She stops, contemplates again, and continues. "Yes'm, you need to see it through. There's gonna be black folks and white folks alike don't like what you doing, but hell with them . . . I think you need to finish what you started and then step back and see what happens."

I stare at the punch cups, thinking how I wish I had those pretty antique Waterford crystal ones that Louisa has; then my next thought is how spoiled and shallow I've become. *Good grief!*

"I guess you're right. I have a feeling I won't be elected director of the pilgrimage again anyway, if Elsie Spencer has anything to do with it. So, I won't have to deal with this anymore after this year."

"And would that be such a bad thing?"

I think about that question for a minute and realize that maybe it wouldn't. I'm actually relieved. How surprising! I really don't care if I'm director or not . . . I feel a burst of affection for Ola Mae and give her shoulders an affectionate squeeze. She almost drops the punch cup she's holding.

"Hold on, now. Let's don't get carried away," she says.

Now I'm embarrassed and I pull away. "We'd better get moving. The ladies will be here in two hours and we haven't even started the rest of the food."

Chapter 18

Del Tanner

I probably had a little too much to drink last night, but driving to work this morning I tell myself I had to do something to calm my nerves. I feel like a cat in a room full of rocking chairs. Between trying to save the lumberyard, keeping Alice off my back about building a new house, and all that business with Daddy in the back of my mind all the time, I don't even want to get out of bed in the morning. Every time the phone rings, I jump, thinking it might be that banker calling to turn me down. When I took them papers to him last week, he was nice enough. Made me wait longer than a businessman should have to wait, but said he'd get back to me about the loan in a couple of weeks.

Talking to Alice about Daddy ain't done no good, either. I don't think she wants to hear it. Hell, I don't want to know it, but now that I do, ain't nothing can change that. I think back over our conversation when I showed her the postcard.

"You don't know that your daddy hung that man, Del," she said.

"Alice, he's sitting there right in front of that dead boy's feet, big as you please, smiling like he's done got a trophy!"

"He was young then—twenty or twenty-one years old. Maybe

he just jumped in the picture. You know how young men are. They're always posing and such."

"Then why did he get that postcard, and why did it have his name on it?"

"I have no idea, but I'll tell you this, Del Tanner. You'd better let this thing go and stop nosing around. Folks around here don't want to talk about those old days. The black people got what they want now, so you don't need to go stirring things up. Your luck, one of these educated black folks around here, who's always hollering about equality, will get hold of this story and you'll be ruined. Not all your customers are white, you know. Those people won't stop at anything. They'll have some NAACP lawyer down here trying to put you in jail."

"Now you're being ridiculous," I told her. But maybe she's right. I probably should leave the past alone. I should burn the damn postcard and those Klan robes, too. I'll be damned if I know why I can't let this thing go.

My mind is as foggy as the weather today. There's such a thick mist hanging over the lumberyard, I can barely make out the office building when I turn into the lot. I'm here earlier than usual, but I couldn't sleep. I'm still having those hellish dreams. Just this morning I woke up in a cold sweat from dreaming that old black schoolteacher named Grace Clark was putting a rope around my neck and laughing. As I'm lying there, trying to go back to sleep, I start wondering, were there other lynchings? How many niggers did Daddy kill? Did he burn their houses? Rape their women? I finally had to go on and get up. I made myself some strong black coffee and came to work.

I feel like if I could just find out a little more about what happened, I might be able to stop thinking about it. My visit with Purvis's son was worthless. Either that man is hiding something or he ain't got no idea that his daddy took lynching photographs. Looks to me like he just shut Purvis's old studio down and left it to sit for forty years. And now, he's trying to sell it. I sit and run the engine, listening to the radio for a weather report.

I must be thickheaded this morning because I just now notice there's a silver Cadillac parked in front of the office door. What is somebody doing here at this hour? It can't be any later than seven o'clock. I switch off my engine, get slowly out of my truck, and walk over to the car. A young black girl who looks to be in her twenties is sleeping behind the wheel of the car. Got her head slumped over on the steering wheel looking like she's dead. In the backseat there's an old white woman pouring something steaming hot from a thermos into a china teacup. The old woman has a big fancy napkin spread across her knees. She's got gloves on and her hands are shaking so bad it's a wonder whatever she's pouring ain't got all over her.

I tap on the driver's-side window, trying to rouse the girl. She jerks her head up, lets out a yelp; the old woman jumps, spills the hot drink in her lap and screams like a bobcat. The car door almost hits me in the nuts as the girl jumps out, opens up the back car door and starts mopping up the mess, apologizing all over the place to the woman she keeps calling Miss Purvis.

"Miss Purvis, are you all right? Did that hot tea burn you?" The girl fusses and dabs at the old woman's dress.

Miss Purvis pushes the girl's hands away; she's stronger than I thought she would be. "Stop fussing over me, Ava!" she says in a gravelly voice. "I'm fine. Now take this cup and thermos and get back in the car!"

I move to stand at the front of the car and let these two women sort out the situation, wondering what in hell they're doing parked in my lot drinking tea at seven o'clock in the morning. The white woman turns and stares at me through big round Coke-bottle glasses. She has hair the color of weathered fence pickets that's fixed in a ball on the back of her head, and as she turns in the seat to put her feet on the ground, I notice that one of her legs is artificial. I automatically move to help her up, but she swats my hand away like I'm some mosquito about to bite her.

Once again, I back up as she pulls herself to her full height, which is about the level of my elbow. "Ma'am," I try, "can I help you?"

She takes a minute to steady herself before she replies. "No, Mr. Delbert Tanner. I am here to help you."

I have no idea why this woman is here, but this is surely not the response I expected. I'm fixing to ask her what she means, but before I can get out a word, she keeps talking.

"My name is Jimalee Purvis. I am the daughter of the late J. R. Purvis, Sr. I have been made aware that you visited my brother, J. R. Purvis, Jr., in order to inquire about a photograph that our father might have taken."

I'm so taken back that my mind goes blank. Then I realize she's staring at me and is waiting for me to say something. I recover myself. "Um . . . yes . . . yes'm. I was just there last week. But your brother said there weren't any records. Said he couldn't help me."

The Purvis woman grunts in response. "That's because my brother is a stubborn ox." Miss Purvis states this as if it's a fact well known to anyone with half a brain. "He chooses to close his eyes to the darker aspects of our father's photography business. When our father stopped doing photography in 1960, we simply closed the doors of the studio and left if untouched. It wasn't until Daddy's death last year that my brother was willing to consider selling the place." Miss Purvis turns slowly and reaches inside the car for a cane. "Now, if you don't keep me standing out here in this damp air all day, I will endeavor to give you the information you require."

I'm still trying to take all of this in, but out of old habit, I move again to help her, and once again she stiff-arms me. She taps on the window with the cane and says to the girl, "Ava, bring my tea and follow me in here with it."

I decide my best move is to unlock the office door. I cross the short distance from the car to my office and fumble with my keys, unlocking the outer door and propping it open for Miss Purvis. I glance around at the office. It's a mess, as usual. I make a mental note to fire my secretary. I push papers into piles and clear the only available chair. I have no idea what this old woman is fixing to tell me, but I feel myself starting to sweat, even though there's a chill in the air today.

The old Purvis woman is sitting in the chair across from my desk studying me through those Coke-bottle glasses of hers. She's got them pushed down on the end of her nose, and it's making me feel like I did when the schoolteacher caught me cutting up in the back of the room. She done made that little girl sit out there in the secretary's area and closed the door to my office like she wants to make sure the girl don't hear us. My mouth has gone dry and I'm wishing like hell for a cup of strong black coffee right about now.

"So you're Ray Tanner's son, are you?" she asks.

"Yes, ma'am, I am."

"And why is it you're nosing around the Purvis studio trying to find out about a seventy-one-year-old postcard?"

I'm thinking this old woman should have been the lawyer in the family. I feel like I might as well be sitting under a lightbulb down at the sheriff's office being questioned. "I found it in some of my daddy's things and I got curious. I . . . I didn't know . . . I didn't know how my daddy came to be in that picture, so I thought Mr. Purvis might have kept some kind of records."

"Mr. Tanner, there were some terrible things that happened in the twenties and thirties around here. Shameful, unspeakable things. Do you understand that?"

"Yes, ma'am . . . I mean, no, ma'am . . . I don't know what you're talking about, ma'am."

"So your father did not apprise you of his white supremacist activities?"

I don't know for sure, but I'm thinking she's talking about the Klan. "If you mean him being in the Klan and all that, no, ma'am, I never knew about all that. The only reason I know now is on account of finding that postcard and his . . . you know . . . the sheets . . . and that hat thing."

"You mean his Klansman robes and hood?"

I shuffle some papers around on my desk, avoiding looking at her. "Yes, ma'am."

All of a sudden she slams her cane down on the floor so hard the door rattles. I almost jump out of my chair and I jerk my head up to look at her.

"Mr. Tanner, are you prepared to hear just what kind of man your father was?"

She's done scared me so bad with that cane, I don't know if I'm ready to hear what she has to say or not, but I don't see no way to get out of it now. This woman's got me feeling so pussy-whipped I just nod my head and don't say nothing. Then she starts telling me a story about my daddy I wish I'd never heard.

December 1931

Jimalee Purvis

I like to leave my bedroom door open at night so I can smell the Christmas tree. Daddy cut a cedar from the woods behind our house this afternoon and Brother and I helped him nail a stand to it. We brought it in and decorated it tonight, and now the whole house smells like cedar. I fell asleep dreaming of the green dress with the cut-lace collar I saw today in the window of

Pott's Department Store. Tomorrow I'll beg Mama to let me have it for the Christmas dance.

I can see the moon outside my window when Daddy shakes me awake, whispering, "Jimalee, Jimalee, get up, girl. I need your help."

At first I think something must be wrong with Mama. She's got another baby coming and this one's been giving her trouble. "Is it Mama?" I ask, jumping out of bed and looking for my housecoat.

"No, your mama's fine. But I need you to help me with some pictures tonight."

"But, Daddy, it's the middle of the night," I say, trying to understand. "What kind of pictures are you going to take in the middle of the night?"

"Never mind that, girl—just put these clothes on and hurry." He hands me what looks like my brother's pants and a long-sleeved shirt. My brother is usually the one to help Daddy when he takes photographs out around town. He knows just how to carry the camera and how to set up the tripod. Daddy has never let me help him before, so I'm confused.

"Daddy, I don't understand," I whisper. "Where's J.R. and why do I have to wear his clothes?"

"Jimalee, stop asking questions and do as I tell you," he says. "When you're dressed, come out to the car and help me load the equipment."

I pull on J.R.'s pants and stuff my nightgown in them, hitching them up with the belt Daddy left on the bed. I button the shirt quickly and try to roll up the sleeves that hang below my hands. My thin thirteen-year-old body surely looks like a boy's in these clothes, but I still don't understand why Daddy is making me do this. I wonder again where J.R. is. He and Daddy haven't been getting along well for the past several months, and J.R. has taken to sleeping out in the barn just to get away from Daddy.

I can see my breath tonight, it's turned so cold. I'm shivering as I close the back door behind me and walk toward the barn. As I approach, I can see the words "Purvis Photography" reflected from the moon shining on the side of Daddy's car. When I walk into the barn, I glance up at the loft, but I don't see any signs of J.R. Daddy is in his special room, laying out pieces *of camera equipment. He turns as I walk in, looks me up and down, and grunts. He takes one of his own coats and a hat off a hook on the wall and thrusts them at me.*

"Here, put these on and carry this out and put it in the trunk. I'll be there in a minute."

I slide myself into the warm jacket, thankful for its weight, and I can't help asking again, "What are we taking pictures of tonight, Daddy?"

He ignores me and continues to move quickly around the room, gathering supplies. I carry the heavy tripod out, slide it into the trunk, and climb into the front seat, feeling nervous and excited to be the one to help Daddy with his pictures. I've always had to stay in the cramped little studio over Main Street. I get people seated just right, touch up the women's hair, try to keep the babies from screaming. A lot of times I have to help Daddy in his stuffy old darkroom, too. That's not much fun, but tonight feels like an adventure.

Daddy gets into the car and still doesn't say a word. We drive fast toward town and turn off just after we cross the river bridge, flying down the gravel road that ends at the boat dock. Near as I can tell, we're close to the Davenports' place, Riverview. But we're not going toward the house. We pull off on what looks like an old hunting road. In the headlights, I can see the thick woods all around us. We bump over the deep ruts in the road for a few minutes; then Daddy pulls the car over in a grassy clearing, turns the headlights off, and looks at me.

"Jimalee, you listen real good now."

"Yessir," *I say, feeling grown-up and important.*

"You keep your mouth shut and do as I tell you. What I'm fixing to take pictures of ain't gonna be pretty, but it's part of my job and something I got to do. We are gonna get in and out of here as quick as we can, but it's important you keep that hat down over your face and stay quiet. Do you understand me?"

I nod my consent, my excitement quickly turning to fear of what's about to happen. We get out of the car and I hold my arms out as Daddy places the heavy tripod across them. While I'm waiting for Daddy to gather his camera and equipment, I look around. The light has changed to a pale gray and I realize that it's closer to sunrise than I thought. The moon is still bright and lights up the road through the woods. Daddy starts walking fast down the road and I struggle to keep up with him, shaking from the cold and not knowing what's happening.

I wonder where my brother, J.R., is. Why was he not at home? Did he disappear so that he wouldn't have to do what I'm doing right now? Why is this job such a secret? Helping in the darkroom, I've seen a lot of Daddy's photographs—tent revivals, circus freak shows, baptisms. He even went out to the Dooleys' house and took pictures of little Johnny Dooley in his casket after he died of diphtheria. What could be so strange now that it requires all of this mysteriousness?

As we move deeper into the woods, I realize we're going toward the river. I can smell the water and I hear it running fast from the recent rains. The air has gotten colder and wetter. Dogs barking in the distance and the muffled sounds of men's voices float toward us. I stumble as I set my foot down in a deep muddy hole in the road and I almost drop the tripod. Daddy reaches to help me and curses under his breath. I think I hear him say "your brother."

We come out on a clearing at the edge of the woods, and I have to stop to set the heavy tripod down and catch my breath. I look over at Daddy and he's stopped, too. He's staring across toward the water. We're right at the banks of the Tombigbee River. I can hear the dogs and the men's voices louder now below us, but I can't see anything beyond where the steep bank drops to the water's edge.

I follow Daddy as he approaches the edge of the bank. He stops dead still to look at the scene below, and I don't think he meant for me to hear him say, "Damn!" As I come up behind him, I squint at the mist rising up off the river, trying to see what he's looking at. There's a group of men, I'm not sure how many, standing around the base of a big live oak tree. Curls of smoke are coming from their cigarettes as they stand around talking and *laughing. Two boats are pulled up on the bank of the river. Is Daddy taking pictures of some big fish they've caught? But they wouldn't be fishing at night, would they? A coon hunt, maybe? Men around here always hunt raccoons at night.*

Daddy says, "Come on, Jimalee," and starts down the bank, picking his way through the thick clumps of dead winter underbrush. I start to follow him and I glance once more at the men below, who are milling around talking with each other in different combinations, and that's when I see him. I stand frozen to the ground and I cannot will my legs to move.

A colored man hangs from a rope wrapped around a thick live oak branch that extends beyond him out over the river. His muddy boots dangle above the water's edge. The man's back is to me and I can see the white palms of his hands tied tight behind him with thick rope. His shoulders are slumped and his head is twisted at an odd angle from a rope that cuts deeply into the back of his neck and holds the weight of his body suspended from the tree.

Daddy turns and sees me standing still. "Move, I say!" he yells. I jump at his words, and drag my eyes away from the man hanging in the tree and start down the hill. The men below hear Daddy yell and look up at us.

"Hey, Ray," one of them calls to a man standing near the tree. "Purvis's here."

I recognize the man who walks over to my daddy. It's Ray Tanner. He's probably twenty now, but he went to our school when I was little. I remember him because he was always so mean to us little girls. I was only nine then, but I remember how glad I was when he dropped out of school to work at the sawmill. I shudder as he claps Daddy on the back.

"Hey there, Purvis. We got us a dead nigger for you to take pictures of."

"What happened?" Daddy asks in a flat voice, pushing his hat back and looking up at Ray Tanner. It seems to me Daddy's avoiding looking at the colored man hanging in the tree.

"Oh, me and the boys had to teach this nigger a lesson. He was messing in white folks' business." Ray says this matter-of-fact-like. "This your boy?" he asks, pointing at me.

I cringe and pray Ray Tanner doesn't get any closer to me. I can already smell the stink of his moonshine whiskey and cigars. I duck behind Daddy as he replies, "Yep. I reckon we'd better get set up."

I move in a daze, following Daddy's instructions. We get the tripod set up, and Daddy sets the big camera on top of it and clamps it down. The men laugh and push each other, trying to be in the front of the photograph. In the end, it's Ray Tanner who's front and center, grasping the colored man's boots and swinging him around to face the camera. My stomach lurches as the rising sun lights up the swollen bloody black face of the man hanging above a smiling Ray Tanner. One of the men behind Ray says, "They'll sure enough let you in the Klan after this."

"Yep," Ray answers, never taking his eyes off the camera. "I think this'll show 'em I'm ready."

Finally, it's over and we start to leave. I want to run up the riverbank and never stop until I'm home in my bed with the covers over my head. I'm so ashamed of my daddy right now I feel like I'm dying inside. As I'm dragging the tripod up the bank, I hear Daddy say to Ray Tanner, "Oh, yeah, need to know his name."

"Zero Clark," says Ray proudly. "He won't be bothering no white women no more."

All that silent ride home, as the slow-climbing winter sun lights up the hoarfrost on the pastures, I can't get Ray Tanner's words and the laughter of those men out of my mind. I don't know what that colored man did to deserve to die like that, but the image of his bloody, lifeless body will come to haunt me for the rest of my life.

Del Tanner

I can't look at her and there ain't nothing I can say. Jimalee Purvis has stopped talking and I can feel her eyes on me, looking to see what I'm gonna do. What *can* I do? Daddy's dead. Purvis's dead. I reckon all this died with them. I sure don't want no part of it.

Now that I know what happened, I wish again I'd never found that damn postcard, wish I'd gone over to the cemetery and buried it with Daddy. Maybe it would haunt him instead of me. Zero Clark's blood is on my daddy's hands, not mine. Thinking about that man's name makes me wonder.

"You say that black man was named Clark?" I ask her.

"Yes. His given name was Thomas Clark, but people around here called him Zero," she says, studying me.

I'm feeling like a grasshopper pinned on a Styrofoam board. "He any relation to that Clark woman was a schoolteacher at some school called the . . . uh . . . what was it?" I search my mind trying to remember what she and the Reeves woman called that school.

"The Union School? That was the elementary school for black children. It was established right after the War. As a matter of fact, it was on your property."

"Yes, ma'am, that one."

"Zero Clark was Grace Clark's brother."

My head is starting to ache. "Does she know? I mean . . . that my daddy . . . you know . . ."

Jimalee Purvis ain't cutting me no slack. "You mean does she know that your father lynched her brother?"

"Yes'm."

"I don't know the answer to that, Mr. Tanner. It's something I've asked myself for seventy-one years. I've never talked to a soul about what happened that night until today. Other than leaving Clarksville to finish college at Tougaloo, Grace Clark has lived in Clarksville all of her life, just like you and me. I can't imagine that she wouldn't have some idea of what happened."

"There weren't nothing ever done about it? To my daddy, I mean?" I ask, knowing what the answer will probably be.

She's looking me dead in the eye and I can't look away. "Mr.

Tanner. No jury in the state of Mississippi would have convicted a white man for a crime against a black man in 1931. A black man could not even testify in court against a white man. Everyone just turned their heads. My own father, who justified taking that photograph by saying he was documenting history, took Ray Tanner's guilt to his grave."

She pushes herself up in her chair like she's getting ready to leave. There's one more thing I got to know before she goes. "Why did your daddy make a postcard?" I ask.

Her shoulders slump and she shakes her head. "Near as I could tell, it was like an initiation. Ray Tanner wanted to be a Klansman, and that was part of what he did to prove himself to the Grand Dragon. The Ku Klux Klan circulated postcards like that one all over the South during the twenties and thirties."

I sit with this for a minute, not knowing how to take in that hanging a man was something to brag about—something to be proud of.

Miss Purvis gets to her feet and leans on her cane. "Well, Mr. Tanner, now you know exactly what kind of man your father was. And now you know that a black man died at his hands, for no other reason than the color of his skin. You'll have to decide for yourself what to do with this knowledge. Most prefer to close their eyes to it—it's just too ugly for most people to acknowledge. Some of us keep it to ourselves, like I have, and it haunts us and makes us bitter. Some try to make things better, like my brother has with his legal work. It's yours to wrestle with now. I'll be going."

I hold the door open for her as she leaves my office. The young girl rushes to help her into the car. As I stand and watch them drive away, my employees are starting to pull in to the lot. Eddie Davis and Mac Sullivan get out of an old beat-up Dodge pickup, laughing and talking. They're probably about the same age as that boy in the picture was, nineteen, maybe twenty. Those two black men been working for me for two years. It hits me—ain't neither one of them ever missed a day or been late.

I make up my mind and step out of the office. "Hey," I holler to them. They both freeze and stare at me real scared-like. It turns my stomach today to see that look in their eyes. Am I that much like my daddy? Do they know? As they walk over to me, I'm feeling all mixed-up. *Hell!*

"I need y'all to start clearing out that warehouse where I keep the old wood. You know, the stuff I get from old houses and barns around here."

They're looking at me sort of relieved, like they're glad they ain't in trouble and sort of like I've lost my goddamn mind. Maybe I have.

"Yessir, Mr. Tanner," Eddie says. "Uh . . . what you want us to do with that wood, sir?"

"Oh, hell, I don't know," I say, getting frustrated. "Just put it behind the bay where we store the two-by-fours. We'll put tarps over it 'til I can figure something out."

"Yessir," they say as I turn and walk away. When I stop to look back at them they're shrugging their shoulders and shaking their heads, but they're headed for the warehouse.

Chapter 19

Billy Webster

The November wind has a bitter edge today and Travis and I wrap our coats tightly around ourselves, holding our hats as we rush up the steps of the old brownstone row house in Bronzeville. I ring the bell, praying this is the right place. After days of searching everything from the Chicago phone directory to dozens of bars and music venues, last night Travis and I stumbled across a South Side hangout called the Chat Room. One of the group of ancient men at the bar said he knew Slider Jackson.

"We go way back," he bragged. "Slider don't come out much no more. Keeps to himself in that old house of his. I can't even get him to play a game of checkers." The other men nod and listen as I explain my connection with Mr. Jackson, and one of them gives Travis directions to Mr. Jackson's house. As we thank them and prepare to leave, the man who seems to be the spokesman for the group says, "Yep, since his woman died, seems like all he do is sit around smoking them cigars he likes and listening to old records. Maybe you young folks can get him out of that house."

I couldn't help but feel a twinge of sadness when I heard those words "his woman." I thought of Grace Clark and all the years she'd wasted loving a man who had obviously completely detached and made a new life for himself here in Chicago. Why did he do that? Why would he leave behind a loving family and a woman who doted on him and never return, not even for a visit? I was curious last night to hear more about this woman the old man referred to, but decided to save my questions for Mr. Jackson—if he answers the door, that is. Travis steps back and studies the architectural details around the porch and windows while we wait, shivering in the cold.

"This place is amazing," says Travis, reaching out to touch the stones making up the arched entrance. "It's got to be one of the first of these built around here."

Travis is filling me in on brownstones and what the Bronzeville community was like back in the thirties, when the door finally creaks open three inches. An old black man's stubbly chin comes into view behind the thick door chain, followed by a pair of full, unsmiling lips and a long tipped-back nose with wide, flat nostrils. I can see the old man adjust one side of a pair of black-rimmed glasses as he bends his head downward to get a better look at me. I feel a surge of excitement. This man appears to be the right age. Maybe we've finally located Slider Jackson.

"Help you?" he asks, stepping back from the crack in the door and making eye contact with me. Travis steps up behind me and the man looks wary. I'm getting the sense that a white man appearing on his doorstep is making him nervous. I hurry to explain our visit.

"Hello, sir. My name is Billy Webster and this is my friend Travis Sprague. We're looking for Albert Jackson, Jr., and we got this address from a friend of his at the Chat Room."

"What business you got with him?" asks the man. He takes a step back, still holding the door, and I can see his bony profile in a faded flannel shirt and worn black pants that hang like curtains from red suspenders on his thin body.

"My grandmother is Mattie Webster from Clarksville, Mississippi. I was hoping he might remember her," I say, noticing the ever-so-slight shift in the visible part of his face when I mention Gran's name. Suddenly the heavy wood door slams shut and I hear the rattle of the chain before the door is jerked open, revealing a slightly stooped but still tall man, an expression of wary curiosity on his grizzled face. I notice the tremor in his hand as he extends it toward me.

"I'm Albert Jackson, Jr., but most folks just call me Junior. You mean to tell me Mattie Webster is still alive?"

My hand is lost inside his larger one as he shakes it heartily and then continues to hold it. "Yessir," I answer. "She's still alive and kicking. She'll be really happy to hear I found you." I watch him closely as I add, "She still plays cards every week with your sister, Miss Adelle, and their good friend, Miss Grace Clark."

"How about that?" he says. His smile looks sad now and his expression becomes distant as he releases my hand to rub his own across his head. He shakes his head slightly. "It's sho been a long time since I talked to them folks down South." He looks me up and down and I think of the charmer he must have been. "Miss Billy Webster, you are the spitting image of Mattie Webster!" He seems to suddenly remember that Travis is standing behind me, and after I introduce Travis again, he asks us in.

We enter a front room that looks like it hasn't changed since the 1930s. Faded patterned carpet covers the floor and the furniture is spare, consisting mostly of a pair of worn wingback chairs near the small fireplace, where a gas heater has been added. The heater glows with a low flame filling the room with stuffy heat. There's a table between the chairs, and I notice a stubbed-out cigar in an ashtray and a cup of black coffee beside it. A beautiful antique upright piano sits in the corner, and beside it a drop-leaf table holding several boxes of records and what looks to be an old turntable. More boxes of records sit on the floor near the piano.

Mr. Jackson offers me the chair opposite him and Travis sits on the piano stool, glancing longingly at the box of records. I know he's dying to dig through them. Mr. Jackson eases slowly into his chair and is offering us coffee, when he's seized by a paroxysm of coughing that seems to leave him exhausted. When he's able to stop he reaches for his cup.

"Are you okay?" I ask. "Can I get you anything?"

He shakes his head. "No, I'm all right. Just an old man with bad habits. Doctor keeps trying to get me to give up cigars, but a man can't give up everything, now, can he?" He notices Travis reaching carefully down to flip through the box of records on the floor. "You a jazz fan, Travis?"

Travis jumps like a little boy caught stealing candy and straightens. "Yessir, I am. You've got an unbelievable collection here. May I?" he asks, gesturing toward the boxes.

"Sure, help yourself," Mr. Jackson says. "How 'bout you pick us out something? I always like a little music playing." He turns back to me and smiles. "Now, what y'all want with an old man like me? Both y'all live down there in Mississippi?"

"No, we both live here. I work for the Chicago City Planning Division, but I grew up in Clarksville. I visit Gran every couple of months or so, and last time I was home we were talking about restoring the Queen City Hotel. Do you remember the place?"

Mr. Jackson sits back in his chair, extends his long legs in front of him, and closes his eyes as Travis places the needle on the record and the sweet, scratchy sounds of a trumpet begin to wend through the room. I'm realizing that this is not going to be a quick process. I glance over at Travis, who seems equally lost in the music. I stifle my impatience with the two of them and wait.

"Duke Ellington," Mr. Jackson mumbles.

"Not many people have this one," Travis answers.

"You know, I've got a solo on that one," Mr. Jackson says, seeming to completely forget about me.

"No shit?" says Travis. "This is so cool, Mr. Jackson. I've looked for this album for years."

Now, I like jazz, but these two are acting like Pentecostals about to speak in tongues. When Mr. Jackson finally answers my question, I don't even realize at first that he's talking to me.

"I got my start there, you know," he says.

"You mean at the Queen City Hotel?" I ask.

"Yep, I wasn't nothing but a boy. Mr. Louis Armstrong took me on."

"Yessir, I've heard the story. That must have been pretty incredible for you."

"The early days, when the Queen City was hopping, was heaven for a young boy like me growing up dreaming about being a jazz musician. Mr. Louis Armstrong gave me my first break."

"Gran showed me the picture of all of you that was taken the first night you played for him," I say. "Y'all looked so happy."

"Lord, but we was young," he says, laughing. "I can still see Gracie's pretty face watching me so proud that night I played with Louis for the first time. I went on the road with him that very summer—1931. We traveled all over the country. It weren't no life for a woman. Although, I did try to get Gracie to marry me and come on the road with us."

I nod. "She told us the story of how you came to Tougaloo and found her, tried to convince her to run away with you. The last part of the story I heard, she put you off until Christmas. I guess she must have turned you down?" I can't read the expression on his face when I say this, but it feels to me like something shut off. I want to know so much more, but I'm afraid to push him.

"So the Queen City's not in such good shape no more, huh?" he asks, clearly changing the subject. I glance over at Travis, who raises his eyebrows and shrugs his shoulders, as if to say, "Oh, well."

"No, sir. As a matter of fact, it's pretty sad. But a couple of people in the restoration business who've been looking it over seem to think that we can bring it back to its original condition. There's a white woman down there who wants to put it on a new African-American tour they're starting. They're thinking of maybe making it a community center—maybe even offering a jazz program—you know, get young people involved. . . ."

"What's that you say?" He squints his eyes and looks at me. "African-American what?"

"It's a tour . . . you know . . . for people to take. . . . They see the places around Clarksville that were important historical landmarks for blacks. . . ."

He laughs, a wheezy sound that gets him coughing again, and I can't help but laugh with him. Travis's looking at us like he can't figure out what's going on.

"I don't get it," he says. "What's so funny?"

Mr. Jackson winks at me and I turn to Travis. "Just an inside joke," I say, noticing that Travis looks only briefly like he feels left out before he returns to his fascination with the record collection. "Seriously, Mr. Jackson, they want to put the Queen City Hotel on the tour and Gran has agreed to it. I realize that this is none of my business, but Gran and Miss Adelle and Miss Grace didn't mention that you were still in Chicago. Then, when I was telling Travis the whole story, he recognized your name and we've been looking for you ever since."

"Miss Mattie and them know you looking for me?" he asks.

I'm suddenly feeling uncomfortable, like I might have gotten into more than I bargained for. "Well . . . no," I say, and then hurry to add, "We think it would be great if you could come back for the reopening of the Queen City. We were thinking maybe you could be like an artist in residence. Maybe mentor some of the kids who are into jazz. And I'm sure my grandmother would love to see you, and so would Adelle. . . ." I watch for his reaction as I add the next part. "And, of course, there's Miss Grace Clark."

He looks away the instant I mention Grace's name. He shakes his head. "I just don't know, young lady. I ain't been back to Clarksville, Mississippi, in more than seventy years. I didn't even go back to bury my mama and papa. There's a lot I regret, now that I'm sober," he says, looking down into his coffee cup. "But I'm an old man now. Looks like it's too late to be showing up there after all these years."

Travis has apparently been listening more than I thought. He sets down the album he's holding, pushes his reading glasses up on his head, and clears his throat. "Um . . . could I ask you a question, sir?"

"Yeah, I ain't got no secrets. Ask me anything you want."

"Why didn't you ever go back? Was it that bad for you there?"

Mr. Jackson leans back in his chair and takes a sip of coffee. "No, son, it wasn't all bad." He pauses for so long I almost think that's all he's going to say. Then he sighs heavily and continues.

"It was right about Christmastime, 1931. We was playing in New York City the whole month of December that year. I remember I'd never seen snow before and I was so excited to call home and tell them about it. I was in a phone booth, putting in my nickels, and that snow was coming down so hard I couldn't see the street. My mama answered the phone, and as soon as she heard my voice, she started crying."

"I know," I say. "Miss Adelle told us what happened to her."

"So I reckon you know what happened to Zero?" he asks.

I'm puzzled. The ladies didn't mention anything about Zero. I think for a second. "Oh, yes, Zero is Miss Grace's brother, right?" He nods. "No, they didn't talk about Zero. Why? What happened?"

Mr. Jackson pulls open a drawer in the table between us and takes out a cigar and lighter. His hands tremble as he unwraps the cigar and lights it. My stomach feels queasy from the smell and the hot, dry closeness of the small room. When he's puffed the cigar alive he leans forward in his chair and props his elbows on his knees, looking at the floor. "White men hung him," he says, and the words are suspended, bitter in the air.

"Pardon me?" I say. "Did you say *hung* him?"

"Yes, ma'am. Zero was lynched on December sixteenth, 1931."

I'm filled with anger so intense that hot tears sting my eyes. No wonder my gran and her friends wouldn't talk about this! I think of dear old Grace Clark and Miss Adelle. The sadness of what they've endured overtakes me. How did they do it? Why would anyone stay in Mississippi? I can't even formulate a response. The three of us sit there silently watching the smoke from Mr. Jackson's cigar float into the air. Finally, Travis breaks the quiet.

"I can see why you wouldn't want to go back," he says softly.

"I'm not proud of what I done. Right after I found out about Zero, I was so full of hate I walked around in a daze, going from one gig to another, and pouring all of my anger into that piano. I'm ashamed to admit it, but back then, I was afraid to go back. Afraid I'd end up like Zero. Funny thing is, I woke up a few years down the road and found myself in demand. Hot bands all over Chicago wanted me and the ladies flocked to me like chickens to corn. Up here in Chicago I found myself steady work and black folks who didn't live every day scared of whites. They weren't necessarily any better off than the folks in Mississippi, but after what I'd seen and heard it sure seemed better.

"The years went by so fast I couldn't keep track. I did everything I could to put Mississippi out of my mind. Between the nightlife, the shows, the booze, and the women, I lost myself in a sea of slide piano and Jack Daniel's. But things changed, music changed, and I got old. The arthritis in my fingers keeps me from playing like I used to. Now I'm just another dried-up old Chicago musician with no retirement, no savings, and living on social security."

"You never went back to visit at all? Never had contact with any of them?" I ask.

"No, ma'am, I didn't. Couldn't bring myself to go back there. Looking back on it now, I think after a while, I was ashamed." I realize now that there are tears running down his cheeks. He reaches into his pocket and pulls out a worn handkerchief and wipes his eyes. "I never could get over feeling guilty for living when Zero died. He'd have made a fine doctor, you know," he says, looking at me. "Addie sent letters over the years, telling me all about Mattie and Robert, Jr., and their kids, telling me about Grace and her being such a fine teacher and all. But I never wrote back. And I moved around so much, I reckon those letters stopped catching up to me." He sighs. "I was pretty full of myself for a while. When Gracie stopped writing, I figured she'd decided she was too good for me." He looks at Travis now as if he'll understand. "There was always a woman willing to cook my breakfast," he says with a slight grin. Travis nods and smiles, and I bristle at their male bonding.

"Sounds to me like Miss Grace got her heart broken," I say, barely able to hide the edge in my voice. Mr. Jackson looks surprised, as if this possibility hasn't occurred to him.

"Don't you know that she's loved you all these years? There was never another man for her," I say, realizing I'm probably getting a little too defensive. Travis shoots me a look that says, "Back off, Billy."

This starts a fresh round of quiet tears for Mr. Jackson, and I almost feel guilty for adding to his obvious torment. He sets his cigar on the ashtray and blows his nose.

"I done a lot of things wrong, Miss Billy," he says, and I start to feel like a jerk for being so confrontational. "The last thing anybody down there needs now is for me to come dragging in there acting like I've got something to offer anybody." He shakes his head. "Too much water under the bridge. Too late for me," he says, picking up the cigar again.

I think about the two women whose stories I listened to just a couple of weeks ago. How both of their lives hinged on the decisions of two men: the one sitting here in front of me now and the one I just found out died brutally before he even got a chance to live his dream. I think about my own fears, the way I've tried to run away from Mississippi and be someone different, live a new life. Who am I to judge this man? And I realize then that those women would take him back with open arms, just like they do me. Not because we're perfect, but because of their capacity to love.

I reach over and lay my hand on his knee. I can see the deep well of pain in his eyes when he looks at me. "Think about it," I say. "It's never too late to go back home."

Chapter 20

Roxanne

The wreath-making party is going better than I expected. Of course, when Rita walked in you could have knocked the rest of the women in the room over with a feather. But they've all been extra courteous, shaking her hand and asking her if she likes Clarksville. Southern women are nothing if not polite. I'm fascinated by Rita's ability to get them to talk to her. She's very comfortable with herself; she's even found things in common with Elsie Spencer. Rita moves right past their awkward responses when she makes reference to the "black community." As I move around the room, surreptitiously catching bits of Rita's conversation and thankful to escape into my role as hostess, I feel that same tug of conflict I keep having lately. I'm probably the only other person in the room who knows what Rita means about the black community. I'm still a little incredulous at how differently I see things now. Will these women see me as a traitor? What, or who, would I be betraying?

Everyone is talking and laughing and drinking my cranberry punch. I'm actually enjoying myself for a change. Frankly, I'm good at this kind of thing—much better than I am at playing Clarksville's African-American historian. If I can just manage to avoid

Elsie Spencer's questions and figure out how to tactfully get a response from Louisa Humboldt about her restoration, I'll be home free.

As I pass around a fresh tray of canapés, I think about Grace, Adelle, Mattie, and even Billy Webster. They have all been so accepting of me over the past few weeks, so willing to bring me into their lives, tell me their stories. Of course, after what I've learned, it's still beyond me why a black woman, money or no money, would want to own a house that was built by slaves. But then it occurs to me, *why not?* If she can pull it off, more power to her!

I'm carrying a tray of empty punch cups into the kitchen when I look over my shoulder and realize Louisa is following me.

"Wonderful party, darling!" she says, trying to drawl. "Y'all have such cute little soirees down here." She lowers her voice as if we are in cahoots. "Great strategy, inviting a black woman."

Strategy? Is that what I was doing? Strategizing? I set the tray down on the kitchen counter, sneaking a glance at Ola Mae, who's standing at the sink washing empty plates. She faces straight ahead, staring out the kitchen window. I swear that's a smirk on her face.

"Imagine me, making a wreath out of magnolia leaves. I've never been very crafty, you know," Louisa continues. "Listen, Roxanne, I was wondering if you found anything in that old diary of Ellen Davenport's that might help with our restoration plans?"

Uh-oh. I've been so busy that I completely forgot about that diary. I tried to read some more of it a couple of times after I found the parts about Zero Clark. But after Ray Tanner managed to split up Ellen Davenport and her beau, Andy Benton, it seemed her life was an endless series of empty days spent doing needlepoint and reading romance novels. She did mention Ray Tanner, Del's father, a couple of times—I think he must have been trying to court her—but she apparently loathed him. Given what he did to Adelle, I can see why, although of course Ellen never knew anything about that. I got so bored with her diary, I stopped reading. The last time I remember seeing it, it was lying on the floor beside my bed. I wonder if I accidentally kicked it underneath the dust ruffle.

"Funny you should mention that, Louisa," I say, scrambling to make something up. "So far, Ellen Davenport doesn't say much about the house, but I'm still hopeful. I have a little more to read. . . ." That might be a small white lie. "I'll get it back to you at our next Pilgrimage Committee meeting."

"And your final estimate, too? For our restoration? Ellery and I have decided we want you to manage the project." She winks one of her false eyelashes at me.

"Absolutely," I say. "Thank you so much." I'm caught completely off guard by this last pronouncement as Louisa sashays out of the kitchen.

Ola Mae snorts. "Looks like you got yourself a job."

I stand there, absently putting more toasted pecans in a crystal bowl, wondering how I feel. I thought I'd be so excited. Instead, what I'm feeling is . . . pretty much nothing. Why do things keep changing?

I'm getting ready to collapse into bed, exhausted, when I remember the diary. I get down on my hands and knees and look under the bed. Sure enough, there it is, pushed underneath the edge of the bed frame just out of sight. I retrieve the diary and crawl into bed with my robe still on. It's cold tonight. I pull the covers up under my arms and prop the diary on my stomach. I'm not sure where I left off, probably around October of 1931. I skim the pages for details about Riverview, and I'm starting to nod off when I get to December 1931. I'm pleased to see that Ellen writes about the removable wall between the parlor and the dining room. Not many of the houses had those and this is an architectural detail that, if restored, will make Riverview unique. Louisa will be thrilled.

I start to close the diary when the name Ray Tanner catches my eye. I sit up and read on.

DECEMBER 14, 7 P.M.

Tonight is our Christmas party. Mama and Daddy invited fifty people this year. They've opened up the wall between the dining room and the parlor to make room for dancing. We've been getting ready for this party for weeks and I've hated every minute of it. I have a confession. I lied to Mama and told her that I've come down with one of my sick headaches so I won't be able to go to the party tonight. She fussed over me for a bit, but she's so worried about having everything perfect for the party that it wasn't long before she turned me over to Sarah Jane and left my bedroom.

Sarah Jane's always so good to me when I'm sick, even when I'm pretending to be. She and I have been getting along better lately. Tonight I told her about how much I loathe Ray Tanner and how Mama and Daddy act like they want me to let him court me. When I asked Sarah Jane what she thought I ought to do, she got real quiet. I thought maybe she was going to tell me, like Mama always does, that I'll be an old maid if I keep being so choosy. Instead, she told me about something that happened last summer.

Ray Tanner forced her to give him the key to our summer kitchen so he could spy on Zero Clark delivering Andy's package to me. So that's how he knew about us! But that wasn't the worst of it! Sarah Jane also told me what Ray Tanner did to her. He's a loathsome beast and I'm going to make sure Daddy fires him. I think when Daddy hears what Ray did to Sarah Jane, he will. As soon as the party is over, I'm going downstairs and tell Daddy what happened. I hate Ray Tanner.

Poor Sarah Jane. She's in love with Zero Clark, but Zero

*loves that colored doctor's daughter, Adelle Jackson. Sarah Jane
and I are in the same situation. Neither one of us can have the
man we love. I feel so sorry for her. Zero Clark is a nice man.
He tried to help Andy and me. Sarah Jane says that after Ray
Tanner stopped Andy and me from getting married, he was
going after Zero next, but Zero got wind of it and left town
to go off to Alcorn State. Sarah Jane says that's a college for
coloreds. I'm glad Zero's away from here and safe.*

The page ends and I close the diary, realizing that Ray Tanner must
have raped Adelle Jackson around the same time that Ellen Davenport was writing in her diary, December 1931. And it sounds
like he did the same thing to that poor Sarah Jane girl. Ellen was
right: He was a loathsome beast! Ellen must not have known that
Zero was back in town that December. I make a mental note to ask
Grace tomorrow to tell me the rest of the story of what happened
that Christmas after Adelle was attacked.

Right now, I need to get some sleep because tomorrow is Tuesday. Grace and I are scheduled to pick up Clarence Jones to accompany us to the site where a man named Horace King, a freed
slave who was apparently an important bridge builder in the mid-
1800s, built the first bridge over the Tombigbee River. The bridge
has since been torn down, like a lot of the historical places she tells
me about. At least the stories will be preserved, even if the physical
landmarks aren't.

What a strange turn of events this morning. I brought Ellen's diary
downstairs to the kitchen, planning to read some more of it before
I left to pick up Grace. I had just opened an RC and was trying to
wake up when the phone rang. It was Del Tanner, of all people. He
asked me if I still wanted to put his warehouse on my tour. I almost
dropped the phone. Was this the same Del Tanner who just a few

weeks ago said it would ruin his business to have his warehouse on an African-American historical tour?

He sounded nervous, very different from the swagger he had the day Grace and I visited the lumberyard. I wasn't sure what to say. I'm thinking surely there must be a catch. I agreed to bring Grace and come by the lumberyard on Friday and hung up wondering if I should have just turned him down flat. I don't trust Del Tanner, and I surely don't want to subject Grace to any of his rudeness.

I'm still pondering Del's change of heart when I start to read Ellen Davenport's diary entry dated December fifteenth, 1931. It's very short.

DECEMBER 15, 8 A.M.

I'm pleased with myself this morning. Last night, after everyone left, I found Daddy in his den, smoking a cigar and drinking brandy. I told him all about what Ray Tanner did to Sarah Jane. I was embarrassed to talk to my own father about such things, but he had to know. I demanded he fire Ray Tanner as soon as possible.

Daddy was quiet for a while, but I could tell he was angry. Daddy is fiercely protective of Josephine and Sarah Jane—almost as much as he is of Mama and me. He won't even let Mama scold them too much.

Daddy told me not to worry, that he would take care of it. That's all he would say, but I have a feeling that Ray Tanner will be looking for work after today. Serves him right.

DECEMBER 16, 2 P.M.

I hardly slept at all last night. The dogs kept barking and barking from their pens, like they were trying desperately to get out. This morning I was trying to make myself get out of bed when Sarah Jane came bursting into my room. She didn't even knock. She slammed the door closed behind her and stood leaning against it, clutching her arms to her chest, and trembling all over. She had the most terrified look in her eyes, and she was breathing so fast I thought she'd faint.

I jumped up and went over to her, and just as I reached her she collapsed on the floor in a blubbering heap. I finally had to shake her to get her to tell me what was wrong.

It took her a while to get the words out, but she told me that a colored man was found dead this morning hanging from a tree near the river. A tree on our property! Clarence Jones saw him from his boat when he put into the river to fish this morning right after sunrise. It was Zero Clark! Sarah Jane is devastated. I asked her if they knew who did it and she said no, that whoever hung him was long gone by the time Clarence found him and cut him down.

I have a feeling I know who it was. Who had it in for Zero? Who was it Zero left town to escape from? Ray Tanner, that's who. I can't help but wonder if I'm part of the reason this happened. After all, I did insist that Daddy sack Ray from his job at the mill. If Daddy did fire him yesterday, Ray probably blamed Zero and went after him. Dear God, how can I live with this?

The RC is halfway to my mouth and I've gone numb with disbelief. All this time I thought Zero Clark left Clarksville. I thought he decided to go somewhere else to practice medicine. How did I get that idea? Grace never told me that exactly, but she didn't tell me this, either. No wonder she's so hesitant to talk about her brother! I feel hot tears burning my eyes. I can't do this anymore. I can't hear one more tragic story. I can't visualize one more horrible scene of white brutality. I get up, drop the diary on the kitchen table, and pick up the phone. I'm canceling everything—my time with Grace today, the appointment with Del Tanner, the whole damn African-American tour! They can find someone else to do it. I'm done. As a matter of fact, I'm done with all of it—the antebellum dresses, the Pilgrimage Tour, the home restorations, the pretending to be a pedigreed Southerner. No more.

As I stand there sobbing, the phone in my hand, the off-the-hook tone bleating in my ear, I feel lonelier and more confused than I ever have. I don't know what matters anymore. And, worse, I don't know who I am anymore. I hang up the phone and sink to the floor. I'm sitting in the middle of the kitchen floor, feeling the cold tile through my robe, and I honestly don't know what to do next.

I pull myself to my feet and see my open address book lying on the counter. A sticky note with Rita Baldwin's phone number floats toward me like a life preserver to a drowning shipwreck victim. I pick up the sticky note, and my hands are shaking as I dial Rita's number.

I'm still amazed that Rita was willing to drop everything and come to my house. I tried to insist that I was okay, since I realized as soon as she picked up the phone that I had no idea how to begin to tell her why I called. I even attempted to pull myself together, giving some empty excuse about following up on the antebellum home prospect, but she must have sensed something, because she asked, "Roxanne, are you all right? You don't sound too good."

That was all it took to cause me to completely lose my composure again, and as I blubbered about finding out something horrible and various other phrases that probably sounded like nonsense, she stopped me to tell me she'd be right over.

So here we are, sitting at my kitchen table, and I'm thinking how I've never sat at my own kitchen table with a friend for one of those intimate conversations like Mama used to have when I was growing up. How could that have happened? I must have drifted off in my thoughts again, because I have to ask Rita to repeat her last question.

"So this was Miss Grace's brother?"

"Yes, and she never even hinted to me that something this horrible happened to him," I say, taking yet another tissue from the box. "Why wouldn't she tell me?"

"Maybe she's ashamed," Rita speculates. "Or maybe she's trying to protect you."

"That's absurd! Protect me from what? Believing that absolutely nothing in hers or her brother's life went the way they planned? I was already there, Rita," I say, realizing how angry I feel. "This whole thing already feels like a complete nightmare."

"Stop it, Roxanne," she says, and I'm taken back by the anger in her voice. "Stop seeing these women as victims. They don't see themselves that way. Yes, they've been through some horrible history. But they didn't let it change their whole view of the world. They've learned to live with the sadness and move on."

"But why?" I can't help but ask. "It all seems so hopeless."

"Roxanne, wake up and take a look around you. My husband works with Elsie Spencer's husband at the bank. You and I are having coffee together at your kitchen table. Do you think those things would have happened in 1931?"

I look up at her, and her expression is so intense I have to look back down. "No, I guess not, but I feel like such a hypocrite. I didn't take on this tour because I'm interested in black history. I did it because I wanted to get Louisa Humboldt off my back and get the contract to do the restoration at Riverview. I thought this was going to be some simple little list of places that Grace would come up with and we'd be done. I never thought I'd get so pulled into their lives . . . their history."

"And how do you feel now?" she asks, taking a sip of coffee.

I pause for a minute to think about the answer to that. "Everything's different now. Somewhere along the way it started to matter. And now I'm totally confused. I don't think I'm the right person for this job. Maybe you should take over."

"Why? Because I'm black? Don't you think Grace Clark had a reason for doing this the way she did?"

I think about it and suddenly realize that Grace probably knew all along that if I'd known about Zero from the beginning I would have bailed on the whole project before we even got started. "Yes, I suppose she did."

Right now I feel completely bewildered. My marriage is falling apart, my daughter is upset with me, I truly believe most of the women on the Pilgrimage Committee think I've lost my mind, I'm depressed over the injustice to a man I never even knew, and I think I'm developing my first real adult friendship with a black woman . . . maybe. Her next comment reminds me that Rita Baldwin does not tiptoe softly around any topic, and I'm stung.

"I think Grace Clark knows that the white women who join the Pilgrimage Committee or the Junior League are 'to the manor born,' so to speak, and most of you have spent a tremendous amount of time ignoring what goes on around you between blacks and whites every day. She used this opportunity to let you in . . . to let you see, if you were willing, into her world . . . our world."

I can see that if I want a friendship with this woman, I'm going to have to be as honest and direct as she is. No more pretending. No more hiding behind Dudley's family, or money, or my own little pathetic created story. "I wasn't born to the manor," I say. "I was born to a poor family on the bayou in south Louisiana." I sigh, thinking this is probably going to be the quick demise of an almost friendship. "Rita, I'm probably the biggest imposter you'll ever meet."

She listens to my whole story, one I've never told anyone before. When I'm finished, I'm surprised by how relieved I feel. She doesn't show much of a reaction one way or the other. I can't tell if she's appalled, or uninterested, or just generally thinks I'm pitiful.

"Sounds like we have a lot more in common than I thought," she says, and her smile is warm. I start to feel a glimmer of hope . . . maybe see a little squeak of light down in the hole I've dug for myself.

"There's one big difference between us, however," she says.

"What's that?"

"You could choose your path *because* of the color of your skin. I had to choose mine *in spite of it.*" She says this gently, looking at me with a clarity I envy. I'm still struggling to understand. My glimmer fades a little. What now?

She stands up and rinses out her coffee cup, places it in the dish drainer. "I think you'd better go wash your face and put on some makeup," she says, reaching for my cup.

I look at her, puzzled. I'm still reeling from our conversation.

"You and I are going to go meet Grace and Clarence. We need to hear the rest of this story."

Chapter 21

Grace

I knew the time was coming soon when I would have to talk to Roxanne about Zero, but I didn't think it would happen this way. I expected her at nine o'clock this morning, but she showed up an hour late, her eyes red and puffy like she'd been crying, and she was having a hard time putting a coherent sentence together. The other surprise was that she brought Jack Baldwin's wife, Rita, with her. She's a real nice woman, and even though I can't see it happening, I think she would make a good friend for Roxanne.

All Roxanne was able to say before we left my house for town was, "I've got to talk to you about Zero, but I want to wait until we get to Clarence's."

Now we're all sitting at Clarence's kitchen table, and she pulls a leather-bound book out of her purse and lays it on the table. The book looks to be old; its pages are brittle and yellowed. I notice she's trembling as she pulls her hand away.

"What's this?" I ask, wondering if I really want to know.

"This is Ellen Davenport's diary," she says, and she takes a deep breath. "Louisa Humboldt found it in her attic at Riverview. I was reading it to see if it contained any history about Riverview." She reaches in her purse for a tissue, like she's worried she'll start crying again.

I'm trying to piece this together. Why has Ellen Davenport's diary got her so upset? Then it dawns on me, and I look at Clarence.

"Sarah Jane," Clarence says, and I nod. Clarence and I are both remembering that Sarah Jane Weathers worked for the Davenports. She was there the morning Clarence found Zero. Clarence later told me she was hysterical that day. We both knew she was sweet on Zero, and she was as close as a sister to Ellen Davenport.

Roxanne is watching us. "So you know, then?" she asks. Her eyes are wide, almost accusing, as she looks back and forth between Clarence and me.

I look at Clarence again and back at Roxanne. "Why don't you tell us what you read, sugar? I never knew Ellen Davenport was writing in a diary about things that happened back then." I'm wondering if Ellen and Sarah Jane knew something we don't. All these years of wondering what happened that night, and here I am, hearing a white woman's version of it.

Roxanne is crying again now, and Rita reaches over and pats her shoulder. "Go on," she says. "Tell them what Ellen wrote."

Roxanne stares into her coffee cup and shakes her head. She tells us in a halting way about the very first time she read the diary, and how Ellen described Zero delivering Andy Benton's engagement ring. "And then you confirmed that part the next time we talked," she says. "To tell you the truth, the main reason I was interested in the diary at all was because Louisa mentioned Zero's name being in it."

"How come you didn't tell me about this diary?" I ask.

"I decided not to mention it to you because you were always so private about Zero. I guess now I know why," she says. "I read far enough in the diary to know that Ellen's elopement didn't work out, that Ray stopped it, and she was brought back here ... that her heart was broken. Again, your stories confirmed all of that. So for a while, I forgot all about the diary."

"So Ellen wrote about Zero in her diary?" I ask. I want to pick it up and look at it, find out if there was something she knew, something to explain what happened, but my hands don't seem to obey my mind. I can't bring myself to touch that diary.

Roxanne reaches for it and pulls it across the table toward her. She leafs through the pages until she gets to the one she's looking for. She smooths the pages out flat, then hands the diary to me. Now my hands are the ones shaking as I set it down between Clarence and me. Together, we read Ellen's entries for December fourteenth, fifteenth, and sixteenth, 1931.

I can't find my voice to respond. Reading young Ellen Davenport's words about my dear brother has torn that old wound in my heart wide open. This confirms what I always thought: Ray Tanner was at the center of this. It had to be him—especially since Ellen got her daddy to fire him over what happened to Sarah Jane.

Clarence reaches into his pocket and pulls out a handkerchief to blow his nose. How much pain can a body bear? The four of us are so quiet I can hear the clock over the refrigerator ticking. That old saying crosses my mind—time heals all wounds. Not this one. It's been seventy years since Zero was murdered, and right now, reading this diary, it feels like yesterday.

Roxanne breaks the silence. "Grace, was I that blind?" she asks. "Did you tell me Zero died and I just ignored it?" Roxanne has got such a pained expression on her face, it cuts right through me.

I finally find my voice. "No, sugar," I say. "I never told you what happened. When you acted like you believed he left Clarksville, I just didn't correct you. I didn't have it in me to talk about his death yet." She nods like she understands.

"I've never seen the point in talking about things you can't do nothing about," Clarence says, and I can hear that old anger in his voice. He gets up from the table and walks to the window, looking out over his little garden. "Talking won't bring him back, or change what happened."

"Clarence," I say. He still won't look at me. "I think it's time. You and I both have been holding on to this story for too long. I don't know about you, but there are some things in that diary that I didn't know." He turns and looks at me, and I can't read his expression. Did he know more about Ray Tanner than he let on? I can't bring myself to ask him right now, and Roxanne and Rita are waiting to hear what happened.

"I'll tell y'all what I remember about those two days," I say. "Then, maybe Clarence will fill in some more."

December 1931

A cat's scream wakes me from an exhausted sleep and I tell myself I'm just being silly for feeling afraid. I turn over, pull the quilt up close to my chin, and try to go back to sleep, but I keep replaying yesterday's events over and over in my mind and sleep won't come. Zero got in last night and Dr. Jackson and I went to pick him up at the bus station. Before Dr. Jackson brought Zero and me home, we went by the Jacksons' house and Zero tried to see Adelle. Mrs. Jackson said she was asleep and that she still refuses to talk to anyone but me. It broke my heart to see the look on Zero's face when Adelle wouldn't let him visit her. Of course, they all asked me what she told me about the attack, and I've never been so miserable as I was telling them the lies Adelle insisted on.

After we got home, Zero and I sat up and talked for hours. He told me all about Alcorn State and I told him about Tougaloo. Zero's face lights up when he talks about college. And he's doing so well. I think we were both bragging a little bit, talking about our good grades. This was our first chance to talk about Gerald Calhoun's letter. As I told him the story of what happened to Mama, I watched him closely for his reaction.

"So you half white, huh?" he said.

"Yes, I reckon I am," I answered, looking down at his hands and mine on the table and feeling the same mixture of anger and shame all over again.

"Gracie, look at me."

I looked up to meet his gaze. His warm brown eyes filled me with reassurance. "I love you anyway," he said with a sly grin. We both laughed as he reached across the table and took my hands in his.

"You going to move up to the big house now?" he asked.

"No, I'm not. I'm staying right here. The Calhouns have been good to us, but that letter doesn't mean I'm part of that family." I told him how when the Calhouns found out about Adelle, they offered to do anything they could to help.

Every now and then as we were talking, Zero would stop and ask, "Now, are you sure Adelle didn't tell you anything else about what happened? Maybe something she remembered about the men who did it— what they looked like, how big they were?"

I've never lied to my brother before. That's part of what's keeping me awake now. I feel the weight of Adelle's story like a stone in my chest. I decide to get up and go to the kitchen for some buttermilk. It always helps me sleep. When I pass Zero's door, I peer in and he's not there. His bed hasn't even been slept in. The stone in my chest gets heavier. Where could he be at this time of night? He's not the kind of man who sits on a barstool at Jones's pool hall. He always says he's got better things to do than carouse with a bunch of men looking for trouble.

The kitchen clock says four a.m. He couldn't have gone to see Adelle this early. I realize that sleep will be impossible now, so I decide to make coffee instead of having buttermilk. I'm just pouring a cup when the back door opens and Zero comes in, looking weary and cold. He looks up at me as he's taking off his dirty boots and tries to smile.

"Morning," he says.

"Morning," I answer, pouring a second cup of coffee. "Where have you been?"

Zero hangs his coat on the hook by the door and reaches for the cup I hand him. He sits down heavily in the same chair where I left him last night when I thought he was going to bed right after me.

"I got to thinking last night that maybe I could retrace Adelle's steps from the house to the bus stop. I thought I might find something . . . you know, something that would help me figure out what happened . . . maybe some clue. So I walked into town and I started behind the Jackson house and tried the different streets she might have taken . . ."

"Did you find anything?"

"Not at first, but then I remembered that she wasn't attacked right out in the open on the street, so I started looking in the alleys. That's when I found this." *Zero holds up a small red pocketknife. It looks like one of those Swiss Army knives.*

I take the knife in my hands. When we were kids, every boy in school whose parents could afford it had one of these. It could be anybody's. It has no name on it, of course. "You don't think this is the knife that cut Adelle, do you?"

"No. From what Dr. Jackson said, this one doesn't have the right kind of blade. But maybe, if I can figure out who it belongs to, it will help me find out who did this to Adelle."

I stop myself from telling Zero he's grasping at straws. I'm suddenly panicked. I've been so focused on Adelle that I haven't thought about what Zero's reaction would be. Now I'm realizing he's going to do everything he can to find her attackers. Adelle was right: This could be dangerous for him. What if Ray Tanner finds out he's back in town?

"Zero, why don't you take that to the sheriff? Maybe they could use it to . . . to . . ."

Zero turns on me like a rabid dog. "To what, Grace? Do you think they've done anything? Dr. Jackson reported the attack right away. He called Buford Culpepper at home and woke him up to tell him what happened. Do you know what our fat white sheriff said?" *Zero is standing now, looking down at me. His eyes are bloodshot and fierce.* "Do you?"

"No," I say in a small voice.

"He told Dr. Jackson that he'd have to look into it in the morning. There was nothing he could do in the dark. He didn't even take a report. He still hasn't taken a report!" Zero throws his remaining coffee in the sink and stands looking out the window. "They're not going to do anything, Grace. This is up to me."

I'm even more afraid now. I can't stop myself from shaking as I walk over to Zero and put my arms around his waist. He turns to hug me, but I can tell he's preoccupied with his thoughts.

"Zero, swear to me you'll be careful!" I plead, stepping back and making him look at me. "I couldn't stand it if something happened to you, too."

"Don't you worry about me," he says, kissing me on top of the head. "I'm going to be fine."

"I didn't see Zero at all that day after he left and he didn't come home that night. I sat with Adelle all afternoon; then Dr. Jackson brought me home to my house to sleep. Early in the morning on December sixteenth, Mr. Calhoun came knocking on the door. He was crying like a baby when he told me they'd found Zero." I have to stop my story and settle myself before I go on.

Clarence has been standing at the window the whole time I've been talking. Now he comes back to the table and sits down heavily, as if he's got the world's weight on his shoulders. He looks at me and starts to say something, and then he looks down again, as if he's having trouble looking me in the eye.

"What is it, Clarence?" I ask. Roxanne and Rita are both leaning forward, watching the two of us.

Clarence shakes his head and sighs raggedly. "Gracie, I ain't never wanted to cause you more pain than you already had."

"Go on," I say, wondering what could possibly hurt more.

"I never told you before, but I saw Zero the night it happened," he says.

· · ·

December 1931

Clarence

Zero and I step out of Jones's Café, and he's talking about how much he's missed Miss Mabel's catfish. He says he's headed back over to the Jacksons' house to see if Adelle will see him tonight, when we hear a noise. At first neither one of us recognizes the sound. It's a sort of hissing coming from the side of the building. I think maybe it's an alley cat. As we walk closer, we realize it's somebody trying to get our attention.

I see a small black close-shaved head peeking around the garbage cans Jones keeps in the alley. The little boy motions toward himself like he's in a big hurry. I look around and over my shoulder as Zero points to his chest. The small black head bobbles like it's on a spring and he waves his arm again for us to come into the alley. As we walk toward the boy, I recognize it's Malcolm Jones, Miss Mabel's son. The Joneses' house is next door to the café, and Malcolm is always hanging around, talking to customers.

"What's going on, Malcolm?" Zero asks. "Why you being all secret-like?"

"You Miss Adelle's fella, right?" he says.

Now Malcolm has got all Zero's attention. "That's right. Why you want to know?"

"My mama said Miss Adelle got hurt." He looks past us, like he's making sure no one's coming. "I heard something the other night," he whispers. "I think it was the men who hurt Miss Adelle."

Zero grabs Malcolm's jacket, and he's so light that before Zero knows it he's got him pulled up off the ground, his feet dangling in the air. "What'd you hear?" Zero asks, and, seeing Malcolm's eyes about to bug out of his head, he sets him back down.

"Don't tell Mama," the boy says, looking around all nervous.

"I ain't going to tell your mama nothing. Now what did you hear?" I think Zero's trying his best to stay calm so Malcolm won't run off.

"I woke up in the night and I's powerful hungry. So I sneaked the key and went in the back door of the café to get me some of them fried apple

pies Mama made for next day's dinner. I's just opening the pantry when I heard voices out in the alley. I didn't dare open the door to look on account of they might see me. But I crouched down up under the window on the alley and listened."

"You recognize the voices?" Zero asks, sounding hopeful. "Them colored men from around here?"

"Nosir, and they weren't no colored men, Mr. Zero. They's white men."

"White men?" Zero looks at me. This don't make no sense to either one of us. Surely Adelle could tell it was white men who robbed her, not colored? Unless . . . A sick feeling starts down in my belly and I can tell Zero's feeling it, too.

Zero squats down in front of Malcolm so's he can look him square in the eye. "Malcolm, this is real important," he says, taking him by the shoulders so he can't squirm away. "Did you hear what them white men said to Miss Adelle?"

I reckon this must have scared Malcolm, because he starts stuttering. "I, I, I think one of 'em named P . . . P . . . Pete, 'cause I hear the other one say, 'H . . . H . . . Hold her, Pete.' Then he say something about how they g . . . g . . . gonna show Zero Clark what happen when he mess in white folks' b . . . b . . . business." Malcolm looks down at the ground.

I feel my heart pounding in my chest and I'm already seeing where this is going. "What else did you hear, Malcolm?" Zero asks, breathing fast now.

"I didn't hear them say nothing else. It got quiet and all I could hear was the trash can bumping up against the side of the building." Malcolm hangs his head. "I climbed out the window on the other side of the kitchen and run home. I's scared, Mister Zero." His voice is not much more than a squeak now. "I swear I don't know what happened after that."

Zero lets go of Malcolm and stumbles toward the trash cans. I shoo Malcolm on home, telling him he done good. I watch Zero real close, not sure what he's fixing to do next. I think we both know what happened now and why Adelle made up that bullshit story about being robbed. She's try-

ing to protect Zero. The one named Pete is Pete Hatfield. He's been taking orders from that son-of-a-bitch Ray Tanner since they beat Zero up over a damn nickel when we was ten.

It also explains the pocketknife Zero said he found last night. Ray Tanner stole that knife off me when we were kids. My mama saved her butter and egg money for a year to buy me that knife. I can see that old festering place in Zero opening up like a scab picked off a sore. The thought of their filthy hands on his Adelle is making him crazy with rage. He hauls off and kicks the trash can so hard the sound echoes down the alley, and I take a step toward him to try to talk to him. He don't even seem to feel any pain in that leg. Before I can say anything he bends over the trash can and throws up the catfish he had for supper.

I'm scared now, not knowing what Zero's fixing to do next. He stands there at that trash can for a long time before he straightens up and looks at me. They's kind of a wild look in his eyes then.

"What you thinking, Zero?" I ask.

"I don't know, Clarence . . . ," he says, and turns to walk away.

"Where you going?"

He stops, but he won't look at me.

"Don't you go and do nothing stupid, now, you hear?" I say. I hear the church clock chiming eight and I know I got to get to my job over at J. T.'s Bar. I ain't told Zero yet that I'm working there now. And I sure ain't fixing to tell him tonight. Ray Tanner is a regular at J. T.'s.

"You go on home, Clarence," he says. "I'll catch up to you tomorrow. Maybe we'll go fishing." He walks off, heading in the direction of Adelle's house.

Grace

We are all listening intently to Clarence. He pauses to drink some of his coffee, and my mind starts to fly all over the place. *So, Zero knew about Adelle after all? Did he go after Ray Tanner? Was he so full of rage that he would take a risk like that? Why has Clarence never told me this? Why has he let me question all these years what happened? What else does he know?*

"I thought he was going to Adelle's house. I swear I did, Gracie," Clarence says, looking at me with pleading in his eyes, like he's afraid I won't believe him. "Then, he showed up at J.T.'s later that night."

"Wasn't that the bar where you worked?" asks Roxanne. I jump when she speaks. I've been so focused on Clarence that I almost forgot those girls were here. I look at Roxanne across the table and I feel like I'm staring at her across a deep, wide chasm. . . . My head starts to ache and my arms suddenly feel like lead.

"Miss Grace, are you all right?" Rita asks, as she comes around the table to kneel beside my chair. "Roxanne," she orders, "get Grace a glass of water."

Clarence jumps up to help, and Roxanne brings me the water he hands her. I don't really like being fussed over like this and I shoo them away.

"I'm fine. Y'all sit down," I say. "I must have forgotten to breathe for a minute."

"I told you ain't nothing good going to come from talking about all this," Clarence says, sitting back down beside me.

I take a deep breath to steady myself. I muster up my old teacher's voice to get Clarence's attention. "Clarence Jones, what happened at that bar?"

Clarence sits up straight, looks at me, and frowns. He goes on to tell us how Zero showed up at J.T.'s, wanting to see Ray Tanner, and that J.T. told him to go on home and wait until daylight.

Clarence can barely get out the last words. "He walked away from there and that was the last time I saw him alive." Clarence's voice cracks as he says, "All these years I've beat myself up for not following Zero that night. But I was scared I'd lose my job. I just kept hoping and praying Zero had gone home."

Clarence turns toward me and leans forward, his elbows on his knees. "Gracie, I swear, until we read that diary, I didn't know Ray Tanner had lost his job that day. I knew he was in the bar that night, but he was there every night. I reckon Mr. J.T. must've told Ray that Zero came looking for him. When I saw Ray and his boys leaving, I just stayed out of their way . . . I was such a coward." Clarence is racked with sobs now and my heart is breaking. I'm not sure if it's for me or for him. "I'm so sorry I couldn't stop it, Gracie . . . I'm so sorry. . . ."

He hangs his head and I can see his tears falling on the tile floor. All of us have carried the pain of what happened for so long. All of us have wondered what we could have done differently to stop Zero that night. At least I now know that Zero didn't go after Ray Tanner. He walked away. My heart goes out to Clarence.

Through his tears, Clarence finishes the story. "I got ready to go fishing early that next morning, right after sunup. I kept thinking Zero would show up at my house and everything would be fine, just like always. We'd fish and talk like we always did, maybe try to sort out what to do. Zero always said he did his best thinking while he was fishing." Clarence looks at me and I nod. I remember Zero saying that very thing.

Clarence pulls out his handkerchief and wipes his eyes. His voice is so soft now I can barely hear him. "But Zero never showed up. So I went on by myself. I put my boat in the river and headed over to that deep hole behind the Riverview plantation where the big catfish go in the wintertime. It was foggy, and when I first came around the curve in the river, I couldn't make out what was in the big old oak tree that branched over the river." Clarence stops and takes a shuddering breath. He has to pause before he can go on. "Then I realized it was Zero. I tied my boat up and ran to fetch Dr. Jackson. He told Mrs. Jackson to call Mr. Calhoun, so's he could tell you. Dr. Jackson and me cut Zero down out of that tree."

No man should ever have to see the sight Clarence saw that morning. I thank the good Lord that I didn't have to see my brother hanging from a tree like that. It's bad enough that ever since that December morning when I jumped out of Mr. Calhoun's car and saw Zero lying on the ground, those grown men weeping over his body, I've fought the images in my mind of what Zero's last moments on this earth must have been like.

December 1931

Zero Clark

I'm thinking about what Dr. Jackson would say right now. That the way for a colored man to deal with a situation like this is to put his energy into getting the vote, furthering his education, working on changing the laws. But how is that going to keep people like Ray Tanner from doing whatever they want?

Ray Tanner's been finding ways to make my life hell for the past ten years. But now he's gone too far. I imagine Adelle in her white nurse's uniform, hurrying home to surprise her family. She looks beautiful in that uniform, the crisp white of it against her skin, the glow she takes on when she's easing someone's pain or making them more comfortable. Adelle is a born nurse. I only hope I can be as good a doctor. I plan to do right by her, to be the kind of man she's proud to marry.

Something has to be done. Ray Tanner has to be stopped. I can't sit by anymore and allow the man who violated the woman I love to escape justice. I know where Ray Tanner'll be this time of night. He's always at J. T.'s Bar, the same bar where his daddy's kept a barstool warm for twenty years. Still does. They might even be there together. I'm not sure what my plan is. I'm not exactly thinking straight. All I can think about is my beautiful Adelle in the alley with Ray Tanner pushing her to the ground.

I stand across the street from the bar and try to see in, but it's too dark to make out anybody. I cross the street and go around to the back. Just as I step into the light near the back door, Clarence Jones comes out, holding a bag of trash in each hand. His eyes get wide when he sees me.

"Zero? Is that you?" Clarence peers through the dark. "What you doing here?"

I step closer to Clarence. "I'm looking for somebody. You work here now?"

"Yeah, just on the weekends. Trying to make some extra money. Who you looking for?"

"Ray Tanner."

"Are you crazy, man?" Clarence looks around the alley and dumps his trash before coming close to me. "You know you don't want to mess with Ray Tanner! He's mean as a yard dog, Zero, and he's gotten worse. Just go home. Stay away from him. Talk to Dr. Jackson. He'll help you figure out something to do."

I reach out and grab Clarence's shoulders. "You and I both know what he did to Adelle, Clarence."

"Yeah, but there ain't nothing you can do. You got to leave this alone." Clarence turns to look behind him at the back door of the bar.

Just then the screen door slams and J.T., the bar owner, walks toward us, his head cocked to one side.

"What you boys doing out here? Clarence, you working for me or talking to your buddies?"

Clarence ducks his head and says, "I'm working, Mr. J.T. I just brought the trash out."

J.T. recognizes me. "What you doing hanging around behind my bar, boy?"

I take a deep breath and look J.T. in the eye. "I'm looking for Ray Tanner, Mr. J.T. Is he here?"

The big burly white man snorts out a laugh. "Does a bear shit in the woods? Of course he's here. It's Saturday night, ain't it? What you want with him?"

"I've got some business I need to take care of with him. Will you let him know I'm here?"

J.T. eyes me. "What business you got with a white man this time of night that won't wait until daylight?"

I ignore the question. "I'd go in there and fetch him myself, Mr. J.T., but I know you don't allow coloreds in your bar. So, if you'd please just send him out here, I'd appreciate it."

J.T. stares at me for a while. Clarence hasn't moved a muscle. Finally, J.T. turns, shaking his head. He looks up and sees Clarence. "You still standing here? Get on back in there and get to work." J.T. turns back to me. "And as for you, I don't want no trouble around my bar. You just get out of here and go home. You take up your business with Ray Tanner in the daylight, you hear me?" I don't move. "I'm telling you. Get out of here before I have to call the sheriff." J.T. slams back into the bar with Clarence following him. Clarence looks back at me and shrugs his shoulders.

I stand there trying to figure out my next move. Maybe J.T.'s right— maybe I ought to wait for morning. But the anger boils up in me and I can't find any place to put it. I think maybe if I walk for a while I'll cool down. As I walk, my mind starts to clear. Maybe I'll try to see Adelle again. It'll be morning soon and I'll knock on her door, convince her to talk to me, maybe talk her into going to the sheriff like Grace said. I can tell her there was a witness—that Malcolm Jones heard what happened. I can tell her there's evidence—the pocketknife is in my pocket right now. I'll show it to her. Dr. Jackson will go with us and we'll tell the sheriff. I imagine Ray Tanner behind bars and I like the thought of that.

I'm walking on Bridge Street, the last street before the river. There ain't many houses down here. Riverview still takes up most of the property along the river. I'm fixing to cut through an alley and head over toward Adelle's house, when I hear a truck coming up behind me. The truck is coming fast and I try to get over in the bushes beside the road. The headlights flash on me and the truck screeches to a stop. Four white men jump out and start coming toward me. I hear them holler, "Hey, boy. We want to talk to you."

I panic and take off running. Behind me I hear Ray Tanner saying, "Catch that damn nigger. I've got something to settle with him."

I head for the river. My mind is not too clear, but I think if I can get to the water, maybe there'll be a boat on the bank and I can cross the river and lose them. I come out of the trees and spot a small boat tied up to a tree at the foot of the steep bank. I take off for the boat, but don't see the roots under my feet, and all of a sudden I'm crashing to the ground. I struggle to get back up, but it's too late. One of the men grabs my boot and then two of them hold me on the ground while the third one gets behind me and jerks my head back. I can smell his sweat and feel it dripping on my face, mixing with my own.

I open my eyes and Ray Tanner is standing over me with a thick rope dangling from his hand. As I watch he makes a loop and winds the rest of the rope around the bottom of it. He's making a noose. I use every bit of strength I've got left to try to get away from the men holding me down, but it's no good.

The night goes into slow motion after that and it's like I'm looking at myself in a nightmare. I feel their heavy boots kicking my sides and belly, but I can't make a sound. I feel blood trickling down my chin and I spit out teeth. I kick out at them and struggle until they have my hands tied tight behind me and my ankles are bound. I'm being dragged now and I hear the river getting closer. I must black out for a few minutes, because when I come to one of my eyes is swollen shut. With the other eye I look up and recognize the big live oak near Riverview towering over me. The one with the good fishing hole under its roots.

Every now and then, Ray Tanner's ugly face is over me, close enough for me to smell the whiskey on his breath, close enough to see his yellow teeth when he spits in my face. I feel the rope scratching the skin around my neck as they yank it over my head. I hear Ray's voice.

"You sorry nigger. I'll teach you to come looking for me like you had business with me."

I hear the river running fast and steady below me. I think of fishing there, catching catfish and taking them home for Mama to fry.

"*Just so you know, nigger, I had me a fine piece of ass a couple of nights ago.*"

The sky on the other side of the river is turning that washed-out gray that comes right before sunrise. I wonder if Adelle is awake. I wonder if she'll finish nursing school.

"*Yessirree, I had me a nigger nurse. She fixed me right up.*" Laughter from some of the other men drifts past me.

I try one more time to break free of the ropes that are binding my wrists behind me. If only I could see her just one more time. Tell her I meant to do things her papa's way. I meant to leave this thing alone, let time pass. Find another way to fight back. I'm off the ground now, standing on top of a tree stump. The ground and the sky are turning crazy circles. A single sliver of orange breaks through the fog over the river. I wish I could have gone fishing one more time.

"*Pete, call old Purvis. We need to get a picture of this one.*"

I close my eyes and see all of them: Adelle, Gracie, Dr. Jackson. Grandma, Mama I'll be joining you soon, Mama. . . .

The noose tightens around my neck and I can't breathe. I clench my jaw against the pain. The tree and the river and the brightening sky swim away from me as I open my good eye for one last look. Then it all goes black.

Chapter 22

Grace

"And did you know that Ray Tanner did it?" Roxanne whispers.

Clarence and I look at each other again. I think we both know more of the truth now than we ever have, but still we have no proof, no certainty. "We had our suspicions, but none of us ever knew for sure," I reply. "There were no black folks who witnessed what happened. Dr. Jackson tried to get the sheriff to investigate, but after he asked a few questions, it was all dropped, swept under the rug, same as always. The Tanners ended up running the saw-mill and lumberyard. As a matter of fact, Ray Tanner was highly thought of among the white folks."

Roxanne's crying again now, holding her face in her hands. "I just don't know how you do it," she says. "How can you deal with all this pain? How do you keep from turning hard with hate?"

"I've done my share of hating," I say. "We all have." Clarence nods at this; so does Rita. "I was so eaten up with it those first few weeks after Zero died that I couldn't leave my house. Finally, Dr. Prosser herself came down here from Tougaloo and packed my suitcase and told me I was going back to college. She said to me, 'Grace Clark, you have got no business letting these ignorant crackers take away your life like they did your brother's. The best thing you can do for Zero is get yourself in my car and get back to school.' I couldn't believe she talked that way, but she was right. I finished college and got my teaching certificate."

"What about Adelle?" Rita asks.

"Addie was as torn up over it as the rest of us," I say. "Maybe more. She told her mama and daddy her life was over, that there was no reason for her to go to nursing school now. Dr. Jackson even came out to my house and pleaded with me to talk to her. But what was I going to say? I was feeling the same way. In the end, it was Adelle's mama who convinced her to finish her nurse's training."

"How did she do that?" Roxanne asks.

"Mrs. Jackson got real sick not long after Zero passed," I say. "She came close to dying from pneumonia, and it was Adelle who nursed her through it. From her letters I could tell Adelle realized that nursing someone else helped heal her own pain."

Clarence shakes his head. "It was never the same around here after it happened. Junior was gone. Zero was gone. Looked like life in this town wasn't worth living. I even considered leaving here myself for a while."

"But you didn't?" Rita asks.

"No, I put my head down and did my work, ended up making a pretty good living for myself. And there was Ernestine, and then our babies. My boys left here, though. Moved all the way to Detroit," Clarence says. I can hear the pride in his voice. He's always been glad his boys made a different life for themselves.

"So why did you and Adelle come back here?" Roxanne asks me.

"I came back for the same reason Adelle did, I reckon. This is our home, Roxanne. This is where our people are and where our lives are. We've been contented here. Adelle had her nursing career and I might never have had children of my own, but I had hundreds of children in my life over the years."

"They were lucky to have you," Roxanne says, drying her tears with a tissue.

"I hope so. I think I finally figured out that hate wasn't going to help me. The best thing I could do for the black people around here was show all those children I taught, black or white, that a black woman can get an education and have a good career. I wanted to see those children grow up and make Clarksville a different place."

"But there are still people like Del Tanner," Roxanne says, shrugging her shoulders.

"There will always be people like Del," Rita says. She hasn't said much through this whole conversation, and I've been wondering what she's thinking. "Del Tanner's generation grew up in what was still a Jim Crow South. Even after the civil rights movement, some of them never adjusted to desegregation. All they can see is difference. . . ." Rita looks at Clarence and me. "I admire your courage for staying. I'm not sure I could have done it. But maybe, since you did, mine and Roxanne's generation will be different."

I watch Roxanne as Rita says this. What's that look on her face? She seems softer somehow, less guarded than I've ever seen her. She seems to admire Rita. I remember how hesitant I was to let Roxanne into my life just a few weeks ago. And now, it looks like she's been good for all of us.

We sit quietly for a few minutes. Clarence pours us more coffee, and to ease the sadness we chat about the places Roxanne and I have gathered for the tour. Then I remember Roxanne said earlier that Del Tanner wanted her to bring me by the lumberyard. "Do you have any idea why he wants to see us Friday?" I ask.

"No, ma'am, I don't," she answers. "And if you don't want to go through with seeing him, I certainly understand. . . ."

"No, I think we need to hear him out." I'm wondering what a Tanner could possibly have to say to a Clark, when Clarence's phone rings.

He leaves the kitchen to answer the phone in the next room. He's gone for several minutes, and when he comes back his expression is mighty worried.

"What's wrong?" I ask, feeling something in my heart crack like an egg.

"It's Adelle," he says. "She's in the hospital. She's had a heart attack."

Roxanne

Rita and I are sitting in the hospital waiting room. Clarence and Grace have gone in to see Adelle first, since the nurses only allow two visitors at a time. I have so many emotions washing over me right now that I can hardly speak. Rita must understand, because she doesn't press me for conversation. I can't bear the thought of losing Adelle Jackson or Grace Clark. Without the two of them I might have gone on with my superficial life, oblivious to a whole other world around me . . . I might never have met Clarence Jones, or Daniel Mason, or Billy Webster, or Mattie Webster, or Rita. I look over at Rita. She seems as lost in thought as I've been.

"Thank you," I say quietly.

She turns to me and smiles. "For what?"

"For being willing to put up with me for one thing," I say, and we both laugh. "Seriously," I say, "thank you for pushing me to listen, for helping me understand. But, mostly . . ." Here I go tearing up again. I've cried more in the past day than I've cried in years. "Thanks for helping me realize what's important."

Rita puts her arm around me and gives me a squeeze. "You've done that all on your own," she says. "I just gave you a little nudge. Besides, I knew there was an interesting person underneath that superficial, white-pilgrimage-director façade."

It's a relief to laugh, but we both stop abruptly as Clarence emerges from the double doors to the cardiac intensive care unit.

We stand as he approaches us. I'm trying to read his expression. "How is she?" we ask at the same time.

"Doctor says she's going to make it," he says, breaking into a wide smile and chuckling. "She had a close call, but she's a strong woman. That doctor said she's one of the feistiest patients he's ever seen."

We all laugh and hug each other in relief. Just then Rita's husband appears, and Rita pulls him aside to fill him in on what has happened. I walk back over to the chairs where Rita and I were sitting. Clarence follows me.

"You can go in and visit Addie now if you want to," he says, sitting down beside me. "I'm going to rest here for a little while."

"Thank you," I say. "I'll go in a minute. I think I'll just sit here with you for a bit and get my breath."

"All right then," he says.

As I sit beside Clarence and I look over at Rita, talking intently to Jack, I'm filled with a sense of contentment. I know that I'm right where I need to be, surrounded by people who matter to me and who I believe care about me as well. I'm experiencing a new anticipation—about what the next half of my own life might be like, and about what my newfound friendships might bring. Although it's still painful, I know that Dudley and I will figure out what to do about our marriage. And I have a chance to allow my daughter to know me differently. I have a second chance to be me without that façade that Rita described.

Adelle

When I open my eyes, I'm so happy to see my dear old friend Grace's sweet face smiling down at me that I start to cry. She wipes my tears and clucks to me like an old mother hen. I'm surprised when I see that Clarence is with her. I haven't seen Clarence in such a long time.

Clarence winks at me and says, "That doctor said you gave him a run for his money. Sounds like you're too ornery to die yet."

"Clarence!" Grace says. "You ought to be ashamed."

Even though I feel weak as a kitten, those two can still make me smile. They tell me that Roxanne Reeves and Rita Baldwin are out in the waiting room. They're worried about me, too. Roxanne is a dear, and she's coming along, for a white woman. I hope she and Rita will get to be good friends. I think Roxanne needs a friend.

Grace and Clarence hover on either side of my bed, talking about the weather and whatnot. Although I'm happy to see them, I remember that when the chest pain started last night I told myself that I had to talk to Grace. I have to tell her before I die. There have never been secrets between us, and I don't want to carry this one to my grave. I wait patiently, and pretty soon Clarence gets restless and says he'll leave so Roxanne or Rita can come in before visiting time is over. He stoops down and kisses my cheek and heads for the door. When Grace starts to leave, too, I hold on to her hand.

"I want you to stay for a minute," I say. "Come closer, will you?" Grace leans in toward me. I smile at her and reach up to touch her cheek. "Gracie, you and me need to talk," I whisper. My voice is weak.

"Sugar, we don't need to talk now. You just rest and save your breath."

"No," I say, and I must sound stronger than I think because Gracie's eyebrows shoot up like they always do when she's surprised. "I need to tell you something before I pass."

Grace is crying now. "You aren't going anywhere, Adelle Jackson! You can't leave me behind. We've always done everything together. . . ."

I don't have time for Gracie's foolishness, so I put my hand over her mouth. "Hush up and listen to me. You always did talk too much."

She obeys me and stands there waiting and listening. The pain seizes my heart again and I have to close my eyes and catch my breath.

"Addie?" she says.

"Don't worry. I'm not dead yet," I say as the pain eases a little. "Do you remember me telling you how I had to nurse Ray Tanner when he was dying?"

"Yes, I remember. I still don't know how you did it, Addie. The good Lord will smile on you for that."

"I'm not so sure about that, Gracie. Not after what I'm fixing to tell you."

There go Gracie's eyebrows again.

"I didn't kill him. Not really. I just didn't stop him from dying. Believe you me, I know an eye for an eye is Old Testament thinking. Lord knows, I have done plenty of turning the other cheek in my time." Gracie's listening real close now.

"His big bony white hands twitched. He was tied down, you see. Those soft ties they use on folks in the hospital to keep them from pulling out tubes and such. I thought about those hands twisting the noose, slipping it over Zero's head.

"The connection between the machine and his windpipe slipped loose somehow. I reckon I didn't have it taped up very well. That breathing machine kept right on making its noise—in and out, in and out. There was that little alarm button. Just one little push, Gracie, and the alarm stops right away."

I feel the pain in my heart again. This might be the one that gets me. I'd better hurry. I keep going. Grace is leaning even closer to me now. "It's a shame, isn't it, Gracie? I heard it's a right frightening way to die. Kind of slow-like. Like hanging when the neck doesn't break right away. When he started to lose his air, his eyes flew open. I think I was the last thing he saw before he passed. He probably thought he was in hell."

Epilogue

Roxanne

We're all gathered at Sandfield Cemetery, the next-to-last stop of the day. The spring rains have kept the ground soft and it's challenging to walk on. The sun is just coming out from behind the low clouds that have been hovering and threatening rain. Rita and Jack are helping Adelle, who is still a little fragile since her heart attack, and I'm helping Grace as we make our way across to the grave sites.

A surprising number of people have arrived at the cemetery, walking carefully among the graves. Some, like our group, are visiting specific graves of loved ones or family, while others—the visitors—have their brochures in hand, searching for the names of key figures from the tour. We've brought pots of roses to decorate the graves, but there are flowers blooming under all of the pine trees shading this plain little cemetery today, yellow jonquils, pink azaleas, red tulips.

We stop first at the graves of Adelle's mother, father, and grandmother. "I sure do miss them," Adelle says softly. I feel a stab of pain noticing the two additional empty plots, knowing they are for Adelle and Junior.

Adelle and Grace stand quietly with their arms around each

other as Rita, Jack, and I remove the old flowers near the head-stones and replace them with the new roses. As I watch the two women, I realize that even with all of their strength, their bodies are as fragile as tissue paper. I wonder how long it will be before we lose them. That thought is intolerable to me right now. I've especially grown to love Grace Clark like my own mother. With-out her, my life would have just gone on from one social event to another. I probably would never have had my eyes opened to any other perspective on life in Clarksville, Mississippi. I certainly wouldn't have been proudly cutting a ribbon for the Thomas Clark Memorial African-American Tour today.

The tour started at the Union School. Del Tanner himself oversaw the restoration of the old warehouse. He even searched all over Mississippi to find old school desks and a blackboard. Although Del kept his distance as people moved into his lum-beryard and through to the old school, he stood there cap in hand, and watched us file by, with a look of respect in his eyes. Respect and something else . . . I'm still not sure what. Funny, when I first met Del he said that if he allowed this school to be on the tour, he'd be out of business in a week. But from what I've heard lately, his business is doing just fine. Actually, it's pick-ing up a bit.

From the school we went on to the other places: the Jacksons' house, Catfish Alley, the Missionary Union Church, and other sites we added over the past several months. This cemetery is the next-to-last stop on what I'm proudly telling myself has been a success-ful first tour.

The final stop and the highlight of the tour is the dedica-tion of the Queen City Hotel Community Restoration Proj-ect. Thanks to Jack Baldwin's financial wizardry, Daniel Mason's dedication and ability to garner community support, and mine and Rita's combined restoration expertise, plans have been drawn up and materials purchased to restore the old hotel. The Queen City will be an African-American community center dedicated to black history, and particularly to the preservation of the jazz culture. Mattie Webster herself has agreed to speak at the dedication. I'm still a little nervous about that since Mattie's such a wild card. But Grace and Adelle have assured me that she will behave herself. We'll see.

It does occur to me that none of my people are here. No husband. A daughter who, of course, couldn't get out of the cruise she had scheduled with her college girlfriends. But I've also noticed that the lonely feeling I've carried around for so long seems to be dissipating. As I look into the wizened old faces of Grace and Adelle and the proud, open faces of Rita and Jack, I think I know why. For the most part these days, my consciousness about being one of the only white people in a group has dissolved along with the loneliness.

Billy Webster is flying in from Chicago for the dedication ceremony. Daniel Mason has gone to the airport to pick her up and they'll join us at the Queen City. She told Rita and me the story of how she and her friend found Junior Jackson living in that old house in Chicago. Another heartbreaking story, without a good ending. There have been so many. She visited him a few times after their first conversation, but she says he still won't budge about coming here. Rita, Billy, and I decided not to tell the ladies about Junior. Why add to their old hurts? Of course, Billy's been coming to visit quite regularly over the past several months. I'm still hoping Daniel Mason will talk her into moving back. I think they make a great couple. I was just telling Rita the other day over lunch, "I think Billy ought to marry Daniel Mason and move back to Clarksville."

"Are you kidding me?" she said. "She'll never leave her job. I think he ought to move up there and find a church. It's easier for a black man to find a church than for a black woman to find a high-paying management job." In our ongoing debate over issues of color, Rita usually wins the argument.

My mind wanders to the time I'll have on my hands after launching this tour. Thanks to Elsie Spencer's blackballing, I didn't get elected as pilgrimage director this year. But, as I expected, it was a relief. And Rita and I are working together now on the Queen City restoration project. I think Louisa and Ellery Humboldt's place might be my last antebellum home restoration. The home I thought Rita and Jack might be interested in purchasing didn't go on the market this spring after all. But I'll keep my ears open—even though my connections aren't what they used to be, since I've stopped working so hard at maintaining them.

Dudley filed for divorce, so we sold the big house and I'm looking for something smaller, maybe a little bungalow near the college campus. In the meantime, I'm staying with Grace at Pecan Cottage. We make pretty good roommates. She's even taught me to make muscadine jelly . . . and cathead biscuits.

As we move on toward the Clark family graves, Grace and I trail behind the others, and I'm overcome again with emotions about the stories I've heard in the past few months. I take Grace's arm. "I still can't fathom how kind and gracious you and Adelle are after all that you've been through in your lives. If anyone has a grudge to carry, it's the two of you." It startles me when Grace stops and squeezes my arm with an iron grip. She turns and faces me, looking up into my eyes. She takes my hands and holds them in her gnarled smooth ones. I look down at our hands there together, not even thinking about pulling away. I'm embarrassed that my tears fall on Grace's hands.

"Now you listen to me, Roxanne Reeves," Grace says. "Holding grudges doesn't help anyone. I learned that a long time ago when we lost Zero. Life is full of pain, but there is joy, too. Adelle loved Zero with all of her heart, and after she lost him, she was never the same. But she still found joy. She found it in her family and her church and her work. Why, she was a pioneer! Remember, Adelle Jackson was the first black nurse to work at Clarksville Hospital."

"I remember," I say, pulling my hands away to search my purse for a tissue to dry my eyes.

Here we are: me, a mid-forties white woman, letting go of my climb up the Southern social ladder, and Grace, an eighty-nine-year-old black woman who's never been the least bit interested in climbing anybody's ladder, strolling slowly through an old cemetery talking and looking at the graves. I recognize other names: Ezekiel Green, Robert Webster—Jr. and Sr. I know all of their stories now. They're no longer anonymous black people from the past. They're alive for me with all of their tragedies and joys.

Grace and I come to a stop behind the others at the graves of her mother, father, grandmother, and Zero. Zero's headstone reads *Thomas "Zero" Clark, 1911 to 1931, He Is with the Angels Now.* I ask Grace, "Do you really believe that?"

"What's that, sugar?" Grace asks.

"That he's with the angels."

"Yes, I do. I believe they all watch over me. That's what carries me through."

Grace insists on placing the flowers at Zero's headstone herself. Jack kneels to steady her and Rita helps Adelle over to the stone bench that has been placed near the graves. I look out across the cemetery and am pleased and surprised to see Daniel and Billy walking toward us along the graveled center lane. Between them is a stooped elderly black man. He's wearing a black suit and hat and I can tell he's leaning heavily on Daniel's arm. I don't recognize him. As he gets nearer, I can tell he's probably about Grace's age. There's something vaguely familiar about him, but I imagine I'm confusing him with someone else—I've seen so many photographs and heard so many stories.

Grace is still bending down, straightening the flower arrangement on Zero's grave. Jack is kneeling beside her, waiting patiently to help her up.

"Rita," I say softly, "I think you need to look at this." Rita follows my gaze and, for a moment, forgets Adelle as she comes to stand beside me.

"Who is that?" she asks. "It couldn't be . . ."

As they draw closer, Billy raises her hand and waves. Daniel Mason has a grin on his face that could only mean one thing. As we watch them approach, I glance back. Adelle has not seen them yet, nor has Grace. They are both focused on getting the flowers just right.

Rita and I walk over to meet them. I think we're both holding our breath, wondering if this man is who we think he is.

As we greet Billy and Daniel, the man removes his hat, revealing closely cut graying hair and a handsome, deeply lined face. Billy places her arm through his and says, "Ladies, I'd like you to meet Mr. Albert Jackson, Jr."

He shakes our hands warmly, and just as we step aside to bring them over to the grave, where Jack is just helping Grace up, we hear a gasp and I look up to see Adelle clutch her hand to her chest. Fearful that it's her heart again, I start to rush over to her. But I see quickly, as she stands and fixes her eyes on Junior, that this is joy, not pain. She tears her eyes from her brother and says, "Gracie . . . Gracie . . . look who's here."

Grace has unfolded herself into a standing position and is brushing off her dress when Junior reaches her. She looks up, freezes, and her hands fly to her mouth as the small spade she was using drops to the ground. I can see the tears forming instantly in her eyes. "Junior?"

We all stand back and watch as the prodigal brother is enfolded in the arms of two women who never stopped loving him or believing that he might return someday. I think to myself, maybe Grace was right. Life is full of pain, but there is joy, too. Today, I choose joy.

First of all, let me say that *Catfish Alley* is entirely a work of fiction. That being said, in some ways it is entirely a work of fact, albeit with author's license in some historical details. *Catfish Alley* is loosely based on places, events, and people in my hometown of Columbus, Mississippi. I grew up just outside of Columbus in a rural community called New Hope. My mother says that when my grandparents moved to New Hope, the school doubled in size. That was the early 1900s, and my grandparents eventually had fifteen children, so that explains the sudden increase in the school population. I lived in that community until my late twenties, graduating from the same high school as my mother had.

My grandparents were cotton farmers, and my sister still lives on what remains of that farm in the house built just after the Civil War, where my mother, the thirteenth child, was born in 1924. As a young girl, I spent many hours in the gardens, fields, and orchards of Mississippi, picking peas, pulling corn, gathering pecans, shaking apple trees, and digging up peanuts. We canned or put up everything we ate, so if it could be shelled, shucked, peeled, or cracked, we or somebody we knew grew it. My brothers hunted and fished, and there was frequently a deer hung from a tree in my mother's backyard, waiting to be skinned and dressed. I admired my mother's ability to catch a string of bream or crappie, clean them on a piece of tin laid across two sawhorses, and then fry them up into delectable morsels, accompanied by hush puppies and coleslaw.

We certainly never considered ourselves poor and never lacked for good food and plenty of it. My mother, at eighty-six, still keeps a small garden and still makes pickles in a hundred-year-old butter churn. None of this seemed unusual to me. It was my life and a good one. It was not until I reached adulthood and left Mississippi for graduate school that I realized very few of my colleagues had similar life experiences. I guess in some ways I've always been a throwback to a previous era.

As a child I spent many long, hot summer days with my grandmother and my mentally disabled aunt Mary. Aunt Mary was a classic example of the Southern credo of keeping your special people at home. Aunt Mary was one of my best childhood friends. We shared books like *The Bobbsey Twins* and *Trixie Belden*. During the long afternoons, while Grandma and Mary napped, I sought shelter from the heat under an old oak tree that had rooted up the sidewalk in front of Grandma's house. I think that's when storytelling came alive for me. Making up stories was a way to pass the time for a little girl who spent much of her childhood in the company of old women.

My grandmother always had her afternoon nap in her four-poster feather bed—the same one where many of her children were born—under the watchful eye of her father staring out from an old-timey photograph. The day my great-grandfather was discharged from the Confederate Army, he had this picture taken. His discharge papers peek out of his coat pocket as he stares solemnly into the camera. I always wondered what else he did that day.

There were no black maids or housekeepers working for my family. As a matter of fact, we had very little interaction with black folks. It's difficult to explain how ignorant you can be of what life is like for a whole other group of people unless you've experienced a segregated world. It wasn't until I went to nursing school alongside black women that I was brave enough to ask why a person would put oil in her hair, instead of constantly trying to get it out like the white girls I knew; or what it meant to have ashy skin—a word not in my repertoire.

Because my world and my perspective were so narrow and defined by the seasons—spring and summer when we worked in the garden, fall when we went back to school, and whatever was in between that passed for winter—I never really developed an appreciation of my local history. Like so many Southern white children, I was oblivious of the issues of race raging around me in the sixties. It was not until my school was integrated when I was in the sixth grade, in 1971, that I found myself mixing with blacks. I can only imagine how difficult it was for the black kids who lost the school they had attended for years, only to be thrown in with a bunch of white kids who had no knowledge of their lives and no appreciation of their struggle. Forces outside of us pushed Mississippi toward integration. I'm not sure it ever would have happened otherwise. In most ways we remained segregated, even after formal desegregation. We played separately, ate separately, shopped separately. And when my own daughter graduated from New Hope twenty-five years later, in 2002, there was still a black homecoming queen and a white homecoming queen.

Even though I took Mississippi history in school, I knew very little of the history all around me in the town of Columbus. I didn't know until I grew up and left my own hometown that Columbus was the birthplace of Tennessee Williams, the famous playwright; Red Barber, the baseball sportscaster; and Henry Armstrong, the world boxing champion. All of these men were born right around the same time as my fictional characters Zero Clark and Junior Jackson.

I didn't know that the women who met to decorate soldiers' graves in the late 1800s were part of the origin of what we now call Memorial Day. I didn't know that in the 1920s, Eudora Welty attended what was then called Mississippi State College for Women, later renamed Mississippi University for Women, in Columbus, where I earned my first degree. At least I knew that "the W," as it's called, was the first state-supported college for women in the country. Maybe I read that somewhere on the admission paperwork. In retrospect, I'm amazed at my own ignorance.

During the Civil War, in order to protect the lives of wounded soldiers sheltered in the grand mansions-turned-hospitals, Nathan Bedford Forrest negotiated to keep Columbus from being destroyed by Union soldiers. Thus, a large number of antebellum homes were left unscathed. In 1940, the historic foundation started the annual pilgrimage tour of homes. That tour is now recognized as one of the best and most authentic antebellum home tours in the country. Not until many years later were the historical sites of African-Americans acknowledged. What began as highlights for Black History Month evolved into an African-American Heritage Tour with a list of historical venues recognizing the businesses, homes, and contributions of the African-American community.

Later in my life, once I'd gotten some distance from my home state and the widened perspective of graduate school, I began to wrestle with what had been integral to my growing-up years: the racial jokes; the almost complete segregation of the races; the dubious way that Southern blacks viewed whites and vice versa. While in my doctoral program in Austin, Texas, I made my very first close black friend; she was from big-city Brooklyn, New York, and I was from rural Mississippi—our life experiences couldn't have been more different. My friendship with Mae helped me across that color line drawn in my youth.

When I returned home to Mississippi to visit, I became conscious of a feeling I would get from young black women, who seemed to view me as an object of disdain. I didn't understand it, yet I thought that I deserved it—not for any particular act of racism on my part, but simply because of my color. My friend Mae had helped me understand that my whiteness was accompanied by privilege whether I chose to exploit it or not. Those women knew this; they had always known. I was the latecomer to this understanding.

As the years went by and I continued to wrestle with my relationship to Mississippi, I found myself drawn more and more to its history. I found myself wanting to understand what was bred into Mississippi whites that moved us so slowly toward accepting the equality of blacks. Was it that we were still so close to a generation of slaveholders who genuinely believed that blacks were born to a life of service? Was it, as many whites said, because blacks are different? So often I heard Southerners say that it's easy for Yankees to preach about integration and equality because there aren't any black people where they live. Was that true?

When I began to research antebellum homes for some of my writing, I ran across the list of sites for the Columbus African-American tour. I began to wonder about the stories of the men and women who might have lived during those early years of the twentieth century. I started to research places that I'd grown up around but never really noticed. I discovered that you can live in a town, reach adulthood, marry, have children of your own, and never fully understand the cultural struggle going on all around you. Whether by choice or by ignorance, the pressure to keep the status quo in Mississippi is like the humidity—ever present in the air.

In my research, I discovered the name of O. N. Pruitt and recognized that his name was inscribed on the photographic portraits of my oldest sister and brother hanging on the wall in my mother's bedroom. These were portraits that my mother had Mr. Pruitt take in the early 1940s to send to my father, who was a soldier stationed in Germany. I found that Pruitt did much more than produce sweet portraits of babies. He also photographed freak shows, circus acts, dead children, tent revivals, river baptisms, and, much to my surprise, lynchings. He was even part of the group of photographers who produced the lynching postcards that were circulated throughout the South in the 1920s and '30s. I found a scholar, Berkley Hudson, whose dissertation work was a study of O. N. Pruitt's photography from 1920 to 1960. The gruesome image of a 1930s double lynching of two young black men that occurred in the same county where I grew up touched something deep inside me and made me want to tell this story.

So, out of all of this imagery, memory, and life experience, the story of *Catfish Alley* was born. I only hope to touch on the reality of what it's like to live in the South, not with judgment or any assumption of righteousness, but with a simple desire to tell a story. They say "write what you know." For me, it's been more about writing what I need to understand. In the end, it's just a story about two women, two women who form an unlikely friendship. But then, I believe that's how we really change how we see our worlds—one relationship at a time.

ACKNOWLEDGMENTS

For my sense of place and the rootedness that sustains me wherever I go, I thank my Southern family. I thank my Colorado family for the daily love and support that grounds me through the ups and downs of writing. Thanks to my dear friends in the original writing group who encouraged me to persist.

Thanks to my wonderful agent, Kevan Lyon, for believing in my work and guiding me through this process. And finally, thanks to my amazing editor, Ellen Edwards, for her meticulous attention to detail, and for those thought-provoking questions that made my novel stronger and continue to help me grow as a writer.

Marion Zachary, Blue Sky Designs Web Development

Lynne Bryant grew up in Columbus, Mississippi, and has lived for many years in Colorado Springs, Colorado, where she teaches nursing at the University of Colorado. *Catfish Alley* is her first novel. Visit her at lynne-bryant.com.

Catfish Alley

LYNNE BRYANT

*This Conversation Guide is intended to enrich the
individual reading experience, as well as encourage us
to explore these topics together—because books,
and life, are meant for sharing.*

A CONVERSATION WITH LYNNE BRYANT

Q. Your Author's Note explains how you came to write Catfish Alley, *but when did you first begin to use writing to explore what you needed to understand about life?*

A. I think my writing has always been an outward expression of an inner search. Whether it was childhood flights of imagination about bubble people who lived at the bottom of the bathtub drain, snippets of prose, feeble attempts at poetry, journaling, or other attempts at novels, writing has always been an exploration for me. I believe we tell stories for that reason—to understand our world. Even my doctoral dissertation was a philosophical inquiry. Only it wasn't very publishable!

Back in 2007, I entered a contest sponsored by Borders to write a post-Katrina love letter to New Orleans. I remember how people were still trying to understand why so many New Orleanians did not want to leave the city during and after the hurricane. As a Southerner, I knew that their reasons for staying had to do with home and rootedness. Where else were they to go? Anyway, I entered that contest, and much to my surprise, I won! My very short essay was an attempt to understand the spirit of the people of New Orleans. I included my love letter to New Orleans on one of my blog posts (see my Web site at www.lynne-bryant.com).

Q. *Like Kathryn Stockett, author of* The Help, *you're a white woman writing about black characters in the South. How did you approach that particular challenge?*

A. Writing fiction, for me, is a process of observation paired with imagination. Although I know that I can never completely understand another person's psyche, black or white, I work very hard to be as accurate as possible. This is especially true when I'm writing in a point of view out of the realm of my experience—from a man's or an elderly person's point of view, for example.

Being a nurse has particularly prepared me for the empathic process. Nurses place ourselves in our patients' experiences so that we can better care for them. Cultivating the habits of observation and empathy as a nurse for thirty years has served me well as a writer. So, when it came to writing a black person's point of view, I used those skills, along with a lifetime of memories of growing up in Mississippi. I hope I've been able to get it right, at least some of the time—that's very important to me. Writing in multiple points of view—black and white, male and female, young and old—is always a risk, but I believe it was worth taking that risk to tell this story.

Q. *The fictional town of Clarksville is loosely based on your own hometown of Columbus, Mississippi. How do you think the people of Columbus will respond to* Catfish Alley?

A. That's difficult to predict. Although Columbus has some unique qualities, in terms of its history and antebellum structures, I feel the characters in my novel and the relationships between blacks and whites that I depict could be found in many other Southern towns. My characters represent a cross section of types of people. Since I spent the first twenty-seven years of my life in Columbus, that small community had a huge influence on me. The African-American Heritage Tour in Columbus wasn't started until long after I had moved away—I think around 2004. The historic places on the tour and the black citizens whose names are included in the historical record were the inspiration for my story. My novel is not intended to portray their factual histories, but to tell a story of events as they might have been.

Q. *You've said that when you moved away from the South, you finally became aware of how unique your life there was compared to the way people lived in the rest of the country. What are some of the strengths your Southern upbringing gave you?*

A. An appreciation of good cooking and cool weather! No, seriously, I have especially come to value the sense of place I experienced in childhood but resisted for a long time as an adult. I also appreciate the hard physical work that we did for the delicious food we ate. The experience of growing our own food from seed to harvest enormously enriched my childhood and early adulthood. I'll probably become one of those old women like Ouiser, Shirley MacLaine's character in *Steel Magnolias*— wearing an ugly sun hat and growing tomatoes and, I hope, writing more books! There was also a sense of connectedness about my Southern life. My people weren't on the social register, but since my mama was one of fifteen and five of my siblings lived in town at one point or another, I couldn't help but know everybody. That can be comforting as well as stifling. I experienced both while living there.

Q. *What role has reading played in your life? Are any novels particularly meaningful to you?*

A. I've always been a big reader, and I read a wide variety of books. I spent a lot of time alone as a child, so books were a constant companion. Some of the Southern classics—William Faulkner's *The Sound and the Fury*, Harper Lee's *To Kill a Mockingbird*, Carson McCullers's *The Heart Is a Lonely Hunter*—gave me a feel for strong Southern writing and for writing about the ordinary, especially about times past. For current women's fiction, I like Fannie Flagg and Dorothea Benton Frank for their humor and the way they depict family and relationships. I love Sue Monk Kidd's *The Secret Life of Bees*, because of the way she captures the essence of the South in one or two words and makes me feel like I'm in the scene. For the lyrical quality of his writing, and for understanding the white Southern male, you can't beat Pat Conroy. When I'm in the mood for a thriller set in the South, I really enjoy Greg Iles. And finally, Edward P. Jones's *The Known World* and Lalita Tademy's *Cane River* were influential in my evolving understanding of the black experience.

Q. *Grace's delicious desserts help win over Roxanne, but also threaten to ruin her waistline. What's your relationship with Southern cooking, and would you share your recipes for cathead biscuits and muscadine jelly?*

A. Southern cooking for me, like nothing else, says home. We always ate really well, even though there was nothing gourmet about it! When our whole family got together there were usually at least three or four vegetables on the table—purple hull peas, creamed corn, fried okra, sliced tomatoes—and, of course, hot buttered corn bread. Desserts might be fried apple pies, banana pudding, or some kind of cobbler. My mama is one of those Southern women who shows her love through her cooking. I've often found myself doing the same thing.

Funny you should ask for those particular recipes. One of my first blog posts was about muscadine jelly, followed by my biscuit recipe. The blog about muscadine jelly received a response from my sister, who informed me that our mama did not put muscadine jelly in the canner—I had gotten jelly making mixed up with green bean canning! So, needless to say, I corrected that quickly. The biscuit recipe is one that I've been using for more than thirty years. The special thing about cathead biscuits is not so much the ingredients as the technique used in making them (although some people would debate that—as there is a debate about the best way to make just about everything in the South). First of all, they're large (the size of a cat's head), and second, they're usually pinched and shaped with your hands, rather than cut with a biscuit cutter.

· Cathead Biscuits ·

2 cups all-purpose flour

4 teaspoons baking powder

2 teaspoons sugar

½ teaspoon cream of tartar

½ teaspoon salt

½ cup shortening
⅔ cup milk
1 tablespoon butter
Additional tablespoon of melted butter

Preheat the oven to 450°. I use a whisk to stir together the dry ingredients. Cut the shortening in with a pastry cutter until the mixture looks crumbly. Make a hole in the center of the mixture and pour the milk in all at once. Stir it just a little bit—the secret to flaky biscuits is not to work the dough too much. When the dough sticks together, turn it out onto a floured surface and work it with your hands gently just 3 or 4 times.

For cathead biscuits, place 1 tablespoon of butter in a 10-inch iron skillet and put the skillet in the oven to heat and melt the butter. When the skillet is hot and the butter melted, pinch the dough into 4 large pieces (each about the size of a cat's head). Pat each piece into a biscuit shape and place in the buttered skillet. Let the edges of the biscuits touch. Brush the tops of the biscuits with melted butter and bake them for about 15 minutes or until the tops start to brown. If you want smaller biscuits, simply pinch off smaller pieces of dough (you may need less baking time for smaller biscuits). A baking sheet can be used if you don't have an iron skillet.

You can substitute buttermilk for the sweet milk, but you'll need to add ¼ teaspoon of baking soda to the dry ingredients and you'll use ¾ cup of buttermilk.

Q. What are you writing now?

A. I'm working on a story set in the Mississippi Delta town of Greenville. It's the story of a young woman who flees Mississippi right after high school, trying to leave behind a tragic event that arises out of racial segregation. She returns to Greenville ten years later to grapple with some unsolved mysteries of her life and, in doing so, ends up getting immersed in her grandmother's history. It's part love story and part mystery, and it includes a lot about that Southern sense of place. Like *Catfish Alley*, the story moves back and forth in time between now and the past.

Q. You teach nursing full-time and have a family too. How did you manage to carve out the time necessary to research and write Catfish Alley?

A. It was challenging, but I have an extremely supportive family. One of the lessons I've had to learn is the discipline of writing. I get up early to write, usually around five a.m. during the school year. I find that if I can get in at least two to three good writing hours, I feel a sense of accomplishment for the rest of the day. I've also learned that having a specific goal and a self-imposed deadline makes a huge difference in my motivation. Middle age is all about management. Managing my full-time job and full-time writing while trying to exercise, spend time in my garden, read, and save some time for my family requires an incredible juggling act. I usually feel like one of those performers spinning several plates at once! But the privilege of writing novels is so worth it!

QUESTIONS
FOR DISCUSSION

1. What was your response to *Catfish Alley*? What did you like best about it?

2. In Clarksville, Mississippi, in 2002, blacks and whites still live largely separate lives, and racial prejudice maintains a powerful hold. Does this surprise you? To what degree does segregation between blacks and whites exist where you live?

3. *Catfish Alley* is in many respects a story of female friendship. Discuss the many relationships among the women characters—between Roxanne and Grace, Grace and Adelle and Mattie, Roxanne and Rita, Roxanne and the other white women in town, etc. What makes the strong relationships strong, and the weak ones weak? What allows Roxanne to overcome racial barriers and form sincere friendships with the black women in the book?

4. At the beginning of the book, no one in Clarksville wants to talk about the past. Discuss the impulse to bury painful past events and the risks and benefits of examining them with a fresh and honest eye from the perspective of many years later. Does

your town acknowledge and honor its full history or only part of it?

5. Discuss how the sins of the fathers are inherited by the sons (and daughters). How does Del Tanner inherit Ray's sins? How do Jimalee and J. R. Purvis suffer from choices made by their father? How is Roxanne's need to hide her origins the result of Mrs. Stanley's attitudes toward class? Do you see similar patterns of behavior in people you know?

6. What do you think of Roxanne's attempt to befriend Ola Mae after so many years of not making any effort to get to know her? Have you ever had an ongoing relationship with a woman who provided a paid service for you—a cleaning lady, hairdresser, or child-care giver? Did the nature of the relationship—one woman buying the services of the other—create a barrier between you? Did differences of race, class, and background also create barriers? To what degree were you able to overcome them?

7. Blacks in Clarksville in the 1920s and '30s lived with the expectation that local law enforcement would offer them little protection against violent crime and even less justice once a crime was committed. Try to imagine what living all your life in such circumstances would feel like. How do you think you would respond?

8. The women who run the antebellum home tour wonder how they can involve black women, since having them dress as plantation daughters in hoopskirts or as slaves in homespun

seem equally discomforting. How might the women alter their perspective to see other possibilities?

9. Grace, Adelle, and Junior all suffer terrible tragedies at the hands of white people, yet they continue to pursue their personal dreams, refusing to allow grief and loss to make them bitter, resentful or angry. In what ways do they suffer, and how are their lives altered, despite their efforts? Were you surprised to learn that Adelle nursed Ray Tanner in his final days? What do you think of her confession about Ray's death?

10. What do you think will happen, or what do you *want* to happen, between Billy Webster and Daniel Mason?

11. By the end of the novel, Roxanne and Del have gained a whole new perspective about the black community in Clarksville. As the African-American tour becomes a fixture in town and interracial friendships become more visible, how might blacks and whites continue to interact in new ways? What specific changes can you imagine?